WE CAME HERE
TO SHINE

Also by Susie Orman Schnall

The Subway Girls

The Balance Project

On Grace

WE CAME HERE TO SHINE

SUSIE ORMAN SCHNALL

St. Martin's Griffin
New York

First published in the United States by St. Martin's Griffin,
an imprint of St. Martin's Publishing Group

WE CAME HERE TO SHINE. Copyright © 2020 by Susie Orman Schnall.
All rights reserved. Printed in the United States of America.
For information, address St. Martin's Publishing Group,
120 Broadway, New York, NY 10271.

www.stmartins.com

Map by Silvia Gherra

Library of Congress Cataloging-in-Publication Data

Names: Schnall, Susie Orman, author.
Title: We came here to shine / Susie Orman Schnall.
Description: First Edition. | New York : St. Martin's Griffin, 2020.
Identifiers: LCCN 2020001286 | ISBN 9781250169785 (trade paperback) |
    ISBN 9781250169792 (ebook)
Classification: LCC PS3619.C446545 W4 2020 | DDC 813/.6—dc23
LC record available at https://lccn.loc.gov/2020001286

Our books may be purchased in bulk for promotional, educational,
or business use. Please contact your local bookseller or the
Macmillan Corporate and Premium Sales Department at 1-800-221-7945,
extension 5442, or by email at MacmillanSpecialMarkets@macmillan.com.

First Edition: June 2020

10 9 8 7 6 5 4 3 2 1

*For the women who paved the way
and for the women who inspire me to be bold*

The time has come for me to announce, with solemnity perhaps, but with great happiness, a fact.

I hereby dedicate the World's Fair, the New York World's Fair of 1939.

And I declare it open to all mankind.

—PRESIDENT FRANKLIN DELANO ROOSEVELT, APRIL 30, 1939

You must do the thing you think you cannot do.

—ELEANOR ROOSEVELT

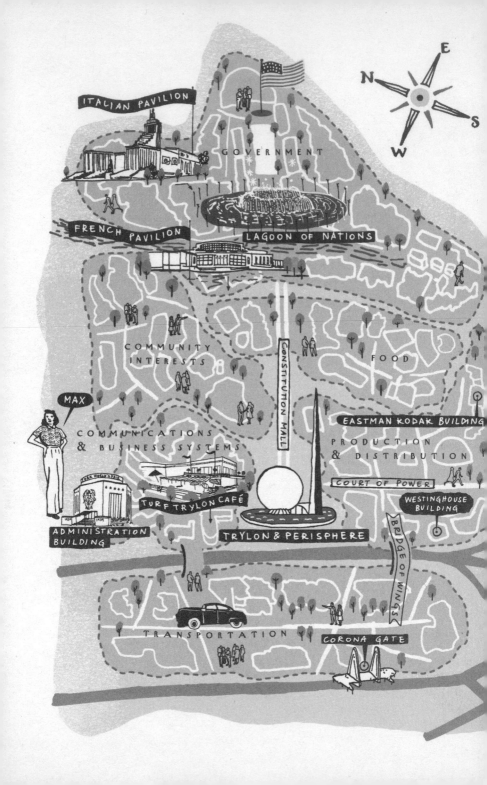

1939 NEW YORK WORLD'S FAIR

RLD'S FAIR SUBWAY STATION

THE RHEINGOLD BAR

AMUSEMENT

BILLY ROSE'S AQUACADE

PIRE STATE BRIDGE

PARACHUTE JUMP

PARKING

TO MANHATTAN

The Trylon and Perisphere, architectural symbols of the 1939 World's Fair, in the Theme Center

Billy Rose's Aquacade in the Amusement Zone

Front cover of the June 10, 1939, issue of *Today at the Fair*

The Life Savers Parachute Jump in the Amusement Zone

COURTESY OF MANUSCRIPTS AND ARCHIVES DIVISION,
THE NEW YORK PUBLIC LIBRARY

Dr. Martin Couney's baby incubators in the Amusement Zone

The Italian Pavilion in the Government Zone

The Westinghouse Time Capsule being lowered into the ground by Fair Corporation president Grover Whalen and Westinghouse chairman A. W. Robertson in the Production and Distribution Zone

1939

WORLD'S FAIR OFFICIALLY OPENS: HERALDS "WORLD OF TOMORROW"

Amid dark clouds and steady rain, hundreds of thousands of enthusiastic visitors turned out to watch as President Roosevelt officially opened the 1939 World's Fair yesterday with a rousing speech promoting "peace and good-will among all nations."

The fair, which all agree is a marvel to behold, is the largest and most expensive exposition ever held, spanning 1,216 acres and comprising hundreds of attractions within its seven zones: Amusement, Communications and Business Systems, Community Interests, Food, Government, Production and Distribution, and Transportation.

"Building the World of Tomorrow," the fair's much touted theme, is incorporated throughout the exhibits and embodied by its iconic architectural symbols: the piercing 700-foot tower-like Trylon and the massive orb-like Perisphere.

Tens of millions of attendees from near and far are expected to descend upon the fair this summer to tour its international pavilions, observe its art installations, be awed by its technological inventions, dine at its numerous eateries, behold its architectural spectacles, enjoy its vast amusements, and witness what Fair Corporation president Grover Whalen and his illustrious committee have been planning for the past four years.

The opening coincided with the 150th anniversary of President George Washington's inaugural address. In attendance were Governor Lehman, Mayor La Guardia, members of the United States Supreme Court and Congress, foreign dignitaries, and notable men from various fields, including the arts, commerce, science, and entertainment.

It is history in the making. Welcome to the World of Tomorrow.

Check this publication each and every day to discover the latest goings-on at the fair so you can plan your visit accordingly.

CHAPTER ONE

‍\/‍

Vivi

Monday, May 22

Vivi Holden would eventually realize that not getting what she wanted that day was the best thing that could have happened to her. But it was still early in Los Angeles. And the not-getting hadn't yet taken place.

Vivi stood just outside of the curving black iron gates of the WorldWide Films studio in Hollywood and paused, shifting from heel to toe and back again in her good black shoes. When she thought about it later, she realized that pause, that uncharacteristic feeling of uncertainty, had been conveying something. But, standing there, on the brink of her future, Vivi would do what she'd become accustomed to doing: ignore the wary voice, charge forward, and deal with the consequences later.

The traffic on Melrose Avenue honked and sped: actors on their way to early call times at the Paramount lot down the street; lawyers on their way to Wilshire Boulevard offices filled with windowed suites and cigarette smoke and secretarial pools;

and everyone else on their way to school or to eat pancakes at the Pantry or to bed after a long night doing whatever it was Angelenos did under the glow of the moon while Vivi slept, her dreams allowing her to escape from the swirl of thoughts that gripped her brain throughout the day. Thoughts of what she'd left behind colliding with thoughts of what she so badly longed for.

Vivi stared at the traffic, the hypnotizing hum.

"Is that Vivi Holden? The new star of *Every Last Sunset*?"

Vivi turned to see her best friend and fellow actress, Amanda Summer, eyes wide in feigned surprise, a mock gasp in her voice. Amanda and Vivi had been signed to WorldWide around the same time, cutting their teeth together and becoming best friends.

"Very funny, Amanda."

"Aren't you going in, lovey?" Amanda asked, gesturing toward the gate.

"I am."

"Then what are you waiting for?"

"I'm not sure." Vivi laughed, scrunching up her nose, a bit confused by her hesitation. She realized she'd been picking at her nails again and forced herself to stop.

Vivi swallowed hard and took a deep breath. Then she put one foot in front of the other and walked confidently toward her future, toward the first day as the leading lady, Lola, in *Every Last Sunset*.

Vivi and Amanda made their way down the main thorough-fare to Soundstage Two, while Amanda prattled on about her boring date the night before. Vivi thought the studio lot looked as if it were preparing to star in a movie about a studio lot in the morning. Capped messengers riding bikes from one office block to another delivering trades, box office reports, contracts. Wardrobe mistresses wheeling metal racks bursting with costumes. Actors and actresses dressed as cowboys and Southern belles and executives and Romans, along with extras trailing behind, hoping to absorb the downdraft of theatrical success. All bathed in sunshine and scented by orange trees.

The machinations thrilled Vivi, as did her good fortune. Landing the female lead in *Every Last Sunset* signified that the studio, which really only meant Mr. Carlton Green, the capricious studio head, believed she was ready. And now she was finally on her way toward everything she wanted. Everything she needed to be financially independent and to make the most of her God-given gifts. That's what she'd been told, and that's what she'd come to believe.

Vivi sped up when she saw Soundstage Two just ahead on her left. A smile took form, lighting up her golden-brown eyes, her whole entire face.

"You ready?" Amanda asked, like a mother on the first day of kindergarten.

Vivi nodded and opened the door.

"Miss Holden, good morning."

"Good morning," Vivi said cheerfully to the young man in a navy-blue blazer embroidered with the WorldWide logo. He seemed to have been waiting for her.

"I'm Kenny, one of the production assistants. I'll take you to your dressing room."

"Coming?" Vivi looked over her shoulder at Amanda, who smiled and nodded.

Vivi's eyes lit up when she saw the dressing room. She'd never had her own before, having shared cramped spaces with multiple girls for the other pictures she'd been in. She took in the cozy chintz love seat, the screened-off dressing area, and the cheerful pink-and-yellow floral wallpaper. And glorious, in the middle of the vanity, was an enormous bouquet of red roses, the tall glass vase tied with a sheer red ribbon.

"I wonder who those are from," Amanda said, an unkind sarcasm in her voice.

Vivi rushed over and read the note: *To my shining star. With love, Gabe.*

"Was I right?" Amanda asked, rifling through the garment rack, tight with costumes.

"You were," Vivi said lightly, deciding not to allow Amanda's dislike of Gabe to infect this exciting day. She'd spent enough time listening to Amanda tell her all of the reasons why the relationship was unhealthy, none of which ever made much sense to Vivi. Gabe had always been wonderful, adoring, supportive. Her first true love. Amanda said there was something about him she didn't trust. But, no, Vivi wouldn't endure Amanda's negativity regarding Gabe today.

"I'll be back for you in fifteen minutes to take you to hair and makeup," Kenny said, closing the door behind him.

"You sure about this, Vivi? You sure Lola is the best character to set you up for your career?" Amanda asked, standing behind Vivi, meeting her eyes in the mirror.

"What's wrong with the character?"

"Just that she's quite seductive. A vixen, from what you've told me. I've always thought your first lead role would be more . . ."

"Wholesome?"

"Perhaps."

"I am sure about playing Lola, and even if I weren't, it's not my decision to make."

"Either way, it's about time you're properly recognized. Soon everyone will know your name."

Vivi had been assigned small test roles in a handful of films. The one with Wyatt Everett, where she played a cigarette girl in a nightclub scene and had to fend off Everett's character's advances while his date retired to the ladies' lounge. The one with Lucille Banner and Monty Greer, where she played Banner's younger sister who tried to steal Greer away while Banner's character languished in a coma at a faraway hospital. And others of the same ilk. The studio's casting heads told Vivi that girls with her looks got certain roles and would continue to get certain roles until the tastes of America's filmgoers changed. Vivi was prescient enough to know that wouldn't happen anytime soon and wise enough to realize, for her career's sake, that was perfectly fine.

Now Vivi felt her hands drawing together reflexively and forced them into her pockets. Her ravaged cuticles couldn't survive another attack by her fingernails. She thought about the role of Lola and what it would mean for her future career. "Jack and Mr. Green think this is the right role for me," Vivi said to Amanda, hoping she sounded confident.

"But what do *you* think, lovey?"

"I—"

Vivi stopped when she heard knocking at the door.

CHAPTER TWO

⅄

Max

Monday, May 22

Maxine Roth would eventually realize that not getting what she wanted that day was the best thing that could have happened to her. But it was still early in New York. And the not-getting hadn't yet taken place.

Max stood just outside the classroom door and paused to quickly catch her breath, smooth her trousers, tuck her unruly auburn hair behind her ears, and wipe the sweat off her forehead with the sleeve of her shirt. When she opened the door, her classmates, who were seated around the long wooden table looking poised and unfettered by perspiration, turned to stare.

She walked quickly to the only open chair.

"Saved a seat for you," whispered James, who was seated to her right.

"Lucky me," she whispered back.

"Now that you're here, Miss Roth," Professor Lincoln began in his sardonic tone, "we can begin." He spoke the latter half of his sentence as if he were opening the first Olympic games. Everything with Professor L., as his students affectionately called him, was momentous, and Max loved the drama. "Congratulations again on surviving the grueling application process and being chosen for this prestigious cohort of juniors who intend to pursue a career in journalism upon graduation. I'm sure each of you is anxious to finally learn what your summer position will be."

In her application, under first choice for summer placement, Max had written: *The New York Times.* She'd broken the rules and also filled it in as her second choice. How could she not? She'd dreamed of working at the *Times* forever. As ever as she'd ever known. In an extreme pinch, the *Herald Tribune* would do.

Professor L., who was one of the most popular instructors at NYU, ensured that his summer cohort students were given opportunities that were typically unavailable to entry-level applicants. And these summer positions often led to offers of employment.

"Within these envelopes are your placements," Professor L. said, picking up the stack that had been on the table before him and fanning them in his hand. "I have spent numerous hours creating matches that are most beneficial to you, my students, and to the organizations that so graciously participate in our program. Placement decisions are final. Once you've opened your envelope and commiserated or celebrated, I will make a special announcement."

"Any minute and you'll get to see if your persistent lobbying for the *Times* paid off," James said teasingly, winking at Max.

"Persistent?" Max said loudly, pretending to be insulted, as their classmates turned to see what Max and James were spitting under their breaths about now. "I beg your pardon."

Professor L. handed Max and James their envelopes. Max started to rip hers open but not before James grabbed her hand and prevented her from doing so.

"Before you do that," James said, "what do you think of a little bet, Miss Confident?"

"Name it, Mr. Fifth Avenue."

Max noticed a strange look pass across James's face, but she wasn't sure if it was because he was a bull foaming to be released into the ring, excited by the smell of a competition. Or if it was because of the Mr. Fifth Avenue razz, which she knew he hated. Which is why she kept it on ice, like champagne, ready for use whenever the situation arose.

James turned to look at Max. She had to hold herself back from grabbing his face and kissing it, a thought she had imagined often.

"Are you sure, Max? You know very well what I'm capable of."

"Sure as God made little green apples."

James laughed and stared an extra beat at Max, which made her blush, which embarrassed her because she didn't like to reveal her cards to anyone. Especially to James Worthington, he of the Fifth Avenue Worthingtons. Specifically the Sixty-Fourth Street and Fifth Avenue Worthingtons (Worthingtons were to be found up and down Fifth Avenue), who, as compared to most New Yorkers, had survived the last decade financially unscathed.

"If you get your first choice, then I have to buy you a drink. And if I get my first choice, then you have to buy me one," James said.

"What if we both get our first choice?"

"That's impossible."

"And that's because?"

"We both have the same first choice, and Professor L. made

it clear that he wasn't doubling up at the *Times* this year," James said.

"Right."

"So, bet's on?"

Max hesitated.

"What? Miss Maxine Roth is experiencing a moment of self-doubt? My goodness! I don't believe that's ever happened before. Ladies and gentlemen . . . ," James started, raising his voice and laughing.

"Shhh. Fine. I'll take your dizzy little bet. But you have to buy me two drinks. Scotches. And they have to be top-shelf."

"Deal."

They shook hands and were about to open their envelopes when Professor L. began talking. James grabbed Max's unopened envelope and placed it, along with his own, just out of reach on the table before them. Max stuck her tongue out at James and focused on Professor L.

"Now for that special announcement. Those of you who took my fall course were treated to a special lecture by Samuel Bing, esteemed journalist with *The New York Times*. Mr. Bing was so impressed by the students he met that he decided to create a scholarship, and this will be its inaugural year."

Max perked up. *A scholarship?*

"You'll each have the opportunity to have articles published this summer by the prestigious magazines, newspapers, and corporate publications we've partnered with. Choose your best published piece and submit it by July fifteenth. Mr. Bing will read them all and select the one he feels represents the student with the brightest future. The winner will be awarded a scholarship, which will cover your entire tuition senior year, including room, board, and books, and a professional recommendation from

Mr. Bing himself. I'll mail each of you a letter outlining the rules and submission details later this week."

With that, Professor L. packed up his beaten leather briefcase, nodded at his students, and left the room.

"That might be the best thing I've heard all day," Max said to James. "Now, how about these envelopes?"

Max grabbed hers and ripped it open, noticing James's more graceful approach out of the corner of her eye.

They each read what was printed on the little slip of paper inside their envelopes and then looked at each other.

"Did you get the *Times*?" Max asked James, her voice flat.

He nodded.

〜

CHAPTER THREE

Vivi

Monday, May 22

It had barely been a couple of minutes since he'd left them in the dressing room. But the production assistant, Kenny, was back. "Mr. Green would like to see you," he said with no emotion in his voice or his eyes.

"Now? I'll be late for my call time."

"He told me to bring you to his office straightaway."

The young man didn't wait for an answer. He turned and Vivi followed, saying good-bye to Amanda with a questioning look. She would have liked to have taken a moment to apply lipstick and slip on a pair of gloves to hide her unvarnished nails, but Kenny walked quickly and Vivi knew better than to keep Mr. Green waiting. Besides, Mr. Green wasn't a lady-in-gloves man. Didn't see how they were practical for reading scripts.

So she pinched her cheeks to bring a blush, ran her fingers through her hair, and caught up with Kenny.

They walked toward Mr. Green's low-slung bungalow, which

was placed strategically between the dressing room complex and the administrative offices. Mr. Green liked having as much proximity to his stars as he did to his accountants.

Vivi couldn't imagine what this could be about. Had she done something wrong? Had she done something right? Was this another invitation for what Mr. Green referred to as a "social visit"? The first—and last—time Vivi had been invited to his office, when she'd been new to WorldWide and excited to be asked to meet personally with Mr. Green, she'd had to learn quickly how to deal with a man who felt she was his due. When she finally left his office that day, she'd commended herself for walking the fine line between not endangering her career while also not encouraging Mr. Green. She guessed she hadn't been worth the trouble, as he'd never invited her back.

Until now.

"Right this way, Miss Holden," said Mrs. Peale, Mr. Green's longtime secretary, as Vivi walked through the main entry. Vivi waited as Mrs. Peale knocked on Mr. Green's door, a quick triple rap that sounded like code, and then was ushered inside by the bellowing sound of Mr. Green's voice.

"Vivi, dear! You're looking as beautiful as ever," Mr. Green said as he stood, his arms outstretched and his smile wide. Someone who didn't know him would assume his smile and tone meant he was in a good mood, but Vivi knew that his external appearance didn't necessarily reflect his internal emotions.

Vivi was surprised to see her agent, Jack Stern, who had just risen from one of the substantial black leather chairs across from where Mr. Green stood behind his equally substantial dark wood desk. She was relieved that this wasn't going to be another one-on-one with Mr. Green.

"Jack," Vivi said in a hopeful voice, suppressing her desire to ask him what this was all about.

Jack, normally gregarious, gave Vivi a decidedly unenthusiastic smile, which led her to believe he had reservations about this meeting. He stood until she sat in the chair beside him.

"Vivi, Jack," Mr. Green said, making eye contact with each of them and clasping his hands together into a fist, his elbows resting on his desk. "I'll get right to the point. As you both know, *Every Last Sunset* is slated to be one of our biggest pictures for 1940. The role of Lola, your role, Vivi, is Academy Award material. There's just one thing," he said, pausing.

"Mr. Green," Vivi said, wanting to prolong the inevitable. She had no idea what exactly he was going to say, but any statement prefaced by *There's just one thing* was never good. "I'm so thrilled that you were confident enough in me to award me the role. I'm looking forward to—"

"Just lay it out there, Carl," Jack said, interrupting Vivi as she turned to stare at him in disbelief—*how rude*—but this was how these meetings ran. Vivi knew the agent was meant to take control and the actress was meant to stay silent. As Jack had told her on multiple occasions, if she followed that simple protocol, her future success would be ensured. So she kept her mouth shut—most of the time—and let the men handle things.

There's just one thing. Mr. Green's statement rang in her ears, getting louder and louder with each repetition until it was all she could hear. *There's just one thing.* Such an insignificant saying. As it turned out, it was entirely *not* just one thing. No, what Mr. Green said next was a whole lot of things. And not a single one was good.

"We screened rehearsal clips for a test audience, and they said you were innocent and sweet. A naïf, I think," he said, shuffling papers on his desk. "Yes"—he jabbed his finger at the paper he'd been looking for—"a naïf."

"I didn't—" Vivi began until Jack interrupted her again.

"Give her another chance, Carl. Let her shoot actual scenes. She can show you what she's capable of." Jack's hands were outstretched, his tone beseeching.

"This is a role for a confident woman who is well aware of her . . . womanliness. I can't have audiences snickering because Vivi isn't believable as Lola. It won't work. The part has already been given to Celine Peters. The contracts were signed an hour ago."

"Mr. Green," Vivi said, standing up to her full height and rolling back her shoulders, a posture her acting coach said conveyed authority and agency. "I can be the actress you need me to be. I promise you, sir, if you give me another shot, you won't be disappointed." It was not an inquiry. It was a declaration.

Vivi had worked so hard. Her training had been nonstop since she'd signed with WorldWide a year and a half prior. A whirlwind of "starlet school," as it was referred to in jest around the lot. Singing and dancing lessons, elocution and accents, dramatic and comedic acting. And how to behave and sit and talk and apply cosmetics to look most appealing, and, most important, how to represent WorldWide Films because, as everyone knew, once an actress was contracted to a studio, she became one little face of that studio. And anything she did reflected upon it. And, for the WorldWide girls, upon Mr. Carlton Green himself.

She had applied herself wholly to every role even though they were small and undemanding and awarded to her based solely on her looks. She didn't complain when the studio made her a blonde, added a beauty mark above her lip, and told her what to eat. Even when they changed her name to Vivi Holden because Alessia Russo sounded too *ethnic*. And she dealt with the unwanted advances from men who felt entitled not only to the best roles but to the newest, prettiest girls as well. Aching and yearning and working and striving were the native language of the people she had surrounded herself with. Today Vivi had felt it had all been worth it, because the reward of it all, the most luscious cherry on top of the most heavenly sundae in the golden-est goblet, was a plum role.

"I appreciate that, Vivi, and I know you're a capable girl. Trust me, I didn't make this decision without a great deal of consid-eration. But I didn't bring you in here today to share only bad news. I have an opportunity for you."

"I—" Vivi began to say; she wanted to give it one last go.

"That's fantastic, Carl," Jack interrupted, turning to give Vivi a smile. "What sort of role?"

From his words, his demeanor, Vivi realized Jack had ac-cepted that her role in *Every Last Sunset* was no longer hers and there was nothing he, or she, could do about it. She figured she'd listen to what Mr. Green had to say and convinced herself that by giving up her fight for the moment, she wasn't capitulating. She was just smart enough to know when to lay down her sword.

"It's a unique situation," Mr. Green said, sounding as if he were trying to convince himself of its merit, "but one that I think is going to help Vivi's career in a number of ways." Mr. Green looked from Vivi to Jack. Vivi wondered if he were waiting for them to salivate. Or beg. "Have you heard of the Aquacade, Vivi?"

"I think I may have read something about it in *Life*," Vivi said hesitantly, resuming her seat but not abandoning her posture.

"Billy Rose's new venture?" Jack asked.

"That's right, Jack. The Aquacade is Rose's swimming and dancing production that he's staging at the World's Fair in New York City. It opened three weeks ago with Eleanor Holm and Johnny Weissmuller swimming the leads. From all accounts it's a magnificent production and being done on quite a large scale."

"Johnny Weissmuller!" Vivi said, nodding, impressed. She knew all about Johnny Weissmuller. Everyone knew all about Johnny Weissmuller. He'd been an accomplished Olympic swimmer when she was still a young girl. And he'd become famous by playing Tarzan in the movies.

"So what does all of this have to do with me?" Vivi asked.

"Eleanor Holm slipped Friday night, breaking some bones. She can't swim the role, and Rose is looking for a new lead. He's a friend of the studio, so he called me hoping I could help him out. He thinks casting a Hollywood actress will excite the press and audiences as well as make up for the loss of Eleanor."

If Carlton Green thinks for one second that he's going to ship me to New York City to dance in some swimming pool, well, then . . .

"Vivi?"

"Yes, sorry, Mr. Green. I'm listening."

"Rose is looking for a gorgeous girl, one we can spare for the summer, and of course she has to be a swimmer. So, immediately I thought of you."

"And what makes you think I can swim?"

"You have your agent to thank for that. When Jack first brought you to my attention, he told me how the two of you had met. He raved about how lovely you look in a swimsuit. And how athletic you are, what endurance you have. If I remember correctly, he went on and on about it, isn't that right, Jack?"

Vivi snapped her head to look at Jack, shocked that their chance meeting at Jack's country club pool—where he had "discovered" her while she was working as a lifeguard, not sitting in a lounge chair downing daiquiris—would lead her to be considered for a swimming job three thousand miles away, just when her career was taking off.

"That's right, Carl. Vivi, this sounds like a wonderful opportunity. A way to get your name out there to a large audience. Plus, you'll be back home in New York for the summer and you'll get to see your sister. Didn't you say you had a sister?"

Vivi no longer considered New York her *home*. She'd left two people behind when she'd come to Los Angeles, and the pangs of yearning and heartache were constant. Her sister had told Vivi she never wanted to see her again. And she couldn't bring herself to even think of the other person. The potential of what could have been, extinguished like so many tiny candles in a rainstorm.

As it became clear that these two men thought this was an opportunity she should be clamoring for, Vivi was shocked. If she wanted any future at WorldWide, any success at all as an actress, it was critical for her to be around, not to be shipped off in the dawn of her career. She needed to rub shoulders with directors and casting agents in the cafeteria, to read and test for roles as soon as they became available. New actresses, young and pretty, emerged daily like embellished butterflies from the chrysalises that were the trains from places like Wichita and St. Louis and Boise, disgorging their wide-eyed freight, who were only too eager to steal parts from actresses like Vivi who hadn't been seen in a while.

If she were in New York, she'd be forgotten as easily as a grade-school crush. How could Jack and Mr. Green not know this? Or, Vivi quickly realized, perhaps they did and didn't much care. She thought back to her "social visit" with Mr. Green and wondered if her number had come up. If this banishment—framed as opportunity—was the price for rejecting his advances so long ago. Being "lent out" to another studio was common, and in every case Vivi knew of, it was done because the star had lost some of her shine.

"I appreciate the opportunity very much, Mr. Green, but I think I can best serve WorldWide right here in LA, continuing my acting classes, meeting more people at the studio, taking small parts, and honing my craft so that I'm ready when you call me up," Vivi said confidently. "Plus, I may have been a swimmer in my youth, but I haven't trained in years. I'm afraid I'd disappoint Mr. Rose and Mr. Weissmuller both. In fact, I know I'd be an absolute disgrace to their production, and the last thing I want is to embarrass you and WorldWide."

"I appreciate your thoughts, Vivi," he replied, "but I don't think you understand how this works."

Vivi saw Jack squirm in his seat out of the corner of her eye. She thought she heard him moan.

"How what works?"

"How a studio works," he said, his tone darkening, his cadence quickening. "I am the studio head. I make the decisions for the actors and actresses who have contracts. If I say that you're going to work in Timbuktu, you're going to work in Timbuktu. Luckily for you, I'm sending you to New York City, where they have indoor plumbing and telephone service. So I suggest you say good-bye to anyone who will miss you for the next four or five months and pack your bags."

Jack coughed and Vivi pursed her lips and Mr. Green went on. "A messenger will deliver a package to your apartment tonight with your train tickets, itinerary, and all of the information you'll need. It's going to be a wonderful experience for you,

Vivi," he said, softening his tone a bit. "Hopefully, I'll get to New York myself this summer with the wife and kids to see you perform. If not, I look forward to hearing all about it when you return in October."

"Carl—" Jack began.

"Oh, I almost forgot," Mr. Green said, standing and walking toward Vivi. He placed his hand on her cheek, like a caress, but one that felt possessive. She blinked, but didn't flinch. "Remember that you're still representing WorldWide while you're in New York. And if we hear good reports from Billy Rose, we'll make sure there's a leading role for you in a film when you return. As a matter of fact, there's one I have in mind that will be perfect for you."

✳

CHAPTER FOUR

Max

Monday, May 22

Once Max confirmed with James that he had gotten assigned the *Times*, she clumsily gathered her things and rushed out of the room, down the hall—ignoring James's urgent voice calling after her: "Max!"—out of the building and across campus, with all of its insistently happy trees and insistently happy students, toward her dorm room. She flopped down onto her bed and pulled the crushed envelope out of her purse.

> *Congratulations:* Maxine Roth
> *You have been placed at:* Today at the Fair, the daily publication of the World's Fair
> *Address:* Flushing Meadows–Corona Park, Queens
> *Contact:* Stanton Babcock, Publisher
> *Expected First Day:* Monday, May 29, at 9:00 a.m.

Max recognized Professor L.'s spare hand and imagined him, sitting in his office, the green glass lamp spotlighting his desk, filling out these little forms. Proclaiming the futures of Max and her classmates.

Professor L. was a legend at NYU, and Max had developed a congenial relationship with him during her freshman year. As a journalism major, she'd taken many of his classes, she'd volunteered for every program he sponsored, and she'd written numerous articles for the *Heights Daily News*. Max was ambitious and wanted more than anything—more than he'd ever seen a girl want something, he'd been known to tell his colleagues—to work at *The New York Times* upon graduation.

Wishing she'd channel that ambition toward something other than working for a newspaper, Max's parents weren't convinced that in this economy, becoming a journalist, and a female one at that, was the wisest path for Max to take, financially or otherwise. "They'll have you writing for the women's pages, Maxine, covering galas and interior design. You'll hate it," her mother had said.

But Max knew she'd never write for the women's pages. As soon as she started at NYU, she did everything possible to ensure that she got the education and experience necessary to land a job writing about things that mattered.

Her parents wanted her to be a nurse or a teacher or even an accountant. It was still difficult for women to get jobs; these days most companies preferred to fill spots with men. But, if she insisted on working for a newspaper, her parents often said, it should be *The New York Times*. They were as spellbound as Max was by the *Times*'s importance and influence. Max knew they'd be disappointed—and worried—when they found out she hadn't been placed there. Her heart hurt when she thought about telling them.

Max scolded herself for reacting so childishly to her assignment. So she didn't get what she wanted. So what? It had happened before and it would happen again. And she realized it was unfair of her to be upset because she knew absolutely nothing about *Today at the Fair* as a publication. The World's Fair had begun only three weeks prior, and she hadn't yet had a chance to go. But that had been by design.

Fairs. Carnivals. Circuses and festivals and parades. Max hated all of those along with anything else where there was a contrived sense of joy and jubilation accompanied by jaunty music and red balloons tied around toddlers' wrists. Where you were reprimanded if you weren't smiling. Where you were meant to embrace your inner child. Max believed her inner child had grown up and was no longer in need of hot dogs from a cart or penny games along the midway.

She'd seen photographs in the *Times* of President Roosevelt officially opening the fair, standing behind a podium surrounded by men in uniforms. The whole thing pretentious and ridiculous, in her opinion. Max recalled the headline saying that the fair or the president's comments were a symbol of peace or some sort of hogwash. As if a fair had the ability to cause such a thing.

It was almost a joke the universe was playing upon her. Not only would she not be working at the *Times*, but she'd also be forced to immerse herself in the celebratory air and affected global unity of the fair. Daily. And in an entirely other borough.

Max heard loud voices in the hall. She got out of bed and opened her door to see what was going on.

"Oh, hi, Max." It was her classmate Louise Molloy and her friends.

"Hi, Molloy."

"Did you get the *Times*?"

"Nope."

"Well, what did you get?"

"I got the World's Fair publication."

"Lucky! You get to go to the fair every day?"

"I do."

"Have you been yet?"

"Nope."

"I've been twice. It's marvelous. You're going to love it!"

"What did you get?"

"The *Herald Tribune*," Louise said.

"That's great. Congratulations." Max smiled politely, but inside she was confused. Louise Molloy could barely string two sentences together. And she got the *Tribune*? Max had it on good authority that the pieces she wrote for the *Heights Daily News* had to be heavily edited.

What kind of game was Professor L. playing? Max had to wonder if he were trying to teach her some kind of lesson. She knew she had the tendency to come off as confident. Maybe he wanted to bring her down a notch. But why shouldn't she act confident? Why was it that confidence played well when it came from a man, but appeared unseemly on a skirt?

There was only one way to find out.

"Miss Roth, how nice to see you," Professor L. said as he welcomed her into his office. There was no one else from the summer placement cohort waiting to see him, which Max figured was because they were all satisfied with their assignments. Or because they were all following Professor L.'s stipulation to accept his decisions as final.

Max's father had taught her never to accept any decision as final. There was always room for negotiation.

"Likewise, Professor," she said, sitting in one of the wooden chairs across from his desk.

"I assume you're here to talk about your summer placement."

"I am."

"Despite the fact that I made it very clear on multiple occasions, including in the original agreement you signed, that my placements were final and that there would be no reassignments?"

"Yes."

"I presume you realize that there was a reason for every match I made."

"Part of why I'm here is to better understand that reason as it relates to my placement."

Max squirmed in her seat a bit as Professor L. stared at her silently, running his fingers through his beard. She couldn't tell by his facial expression if he was going to reward her persistence and explain his reasoning or if he was going to tell her that his wishes on this matter had been clearly expressed, that she needed to learn that rules were rules, that she wasn't entitled to exceptions, and then toss her out on her unbecomingly confident rear end.

He placed the tips of his fingers together, and she thought she saw a small smile escape from the edges of his lips.

"I'm tempted to dismiss you from my office for defying my clearly expressed wishes, Miss Roth. But I also appreciate your persistence. First, tell me, why are you dissatisfied with your assignment?"

"Mostly because it's not the *Times,* sir," she said, ensuring her tone remained measured. She didn't want to sound like she was complaining.

"Do you know how many of your classmates put the *Times* as their first choice?"

"I do not."

"Most. To be honest, Miss Roth, I thought I was doing you a favor awarding you the World's Fair position."

Max perked up. "You did?"

"Indeed. You strike me as a young woman who doesn't want

to be pinned to a desk, and most of those other assignments require just that, including the *Times* and the *Tribune*. At the fair, you'll be exposed to all that it has to offer. Have you been?"

"Not yet."

"You're in for quite a treat," he said, his normally serious expression transforming into a wide smile. Max had never seen the man smile like that. "I was there yesterday, and it is a marvel. I believe this summer will be a great opportunity for you. An opportunity to expand your horizons and see things that will inform your future writing and imbue it with a larger world perspective."

"So I take that to mean you won't reconsider and assign me to the *Times*?" Max asked in a sweetly sarcastic tone, her lips turning into a smile. She knew the answer.

"I'm afraid not," he said kindly. "And I don't think you'd want that sort of special treatment anyway."

"I think I might," Max said, laughing.

"Perhaps. But not getting what you want all the time builds character, Miss Roth. And no one has ever been accused of having too much character."

"I'm also afraid that this placement might be detrimental to my long-term career."

"How so?"

"I understand that many of the students from past cohorts received job offers from their summer placements for positions after graduation. The fair only goes through the fall, so I won't have access to a post-graduation opportunity."

"I see, and that's a valid point, but I don't want you to worry about it. You are an exemplary student, and I've been pleased with your work on the *Heights Daily News*. I don't allow my best students to flounder after graduation, Miss Roth."

Max, who had entered the meeting filled with fire, intending to do whatever she needed to do to change Professor L.'s mind, realized she needed to stand down. He was still her professor. He still possessed the power to influence her future. She loved a good fight, but knew when to unfurl her fists.

"Thank you for your time, Professor. I'm sorry I came in so stirred up."

"I admire your fervor. And I appreciate a good sparring session."

They both smiled, and Max stood up and walked to the door.

"Miss Roth?" he called after her.

She turned.

"In twenty years, in forty years, when people talk about the World's Fair of thirty-nine, when people ask if you were there, you'll have the best answer of anyone, and you'll be the envy of all. You'll be able to say you were immersed in the fair. That you worked there, that you thrived there. Perhaps, and I'm not saying this flippantly, it might even change your life."

꧁

CHAPTER FIVE

Vivi

Monday, May 29

Vivi knocked a second time on the door, this time more force-fully. When there was still no answer, she consulted the neatly typed itinerary and confirmed that she was to report at 8:00 A.M. to the Aquacade office. She glanced at the sign on the door: AQUACADE OFFICE.

Her nerves were already frayed, as she'd encountered more traffic than she'd allotted time for on the way from her hotel in Manhattan to the World's Fair grounds in Queens. She'd told the taxi driver to drop her at the Flushing Gate, as she'd been instructed. But he had insisted, despite her firm entreaties, on dropping her at a different gate so that she could have a grander entrance, considering it was her first time at the fair and all.

Vivi had slammed the taxi door behind her, and then groaned as she realized the colorful scarf she had planned to tie around her neck was stuck in the door of the taxi, which was now barreling down Corona Avenue, spewing exhaust in her face, its pilfered silk blowing in the wind behind it like a protest.

Looking around, Vivi tried to orient herself. Workers bustled around, but the grounds were empty of patrons. A sign to her left announced that the fair didn't open until nine o'clock.

"The Amusement Zone?" Vivi asked the ticket-taker at the entrance gate as she showed him the employee pass included in her packet. He offered her a map and cleared his throat, as if he were preparing to deliver an important presentation.

"Go toward the Aviation Building"—he pointed to her right— "then hang a left and go over the Bridge of Wings. Keep walking, then turn right and walk some more till you go over the Empire State Bridge. The Aquacade Amphitheater will be directly in front of you."

Vivi tried to follow along as the young man traced her route with his fingertip on the map. When she looked at him, confused, he pointed over his left shoulder and said, "Just go that way. You can't miss it."

Looking down at the map, Vivi thought she'd never get her bearings. From where she was standing, the seven different zones extended above and to the sides for what seemed like miles, and it looked as if there were hundreds of buildings on the map.

The closest she'd ever come to a setting like this was at the LA County Fair, which she and Gabe had gone to the year before. Back then she couldn't imagine that anything could be better. Or bigger. It was clear to her now that this, the 1939 World's Fair of New York City, would make the LA County Fair look, in comparison, like a faded small-town carnival gasping on its own dusty breath.

The World's Fair was all anyone had been talking about. People she knew in Los Angeles were maneuvering to visit. And newspapers around the world were touting it as the largest and most expensive of any exposition ever held. She had read statistic after statistic and fact after fact, but couldn't recall any of them at the moment.

Vivi walked quickly, wrapping her sweater tighter around her against the cold, dreary morning, and trying to remember everything the ticket-taker had said. Unfortunately, because she barely looked up, focused as she was on her route and the time, she missed the marvels surrounding her. She glanced up at the enormous spire-like Trylon and spherical Perisphere, which were the most celebrated and recognized symbols of the fair and served the same focal purpose as the Eiffel Tower had for the Paris fair of 1889. Their likenesses were printed on fair advertising, countless magazine covers, promotional brochures, and, she'd heard, myriad souvenirs, including ashtrays, diaries, playing cards, saltshakers and pepper shakers, pottery, and children's toys. Vivi admonished herself to relax. *This is New York. People are late. It won't be a problem.* But she wanted to make a good first impression.

Now, after knocking on the office door a third time, Vivi spun around and looked for someone to ask. At that moment, a man walked by purposefully, his head down as he flipped through pages on a clipboard and hummed loudly.

"Excuse me," Vivi said, lifting her chin.

He turned and smiled. People always smiled at Vivi Holden.

"Can you please tell me where I can find Mr. Edward Tandy?"

"You wouldn't be Vivi Holden?"

"I would." She exhaled, relieved.

"Is it Tuesday already?" he asked, looking surprised.

"Monday."

"I thought you were arriving Tuesday. Anyway, come with me, and I'll take you to Ed."

Vivi tried to keep up with the man's pace as he walked toward a gate.

"I'm Thad Muldoon, Ed Tandy's right-hand man. We're thrilled to have you here," he said, continuing to smile widely at her.

"Very nice to meet you," Vivi said, extending her hand, which Thad took in his after he moved his clipboard underneath his arm.

Now that she was close to him, Vivi could see his face more clearly. He had dark wavy hair, large brown eyes, and a kind and handsome smile. He looked like he was in his mid-twenties, and wore trousers and a shirt with the sleeves rolled up. Mostly what Vivi noticed, though, was that he was nice, a trait that had been lacking in most everyone she'd encountered since arriving in New York.

"How was your trip in from the coast?" Thad asked.

Despite her dismay at leaving Hollywood, Vivi had relished her time on the train. She had traveled the LA-to-Chicago leg on the *Super Chief*, a favorite among celebrities due to its speed, elegant interiors, superior customer attention, and extensive meal service, which included coffee in bed in the morning and caviar served on fine china during dinner. It was laughably more glamorous than the way she'd traveled to Los Angeles two years prior, when she'd left New York in a bit of a hurry, with a small battered suitcase and a bit of cash from her sister rolled up in a ball in her brassiere.

"It was quite wonderful, thank you. There's something very inspiring about traveling across the country by train, especially on the *Super Chief*. Have you—"

"Now, when we walk through this gate here," Thad said, speaking more quickly as he came to a stop in front of a white wooden gate that bore a sign that read AQUACADE CAST AND CREW ONLY, "I'm going to lead you right to Mr. Tandy. He's a busy man, so he might be short with you, but don't take it personally. I should prepare you: things have been a bit chaotic since Eleanor was injured. Ruby's taken over beautifully, but she's Ruby, you know—"

Vivi didn't know, and was trying to keep up with Thad, trying to decide if she would be all right once she passed through the white gate or if she should run for her life. But Thad was still talking.

"—and Camilla, our choreographer, is doing her best to get things back on track. But you're gonna be fantastic. When I heard we were getting a real Hollywood star—"

"I'm not really—"

"—I knew the production would be back up and running as smoothly as before. You ready?"

Vivi took a deep breath, but before she had the chance to answer, Thad opened the gate and gestured for her to go ahead. It was a good thing he hadn't waited for her answer. She wasn't sure what she would have said.

It was as if a director had yelled "Freeze!" as soon as Vivi and Thad walked in, because every swimmer, dancer, diver, workman—heck, every single person on the pool deck and stage—seemed to turn in slow motion and stare at Vivi.

She knew what she had to do. She straightened her shoulders, lengthening all five feet eleven inches of her body, lifted her chin, jutted her left hip, and smiled.

She was immediately stunned by the scene she had walked into. She knew the Aquacade was a grand production—she'd read all of the newspaper articles Miss Peale had attached to her itinerary—but she was in no way prepared for the reality.

The articles said the pool was 275 feet long, or about the size of a football field, but Vivi had never attended a football game, so she was unable to put that into context. Now that she was standing next to it, it was enormous. She couldn't imagine having to swim from one end to the other. The pools she swam in during high school meets were a fraction of the size.

And then there was the stage behind the pool, which was a little wider than the pool and equally as long from front to back. Vivi knew the cast comprised one hundred swimmers and another hundred dancers and she knew they had to all fit somewhere, but the scale was massive and she felt overwhelmed by the sheer size of it all. And by the fact that she, as the lead swimmer, was going to be the main attraction.

It was when she looked toward the audience seating that Vivi realized Mr. Billy Rose was as much of a showman as the press made him out to be. Because Billy Rose wouldn't bother putting on a show unless there was a gigantic audience to watch it. And that was certainly true of the Aquacade. The audience area could hold ten thousand people! Vivi had never performed for a crowd that size. Not even close. And she only had two weeks to prepare. Before she had a moment to fully comprehend how terrifying that thought was, a man approached her. He held a cigarette in his left hand and was now pumping her hand with his right, all the while introducing himself.

"Ed Tandy, but call me Ed. It's wonderful to have you here, Miss Holden."

"Vivi," she said, smiling.

"Vivi, of course. Just wonderful to have you. But you're not supposed to start until tomorrow."

"I was told—"

"Doesn't matter. Was your travel smooth?" he asked, smiling, his hands on his hips as he took a drag from his cigarette. He looked distracted and focused, and Vivi wondered how one could be both at the same time.

"It was. I—"

"Grand, grand," he said, not waiting for her to answer and not seeming to realize she hadn't. "Now, Vivi, as I said, it's wonderful to finally have you here, but our rehearsal schedule for the week was designed for you to join in tomorrow. Between you and me," he said, dropping his voice into a dramatic whisper and blocking his mouth with his cigarette-holding hand, "however much I'd like to get you in that pool, I know better than to mess with Camilla's rehearsal schedule. She'll have my head, if you know what I mean. So, be a dear and come back tomorrow. Eight A.M."

"But . . ." Vivi said, about to tell him she was ready to start immediately and wanted as much time as possible to rehearse.

"We have a lot riding on you, Vivi. The press release is out, and there'll be a lot of journalists here Friday night, so you—"

"Next Friday night," Vivi interrupted.

"Right, Friday night."

"In two weeks."

"In four days."

"But that can't be right," she said, fumbling for Miss Peale's itinerary in her bag. "I was told I would have a full two weeks of rehearsal before my first performance."

"You were told wrong," Ed said.

"How am I . . . ?" Vivi began, protesting but knowing already that it was a futile effort, despite what Miss Peale's itinerary said. She was in the hands of Ed Tandy now, and she was certain that he'd expect her to do as she was told.

"We've hired Camilla for extra hours this week to rehearse with you. You'll debut Friday, and Ruby will swim the lead until then. You only have to learn five or six numbers. Everything will be fine."

Vivi was stunned. She thought about calling Jack to explain the situation. But she decided she wanted to handle things on her own. Plus, she didn't want to come off as a troublemaker to Ed. Even so, she didn't understand why Ed, and especially Billy Rose, would want her to debut on Friday when that clearly wasn't enough time for her to learn the role. Or perhaps they thought it was. Surely they wouldn't put her in a situation where she could fail; it would be detrimental to them and to their production.

Before she had a chance to open her mouth to demand more rehearsal time, Ed was shouting for everyone to gather around.

The bodies sprang into action and Vivi looked into the mass of faces—some smiling, some stony—and forced herself to transform into a Real Hollywood Star, which was what Ed and Thad and all of the faces staring at her expected her, needed her, to be.

Vivi smiled and was startled when Ed Tandy grabbed her hand and lifted it into the air in triumph.

"Everyone, this is Miss Vivi Holden. She's come all the way from Hollywood, where she's a star under contract with World-Wide Films. Lucky for us, the head of WorldWide, Carl Green, and Billy Rose go way back, and Mr. Green was kind enough to lend us her beauty and talents for the summer to replace Eleanor. Now, if you'll join me in giving a proper Aquacade welcome to Vivi Holden."

There was a loud round of applause; Vivi couldn't help but feel welcomed. She felt her nerves abate, a respite from the burdensome worry of not fitting in, of this whole endeavor being flawed.

"Back to work!" Ed yelled. This time Vivi heard the shortness in his voice that Thad had mentioned, and the cast members hurriedly resumed what they'd been doing before she'd entered. "I'm sorry, Vivi. I have to get back to my office to return some telephone calls. I'll tell you what: Thad will take you on a quick tour, and we'll talk more tomorrow." He gave her a wide smile and before she had a chance to say another word, he'd begun walking quickly toward his office.

Vivi felt unmoored, as if she'd been flung off of a towering waterfall.

"Ready for the grand tour?" Thad asked in a kind voice.

"Ready."

The scale of the Aquacade was dazzling and impressive. Thad explained the intricate lighting system, which was controlled by a technical director from an outpost on the roof and required twenty electricians to operate. He pointed out the two seventy-five-foot diving towers on either end of the pool, with the Vincent Travers Orchestra in one tower and the Fred Waring Glee Club in the other.

They climbed the stairs to the last row of the audience seating and looked down upon the rehearsal taking place. Vivi's eyes were immediately drawn to the couple swimming the duet in the middle of the pool. She recognized Johnny Weissmuller instantly.

"Who's the girl swimming with Johnny?" Vivi asked Thad, unable to take her eyes off her, wondering if that was the Ruby she'd heard about. She was lovely, with light brown hair tinged with golden highlights from the sun, and she was gorgeous in the water.

"That's Ruby Lancaster. She is, rather, *was*, Eleanor's understudy. Now she's your understudy."

Vivi doubted that she'd ever look that natural in the pool. That she'd ever be able to swim the duets with Johnny as gracefully or as sensually.

"Oh, look," Thad said, pointing to the diving tower on the left. "That's Dean Mitchell, our best diver."

Vivi watched as a tall, muscular man positioned himself on the edge of the platform, his arms firm by his sides.

"He looks so confident," Vivi said.

"When you do something you love, something you're exceptional at, that's just the way you look."

Vivi nodded wistfully. "I don't think I've ever looked like that. I've certainly never felt like that."

"I can't imagine that's true," Thad said, looking at her with an admiration she was convinced was misplaced.

They watched Dean spring off his toes and expertly maneuver his body into twists and flips before he landed in the water with barely a splash. His body, his expression, his whole being seemed to glow.

"I read in the paper that you're originally from New York," Thad said.

"The paper?"

"The fair has a daily paper. They ran an article about you the other day. I could probably try to get you a copy."

"Oh." Vivi was surprised to hear that. "Yes, I grew up in Brooklyn." She returned her gaze to the pool, hoping he wouldn't ask more questions.

"Still have family nearby?"

Especially that one.

"My sister, Maria, is still in Brooklyn, with her husband, Frank, and little Sofia."

"How nice that you'll get to spend time with them all now that you're back in New York."

The last time she'd seen her family, Sofia had just been born. Vivi thought her birth could be a happy time for her family, a new beginning, especially since things had been so sad and unstable since her parents had died a couple of years prior, leading Vivi to move in with Maria and Frank. Vivi knew the baby had changed things between her sister and Frank, but she didn't expect it to get to the point where Maria would tell Vivi to leave.

Vivi thought about that day. The cruel words her sister had said. The pain she'd felt when she thought she had no options except for the one her sister demanded.

"Yes," she eventually said to Thad, her voice quiet. She tried to sound convinced of what she was saying so he wouldn't ask her anything else. "It's unnatural to be away from family for so long. Something inside me hasn't felt quite right since I moved away."

Thad nodded at her and together they walked down from the seating area toward the gate, making small talk about the rainy weather they'd been having and how it had affected the Aquacade audience size, since there wasn't a cover over the seating area.

"I guess we'll see you tomorrow then," Thad said.

"See you then, and thanks for the tour."

"You look petrified," he said, cocking his head a bit to the side.

"Do I?" Vivi said, trying to keep her voice calm and her demeanor the same.

"You have absolutely nothing to worry about. I promise."

The New York Chronicle
Monday, May 29, 1939
By Pierce Hayes

WEATHER KEEPING CROWDS AWAY

While planning the World's Fair, Grover Whalen and the Fair Corporation have spent the last several years ensuring that every aspect of the fairgoer's experience would be perfect.

What they have not been able to control, however, is the weather, which, since opening day on May 1, has been mostly wet and cold, and presumably a reason many are avoiding the fair altogether.

The Corporation initially projected that 40 million to 50 million people would come to the fair this summer and that profits would exceed $8 million. One month in, though, and experts predict those numbers will be virtually impossible to attain. Weekly attendance has been steady at around 1 million visitors, which would result in summer attendance at 27 to 29 million, far below the Corporation's projections. If numbers fail to improve, concessionaires and exhibitors might find it difficult to recoup their investments, which would leave a stain upon the long-term reputation of the fair.

The dreary weather, however, isn't the only thing affecting crowd size. Many potential fair visitors have groused about the high cost of admission (75 cents, which is 25 cents more than standard), as well as the high prices of food, out of reach to many New Yorkers of modest means.

ψ

Max

Monday, May 29

It had been a week since she'd gotten her summer assignment when Max came into the kitchen for her morning coffee. "There she is, our *New York Times* reporter, ready for her first day at work," Max's father, David, said when he saw her.

Max was still adjusting to being back in her family's small apartment on the Upper West Side. Adjusting to the rhythms and the expectations, to the lack of privacy, to the daily aroma of breakfast wafting under her bedroom door, and to the familiar sounds of her father setting his coffee cup down on the kitchen table and unfolding his newspaper.

As Max poured herself a cup of coffee and added milk and two tablespoons of sugar, feeling nervous about starting her new job, she thought back to the night she'd joined her family for dinner after she'd received her cohort assignment from Professor L. and visited him in his office. She had hoped the warmth of her family would cheer her up.

"Maxine!" her mother, Sarah, had shouted, when she let her-self into the apartment. "Come into the kitchen. I want to hear how it went."

"What'll it be, Maxie? Gin and tonic? Vodka orange juice?" her father asked, coming out of the kitchen and giving her a kiss.

"Scotch, neat, please."

"What did you get?" Max's sixteen-year-old sister Anna asked, coming out of the bedroom she shared with her twin sis-ter, Leah.

"Did you get the *Times*?" Leah asked, crossing her fingers and legs and eyeballs dramatically for good luck.

Max looked into the loving yet irritatingly unrelenting eyes of her mother and sisters, then walked purposefully toward the living room, where her father was standing next to his glass trol-ley bar with her scotch. She needed another minute, at least, without admitting to them what had just happened.

Max's father was known for his latent desire to be a bartender. He welcomed any opportunity to wield bottles and mixers and garnishes and, especially, his treasured seven-piece brass bar tool set that not a soul save he was permitted to touch. His specialty was a classic Manhattan. He even made his own maraschino cherries every summer, painstakingly jarring them so he'd have enough for the winter. David Roth was the guy who wouldn't hold back from fixing drinks at someone else's party. Or on bridge night. Or even, maybe especially, a bris. David Roth felt that every occasion deserved a cocktail.

Max wrapped her hand around the weight of the glass and took a long sip, enjoying the burning sensation and feeling her eyes water, unsure if it was a result of the scotch or her summer assignment or of having to disappoint her family. She set the drink on the trolley and wiped her eyes with her sleeve.

"Maxine, don't avoid the question. Did you get the *Times*?" asked her mother, trailed by her sisters, an expectant smile on each of their faces.

"Of course she got the *Times*," her father said, beaming at her with pride.

Max wanted to tell her family the truth. That she didn't get the job that she and they had been hoping for. The job that her parents had told their bridge-night friends would practically cement her future as a journalist. She didn't want to tell them that instead she was going to work at a tiny paper at the World's Fair, at a publication that wouldn't even exist come November.

"I got the *Times*!" Max said, regretting what she'd said instantly. Lying in the Roth family was not tolerated. Even if the liar didn't want to disappoint her parents.

It was times like these that Max wished she were less impulsive.

Everyone cheered and hugged her, which only made her feel worse. But she was certain they'd be concerned if they knew the truth.

"I appreciate the excitement, but I probably won't even get to write any articles, so don't start looking in the paper every day for my name or anything like that," Max said.

"Don't be so modest, Max," Anna said.

"It doesn't matter what you do there. It's the *Times*!" Leah said.

Now she sat at the breakfast table with her coffee and her father and felt sick when she saw the look of pride in his eyes.

"I've got to go. I don't want to be late for work, and neither should you," he said, kissing Max on the cheek. "So proud of you, Maxie." Though he was trying to sound upbeat for her, Max saw her father's stress in the slouch of his shoulders and in the urgency of his actions.

He reached for his newspaper, kissed Max's mother, and raced out of the apartment, grabbing an umbrella and reminding Max to take one as well.

David was an accountant for a large commercial real estate concern. He didn't conceal the company's recent financial problems from the family, and Max worried that he might lose his job if things didn't get better. She knew he'd already had to take a pay cut since his salary barely covered their family's expenses and her NYU tuition.

Sarah wanted to go back to work as a teacher—a job she'd given up when Max was born—to help with the family's expenses, but teachers were holding on to their jobs in this economy, so she was having trouble finding a suitable situation.

Yes, Max thought, she'd made the right decision lying to them about the *Times*. She didn't want to be responsible for one more thing her parents lost sleep over.

Riding the subway to the World's Fair grounds in Queens, Max thought about how over the past week, since she'd gotten her assignment from Professor L., she'd done a decent job of convincing herself that there might be some positive aspects of working at the fair. Sure, it would be too cheerful and optimistic an environment for her liking. But at least it would provide interesting topics to write about for the article she'd submit to the scholarship contest Professor L. had announced. Max worried that if things continued the way they were at her father's company, they wouldn't be able to afford tuition next year. So winning that contest had become Max's focus.

And, hopefully, at the end of it all, Professor L. would write her a glowing recommendation that she could use as entrée to the post-graduation job of her dreams. And there would be birds chirping and flowers blooming. The false cheeriness made her gag.

Max emerged from the subway at the station near the Amusement Zone. The sky was gloomy and the rain was deciding whether or not to make an appearance. She was happy her father had reminded her to bring an umbrella.

It wasn't yet 9:00 A.M., so the gates weren't open to attendees. The ticket-taker accepted Max's employee pass and showed her on a map the best way to get to the Administration Building, which housed *Today at the Fair*. It was clear across the grounds from where she stood.

Even though the crowds hadn't yet descended, she could smell the donuts cooking at the Donut Palace and hear the barkers preparing their spiels. She looked up at the Life Savers Parachute Jump, which she'd read was 250 feet high, and saw one of the parachutes drifting gracefully toward the ground, presumably a ride operator doing a test run before opening the attraction for the day. Max thought the ride looked a bit thrilling, and contemplated returning when she had free time.

She walked across a bridge to the main part of the fair and headed straight. Despite her plans not to become charmed by the fair—its architectural wonders, its thoughtful and color-coordinated plan—she was still a journalist in training and thus her natural curiosity took over, replacing her habitual cynicism with pure fascination.

Eventually, Max eyed the massive white Administration Building ahead on her right, nestled among the buildings housing the fair post office, press office, and treasury. It was close to nine o'clock, so Max took a deep breath, ascended the handsome front stairway, pushed through the massive doors, and entered her future.

A young woman sat behind a large desk just inside the doors and directed Max down a long hallway to the right, to the offices of *Today at the Fair* in Room 105. When she reached the wooden door at the end of the hall with the words TODAY AT THE FAIR painted in bold letters, she knocked gently and then turned the handle. The very first thing she saw upon opening the door was her classmate Charlie Hull.

"Well, hullo, Maxine."

Max hated that Charlie always called her Maxine. She hated that he thought it was funny to say *hullo* instead of *hello*. And she especially hated that she would be working alongside him the entire summer.

Charlie's hair was dull blond and very short. And because his skin was the same color as his hair and his eyes were a light golden brown (and would have been beautiful on anyone other than Charlie Hull), he looked like a once-luminous watercolor faded by the sun.

"I guess we'll be spending our summer together, Maxine. Lucky for you," Charlie said, chortling.

Max looked at him as she supposed one would look at an irritating younger brother and was about to respond when they were unexpectedly joined by an older man who had just entered the office, a tan fedora with matching band set firmly upon his head.

"Charlie Hull and Maxine Roth, I suppose," the man said, slapping Charlie on the back and reaching to shake Max's hand. "I'm Stanton Babcock. Come with me."

Charlie raised one eyebrow at Max and began following the man. Max, a half beat delayed, quickly caught up and made sure she and Charlie entered Mr. Babcock's office together. The office was nondescript—white walls, wood desk, standard-issue chairs—but it was the view of the Trylon and Perisphere, which were, at that moment, reflecting the glow of the early morning sun trying to break through the clouds, that caught Max's attention.

"Pretty spectacular, no?" Mr. Babcock asked, his hands on his hips as he followed Max's gaze. "Never thought Grover Whalen and his men would ever pull this thing off. But they did. And now we've got work to do. So grab a seat, you two, and let's see what we have here."

Max stopped her gawking and took one of the two seats across the desk from Mr. Babcock. She pulled a notebook and pencil out of her bag and placed them on the desk before her, scooting her chair in a bit so she was in position, perched over her notebook, ready to begin.

"Pass me a sheet of that," Charlie whispered.

Max sighed under her breath, tore a sheet from her pad, and handed it to him without turning her head.

"And a pencil?"

Max fished one out of her bag, while Mr. Babcock looked on, seeming to grow more impatient with every request Charlie made.

"Sorry, Mr. Babcock. I arrived quite early and settled myself at the desk Marianne showed me to, so I don't have my things with me."

Mr. Babcock nodded and looked down at papers on his desk. This gave Max the opportunity to do a quick study of the man. She'd noticed when they first met that he was tall, over six feet and a perfect eye-level match, it seemed, with Charlie. Clearly a disadvantage for her, Max thought. She had always perceived it a loss to have ambitions to work in a man's world yet always have to look up to them in the physical sense. She had no intention of allowing that to be a detriment and chose instead to compensate in other ways—with her determination, hard work, and resourcefulness. Still, she detested that most men would look down on her. And even worse, in her opinion, that she would have to look up.

Mr. Babcock had white hair, and she thought he looked somewhere between fifty and sixty. He seemed like a no-nonsense man, from the cut of his suit and the pinch of his hat, from the cup filled with sharpened pencils to the right of his blotter and a similar one filled with sharpened red pencils to the left. At that moment, a woman—Max presumed it was the aforementioned Marianne—entered Mr. Babcock's office with a mug of coffee and quickly left. Not a word was uttered between the two of them. The interaction seemed odd, but it gave Max the impression that Mr. Babcock was efficient with his words and actions. That, in her future dealings with him, she should get to the point and then get out. She could do that. In fact, she preferred these types of men to the ones who wanted to chit and chat and find out what her father did for a living and how she had become such an ambitious girl.

"I'm pleased to have you both on my staff this summer," Mr. Babcock said, looking up from his papers as he placed his hands flat on the desk. "And I hope you'll find that the fair is an exciting environment in which to work."

Max and Charlie nodded.

"The subheading of *Today at the Fair* is 'Official Daily Program of the New York World's Fair 1939,' and that sums up what we set out to do here. It's a daily, and our deadline is early each afternoon, so my expectations of the two of you will be high, and there isn't time for dillydallying or mistakes. As the publisher, I oversee all aspects of the publication. You'll report to Hugh

Collier, our editor in chief, who should arrive any minute. Hugh, Marianne, and I have been doing all the work up until now and we've realized that there's more than the three of us can handle, so we're happy you're here. I have some telephone calls to return, so why don't you take a look at these documents outlining your responsibilities, and we can resume our conversation in fifteen minutes."

"Thank you, Mr. Babcock," Max said, accepting her document from him and standing up to walk out of his office.

"Thank you, Mr. Babcock," Charlie echoed, and followed Max. "We're sitting over there," Charlie said to Max once they were back in the main room. He pointed across the office to two desks set close to each other. The office consisted of a large central room with the entrance and reception desk on the west wall. The north wall held two private offices: Mr. Babcock's and another that Max presumed belonged to Hugh Collier. There was a table that faced the windowed east wall and was covered in office supplies and past issues of *Today at the Fair*, and then two desks that were placed up against the south wall.

Charlie took a seat at the desk on the right, where he had dumped his belongings that morning. Max pulled out the chair of her desk and set her notebook, pencil, and responsibilities document on top of the blotter. She hung her handbag on the back of her wooden chair and took the cover off of her type-writer.

"Sorry we didn't have a chance to meet when you arrived, Miss Roth. I must have been in the washroom," Marianne said, approaching Max. "I'm Marianne, the receptionist."

"Call me Max, please," Max said, extending her hand and smiling. Marianne appeared to be around Max's age. She was pretty in an innocent way, and wore a prim butter-yellow shirtdress with a white tie at the neck and poufed cap sleeves. She had light brown curls cut close to her head and a kind pale-pink smile.

Once Marianne walked back to her own desk, Max looked over at Charlie and saw he was focused intently, taking notes in the margins of his responsibilities document.

Max picked up her document, eager to see what types of articles she'd be assigned, what sorts of stories of the various attractions she'd have the opportunity to regale fairgoers with. As she read over the list, however, she realized Mr. Babcock and Mr. Collier had quite different plans for her.

"Gonna be a busy summer, Maxine," Charlie said, lifting his paper at her and smiling.

"Let me see that," Max said brusquely, leaning over and grabbing Charlie's document from his hands.

She quickly read through his list of responsibilities, becoming increasingly outraged, and realized there'd been a huge mistake.

CHAPTER SEVEN

Vivi

Monday, May 29

After her grand tour of the Aquacade, Vivi left Thad and hailed a cab outside the Corona Gate. "The Stafford Hotel, please."

As the taxi sped out of Queens and back toward Manhattan, the trees a long slash of green, her window cracked open to allow air into the stuffy car, Vivi thought about her morning and couldn't believe she'd only been at the fair for an hour.

And though she had wanted to start rehearsal as soon as possible, she was grateful for an extra day of rest, as the travel from the West Coast had affected her more than she'd expected.

Vivi didn't know whether it was WorldWide or Billy Rose who was responsible for her comfort while she was in New York, but someone was being extremely generous. Vivi hadn't been privy to the discussions regarding her salary (that's what agents were for, after all), but regardless of what that turned out to be, she was also receiving a generous stipend meant to ensure her utmost happiness and well-being as it related to transportation, lodging, and food.

Closing her eyes, Vivi allowed the rocking movement of the car and the rhythmic tap dance of the raindrops upon the roof to lull her into a short nap. She awoke with a start when she heard the cabbie say, "The Stafford, miss."

"Thank you," Vivi said, rubbing her eyes and trying to get her bearings as she paid the fare and collected her belongings, hoping not to repeat her morning error of leaving something behind.

The Stafford was impressive, intimate, and far more luxurious than Vivi had expected. But again, Miss Peale had directed her there in her comprehensive information packet, and there was no indication that the lodgings were temporary. The hotel, with its dignified reception area, exquisite floral arrangements, elegant marble fittings, and plush towels, was a nicer accommodation than any Vivi had ever inhabited, and the idea of staying there for the next four months almost made up for the melancholy she felt about having to be in New York in the first place.

Vivi approached the front desk and asked the attendant if there was any mail for Room 17.

"Good day, Miss Holden. I trust you've enjoyed your morning so far," he said as he turned toward the ornate brass mail slots on the wall behind him.

"I have, thank you," Vivi said, watching him retrieve two envelopes.

"I hope these are missives filled with joy," he said, smiling as he handed the bundle over to Vivi. He then looked down at a ledger on the desk. "You also have a telephone message from a Mr. Gabe Grant. He called soon after you left the hotel this morning. Please do let us know if there's any way we can make your stay more comfortable."

"Thank you, I will," Vivi said as she accepted the mail from the man, whose name tag read *Charles* in swirling type.

Vivi glanced at the return addresses on the letters and was pleased. She walked purposefully through the lobby toward the elevator, eager to return Gabe's call so she could reach him at home before he went to his office.

On the way to her room, she read Amanda's letter about her latest dates and her gay account of life at WorldWide. Amanda seemed especially to relish in the telling of the bits she'd heard about Celine Peters and her prima donna demands on the set of *Every Last Sunset*. Vivi hoped Mr. Green regretted his decision to cast Celine instead of her.

Vivi tried to absorb Amanda's letter in the way in which she knew Amanda had intended it, a frothy gossip of all Vivi was missing so she wouldn't feel too far away, but instead Vivi focused on all that she was missing and that she felt too far away.

Kicking off her shoes and massaging her feet, Vivi picked up the telephone, anxious to connect with Gabe.

"Vivi, my darling, how are you?" Gabe asked when the call was connected. She could picture him in his navy pajama bottoms, his chest bare, his dark hair flopping sexily over his eyes.

"It's so nice to hear your voice."

"I thought I'd reach you this morning to wish you luck before your first day of rehearsal, but the front desk said you'd just left the hotel."

"The Aquacade people sent me home, saying they weren't expecting me until tomorrow." Vivi felt her voice cracking; she didn't want to break down. She wanted to sound strong, like she was in control, like she could travel to the other side of the country and take care of herself.

"Okay, so you'll have an extra day to rest. That's not a terrible thing. What did you think of the venue? How did Billy Rose seem?"

"I didn't meet Billy Rose, but everyone else I met seemed nice." She didn't want to tell him how nervous she was about how much she had to learn and how quickly, or how frustrated she felt being so far from everything that meant anything to her. She didn't want to worry him. Gabe would take the first train out to be with her, and she knew he was too busy at work to come all the way to New York just to soothe her nerves and hold her hand.

"That's great. So how will you spend your day?"

"First I'm going to read the letter you sent that the front desk just handed me—"

"The one where I pledge my love and ask you to marry me again."

"Oh, Gabe," Vivi said, lightening her voice. She didn't want to sound ungrateful for his love.

"I know, I know. You love me, but the timing's wrong."

"I do love you. Very, very much."

Vivi thought about Gabe's prior proposals. The silly casual ones over champagne toasts at Musso's or during leisurely drives to visit industry friends in the Malibu Movie Colony on Sundays. And the big serious one that had come with a ring during a trip they'd taken to San Francisco earlier that year.

She'd turned him down that day, explaining, as she'd explained to him before, that however much she loved him, however much she knew he was the man for her, for her future, to be the father of her children, she wasn't ready to become a wife yet. Or a mother. There was still so much she felt she needed to achieve.

"The timing's right, Vivi. Especially now that you're all the way in New York. Marry me and come back home. You can quit your job, shove the whole thing in Carl Green's smug face, and let me take care of you."

Gabe was always going on that his job as an attorney for MGM brought in enough money to provide for them both—*to keep us flush in champagne and jewels*, is what he was fond of saying—and that she should just marry him already.

At times the idea had its merits. At times when Vivi had an early call time for an uncredited role without even a line of dialogue, and at times when she wondered if she would ever be as good as the greats in her industry or if she was just another pretty face atop a long set of shapely legs. And now, when she felt banished to the Aquacade for a role that she knew wouldn't serve her. But, at other times—luckily for Vivi, most of the time—she knew that she was exactly where she ought to be. It wasn't a quick sprint but a longer race to become the type of leading lady she'd set her heart on. And to achieve the kind of financial independence that was important to her, especially after witnessing the relationship her sister and Frank had and how helpless and vulnerable her sister felt in the marriage because she didn't have her own money.

It was still too early to give it all up for a man, even one as lovely and kind and intelligent as Gabe Grant. Even if he'd been a salvation of sorts for her. An emotional home. And a family for the past year.

"Soon, my love. I promise the timing will be right. Soon."

Luckily, Gabe was a man who knew when to drop things and move on. Knew that she loved him. Knew that she just wasn't ready and that it had nothing at all to do with him. His confidence was intoxicating. "Tell me more about the Aquacade."

"Well, the craziest thing is that Ed Tandy, the man in charge of the show under Billy Rose, told me I'm debuting this Friday, which is much sooner than I'd been told."

"If that's the case, call Jack; that's what an agent is for. He'll take care of everything."

"I want to deal with it on my own."

"That's my girl. Listen, darling, I have to go. I have an early meeting that I can't be late for."

"I love you, Gabe. I'll write you a long letter just as soon as we hang up."

"You sure you don't want me to come out there and rescue you?"

"Stay put. I can take care of myself."

Vivi took a deep breath as she replaced the receiver, feeling tears form in her eyes. She missed Gabe so much, but she felt a sudden burst of purpose that while she was in New York, she'd focus her energy on the Aquacade.

She also felt a sudden burst of hunger. She'd been too nervous to eat that morning, and now she was craving blueberry pancakes and well-done bacon.

Heading back down to the lobby and the bright restaurant off the main corridor, Vivi decided that yes, while she was here in New York, she would make the most of this opportunity. She'd demonstrate the same strong work ethic she had in LA. After all, she'd believed Mr. Green when he told her that if she did well, then when she returned to Hollywood in the fall, a role equivalent to the one she'd lost in *Every Last Sunset* would be waiting for her. And she'd believed Jack when he told her to trust him. That he'd work on Mr. Green and make sure that role was indeed waiting for her. She couldn't afford, professionally or financially, not to be successful in this swimming show, despite the misgivings she'd originally had. She made a pledge to herself that she would do absolutely anything to ensure that Jack and Mr. Green—and even Gabe—were proud of her.

The hostess showed Vivi to a table and handed her a menu. Before she could order a cup of coffee, an adorable little girl from the next table, wearing bright yellow rain boots, ran over to Vivi and sat on her lap.

"Are you a princess?" the little girl asked, smiling up at Vivi and touching her hair, her blue eyes wide and beseeching.

"Margaret, come back here," a woman—Vivi assumed it was Margaret's mother—said, rushing over to Vivi to retrieve the child. "I'm so sorry."

"That's okay. She's beautiful."

"Thank you," the woman said, laughing. "Beautiful and too brave for her own good."

The woman led the little girl back to their table, where she was scooped up by a man, presumably her father, and covered in kisses. Vivi smiled as she stared, and felt a lump in her throat as she swallowed hard. Despite her professional goals, she envied that woman, that small family, the darling child, a doting husband and father.

Vivi had been so convinced that she was making the right choice by pursuing her career instead of settling down with Gabe, even if her career, at that moment, required her to be in a swimming pool for the next four months rather than on a soundstage on the coast.

Perhaps she was being too cavalier about Gabe's proposals. Perhaps the smart thing to do would be to pack her things, get on the next train west, and accept that lovely man's proposal before it was too late.

⅄

CHAPTER EIGHT

Max

Monday, May 29

"Have you both read through your documents?" Mr. Babcock asked fifteen minutes later when he, Max, and Charlie had reconvened in his office along with Hugh Collier, the editor.

"If I may, sir," Max said, trying to control her voice. "I noticed I'm not going to have the opportunity to write any articles." Max smiled and took a breath, feeling proud of herself for being calm and nonconfrontational, knowing this wasn't the time nor the place to be either.

"That's exactly correct, Maxine," Mr. Babcock said unapologetically. "You will manage the official daily schedule and special event listings as well as photo captions, and Charlie will be assigned articles."

"Could I do the listings *and* write articles? It was my understanding, as well as Professor Lincoln's, that everyone in the summer cohort would have the opportunity to write. You see, there's a contest—"

"No, you'll be too busy."

"I appreciate that, and I'm really looking forward to being busy here and working hard, but perhaps Charlie and I could share the listings work and then we could both write articles."

Max looked at Charlie. His lips were pursed and he was sweating. He gave her a look back that she interpreted to mean *Back off, Maxine. Let it be.* He had the luxury of being able to feel that way.

Max also looked at Mr. Collier, who hadn't said a word. He stared down into his lap and let Mr. Babcock do all the talking.

Mr. Babcock cleared his throat. "Maxine, I appreciate your eagerness. I think it's wonderful when girls show interest in journalism. But I have found in my experience, and I've been in this business a long time, that females do better with the tasks I've assigned you due to their excellent attention to detail. Now, we have a lot of work to do, and I don't want to waste any more time. If you're displeased with the situation here, I presume you could express your feelings to Professor Lincoln and perhaps he could reassign you to a different publication."

Mr. Babcock paused, and seeing that Max was not going to say anything more, he moved on to Charlie.

"Now, Charlie . . ."

Max tuned out Mr. Babcock as she thought about what he had said, realizing that he was making assumptions about Charlie's and her skill sets based upon the contents of their undergarments. She was furious, but admonished herself to relax. It was the first day. These men were still her bosses for the summer, and she still needed to make a good impression. She'd had her say. Mr. Babcock had had his. She'd just have to find a different approach when the time was right.

After Mr. Babcock finished discussing Charlie's role, he moved on to Max.

"Your responsibilities, Maxine, are divided among two very important sections. The first, the 'Official Program of Today's Special Events,' lists one-off concerts, exhibitions, promotional days, and the sort. There will be about thirty on any given day. Each morning, you'll receive memoranda from the different fair departments that want items included in the section the next day. It's your job to organize and edit those requests and then type them up in chronological order."

Max nodded.

"The second section, 'Around the Clock Today at the Fair,' contains the day's full schedule. These listings rarely change from day to day, but you'll incorporate any new items and adjust times or locations as requested. There are hundreds of events each day beginning at nine o'clock, when the gates open in the morning, and running through midnight and sometimes later. The exhibits close at ten, but the Amusement Zone doesn't close until two in the morning. You must review this section with an ever-so-vigilant eye, as there is much opportunity for error. Any questions?"

"No, I understand, Mr. Babcock."

"From what you said earlier, I realize you think writing articles is the more important role around here, but I assure you that the sections I've assigned you are critical to the running of the fair. Everyone who opens our paper will look at your sections, Maxine. They'll use them to plan their day."

He gave her a large smile and dismissed them from his office.

"I can't believe you spoke to Mr. Babcock like that, Maxine," Charlie whispered to her when they were both settled at their desks.

"Why?"

"Because he's the boss."

"I wasn't disrespectful. I was just expressing my concerns. What's wrong with that?"

"I just think you're brave."

"You do?" Max smiled at Charlie.

"Braver than me, that's for sure."

Max flipped through the stacks of memoranda from the different departments and got to work.

"How about lunch, Maxine?"

"Is it time already? Where did the morning go?" Max said, stretching her fingers.

"Whaddaya feel like eating?" Charlie asked, standing up.

"I'm not sure," Max said, hesitating, wondering if she wanted to spend her lunch hour with Charlie.

"Well, come on, we can decide on the walk over."

What the heck, Max thought as she collected her things. After she and Charlie told Marianne they were going for lunch, they walked out of the Administration Building into the day, which had thankfully become sunny and warm.

"I've heard good things about the Famous Chicken Inn over in the Amusement Zone. How does that sound?" Charlie asked.

"Perfect," Max said, and they picked up their pace. They had an hour for lunch, but the restaurant was clear on the other side of the grounds.

"I'm glad to be working with you this summer, Maxine."

"Thanks, Charlie. Me too," Max said. Perhaps she'd never given him enough of a chance before. Perhaps he'd be a perfectly fine coworker: they could eat lunch together, discuss their work together, and commiserate about their bosses together.

They crossed the bridge that would take them from the main exhibit area of the fair into the Amusement Zone. Max noticed the tremendous Aquacade sign up ahead. Just beyond was the Famous Chicken Inn.

"This chicken is delicious," Max said, her eyes wide, after she'd taken her first bite. She'd ordered the "Milk Fed Southern Fried Chicken with all the Trimmins" plate at Charlie's recommendation, and she was not disappointed.

"I told you, Maxine," he said, his mouth full of food.

While they ate, they talked about the other members of the cohort, who was dating whom (Max was shocked to learn Louise Molloy and Ken Selby had gone out after the first cohort meeting), who had the best assignment (James, they both agreed on that one), and whether Professor L. was actually very mean or very nice (Max thought nice, Charlie thought mean).

"You and James seem pretty lovey-dovey," Charlie said, raising his eyebrows up and down.

Max laughed and shook her head. "There's nothing going on there."

"Oh, please, Maxine. I've never seen two people more in love."

"We're just friends."

Max thought Charlie's perception of James and her was amusing. And interesting. She'd certainly like to be more than friends with James. But she'd received no indication that the feeling was mutual.

He'd telephoned her once since they'd received their cohort assignments, after she'd rushed out of the room. She felt bad that she'd acted so immature and had told him so. He told her she could make it up to him when they settled their bet with drinks on her, and they'd made a plan to meet the following week. That week was now here and they would be having drinks at the fair the following night. Max was giddy thinking about it.

"What are you writing about in your articles today?" Max asked Charlie as they walked back to their office.

"I'm working on three pieces. The first is a couple of hundred words about the nightly fireworks show in the Government Zone. I'm doing a longer piece about tomorrow's dedication of the French Pavilion by the ambassador, and then a front-page piece about how excellent attendance has been so far."

"But it hasn't."

"What hasn't?"

"The attendance numbers. I've read a few articles in *The New York Times* and in other papers about how the numbers are much lower than the Fair Corporation estimated because of the weather and the admission price and things like that."

"I don't really know anything about that. I just have a press release from Grover Whalen's office that I'm working off of."

Max thought that it all sounded a bit strange, but Grover Whalen was in charge of the whole fair. Surely he knew the real story about the attendance numbers.

"You're so lucky, Charlie."

"'Cause I get to write articles?"

"Yes. And go out and interview people, and all that stuff."

"I feel real bad that they're not letting you write anything. I bet if you do your listings well, Mr. Babcock will change his mind."

"I hope so. I'm just dreading being cooped up in that office all day editing listing times while you get to go to things like the opening of the French Pavilion."

"Maybe if you tell Professor L. what's going on, he can do something about it."

"Maybe, but I want to handle it on my own at first."

"That sounds like you."

Charlie looked at his watch and stopped walking, turning to Max.

"We ate so fast that we have a little time left, and I'm supposed to pick up a package of information at the French Pavilion. Wanna come?"

"I do!" Max said as they took a sharp turn to the right. Of everything at the fair, Max was most interested in the international pavilions.

As they faced Constitution Mall, the long thoroughfare that led from the central Trylon and Perisphere up toward the Government Zone, the area that held the international pavilions, Max felt her breath catch in her throat.

"It's beautiful," Max said, thinking the planners of the fair were quite skillful at creating, or perhaps manipulating, the visitor experience. The part of her that wasn't grumbling at how contrived it felt was quite taken by the majesty of it all. She was certain that her father, who loved fairs and had been speaking about seeing the different pavilions, would love this view.

Constitution Mall was a great expanse bursting with statues, most notably a giant sundial and the sixty-foot-tall statue of George Washington, his eyes staring directly at the Trylon and Perisphere—*facing the future*, she could imagine the planners thinking quite literally.

"Haven't you seen any of this before?" Charlie asked.

"No, this is my first day at the fair."

"I've already been three times! So now I'll impress you with my knowledge. Did you know that sixty countries plus the League of Nations are represented at the fair? And that some of them have spent upwards of three million dollars on their pavilions?"

"I did not," Max said, laughing.

"President Roosevelt himself issued the invitations three years ago, and the Soviet Union was the first to sign on."

"Have you ever traveled anywhere outside of the US?"

Charlie shook his head. "You?"

"No, but I'm dying to. And the first place I'm going to go is to France. Ever since I saw photos in *Life* of the Eiffel Tower and the crepes, that's been at the top of my list."

"Knowing you, you'll get there someday, Max."

"Oh, wow, look at that!" Max pointed at an oval-shaped lake just ahead filled with gorgeous water lilies in shades of pink and white.

"That's the Lagoon of Nations, and it's four city blocks wide."

"Everything has such fancy names: the Lagoon of Nations, Constitution Mall," Max said with a flourish.

"That's right," Charlie said in all seriousness, "and the Court of Power and the Avenue of Patriots and the Plaza of Light. The planners had grandiose intentions and wanted to pay tribute to the stated theme of the fair and its goals, so they named all of the courtyards, bridges, and thoroughfares accordingly."

Max laughed at Charlie. "You could really be a tour guide here."

"Perhaps if this journalism career doesn't work out."

"Perhaps."

"This," Charlie said, pointing to the lagoon once they were standing next to it, "is where the fireworks show is held every night."

Max felt the spray of the fountains on her face and closed her eyes to enjoy the sensation.

"And this," Charlie continued, gesturing to the right and left with both of his hands, "is the Government Zone, where all the international pavilions are. The larger pavilions for countries like France, Belgium, and Italy are off to the sides, and their buildings are architecturally true to their countries. And the smaller ones, like Mexico, Lebanon, and Finland, are in what's called the Hall of Nations. See how each country has its entrance identified by its flag?"

When they stopped briefly in the French Pavilion so Charlie could retrieve the documents, Max thought about how she had completely underestimated the magnitude of the fair.

It would be impossible to see and do it all. Certainly a visitor *could* make his or her way from one end of the grounds to the next, loop around, and walk in and through all of the avenues, courtyards, and plazas, and over all of the bridges, glancing from side to side at the buildings and attractions along the way. That could probably be done in a full day, maybe two, even shorter if one were to hire one of the ubiquitous fair "guide chairs." These three-wheeled chairs, pushed by handsome young men in uniforms and pith helmets, were a lifesaver for fairgoers. But taking advantage of all the fair had to offer was an enormous undertaking, one that Max was now personally responsible for conveying the opportunities for each day in *Today at the Fair*, which, she had learned, could be purchased for five cents a copy at any of the numerous concession stands dotting the grounds.

Max's brain was dizzy with the scope of all of the events she'd typed up that morning: the musical performances and classes, fashion shows and speeches, and movies, recitals, assemblies, demonstrations, receptions, luncheons, dinners, tours, parades, and "singing" fountain performances, and that didn't even include what went on from open to close each day in the Amusement Zone.

It confounded her how anyone who read through the paper's daily fair offerings could pick and choose among them.

Now, back in the office, Max was glad she'd gone on that little jaunt with Charlie during lunch, glad she'd tamped down her cynicism and allowed herself to be awed by what was truly awe-inspiring. She thought it was a shame that the fair had been designed to be open for only one year. She knew for certain that she didn't want to be there when the fair ended, when the wrecking balls rolled down those gorgeous thoroughfares and destroyed the acres of glass and steel, concrete and landscaping, embellishments and statuary, all of it saturated with hope. With visions of the future. And, particularly in the Government Zone, with patriotism.

Those international pavilions celebrated each country's individual patriotism. But more important, Max thought, was the confluence of all those celebrations in one place. One tiny patch on the vast globe where countries had come together to show unity and to symbolize the grandeur that could come from the powers of the world working together harmoniously. The idea of it stood in powerful contrast to the conflicts that were actually taking place abroad.

The theme of the fair was no secret: the World of Tomorrow. Max had seen it printed on fair maps and programs, had read about it in articles, had heard it on radio broadcasts and newsreels. She'd never really thought about what it meant. But as she sat at her desk, at her first real job, as she prepared for the career that she wanted more than anything else in her life, she thought about the meaning of that grand concept. She had no idea what her own future held; she knew only that she expected it to be bright. Blazing. Like a fire that knows no shortage of fuel. She expected she'd continue to work hard and accomplish whatever she set out to do. Perhaps this fair and its theme of tomorrow held more for her than Max had anticipated. Perhaps if she opened her eyes a bit and let down her guard a bit more, she'd absorb a little of this hope and it would carry her like a wave toward her own future, her own world of tomorrow.

TODAY *at the* FAIR
Tuesday, May 30, 1939
By Charlie Hull

WORLD'S FAIR ATTENDANCE SHATTERS EXPECTATIONS

It's been a month of pageantry and revelry. A month of innovation and recreation. Yes, fairgoers, today marks a month since President Roosevelt declared the fair open to all.

Fair Corporation President Grover Whalen released the official numbers for the first month of the fair's operation. Attendance numbers have surpassed expectations, with about 1 million visitors each week hailing from near and far.

Newspapers, domestic and international, have featured rave reviews of, among other things, the fair's architecture, its vast scope of performances, and the high quality of its food.

The Amusement Zone, in particular, continues to attract record numbers to its 280 acres of attractions, food venues, and festivities for all ages.

Crowds are flocking to Frank Buck's Jungleland, with its camel rides and Monkey Mountain; to the replica of Shakespeare's Globe Theater and the crenellated architecture of Merrie England; and, of course, to everyone's favorite thrill ride, the Life Savers Parachute Jump.

The highest-grossing attraction continues to be Billy Rose's Aquacade at the New York State Amphitheater, which features four shows daily starring Aquabelle Number One Vivi Holden and Aquadonis Johnny Weissmuller.

Fairgoer William Reilly, 9, of Bayside, Queens, who attended the fair for the first time yesterday with his parents and kid sister, said, "I wish I could live here. I've never seen anything like it in my whole life!"

That's the type of rave review that concessionaires—who report lines all day long and sold-out performances—like to hear.

Whalen predicts that both attendance numbers and profit for the fair overall will increase each week as the weather becomes more pleasant, schools let out for the summer, and patrons continue telling their friends about their marvelous experiences at the fair.

(For a full list of all the day's events and attractions in the Amusement Zone, see pages 4–5. Dining options are on page 7.)

✷

CHAPTER NINE

Vivi

Tuesday, May 30

"Welcome, Miss Holden," Camilla, the Aquacade choreographer, said to Vivi, noticing her standing on the pool deck with the other swimmers that morning, her first official day of rehearsal.

"Thank you," Vivi said, hugging herself and trying to stay warm. The May morning was a bit chilly, but Vivi was happy that Billy Rose provided big urns of steaming coffee in the dressing room, which helped considerably. She was cold, it was all new, and she was nervous, but she told herself that everything was going to be okay and hoped that if she thought it often enough, it would become true.

Vivi had been surprised when she entered the women's dressing room that morning. It was dank, with small puddles on the concrete floors, and aside from the round bulbs framing the mirrors at the makeup tables, it was poorly lit. She wondered how

Celine Peters was managing in her deluxe dressing room on the set of *Every Last Sunset*.

"Miss Holden . . . ," Camilla began.

Vivi thought Camilla seemed formidable and a bit scary. She was surprised by how desperately she wanted to please this woman.

"Please call me Vivi."

Camilla smiled. "Vivi, then. You have a lot to learn and not that much time. I think the best way to start is to have you shadow Ruby for the first number, which is called 'Yours for a Song,' just to get a sense of where you need to be in the pool. Try to follow the moves as best as you can, and we'll spend one-on-one time later so I can teach you the strokes."

Vivi nodded, wanting to seem agreeable, knowing she was about to make a huge fool of herself.

It didn't help that Vivi felt hundreds of eyes staring at her. She heard an audible sigh and looked over to see that Ruby was glaring at her. Vivi had never felt immediate hatred from someone so intensely as she did from Ruby Lancaster. Those extras walking the lot at WorldWide, their jealousy for the contracted actresses as pronounced as the rouge on their cheeks, could take lessons on the art of the eye roll and the craft of the hostile stare from Ruby Lancaster. In fact, if Carlton Green could see Ruby now, he'd sign her immediately to a WorldWide contract and send a memo straightaway to the casting department commanding them to cast Ruby as a top-billing villainess in their very next film.

"Everyone, in the pool!" Camilla shouted, and clapped her hands twice.

Looking around and seeing the other girls adjusting their bathing caps, Vivi did the same, sure to tuck every last piece of hair inside. She knew that the chemicals they put in the pool would turn her hair green, and she didn't know when she'd next have a chance to get it dyed.

Ruby dove into the pool and Vivi followed, happy to find that the temperature was significantly warmer than the air. Thankfully, Mr. Rose had sprung for heating. Vivi surfaced and was disoriented as she looked around to see where Ruby had gone.

"Over here," Ruby said to Vivi, waving her to the right side of the pool, an annoyed and unkind edge to her tone.

Vivi swam toward Ruby, treading water when she arrived in position. Vivi assumed Ruby's abrupt attitude toward her was because Vivi was essentially taking her part away. Despite being on the unpleasant end of it, Vivi could understand where it was coming from. Perhaps when Eleanor was injured, Ruby thought the role would be hers. Vivi realized what was happening to Ruby was similar to what had happened to her with *Every Last Sunset*. She, Vivi, was to Ruby as Celine Peters had been to her.

Vivi felt bad. She hadn't meant to steal the role away. The only consolation was that Ruby would still be in the ensemble. But she'd no longer be, in Aquacade parlance, Aquabelle Number One. No, that charmed honor now belonged to Vivi.

"Usually, we start with a tiller," Ruby said, "but I guess Camilla didn't want to overwhelm you right away."

Vivi nodded, though she had no idea what a tiller was.

Then she found herself directly next to Johnny.

"Johnny Weissmuller. It's nice to meet you," he said, holding out his wet hand.

"Vivi. Nice to meet you as well," Vivi said, shaking his hand and smiling.

She didn't have time to dwell on the fact that she was meeting *the* Johnny Weissmuller. She'd met loads of actors; why should this time be any different? For some reason it was. Maybe because he was gorgeous, a sleek and hulking boulder of a man, with skin that practically glistened in the water. But before she could give it another thought, the pianist began.

"Try to follow but don't get too close or you'll get kicked," Ruby said, affixing a saccharine smile on her face.

Ruby then swam to her left while Johnny mirrored her movements alongside. Vivi didn't know where she was supposed to position herself in this formation so she stayed close, but not too close, and tried to imitate their movements. The treading and the kicking and the fluttering all while trying to follow along and stay out of the way was physically exhausting. Vivi found herself out of breath quickly and hoped no one else, especially not Ruby or Camilla, had noticed. She'd have to do something about her conditioning.

The rest of the cast swam around the perimeter in measured and synchronized strokes, their heads above the water, their kicks fully underneath. Vivi did her best to follow along as Ruby and Johnny performed complicated choreography that involved a great deal of intense eye contact with each other and complicated-looking strokes in time to the music.

Then the female swimmers came toward the center and formed a ring around Ruby, Johnny, and Vivi, their heads toward the center of the pool and their faces looking outward. As the music hit a crescendo and Ruby's and Johnny's kicks became more pronounced, the girls put their arms on one another's shoulders and lay on their backs. The men, who had formed an outer ring around the women, moved in closer and faced the women. Then each man grabbed the ankles of the woman in front of him, holding her up while he kicked his legs forcefully underwater in a side stroke to propel himself and his charge around in a counterclockwise circle.

The whole time, Camilla was clapping her hands to the beat and counting out the strokes loudly to be heard over the sound of the piano.

When the music finally stopped, Vivi was close to tears. She knew she had looked like a floundering fish and she was angry with all the people who had put her in this position. The list was long: Carl, Jack, Ed, Billy, even Camilla. How any of them thought this was a good idea, she did not know.

"Vivi, can I see you over here, please?"

As she swam to the edge of the pool where Camilla was standing, Vivi felt relieved that the other swimmers were talking to one another, so she wouldn't be humiliated by them hearing Camilla's instructions. Though she'd only been there for a couple of hours, Vivi had gotten the sense that it was a lively and social group filled with friendships and, by some of the antics she'd observed already, many romantic relationships. Vivi had been on several movie sets and had never experienced anything like this. Perhaps the fact that everyone was stripped down to swimsuits each day, practically naked, had led to the frenzy. (She'd find out later that couples made ample use of the privacy of the diving bays for their rendezvous.)

"I'm sorry," Vivi started. "I didn't know where to be, what to do."

"It's fine. But why don't you dry off and join me on the side? That probably wasn't the best way for you to learn anything. Grab a chair and watch us rehearse the number a few more times. You'll get the hang of it, and then I'll put you back in the water."

Vivi nodded and exited the pool as Camilla clapped her

hands twice and called for the swimmers to start the number from the top.

This time Vivi was able to see what Ruby had meant by a tiller.

The swimmers lined up in one long row on the edge of the pool, alternating men and women. As the music began, they dove in one after another, a split second from one to the next, the motion mimicking a wave. It was gorgeous to watch, each splash practically hypnotizing Vivi with its pleasing sound and flourish of water.

As she watched from her chair on the pool deck, Vivi studied Ruby carefully, trying to memorize what she was doing, and wondering if she'd be able to live up to Ruby's example. Would she be able to put on an expression that looked as if she weren't exerting herself physically at all, keep her shoulders rolled back and her chin high as if she were standing still in the water, make something so difficult look so effortless? After the first run-through, Vivi abandoned her chair and tried to imitate Ruby's movements from the stage behind the pool, though it was difficult to do on land what Ruby was doing in water, absence of buoyancy being the prime reason. And, as Vivi chided herself, absence of talent.

Vivi's several hours in and out of the pool that morning turned out to be extremely frustrating. She had so much to learn. The only bright spot was a swimmer named Sadie who introduced herself to Vivi and offered to help in any way she could. She seemed genuinely nice, unlike the pack of girls Vivi had dubbed the Rubettes, for the way they followed Ruby around, fawning all over her pretty little head. Vivi thought it would be nice to get to know Sadie better, to have a friend in the production.

Eventually Camilla clapped her hands three times, which

apparently meant it was time for lunch, as all the swimmers exited the pool, discussing where they were going to eat and with whom. Vivi wondered if she'd ever find her place among this cast. And then she reprimanded herself for harboring negative thoughts. Those feelings of insecurity were familiar territory for Vivi. Despite a confident outer shell, she'd felt them before every audition and during every film she'd ever been in.

"Vivi," Camilla called to her.

Vivi wrapped her towel around herself and walked toward Camilla.

"That last time was a little better," Camilla said.

"I'm really trying," Vivi said, wiping the pool water from her forehead, and rubbing her fingernails because the chlorine stung where she'd nervously picked at her cuticles. Vivi stared at the petite woman. She had small dark eyes and straight dark hair that was pinned back tightly into a low bun above her neck, making her face appear more severe than it probably was. Camilla wore all black. Black capris. A black sleeveless blouse with black buttons. A black cardigan during the morning chill. Black flats. And a black kohl line along her upper lashes.

"I know you are, Vivi. I just need you to focus more. Forget everything you learned as a swimmer. This is different. I need you to swim pretty. Head and shoulders out of the water. Smile on your face. Eyes engaged. This is about pageantry, so give me more beauty and less brawn. Understand?"

"This type of swimming—"

"Water ballet," Camilla said.

"It's just that it's entirely different from what I did on my high school swim team. It's all so unfamiliar." Vivi felt as prepared for what she was expected to do as a virgin on her wedding night.

"I understand. It was new for all of these swimmers when they started."

"I don't know why Ed thinks I can learn in a few days what they learned over the course of months."

"I'm not sure either," Camilla said, her tone more gentle. She paused for a moment, as if she were trying to work something out in her mind. "How about this? This week, I'll focus our rehearsals on the opening number and the finale, and I'll convince Ed to debut you with just those two. From there, you can add a new one each week."

Vivi's first instinct was to give Camilla a huge hug, but she didn't get the impression that it would be entirely welcome. "Thank you," Vivi said. "That sounds a lot more reasonable."

While the others went to lunch, Vivi worked with Camilla and found she picked up on the movements so much more quickly that way. She was starving, but she didn't want to waste even a minute indulging in something as frivolous as hunger.

Camilla taught Vivi the moves, which were precise and athletic, and had names like pinwheels, back dolphins, and spirals. And she taught her to swim in precise rhythm to the music and be dramatic and artistic with her arm movements—the sculls—above the water while moving her legs forcefully below in a move called the eggbeater, which gave the swimmers height and stability.

Each number employed many of the same moves, just in different sequences. Vivi only had to memorize the arrangement for the two songs and she'd be prepared for Friday. Through the discipline in her acting classes, she had developed a skill for memorization. Unfortunately, the techniques that had worked for her so well at WorldWide were useless here.

When rehearsal broke for the 3:30 show, the first show of the day, Vivi, who was free to go back to her hotel, decided to take a seat high up in the audience and watch the spectacular that was Billy Rose's Aquacade.

The show comprised four themed sections: "A Beach in Florida," "Coney Island," "A Beach on the French Riviera," and the finale, called "The Aquacade," which featured a patriotic number to "Yankee Doodle's Gonna Go To Town Again." There were dancing and swimming numbers, diving acts, and comedy routines all involving extravagant costumes, perfectly timed musical accompaniment, artfully designed large-scale sets and props, and a light-and-fountain show the likes of which American audiences had never seen.

Having now spent hours learning the choreography to different numbers out of sequence, it was fascinating for Vivi to see the show in its entirety. She was impressed by the synchronicity of the performers (a feat that she now knew, since she'd been working at it all day, was vastly more difficult than it appeared) and was delighted by the elated reactions of the audience to the costumes, to the sets, to the orchestra, to the performances, to all of it.

And though it all made her feel excited to be part of this magnificent and professional production, she also felt sick to her stomach because she knew she had so much still to learn by Friday.

☀

CHAPTER TEN

Max

Tuesday, May 30

"Now I understand all the fuss about this fair," James said when he spotted Max.

Max was excited to see James that night, after her second day of work. They'd decided to meet at the Turf Trylon Café, which was in the Communications and Business Zone, and known to have one of the nicest bars at the fair. The building was large and surrounded by elegant hedges, and there was a spacious outside patio dotted with umbrellas striped in pale yellow.

"Hi, James," Max said, stopping in front of him. She was unable to prevent a smile from taking over her face. Her cheeks flushed, and she feared he could see right through her, straight into the parts of her brain that contemplated and calculated the possibilities of such things as a "Max and James."

"Max," James said, smiling and leaning down to kiss her on the cheek.

They both paused for a second. A pregnant pause, Max

thought, one in which there was no sound, no movement, no fair or people or molecules or gravity or sense of time around them. And then, in an instant, to Max's dismay, James spoke again, and the world and its expectations and its requirements returned.

"How did your first two days of work go?"

Max shrugged.

"I know just the cure."

James and Max walked into the crowded restaurant and chose two stools at the long bar.

"I still can't believe I lost your dumb bet. I detest losing bets," Max said as she hoisted herself up onto the tall stool.

"Which is what makes this all the more joyful for me."

"What'll it be?" the bartender asked. He had a thick Irish accent, white hair, and a nose reddened from age or drink or possibly both. His name tag read *Patrick*.

"Two scotches, please. Neat," Max said. If there was one thing her father had taught her, it was how to drink her liquor.

"Make mine on the rocks," James said, eliciting an eyebrow raise from Max. "Just say it," he goaded her.

"Can't handle a little whiskey, Worthington?"

"I drink mine like a gentleman, Roth. Now, tell me about this job of yours," he said, grabbing a handful of nuts from the small dish Patrick had set before them. "How's it going with Charlie?"

"What?"

"Charlie Hull."

"How did you know I'm working with him?"

"Everyone knows. You may have spent the night sulking after Professor L. distributed the summer assignments, but the rest of the cohort went for drinks. I know where everyone's working."

"So you know Louise Molloy got the *Tribune*."

"I do. Everyone was wondering where you were and what

your assignment was. It was actually Louise Molloy who told us. And when she did, Charlie let out quite a whoop, which is how I know two things."

"Which are?"

"That Charlie Hull is also working at the fair, and that Charlie Hull has a crush on a certain coworker."

Max groaned. "That is not true."

"Well, at least the two of you have all summer together to explore the potential of a relationship. I look forward to toasting you both when you announce your engagement at Christmas."

"Hilarious," Max said, shaking her head. She lifted the drink Patrick had just placed before her. "I guess, since I lost the bet . . ."

"Which makes you the . . . what is it called?" He scratched his cheek dramatically, an affected expression of bewilderment claiming his lovely face.

"That would be the *loser* of the bet."

"Ah yes, that's the word I was thinking of. Please proceed."

"As I was saying, since I lost the bet, allow me to propose a toast to the winner of the bet, one James Worthington, who, by sheer luck alone, and possibly as a result of a sympathy move from Professor L., is working at the esteemed *New York Times* this summer, where he will most certainly shine and may even convince some old bugger over there to hire him for a full-time job after graduation. That is, if he graduates at all."

"That is one hell of a kind toast, Max. I appreciate your thoughtfulness."

"Don't mention it."

They lifted their glasses and clinked them together, making eye contact that practically melted Max's insides and almost, but not quite, began to make up for her job.

"To a productive summer," Max said.

"To a productive summer," James repeated.

They each took a sip and set their glasses down.

"So if Charlie's not the problem, what is?" James asked.

"They're not letting me write articles."

"How can that be?"

"They thought I'd be better suited to the official program and event listings sections and writing the captions for the various photographs."

"Did you talk to them about it?"

"You know me well enough to know that I marched myself into the office of the publisher, Mr. Babcock, and told him, calmly, that I thought there'd been a mistake and that I wished to write articles as well. He said that the sections I'd been assigned require more precision and attention to detail and he knows that's a stronger skill of women than men. Can you believe that?" Max had worked herself up at that point and had raised her voice quite considerably. She exhaled and took a long slug from her glass.

"Did you ask him if you could write articles *in addition* to doing the listings?"

"He said there was no way I'd have extra time and that the listings would take up the bulk of my day. He apologized when he realized that his decision was causing me distress, but said that what's done is done and, in not so many words, if I didn't like it, I could inform Professor Lincoln and perhaps he'd reassign me." Max finished off her drink and placed the glass a bit too firmly back onto the bar. The sound attracted Patrick's attention, and she signaled to him that she'd have another.

"Slow down there, cowboy. Are you sure about that?"

"I appreciate your fatherly worry, James, but I do know how to pace myself at a bar. And that first one has barely done its job of erasing my memory of the last eight or so hours. So, if you don't mind, I'd appreciate it if you'd concern yourself only with your own alcoholic intake and leave mine to the discretion of my dear friend Patrick and my very own self."

"As you wish," James said, smiling at Max and at Patrick, who had overheard.

"The worst part of it all is the contest. I need that tuition money, James. And I thought I'd have as good a shot as anyone in the cohort to submit a winning article. But if I'm not given the opportunity to write in the first place, then I can't enter the contest, and if I can't enter, then I can't win. And then it's possibly bye-bye to Max Roth at NYU next year."

"Why's that?"

"Things aren't going well for my dad's company and I don't know what's going to happen with his job. There might not be money for tuition, so if I can get it from Mr. Bing, that would be ideal," Max said, taking a sip of her second scotch. She noticed James noticing how much she was drinking.

James paused. "Excuse me, Patrick. Can we please see a menu? My friend here could use some food in that little body of hers, which is currently about to overflow with scotch."

The two men nodded at each other in some sign of male understanding, Max thought, but she didn't think a bit of food was a terrible idea. She took a breath and realized that the scotch had not only failed in helping her forget the happenings of the day but that it had made her feel almost worse about them.

"I'm so sorry to hear about what's going on with your family, Max. Hopefully, the economy will turn around soon."

"Let's change the subject. Tell me something about your day. Your perfect day at the *Times*, where they probably have miniature canaries singing gleefully in gilt cages and tiara'd ladies in pale yellow chiffon passing out sugar-dusted confections and ice-cold lemonade."

"Are you sure you don't want to tell me more about this situation with your father?"

"One hundred percent sure. I'd like to hear about the confections."

James laughed. "Well, there aren't confections or lemonade, and certainly no canaries, but they do have coffee available all day, and there were a couple of boxes of donuts in the kitchen this morning."

Max swooned. "Donuts."

Patrick set a basket of soft rolls in front of them. Max, suddenly feeling ravenous, took one and slathered butter on it.

"I hate to say this because I know how disappointing your day was, but I had a pretty good day. They let me sit in on the morning editorial meeting and asked me to introduce myself to the group and say what my career ambitions were. And the man I'm reporting to said I'd have plenty of opportunities to write. I'm going to start out doing mostly research focusing on what's going on in Europe, but he said that he'd start assigning me short articles in a couple of weeks."

"That's wonderful, James," Max said. She was entirely happy for her friend and proceeded to pepper him with additional questions about his day. If it couldn't be her at the *Times*, she didn't want it to be anyone else besides James. He was one of the most talented students in their cohort and, as such, deserved the placement he'd received. And perhaps, she thought, if James impressed his superiors and if Professor L. came through for her as he said he would, they might be working together at the *Times* after graduation.

"So what are you going to do about the contest?" James asked as a waiter set down the steak James had ordered. "Eat," he said, pushing the plate and a glass of water toward Max and handing her utensils and a napkin.

Max smiled at him. She appreciated his concern despite her having told him earlier to mind his own business. She was happy he had ignored her sass, and she spent the next couple of minutes silently enjoying her steak while James engaged in pleasant banter with Patrick about the fair.

"That was delicious," Max said, sighing loudly, resting her fork and knife on the plate.

"So the contest?" James asked.

"Do you think I should meet with Professor L.? I guess I could just wait until our Friday meeting. Maybe something will change before then. No use getting him involved if it turns out to be nothing."

"That's a good idea. Get a week under your belt, see what unfolds, and if things seem as dour on Friday, you're well within reason to speak with Professor L. Plus, I don't think he would appreciate the fact that your editor or publisher is making assumptions about what you'd be better at based upon being female. How does he know whether you have good attention to detail?"

"Exactly. He probably thinks women shouldn't even be working in the first place. That we should just graduate from high school, if even, and then get married, have babies, and be homemakers."

"Exactly."

"So that's what you think too?"

"No. That's not what I said." James smiled and shook his head.

"Oh, it very much *was* what you said." She knew he didn't mean it that way, but this was fun nonetheless. And Max enjoyed having fun with James. She'd have plenty of time later to tell him that she knew he was a modern man who didn't expect women to be subservient. At least, she didn't suppose he did.

They spent another hour together at the bar, talking about their summer jobs and the future beyond them, a future Max secretly hoped would include James. She'd never tell him, though. She may have been modern in her thoughts about professional aspirations, but when it came to men, she was a little bit more old-fashioned. She knew that if a man were interested in her, he'd pursue her. So far, James treated her like a kid sister, a classmate, a colleague with whom he could discuss their shared interest in journalism. Her summer assignment wasn't the only thing she'd have to be patient about. She just hoped she could turn the tide on both.

TODAY *at the* FAIR
Thursday, June 1, 1939
By Max Roth

OFFICIAL PROGRAM OF TODAY'S SPECIAL EVENTS

All Day—Various Closings

There will be minor closings and delays in certain areas of the grounds as fair management prepares for Monday's visit of the King and Queen of England.

2:00 P.M.—Japanese Pavilion Silk Demonstration

Expert silk workers from Japan use modern machines to create silk from thousands of cocoons, celebrating one of Japan's most traditional methods of production. In Japanese Pavilion, Hall of Nations.

5:45 P.M.—Free Admission at Futurama

General Motors will offer free admission this evening for Futurama. Ride a specially designed chair-car for a bird's-eye view of the United States in 1960. Designed by Norman Bel Geddes, this modern world contains tens of thousands of miniature homes, trees, automobiles, and more, spanning mountains, cities, lakes, and highways.

6:45 P.M.—New York City Police

Police Department Band and Glee Club concert at New York City Building.

(Events continue on p. 2.)

⎯⎯⎝⎠⎯⎯

CHAPTER ELEVEN

Vivi

Thursday, June 1

Vivi bit her nails as she walked toward the amphitheater for that morning's rehearsal. Something about the pain made her feel better. It distracted her from what she was really feeling, which was panic and sheer fear about her debut performances the very next night.

It had been a whirlwind couple of days in the pool. Despite Camilla's entreaties to Ed after the first rehearsal, he rejected her idea of having Vivi debut only the opening number and the finale.

Audiences are coming to see our new star! Vivi had overheard him shouting to Camilla when she approached him with the idea. He followed that sentiment with a *she'll do all the numbers and that's final!* gavel bang and stormed off to his office, puffing away on his ever-present cigarette.

So Camilla intensified her one-on-ones with Vivi, trying to stuff months of material into a few days.

And then there'd been the phone call with Jack. Though Vivi had resolved to handle the situation on her own, she was relieved when he'd called, reaching her in her hotel room two nights prior.

"What's this about them giving you only a few days to rehearse?"

"Who told you that?" Vivi asked.

"Gabe."

Gabe had called Vivi earlier that Tuesday night to see how her first day went. He must have called Jack as soon as he hung up.

"I told him not to tell you. I can handle it, Jack."

"This is my job as your agent, Vivi. Carl had told me Billy Rose was desperate to get a new star in right away, but I had no idea they were going to set you out to sea with no lifeboat."

"It does feel a little bit like that."

"Let me make a few calls. I won't have those Aquacade people humiliate you like this."

Vivi appreciated his concern, though she was doubtful he'd be able to accomplish anything. She'd seen the new programs the Aquacade people had printed up, and the big banners they'd hung outside the Aquacade with her photo on them. They'd invested a lot already in her debut, and Vivi couldn't imagine any threat from Jack would deter Ed and Billy from their plan.

She turned out to be right. Mostly. Ed told her that he appreciated Jack's concern, but audiences were excited to see her in the show, and that she should spend her time focusing on the choreography rather than on her negative thoughts. That she'd be fine. He did, however, concede to one compromise: Vivi would only swim in the 8:30 P.M. and 10:30 P.M. shows on her opening night. And for that, Vivi was thankful.

Now, distracted by her thoughts on the matter as she walked toward the women's dressing room, Vivi bumped directly into Johnny Weissmuller.

"Sorry, Johnny. I—I was just—My head was in the clouds," Vivi said, nervous to be talking to him. Of course, they'd interacted over the past couple of days in rehearsals, but small talk and swimming together had been the extent. They hadn't had a full conversation.

"It's fine, Vivi," he said, smiling kindly at her.

"You know, I've been watching the shows every afternoon from the audience and you look great out there," she said, her voice firm. She didn't want Johnny to think her personality was as limited as her performance so far in rehearsals. It was important that he see her as an equal partner—one he'd be able to count on in the water—and not as a weak link whom he could dismiss.

"Did you really think so?" he asked sincerely, turning his full attention, and with it a penetrating stare from his dark brown eyes, toward Vivi.

Chuckling to herself, Vivi thought Johnny almost made it too easy. Of course, he was just a man. It was all about ego. "Absolutely," she said in a tone that was complimentary but not in the least bit obsequious.

Now that they were talking for more than just a minute, Vivi was able get a good look at him. She'd seen him in *Tarzan the Ape Man* and a couple of the sequels, but she could convincingly confirm to anyone who asked (and in the letter she'd write that very night to Amanda about this very moment) that he was more handsome in person, despite being in his thirties. Because she was tall, Vivi stood eye to eye with many men, unfortunately eye to breast (theirs to hers) with many others, but Johnny was so tall, at least six foot three or four, that she found herself looking *up* to him. She'd never dated a man of that height, and she realized right then how alluring she found height on a man. He had dark hair, which matched his eyes, bronze skin that appeared as if the sun had personally reached down to kiss it, and a physique like a god borne of Olympus.

It was quite a thrill to be talking to Johnny Weissmuller. He was a film legend, after all, and Vivi was impressed with him though she was working hard not to give him any idea that she was. In fact, if anyone had been watching, they may have asked who was the stunning blonde talking to Johnny Weissmuller in such an aloof and in-control manner. They may have thought she had him eating out of her hand.

"Sorry I haven't been more welcoming. It's a tough time for me personally right now with the divorce and the engagement and all, so I've been a little distracted," Johnny said, raking his dark hair off his forehead with his fingers.

Anyone who read *Photoplay* was aware that Johnny Weissmuller had been in divorce proceedings for months with his second wife, the actress Lupe Velez. Their marriage had been a contentious one, and after filing for divorce on two prior occasions, she apparently meant it this time; they were just waiting for the paperwork to go through. Johnny hadn't wasted any time finding a new Mrs. Weissmuller, and had announced his engagement to socialite Beryl Scott back in February.

"That's okay, Johnny, I understand. Sorry you're going through all of that. Look, I just want to say that I'm doing my best to be ready for tomorrow night. You have nothing to worry about, and I'm looking forward to working with you and getting to know you better."

"Likewise. And just so you know, the combinations are tricky to learn. They certainly were for me and Eleanor, so I understand what you're up against. But you're doing great."

"That's very kind of you to say. I guess I didn't expect it to be so hard. And Ruby's a tough act to follow."

"She sure is."

"Though she seems intent on watching me fail. Kind of a nasty one, that girl," Vivi said, lowering her voice, all the while winking conspiratorially at Johnny. Certainly, he'd had to deal with her difficult attitude in some way since the show had started.

"I . . . ," Johnny began, looking taken aback.

"Vivi!"

Vivi turned to see Sadie, who appeared right next to them.

"Hi, Sadie," Vivi said.

"See you later," Johnny said to Vivi. He walked away suddenly.

"That was pretty brave of you," Sadie said, gesturing her chin toward Johnny as they both watched his retreating figure.

"Talking to Johnny?"

"Slamming Ruby Lancaster like that."

"She deserves it."

"That's true. Ruby hasn't given me the time of day since we started rehearsals back in the spring."

"So then what are you talking about? Why was it brave of me to say something negative about her?"

"Because I may not be one of her followers, but Johnny is. In fact, he follows her up to the diving bays every single afternoon."

"But he's married! And engaged!" Vivi said.

"Welcome to the Aquacade."

Sadie linked arms with Vivi, and together they walked into the dressing room to change for rehearsal.

Vivi had come so far since her first rehearsal on Tuesday; still, she was relieved when Camilla clapped her hands three times for lunch. That day, she would be going out for lunch with Sadie and her group of friends.

Walking back to the amphitheater after lunch, Vivi's breath caught in her throat when she saw a dark-haired woman waiting next to the ticket booth. She told the other girls to go on in, that she'd catch up with them in a minute.

The best part about the past week was that the constant movement, the unrelenting schedule, and the dreamless sleep brought on by sheer exhaustion all provided Vivi the gift of distraction. If she'd had more time to think about it, it would have been torturous. Being in New York, being so close to all of the reasons she'd left for Los Angeles, brought everything back so mercilessly. When she thought about it, she felt as if she were being pelted by hail.

It had ultimately been her choice to go, but Vivi had left so much behind. Had it really been her choice? Regardless, her departure had severed her relationships with the two people she loved most in the world. The only two people, besides her late parents, who had truly ever meant anything to her.

Now one of those two people, her sister, Maria, was standing before her.

"Alessia," Maria said, with a careful smile on her face. Her eyes were glassy, as if they'd been harboring tears for quite some time. "I saw your picture in the paper. That's how I knew you were here, though I almost didn't recognize you," she said, touching Vivi's hair, which was a completely different color than when Maria had seen it last. "And of course your name is different, but I knew it was you. Why didn't you get in touch when you got to New York?"

Vivi hadn't seen her sister in so long, and she'd missed her tremendously. She almost crumbled right there, crying, hugging Maria, reuniting. But then she remembered how horrible their parting had been.

Still, Maria was waiting for an answer.

"You said you never wanted to see me again. Why would I have been in touch?"

Vivi saw her words hit her sister as if they'd been a physical punch. Vivi looked around, searching for someone.

"Frank's not here," Maria said. "I left him."

Vivi felt herself exhale. She saw in her sister's eyes a glimmer of the girl she once was before Frank had come into her life. Vivi realized that now that he was gone, now that that awful man, who had been so controlling, so dangerous, was gone, perhaps Vivi and Maria could be sisters again. Maybe none of it mattered anymore. This was her sister, the only link connecting Vivi to her parents. But still. It had become so complicated. There was so much pain. Too much, it seemed, to go back to how things had been before.

"I'm sorry I said such awful things to you," Maria said.

"You can't just say sorry and expect it all to be forgotten."

"Maybe if you knew why I said it all, you'd understand. Every time Frank got drunk he would . . ." Maria paused, trying to form the words. "He would say things about you. You weren't safe in our home anymore, and I wanted you—no, I needed you—to go as far away as you could from him. I knew if I told you the truth, you wouldn't leave. You would have stayed to protect me. That's why I had to say those things to make you go."

Vivi stood still, trying to make sense of it all.

"And Sofia?" Vivi asked, choking up.

"She's with a neighbor for an hour. I wanted to come alone."

"How is she?"

Maria softened. "She's wonderful. Adorable and sweet. I'd like for you to see her."

"I'd like that too," Vivi said, tears filling her eyes, thinking of the little girl whom she hadn't seen in two years.

But then the memory of the last conversation she'd had with Maria came rushing back like a torrent, the conversation that had changed everything between the sisters. "I guess you were right, though," Vivi said, her tone filled with acid.

"About what?"

"That all I had going for me was my looks."

"Alessia," Maria said sadly, her eyes filled with regret.

"No, it's true. Look at me," Vivi said, putting her arms up as if she were on display. She swallowed painfully, trying to keep her voice firm. "I'm a Hollywood star. I'm a real-life showgirl in a big production. You said I only had my looks going for me, and guess what? The right people agreed with you. Now, if you'll excuse me, I'm going to be late for rehearsal." Vivi stared at her sister—the heartbreak of their relationship manifesting itself like heat, no, like fire, in her body—and then she walked away.

She wouldn't allow Maria to show up and expect everything to go back to how it was just because Frank was out of her life. It wasn't that easy. At least it wasn't for Vivi.

"Alessia, wait," Maria said.

Vivi stopped.

"I came to tell you something else. Please turn around. I don't want to shout this."

Vivi turned and Maria walked toward her.

"I saw your picture in the paper, which means it's possible that Frank did too. I'm not sure if he'd recognize you as easily as I did, but he might. If he comes here looking for you, you could be in danger, especially if he's drunk. And if he asks you if you've seen me, say you haven't. He doesn't know where Sofia and I are.

I spend every waking moment worrying about what will happen if he finds us."

Vivi nodded and then walked toward the Aquacade entrance gate. She hated to be callous to her sister, knowing how awful it must be for her to live in constant fear of that horrible man. But she needed time to think about what all of this meant. Her mind was in too much of a disarray at that moment to make any sense of it at all.

✲

CHAPTER TWELVE

Max

Thursday, June 1

"Max and Charlie!" Hugh Collier called out from the doorway of his office that morning, their fourth day at work.

Max and Charlie grabbed their notebooks and pencils and quickly walked toward the editor's office, taking the two seats across from his desk.

Hugh Collier's office matched its occupant. It was exceedingly tidy and there was very little color. Hugh reminded Max of a little gray bird. His grayish hair was cut close and his grayish eyes focused intently. He wore a white shirt, gray trousers, a gray vest, and a gray-and-white polka-dotted bow tie. So far he seemed kind enough.

"Good morning," he said, looking from Max to Charlie and back.

"Good morning," Max and Charlie repeated in unison.

"We've gotten off to a good start so far," Mr. Collier began, "and I just wanted to commend the two of you on your hard work."

Max thought her first few days at the paper had indeed gone well. She was now well acquainted with her responsibilities, and she hadn't suffered a negative word from Mr. Babcock or Mr. Collier. She hadn't heard much from them at all, positive or negative, but Max didn't require acclamation to motivate her to do a good job. Maybe girls like Louise Molloy fell all over themselves to get a "well done" from the boss, but not Max. She knew she'd done well. Didn't need a man in a tie to tell her so.

And despite not writing articles, it was still a thrill to see her byline each day in the paper. She had to hope that none of her parents' friends would see her name and rat her out.

"Max," Mr. Collier continued, "I've been thinking a great deal about your desire to have more responsibilities, and I've come up with a solution."

"Oh?" Max said, surprised.

"Marianne has requested an earlier departure time each day while she's caring for her ailing father. So I've decided to turn Marianne's afternoon production responsibilities over to you." Mr. Collier paused and looked toward Max.

Max knew that she was supposed to thank Mr. Collier. That he expected her to be appreciative of his overture. So she tried to think of happy things—cookies, rainbows, James—to urge a small smile onto her face.

"Thank you, Mr. Collier," she said, trying to sound grateful.

"You're quite welcome, Max," Mr. Collier said. "Each day, at five o'clock, when Charlie and I have finalized the articles and layout for the following day's issue, you'll take those pages in their special folder to the typeset office in Manhattan, where you'll give them all to our contact, Albert, who will handle it from there. Marianne will provide you taxi fare in an envelope each morning."

Max realized her new responsibilities meant being a messenger. She didn't feel she was above it, but she knew there wasn't much opportunity to learn at the post. Still, it was a necessary part of the production of *Today at the Fair*, and she would take that assignment seriously, as she did everything else.

"Thank you, Mr. Collier. I think I've got it all."

"Very well, Max. I can already tell, from your work this week, that you're well suited to these responsibilities. If you continue to fulfill your duties to my satisfaction, perhaps we can discuss the possibility of a test article in a month or so."

"Thank you."

"Now, I wanted to talk to the two of you a bit further about the special commemorative issue we're creating for Monday's visit by King George VI and Queen Elizabeth. Things will be quite hectic for the next several days, both here at the paper and around the grounds."

Max had never been a follower of British royalty, but her sisters had been going on and on about how exciting it was that the King and Queen would be visiting the fair. Just that morning at breakfast, they'd asked to go. Max's mother had replied with a firm no, saying what a mob scene it would be. Plus, they had school.

"There's a meeting today at Perylon Hall at noon about the fair's preparation for the royal visit, and I'd like you both to go. Here are your passes," Mr. Collier said, handing an envelope each to Max and Charlie. "Max, you'll see yours was originally designated for me, but since I can't go due to a prior commitment, Marianne suggested we call to ask if the pass is transferable, which it is. So you'll go in my place. Be sure you get information about the schedule so you can incorporate it all into the event listings for the regular day's paper as well as the special issue. And, Charlie, you'll meet with me later today so we can brainstorm all of the different articles you and I will write."

After Mr. Collier dismissed them, Max walked over to Marianne's desk.

"Thank you so much for suggesting I go to the royal visit meeting. That was really nice of you," Max said, smiling down at Marianne.

"My pleasure," Marianne said. "It seemed silly for the pass to go to waste." Marianne looked around to make sure no one in the small office was listening in. "For what it's worth, I think it's awful that Mr. Babcock isn't letting you write for the paper."

"I appreciate that."

"He can be a real jerk."

"I got the impression you didn't like him. You always seem to get very quiet when you interact with him."

"You noticed that?" Marianne asked, looking surprised.

"I'm a journalist. I'm observant," Max said, shrugging.

"I didn't realize it was so obvious."

"I wouldn't worry about it. I doubt he's noticed. He's always too busy going off to meetings and lunches."

"Thanks, Max. Anyway, I hope things change around here. We're overdue for a woman in this office to be treated well. Oh, and thanks for taking over the afternoon production stuff. My dad's not well, and I need to be home more."

"I'm sorry to hear about your dad, and I'm happy to take this off your plate."

The two spoke for a while longer, and then Max went back to her desk to work on the day's listings. Finally it was time for Max and Charlie to go to Perylon Hall.

There was a loud buzz in the meeting room as members of

different fair departments took their seats. Eventually a short man with cropped brown hair ascended a small stage at the front of the room and spoke into a microphone.

"Hello, I'm Phillip Weaver from the Fair Events office, and I welcome you all today to hear about the truly wonderful plans we have for the royal visit in four days' time. I know many of you are planning special events in your own departments to coincide with the visit, so I wanted to ensure that you were aware of the day's schedule, the route the King and Queen, along with their entourage, will be traveling, security measures that we are undertaking, et cetera. At the end of this presentation, you'll each receive a document containing details of what I'll review now."

Despite the promise of handouts, Max took copious notes throughout the presentation and was impressed by the scope of plans being made for the visit. She looked forward to figuring out how she could best present the comprehensive schedule in the paper.

"Do you want to grab a hot dog from one of the stands before we head back to the office?" Max asked Charlie as they walked out of the building.

He gave her a strange look.

"It doesn't have to be a hot dog," Max said. "A sandwich, whatever."

"It's not that. I already have plans." Charlie paused and appeared to be contemplating whether he should say more. "I'm going to lunch with Mr. Babcock and Mr. Collier," he said, rushing the words out of his mouth. "I didn't want to tell you because I knew it would make you feel bad, but I don't want to lie to you either."

"That's okay, Charlie. It's not your fault. I'm fine. I'll see you back at the office."

Max walked back toward the office and forced herself to think about the royal visit instead of how she'd been left out of an office lunch. She tried to convince herself there was probably a very good reason for it, even though her gut told her there probably was not.

As she approached the nearest hot dog stand, she saw a man turn abruptly and walk quickly away from her.

"Dad?" Max said loudly, confused, following him.

The man slowed, paused, and turned around, pursing his lips when he saw Max.

"What are you doing here?" Max asked, excited to see her father.

Max noticed her father starting to breathe heavily, and a slick of sweat formed on his forehead. Max took him by the arm and led him to a nearby bench, helping him take off his jacket and retrieving his handkerchief from his pocket, where she knew it would be, where it always was, and dabbing his brow with it.

Max let him rest for a moment, realizing quickly what was happening.

"I'm so sorry, Max. I didn't want you to see me like this."

"So what you thought might happen with your job actually did?"

Her father nodded and struggled to take a full breath.

"I'm so sorry," Max said, turning to face her father. "I wish I had known."

"I couldn't bear to tell any of you. You have to promise me that you won't tell your mother," he said, looking into Max's eyes for the first time since she'd called out to him.

"Okay," she said. Max hated the idea of lying to her mother about one more thing. She was already lying about her own job—the apple doesn't fall far, and all that—but she also couldn't imagine betraying her father.

"You know how she is. She couldn't handle this. Not now."

Max nodded, knowing he was right, and wanting to make this easier for him, even if just a tiny bit. "What happened?"

"Nothing I didn't know was coming."

"This morning?"

"Two weeks ago."

"But I . . . This morning . . . ," Max began, thinking back to that morning and every morning she could recall, as she watched her father take a few sips of coffee before rushing out the door to get to work.

"I couldn't—I was so ashamed."

Max sighed. Her heart ached for her father and what she knew he was going through. The pain he must have been experiencing and having no one to talk to about it. "What have you been doing every day?"

"I've been talking to other firms to see if anyone is hiring. I'll let you take a gander at how that's going. But mostly I've been walking. Going to museums that don't charge entrance fees, reading at the library. Today I finally allowed myself to spend a little money, and here I am," he said with enthusiasm that Max knew was forced.

"Pretty amazing, right?" Max said, gesturing around them at the fair, hoping to change the conversation a bit. Hoping to spare her father one more minute of feeling as if he'd let his family, let her, down.

"Pretty amazing," he said, nodding and smiling.

Max heard him take a breath, deep and clear, and he stuffed his handkerchief back into his pocket. She then saw something cross his face and he turned toward her.

"Hold on a minute. What are *you* doing here?"

Max took a breath and knew exactly what she had to do. "I'm on assignment, believe it or not. One of the editors at the *Times* is doing a piece on the fair and asked me to take some notes for him. I'm expected back soon so, unfortunately, I have to go. Otherwise, I would have loved to walk around with you."

"I'm so proud of you, Maxie," he said, leaning in to give her a kiss. "Now go. You have a job to do."

Max kissed her father and told him she loved him. And that his secret was safe with her. Then she rushed off toward the Administration Building, knowing her father would think she was heading toward one of the fair exits. She wouldn't have time to grab something to eat. She'd lost her appetite anyway.

TODAY *at the* FAIR
Friday, June 2, 1939
By Max Roth

OFFICIAL PROGRAM OF TODAY'S SPECIAL EVENTS

All Day—Various Closings

There will be minor closings and delays in certain areas of the grounds as fair management prepares for Monday's visit of the King and Queen of England. Monday's commemorative edition of *Today at the Fair* will contain the complete schedule of events.

3:30 P.M.—Happy Birthday, Tarzan

It's Johnny Weissmuller's birthday. Weissmuller, originally of *Tarzan* fame and now highly lauded for his strong strokes in the Aquacade, turns 35 today. Master of Ceremonies Morton Downey will lead the audience at each of today's Aquacade performances in a rousing rendition of "Happy Birthday."

8:30 P.M.—Aquacade Debut

Tonight is the much anticipated debut of the newest Aquabelle Number One, the gorgeous Vivi Holden, who took over Eleanor Holm's part. Straight from Hollywood, Holden will

swim into the hearts of audiences at the New York Amphitheater in the Amusement Zone during tonight's 8:30 P.M. and
10:30 P.M. shows. The lead role in the 3:30 P.M. and 5:30 P.M.
shows will be swum by understudy Ruby Lancaster.

(Events continue on p. 2.)

The New York Chronicle
Saturday, June 3, 1939
By Fran Haupstein

THIS TIME IT'S A FLOP INSTEAD OF A SPLASH FOR ROSE'S AQUACADE

Billy Rose's Aquacade, being staged at the New York Amphi-theater on the World's Fair grounds, had its second official opening last night when Hollywood actress Vivi Holden took over the lead role for the still injured Eleanor Holm.

All were heartbroken for petite paddler Holm when Rose's flack announced two weeks ago that the adorable former Olympian had retired her swimsuit after having sustained serious injuries from a nasty fall on the slippery pool deck.

Looking the part—in face and form—of a leading lady might be all Miss Holden has going for her. Having attended the original opening night of the Aquacade along with almost ten thousand other delighted showgoers on May 4, I can say with certainty that the only commonalities Miss Holden shares with Miss Holm are the first three letters of their surnames.

In other words, if Miss Holden doesn't clean her act up, pronto, there'll be a mad rush of audience members out of the Aquacade instead of in.

A source for the show told me in confidence that Rose and his deputies are aware of the deficiencies of their new star,

but he assured me that with a bit more practice, she'll out-
shine even Miss Holm. (That source wanted to remain anonymous so as not to fall out of favor with Rose, considering Miss
Holm is also the future Mrs. Rose.) In the meantime, I have it
on good account that they're set to send Ruby Lancaster back
in to save the show while Miss Holden continues rehearsing
at a frantic clip.

Upon Miss Holm's departure, Miss Lancaster had taken
over her part quite, er, swimmingly. This should reassure
those of you reading this while drinking your coffee and planning your day at the fair that it's safe to go back to the Aquacade, folks.

It was a delight to see for the second time the brawn and
impressive swimming of "Aquadonis" Johnny Weissmuller and
the skill of the divers, especially Dean Mitchell. The music, as
well, is still divine, with catchy tunes and rousing orchestra-
tions led by Vincent Travers.

Turns out, yesterday was Weissmuller's 35th birthday, and
master of ceremonies, the debonair Morton Downey, stole the
baton from Travers and conducted an off-key but enthusiastic chorus of audience-goers singing "Happy Birthday" to the
much-loved star. I suspect Miss Holden's performance was
Weissmuller's least favorite gift.

CHAPTER THIRTEEN

Vivi

Saturday, June 3

"Good morning, Vivi," Thad said to her with a tight smile as she entered the amphitheater through the cast-and-crew gate. "Ed wants to see you in his office as soon as possible."

Vivi swallowed hard and thought about her debut performances the night before. They hadn't been flawless. But she also could have done a lot worse.

Before the eight-thirty performance, Mr. Mackey, the Aquacade spokesman, had told her to meet him outside the dressing room immediately after the show so he could escort her to a press conference where she'd take questions from journalists and pose for photos. He said she'd most likely also have a one-on-one with *The New York Chronicle* theater critic, Fran Haupstein. But after the show, Mr. Mackey was nowhere to be found. Vivi waited for him for twenty minutes, shivering in her wet swimsuit. And because Ed had been busy with press after the eight-thirty show and she didn't see him after the ten-thirty, they hadn't had the chance to talk before she left the grounds, so drained that she was barely able to tell the cabdriver her destination.

"Have a seat, Vivi," Ed said in an unreadable tone when she entered his office. He was taking long, aggressive drags of his cigarette and stacking newspapers on his desk. Moving them around and stacking them again. And again. A flustered tic. "I assume you've seen *The New York Chronicle* this morning."

"I haven't. I meant to, but I was running late and—"

Ed stopped her mid-sentence by holding out his hand— encumbered by its low-burning cigarette—and ordering her to stop talking.

Vivi swallowed bitter bile and pursed her lips, physically tamping down the excuses and apologies and supplications. There was still part of her, though it was shrinking with every second that passed without a smile touching Ed's lips, that hoped it hadn't been that terrible. That Ed had just had an unfortunate morning due to a broken alarm clock or had spilled coffee on a newly laundered shirt.

But she knew that his morning had probably been bad because of her. And because of whatever those haughty theater critics had written about her in those newspapers he was fingering like a security blanket.

The phone rang and Ed stared accusingly at Vivi as if she had caused the disruption herself.

"Ed Tandy," he said brusquely into the receiver when he picked it up.

Vivi could hear an angry male voice on the other end, but she couldn't make out the words. She was only privy to Ed's side of the conversation. Could only feel his eyes boring into hers. She lowered her gaze to her lap and began picking her cuticles, dried from the chemicals in the pool.

Ed continued his one-sided conversation.

"She's here now."

"I'm about to."

"I'm aware of that, Billy."

"I agree. Consider it done."

About to what? Consider what done? Vivi realized that she was about to be fired. That she'd have to return to Los Angeles, probably on a bus this time, and that Mr. Green would be extremely disappointed in her. No, he'd be angry. Furious. And that would be the end of Vivi Holden at WorldWide Films. At any studio, once Mr. Green got on the phone and told the other studio heads about her inability to follow through on an assignment. That would be it for her acting career and that was not an exaggeration. Hollywood was a hive of buzzy gossip and painful stings, and once you were released from the colony, it was as if you'd never existed.

Vivi's eyes were still downcast, so she didn't see Ed push the newspaper toward her, only heard it, only felt the air displace. She looked up and saw it was that morning's *Chronicle*.

Ed stabbed forcefully, repeatedly, at a spot on the paper with his finger. "Read this."

After wincing at the headline, "This Time It's a Flop Instead of a Splash for Rose's Aquacade," Vivi read the article in full and then she stood up confidently, reaching her hand out toward Ed.

"Thank you, Ed. I appreciate this experience for what it was. I'm sorry I let you down." Once she realized he wasn't going to shake her hand, she pulled it back, pursed her lips, nodded once in an act of sealing her decree, and turned toward the door.

"Where the hell do you think you're going?" he yelled after her. Vivi turned and stared at him. "Aren't you going to fire me?" He paused for a second and took a deep breath. Then he softened the expression on his face and the tone in his voice, and the red in his cheeks faded to a less alarming shade of pink. "To be honest with you, Vivi, I'd like to. If it were up to me, I would have fired you after the eight-thirty show last night. But it's not up to me. It's up to Billy Rose."

Vivi had been relieved the day before when she'd heard that Billy Rose wasn't going to be in the audience for her debut shows. He was in Miami with Eleanor Holm, taking her to see a doctor friend of his. Vivi's nerves would have been worse had he, the mastermind behind the Aquacade, been watching. Now she thought his absence was what might have saved her job.

"I see," Vivi said calmly, unsure if she would have preferred getting fired so she could be relieved of this miserable assignment.

"And I realize now that we were unreasonable in our expectations of you."

Vivi felt a huge wave of relief—and redemption—pass through her body. "Thank you."

"Camilla tried to warn me, but I thought you could manage it all. So here's what's gonna happen. For the time being, I'm putting Ruby back in as the lead and I'm giving you an additional week to rehearse this role as if your life depended on it. Starting right after you leave this office and then every morning for the next week, you will work with Ruby starting at eight A.M. until your muscles twitch and your eyes burn. On Friday you'll take over for Ruby for the eight-thirty show. If your performance is anything less than perfect, I'll make the call to Carl Green myself and send you back to the coast. That's plenty of time to learn the numbers. Have I made myself clear?"

"Yes," Vivi said, still standing.

"Now go find Ruby and work out a rehearsal schedule."

"Ruby? You mean Camilla?"

"I mean Ruby. Camilla's gone. We only had her on contract through the end of May. She stayed a few extra days to work with you. Didn't you notice everyone saying good-bye to her yesterday?"

Vivi had, and it had seemed unusual considering they'd see her the next day. No one had bothered to tell her, Camilla included, that it was Camilla's last day at the production. Vivi didn't want to consider what that meant.

"Can we get her back? To teach me, I mean?" There was urgency in Vivi's voice and a look of worry on her face.

"She's working at a ballet in Manhattan. I've already spoken with Ruby, and she agreed to rehearse with you."

Vivi knew better than to express her reservations about that arrangement, certain that her opinion on the matter would have no effect on Ed's decision one way or another.

"No problem at all, Ed," she said, fixing a smile on her face. "No problem at all."

Vivi walked with her head down toward the dressing room. She felt ashamed and embarrassed. She imagined everyone in the cast had either read the *Chronicle* review or had been told about it, and the whispers she heard as she passed confirmed that. Vivi knew she'd been set up to fail, but she blamed herself a little bit as well. She hadn't succeeded in quieting the negative voices in her head about her abilities. Instead, she'd given them space to manifest.

She was kinder to herself when it came to how distracting the thoughts of her interaction with her sister had been. Seeing Maria had rattled Vivi. She'd played their conversation from two days prior over and over in her head. Some moments she regretted how angry she'd been and how she'd dismissed her sister.

And other moments she felt fully justified in doing so. But it was consuming her, and she knew she'd need to compartmentalize those thoughts so she could do her job.

Sadie sidled up to Vivi as she unpacked her bag in the dressing room. "I saw the review, Vivi. I'm so sorry."

"Thanks, Sadie. I knew I wasn't perfect, but I wasn't expecting that."

"That Fran Haupstein is known to be a real shrew."

"Shrew or not, she still gutted me. It's humiliating."

"Just forget about it. It means nothing," she said, and then softened her tone. "I saw you go into Ed's office when I came through the gate this morning. How did that go?"

"Better than I thought. I'm not getting fired. He's putting Ruby back in as lead all week and then I'll swim in the eight-thirty show Friday night. If he's not happy with my performance, though, that's the end of me. But—" Vivi paused, looking around to make sure they were alone, which they were, and then lowering her voice just to be safe "—because Camilla's gone, I have to rehearse with Ruby."

"Oh boy."

"Exactly. She hates me."

"She doesn't hate you. She's just jealous because you have the role she thinks should be hers."

"Which is why I can't imagine that she's going to make any effort to teach me. It's in her best interest to sabotage the whole thing, to teach me the wrong strokes and make me look like a fool because then she'll get my part."

"But then Johnny will be angry, and she doesn't want that. From what I hear, she's in love with him, and if you can't swim the part, it makes him look bad. Plus, Ruby's dream in life is to hook her wagon on to Billy Rose's horse and follow him around the world, performing in his productions. She can't afford to aggravate him, either."

"Let's hope you're right," Vivi said.

"Vivi!"

Sadie and Vivi both turned to see Ruby, with a wide, cloying smile, approaching them, holding a massive bouquet of flowers. Vivi smiled politely. She wouldn't stoop to Ruby's level.

"These are for you," Ruby said, placing the arrangement down on the counter at Vivi's dressing area. "A messenger stopped me as I was walking near the gate just now and asked me if I'd take them to you. From your mother?" Ruby asked in a syrupy voice, pulling the small card from where it was pinned to the bouquet and thrusting it at Vivi with a straight and deliberate arm.

Vivi looked into Ruby's eyes and saw malice.

"My mother died when I was fifteen," Vivi said.

"I'm sorry," Ruby said, looking suddenly contrite. And almost human. "My mother died too."

"I'm sorry," Vivi said, nodding and looking into Ruby's eyes, thinking it would be nice to be able to connect with this woman rather than lock horns with her.

Vivi took the card and read it quickly to herself. "They're from my boyfriend, Gabe," Vivi said, tucking the card in among the riotous blooms.

"So sweet," Sadie said.

"I guess he probably meant for them to be delivered yesterday before your performance. Not today, after that business in the *Chronicle*. Hope it didn't upset you too much," Ruby said smugly.

Vivi realized the detente between Ruby and her, unfortunately, was to be short-lived.

"I'm fine, Ruby, but thanks for your concern," Vivi said, a smile crossing her lips and light dancing in her eyes. Vivi decided that, despite Ruby's venom, if she had to deal with her, she was going to take the high road. Sadie was right. Regardless of how much Ruby wanted Vivi to fail, if Vivi did, then it would make Ruby look just as bad. Vivi would milk that knowledge for all it was worth. "Ed told me to tell you that we'd be meeting each morning starting at eight A.M." Then she decided a small lie would be appropriate. "He also said that I'm to report back to him each afternoon to let him know how your instruction is going so he can be sure you're taking the task seriously."

"He said that?" Ruby asked, a confused and, Vivi thought, defeated look on her face.

"He did."

"Meet me in the pool in ten minutes," Ruby said. "We have a lot of work to do."

Ruby started to walk away, but Vivi decided to say one more thing while Ruby was still in earshot, not to Ruby but to Sadie, a bit of payback for how awful Ruby had been to her. "Sadie, did I tell you what Johnny told me in rehearsal the other day about the sweet way he proposed to Beryl?"

Vivi heard Ruby harrumph. And though the provocation of Ruby brought her a moment of joy, it was fleeting. The memory of Fran Haupstein's words came rushing at her like a mudslide.

CHAPTER FOURTEEN

Max

Saturday, June 3

It was late morning, a few days after she'd run into her father at the fair, and Max was having trouble focusing on her event listing edits; the tediousness of her tasks bored her. There was a lot of activity in the office regarding Monday's upcoming royal visit, but none of it involved Max. She'd done a draft of the schedule of events, and though she'd brainstormed ideas for articles for the commemorative issue, they'd all been assigned to Charlie. He'd asked her to stop coming up with ideas, because every time she did, it created more work for him.

She put down her pencil and turned to her left to stare out the window. It was a curse and a gift to have a brain that was always working. A brain that never took a break from coming up with ideas, figuring out problems, planning ahead. A curse because it never allowed a moment of quiet. A gift, though, because it often devised something useful. And that was exactly what had just happened. Max gasped quietly and knew precisely what she was going to do.

This plan, so quickly formulated by her brain and now being meticulously and rapidly plotted as if a team of workers had their feet up on desks in her skull, would provide a way to minimize the monotony, at least for a short while. It would also move her one step closer toward her ultimate goal, which was writing articles for *Today at the Fair*.

Max collected some papers on her desk and stuffed them, along with a pencil and a pad, into her bag. She then stood up and walked toward Marianne's desk.

"How's your father doing, Marianne?" Max asked.

"Not so great," Marianne said, attempting a smile.

As much as one could in a week, Max and Marianne had become friendly. They'd had lunch together one day, Marianne telling Max about how she was from a neighborhood right near the fair, about her big family, about her love for animals, especially her two Boston terriers.

But despite Marianne's kindness, Max noticed an underlying sadness, a hesitation, in her new friend. Max knew Marianne had a great deal of responsibility for her father and that it weighed heavily on her, but that didn't explain why Marianne often seemed on edge in the office.

"I'm so sorry to hear that. Is there anything I can do for you?"

"That's sweet of you, Max, but we're okay. Off somewhere?"

"Yes. Strangely enough," Max said to Marianne in a tone she'd affected to convey surprise tinged with a small amount of alarm. "Several departments didn't turn in their memoranda. It's so unlike them." Max tsk-tsked and shook her head at the irresponsibility.

Max felt bad lying to Marianne like this, but she knew it wouldn't affect Marianne in any way. Plus, if Marianne (who had told Max she admired her determination) knew what Max was up to, Max knew Marianne would support her wholeheartedly. The only reason Max wasn't telling her the truth was so she wouldn't entangle her in the scheme, potentially setting Marianne up to endure any wrath from Mr. Babcock and Mr. Collier if something should go wrong. Not that anything would, but Max was being cautious.

Those departments had indeed turned in their memoranda, but said memoranda were now safely concealed in Max's handbag and would be transferred to the nearest trash can on the fairgrounds as soon as Max moved on to the next step in her plan.

"That *is* so unlike them."

"I guess I'll pay a visit to the departments with missing memoranda. It's no problem. I don't mind."

"You're such a good sport, Max. What a hassle. I'd be a lot more annoyed than you seem to be. It's not that difficult an assignment for the different fair departments: memoranda in by nine A.M."

"I know, but what choice do I have? I want to make sure the listings are all accounted for and correct."

"You're terrific. And I'm going to tell Mr. Babcock and Mr. Collier that very thing when they get back from their meeting. Go ahead. I'll cover for you if anything comes up."

"Thanks, Marianne. I appreciate it," Max said, heading out the door.

Max was happy to be back in the fresh air—chilly as it was—and pleased that phase one of the scheme had proceeded so flawlessly. She tossed the evidence into the nearest trash can, as she'd planned, but not before first writing down in her notebook which departments she had to visit. She'd selected them purposefully.

The strategy behind all of this was that Max would introduce herself to the media relations personnel in the departments that most interested her. That way, when she was able to write articles, she'd already be familiar with the people she'd need to contact to obtain interviews and information.

Max took her worn fair map out of her handbag and decided to go to the farthest department on her list first. Then she'd work her way back to the Administration Building with plenty of time to edit the listings and be in a cab by five to head into Manhattan to deliver the package to Albert at the typeset office.

"What happened to Marianne?" Albert had said in a concerned voice Thursday afternoon, the first day Max had shown up with the package.

"She's fine. I'm just running production now. I'm Max. I'm a student at NYU working at the fair for the summer."

"I'll miss that sweet girl, but it's quite fine to meet you, Max," Albert said, extending his hand and revealing a wide smile with crooked yellowed teeth. Albert was an older man, tall, about six foot, with hunched shoulders. He seemed kind and Max thought that seeing him would be a nice way to cap off each day.

She and Albert had even begun a little game. They'd never set out the rules, never even mentioned they were playing; it just seemed to happen. The first day Max arrived with the package, Albert had handed her two peppermints.

On Friday, the second day, Max decided to give him something in return. She'd scoured one of the concession stands at the fair during her lunch hour that day and had selected a postcard that bore a photograph of the fair's most recognizable symbols, the Trylon and Perisphere, in the most graceful morning light.

Albert had smiled at her when she gave it to him, had stared at it a long time, and then told her every evening, when he needed a break, he went to the highest floor in the building that their company occupied and stared out a particular east-facing window where he could see a sliver of the lit-up Trylon and Perisphere in all their glory. He hoped to be able to take his wife to the fair one day soon.

And so it went. Today Max would pick up a pickle pin from the Heinz Dome in the Food Zone; she hoped it would elicit a hearty laugh from Albert. The pickle pins were one of the most coveted souvenirs the fair had to offer; thousands flocked to the Heinz Dome every day to claim one.

Now, as she headed toward the press office in the Court of States (the area in the Government Zone where twenty-one US states had pavilions), Max felt like a sailor on shore leave, with a skip in his step but still feeling the sense of urgency to pack it all in, to suck the marrow out of the day, and to use his time wisely before he had to walk the plank back to the confines of his ship.

The head of events for the Court of States was a Miss Aberdeen. Because of a mishap with the memoranda earlier in the season, each office responsible for submitting them had been told to keep a copy each day. So when Max told Miss Aberdeen that there'd been another situation and the Court of States memo was missing from the box, Miss Aberdeen didn't flinch and it took her only a minute to retrieve her copy and hand it over to Max.

Max then took advantage of this face-to-face with Miss Aberdeen and told her that should she have any events that she'd especially like covered in an article, she should feel welcome to call the *Today at the Fair* offices and ask for Maxine

Roth. She'd then be delighted to pitch the article to the editor in chief.

That then led to a conversation about the wonderful offerings in the Court of States, the exciting news that Miss Aberdeen had just become engaged and would be marrying a Mr. Thom Alemany at the end of the summer (*how lucky I won't have to change my monogram*, she'd confided), and the decision that the two of them, Miss Aberdeen (*please call me Alice*) and Max, would meet up soon for a concert in the Music Hall or for a drink at the Swiss Pavilion Garden.

This same performance played out several more times at the press offices in the Hall of Nations, the Community Interests Zone, the Food Zone, and the Communications and Business Systems Zone.

In that last one, she'd engaged in a lengthy discussion with their head of media relations, a young man named Arthur Zeitlin. She hadn't seen Arthur in years, since they'd worked together on their high school paper, when he'd been a senior and she'd been a freshman. Max had always had a crush on Arthur, but she'd lost track of him when he left for Yale. Now, here he was, newly graduated from the Harvard Business School and working at the fair.

When he told her he'd just finished for the day and would she like to get a drink, she asked him, startled, what time it was. And when he replied, in a calm voice, that it was five o'clock, Max grabbed her handbag and bolted from the office without so much as a good-bye to Arthur. Luckily, Max wasn't far from the Administration Building, and she ran as if she were competing. As if there were a gold medal at the end.

During that sprint she realized the trouble she was in, duly confirmed when she finally arrived back at the *Today at the Fair* office.

"Where have you been?" Mr. Collier shouted at her as soon as he saw her. She looked to her left and saw Mr. Babcock standing in the doorway to his office, a scowl on his face and his hands on his hips. He couldn't look more like a principal disappointed to find out his star student had defaced the girl's washroom. She looked to her right and saw Charlie with a strange expression on his face. Marianne looked frightened and distressed.

"I'm so sorry. I was out collecting listings since the memoranda were missing this morning and—"

"Do you realize what time it is?" Mr. Collier's voice was firm and angry.

"I do and I'm so sorry and I'll get to work on these edits right away and have them done in just a minute and—"

"We both know those edits will take at least a couple of hours. What you may not be aware of, Miss Roth, is that the delay in getting the final pages to the typeset office this evening will cost us quite a bit in late fees. Due to our small budget, we have only until six o'clock each night as a deadline before we start getting charged for every half hour over that. So I suggest we table the remainder of this conversation so you can get to work."

"Yes, sir. I'm so terribly sorry," Max said quietly, keeping her head down as she rushed to her desk and began her work.

It was 6:45 when Max finally finished. She was prepared to rush out and grab a cab to Manhattan. As she rose, however, she noticed Mr. Collier was still in his office.

"Miss Roth," he called to her, and she entered his office without trying to take up any space. "I have a dinner engagement in Manhattan right near the typeset office, so I will deliver the package myself this evening," he said, extending his hand and standing up to collect his things.

As she placed her work in his hand, Max tried to explain again.

"I'm angry, Miss Roth. And every additional moment we beat this dead horse costs us more money. We will have ample time to discuss what happened." With that, he placed her work into the day's package and left.

Max was the only one remaining in the office. She straightened her desk and turned off all of the lights. As she shut the door behind her for the night, she realized that she'd most likely destroyed any chance she'd ever had to write an article for *Today at the Fair.*

The first thought that came to her mind was how nice it would be to have a drink and talk with James, to vent about her day, to let a nice glass of scotch absorb her sorrows. But she hadn't heard from him since they'd had drinks at the Turf Trylon Café on Tuesday night. She presumed he was busy with work.

Going home was the very last thing Max wanted to do, not having any desire to deal with the questions she'd certainly face from her parents and her sisters about her exciting day at the *Times.*

She'd kept her father's secret since she'd run into him at the fair a few days prior. It hadn't been difficult. He dressed every morning for work and left with his paper after a quick cup of coffee. If Max's mother even suspected what was going on, she chose not to notice. Max was concerned about him, but she still hadn't had an opportunity to speak with him alone. In the mornings, he left before she had a moment of privacy with him. At night, he claimed he was too busy with things around the apartment or with helping her mother clean up after dinner or a million other excuses. Max realized he didn't want to talk about it. She'd have to respect his wishes.

Since she'd been leaving the fairgrounds every day in the late afternoon to go to the typeset office, she hadn't yet spent an evening wandering around the fair. Perhaps it would be a good way to clear her mind. She grabbed a copy of that day's event listings and ran her finger down the list until she found out what was happening at seven o'clock. As soon as she saw it, her finger stopped. She grabbed her bag and rushed out of the office, not wanting to miss a single word.

CHAPTER FIFTEEN

Vivi

Saturday, June 3

Vivi tried not to think about that morning's *Chronicle* review and the conversation she'd just had with Ed as she quickly changed into her swimsuit to meet Ruby for their first rehearsal. Ruby had said she'd meet Vivi in the pool in ten minutes, and Vivi didn't want to be late.

"I'm going to do things a little differently than how Camilla did them," Ruby said in an imperious tone, once they were standing by the pool. "I know you've only practiced in the pool, but I think it's easier to learn on the stage. That's how we started rehearsal back in the spring when it was too cold to get in the water."

"Okay," Vivi said, willing to try anything to meet Ed's expectations of her come Friday.

They began by running through one of the complicated duets that Vivi would perform with Johnny. This number had confounded Vivi the most in past rehearsals since, because she and

Johnny were the only two in the pool, she wasn't able to look at any other swimmer when she forgot which way to turn or which arm to spiral first. Ruby moved through the steps quickly, at a pace that made it difficult for Vivi to keep up. Vivi tried to minimize the feelings of frustration, reasoning that if she could do that, she would have more mental space to learn the moves. That was it: tamp down the doubt, make room for confidence.

They didn't have an orchestra to rehearse with, so Ruby hummed while Vivi counted out the beats.

It was within the first half hour of this arrangement that Vivi realized Ruby would exhaust all of her patience. Ruby's approach was different than Camilla's for sure, and that wasn't entirely bad, but her comportment was downright insolent.

Each time Vivi made a mistake, Ruby would yell, "No!" and then she'd demonstrate the movement again for Vivi. "Like this!"

"I know this must be aggravating for you, Ruby, but there are better ways to elicit a good result from me than yelling as if I were a dog you were training," Vivi said calmly after the prior depiction had occurred a handful of times.

"Don't be so sensitive," Ruby said, a patronizing tone in her voice. "Now again."

The morning proceeded, and though Vivi had been willing to give Ruby's out-of-the-pool practice idea a chance, she realized that it wasn't working. It was effective for understanding the marking of a number and the hand motions, but because she was sashaying across a stage on land as opposed to gliding through the water, the whole process seemed detached from what she actually needed to learn.

"I appreciate that this style worked for you when you were learning, Ruby, but I think I'm better off in the pool," Vivi said in a polite but decidedly not subordinate manner.

"You're going to have to trust me on this," she said condescendingly, as if speaking to a disrespectful child objecting to her teacher's confusing instruction of cursive. "I have more experience than you do, and I know what works and what doesn't. Plus, you can't be certain that my style of teaching is the issue; perhaps you're not paying close enough attention. Or perhaps you're not skilled enough. Now again!"

Stunned by Ruby's nerve and arrogance, Vivi decided she needed to change the dynamic between them, so she took a different approach.

"Can we just get this whole thing out in the open?" Vivi asked.

"What whole thing?" Ruby asked, tilting her head and putting her hands on her hips.

"I know it's not fair that I got Eleanor's part when it's obvious to anyone who watches you swim that you are beautiful in the water. Trust me, I'd rather be back in LA working on a movie. But Billy Rose had other plans for you and me. So now, since we're both here and this is the situation, what do you say we bury the hatchet and make the most of it?"

Ruby paused and Vivi presumed she was weighing her options. She could continue punishing Vivi. Or she could make everything more pleasant for both of them. "What exactly are you suggesting?"

Vivi held back a smile. She didn't want Ruby to think that Vivi had won this argument. In fact, Vivi wanted Ruby to come away thinking this had all been her idea. "Stop treating me like the enemy, and in return I'll work incredibly hard and everyone will give you the credit for it. Billy Rose won't think twice about casting you in his next show because you've shown that you're a team player."

"You think he'll see it that way?"

"Absolutely."

Ruby took a deep breath. Vivi noticed the enmity drain from Ruby's face and her shoulders drop two inches.

"I guess I was taking my anger out on you," Ruby said, still a small amount of fire in her voice, but much, much less than there had been before. "When I took over Eleanor's role, they never told me it was temporary. I was surprised when you showed up."

"I can understand that. I'll tell you what. You help me out by teaching me the part and making me look good this Friday night, and I'll make it up to you somehow."

"How?"

"I'm not sure yet. But I'll come up with something. I promise."

Ruby seemed to be assessing Vivi. Vivi stayed silent and hoped they could move forward in a more positive way. After a minute, Ruby nodded and resumed their rehearsal. Vivi knew not to expect they'd become best friends overnight; Ruby still harbored some resentment for her, which Vivi understood. But the tone of their interactions changed immediately, and Vivi found that being more relaxed made her pick up the moves more easily.

They took a break from each other at lunch—Vivi joined Sadie and a couple of the other swimmers (Betty, Ginny, and Meg, non-Rubettes the lot of them) for egg-salad sandwiches at the nearby Midway Inn.

As they walked, the girls talked about the latest gossip among their castmates. Vivi tuned them out and found that she was looking around, staring at the faces of every woman and man she passed.

In the women's faces, she was looking for her sister, Maria, wondering if she would come back and try to talk to Vivi again.

Their conversation had riled Vivi. The feelings it stirred in her confused her and made her sad. Part of her wanted to find her sister and Sofia and make everything better. And part of her didn't think she could ever forgive her sister for what she'd done. Regardless, Maria hadn't told her how to contact her, so even if Vivi did want to continue their conversation, she had no way of doing so.

And in the men's faces, she was looking for Maria's husband, Frank. Frank had been charming when he and Maria first met. Vivi's parents had been alive then, and even they thought he was a good match for their daughter. But after the wedding, and after the miscarriage, and after Frank lost his job, he started drinking. And that's when everything changed.

Frank had one of those New York faces: dark hair, brown eyes, thick eyebrows, bent nose that had been broken at least once in an after-school brawl or an amateur boxing match, and a pronounced five-o'clock shadow that developed around noon. The same face that every third man at the fair had. Whenever Vivi walked through the fairgrounds since Maria had warned Vivi that Frank might try to find her, there had been a constant hum of fear clutching her stomach every time she saw one of those faces. At least a few times, she was certain it was Frank, and her palms would begin to sweat and her heart would begin to race. But the man would disappear into the crowd, or he'd be too tall to be Frank, or the cut of his suit would be too smart.

"Vivi, what are you staring at?" Sadie was poking Vivi in the shoulder, trying to get her attention.

"What?"

"We're here, but you look like you're off in outer space. Is everything okay?"

"Yeah, sorry. I was just thinking about my morning with Ruby."

"Just try to put all that aside for a bit and enjoy your time with your real friends."

Vivi and Sadie followed the others into the Midway Inn and sat down for lunch.

"Did you all hear about Mickey Rooney and Judy Garland?" Betty asked.

"No, did something happen to them? I love them!" Meg said.

"Nothing like that. My sister's a waitress at the Rheingold and she said that she heard from a waiter whose brother works at the Parachute Jump that Mickey and Judy were here last night and rode the ride twice!"

"I can't believe I missed that," Ginny said.

"Apparently," Betty continued, "they tried to disguise themselves to go undetected, but someone recognized them and asked for an autograph, so a crowd formed. It became so chaotic, they had to be escorted off the grounds by police!"

"We miss all the fun working so many hours at the Aquacade," Meg said, pouting.

"Just be happy you have a job, Meg," Betty said, turning to her and raising her eyebrows.

"Exactly," Ginny said. "And if you don't want yours anymore, Meg, my sister will snatch it up. She's been trying to get a job at the fair for weeks."

"I'll ask my sister to find out if they're hiring at the Rheingold. Seems like everyone I know has a sister or a brother working at the fair, so why shouldn't you, Ginny?"

"Thanks, Betty."

"Of course. Actually, we have to hurry so we can be back in time for the wedding."

"What wedding, Betty?" Vivi asked, joining the conversation for the first time since she'd sat down.

"Jack Sullivan and Peggy Maeder's wedding. Not the actual white dress and church, of course. That's going to be a family affair on Long Island tomorrow morning. But they're doing a little something for the cast at the end of lunch. We're going to toss rice at them in the pool."

"They're adorable," Meg said. "I heard they fell in love the first day of rehearsals."

Betty lowered her voice and leaned into the middle of the table so the others could hear her. "Did you hear about Leanne?"

All the girls except for Meg shook their heads.

"You didn't hear it from me, but she's pregnant."

"I didn't know she was married," Sadie said, covering her mouth with her hand.

"She's not, dummy," Meg said. "I heard that one of the divers is the father and that baby is a result of a diving-bay affair."

"I heard that too," said Betty, nodding. "She's telling Mr. Tandy today that she's leaving the show, using the excuse that she has to help her mother with her baby sister."

"Why does she have to leave?" Ginny asked.

"You can't be pregnant in the Aquacade, Ginny," Meg said, looking at her friend as if she were crazy.

"It's not like she's showing yet."

"I know, but if they find out, she'll be so humiliated."

"I'm sure the father of the baby doesn't have to leave the show. That's not fair," Vivi said, picking at the crust on her plate.

The girls chewed their sandwiches in silence for a moment.

"It's her own fault if you ask me," Sadie said. "What did she expect, going up to the diving bays in the first place? Plus, they were very clear when we auditioned that we have to maintain the utmost integrity: no husbands, no babies, no weight gain, and no shenanigans with the other cast members."

"It's time to go," Betty said, standing up suddenly. "I don't want to miss the send-off for Jack and Peggy!"

When the girls returned to the pool, there was already a crowd assembled around one corner. Swimmers were cheering as Vivi and Sadie rushed to get a spot. Someone shoved rice into their hands, and they threw it into the pool at Jack and Peggy, who were kissing. Vivi had always thought Peggy was stunning, with her dark head of curls and her long legs. And Jack was unquestionably the most attractive swimmer, besides Johnny of course. It was a sweet interlude and a nice break in an otherwise horrendous day of rehearsal for Vivi. She thought about Gabe for a moment and smiled to herself, thinking about the phone call they'd probably have that night.

Vivi wondered what it all meant now for Jack and Peggy. Would Peggy be forced to leave the show now that she was married? Would Jack? What would it matter if they were married anyway? Vivi knew that's just the way things were, but lately she'd begun to question why that was. And what it all meant for her.

After two more hours of rehearsal, Ruby went off to make herself up for the three-thirty show. Vivi was pleased that she'd stood up to Ruby, who had softened her edges considerably, creating a much more pleasant environment for the two of them.

Vivi walked quickly to the dressing room and found a back corner where she could change into her street clothes. She didn't want to be near the swimmers who were, at that moment, beginning the exacting multistep hair-and-makeup preparations required for the shows.

She wanted to slip away unnoticed, without calling any attention to herself. It had been a grueling day and she didn't have the energy to deal with the complicated dressing-room social structure.

Once she was dressed, Vivi made her way to the top row of the amphitheater. She'd vowed to catch at least one show a day, hoping she'd learn from watching. In the far corner of the top row, she could move in her seat, mimicking the hand motions of the swimmers down below without anyone else noticing.

Vivi loved watching the show and wondering what the audience members around her were thinking. They probably assumed the swimmers were glamorous showgirls, each more beautiful than the next, with glowing skin and alluring curves; that these girls' lives were exciting and filled with nonstop action and romance; and that they had no problems. They'd probably be surprised to learn that while those showgirls were swimming, executing perfect crane positions and porpoise dives, Betty was formulating her grocery shopping list, Ginny was wondering whether she'd be able to make her rent this month, and Meg was worrying about her father, who still hadn't found a job. People were people. Different costumes, same problems.

There were so many young women working at the fair that summer: as waitresses and Girl Guides, running demonstrations in the business buildings and leading tours in the international pavilions, assisting fairgoers in every capacity. Vivi thought each woman came to the fair with her own goals, but so many of those were similar: to be fulfilled. To contribute in some way to society and to the livelihoods of themselves and their families. To expand their horizons. They were all exactly like Vivi and they were all entirely different. As women always were.

When the three-thirty performance finished and the crowds snaked their way to the exits, Vivi stood in the last row and tried to work her way through each number, moving her feet, waving her arms, counting the beats over and over in her head. But there was too much to remember and she was overwhelmed with frustration. Because she would learn one number for a short while—in first Camilla's and now Ruby's training regimens— and then move on to the next, they were all getting jumbled in her mind. She tried to ignore the stinging behind her eyes, and tried to talk herself down by saying that everything would be okay, that any day now it would all click.

As the audience swelled once more, for the five-thirty show this time, Vivi resumed her seat, took a deep breath, and said to herself, "Now again."

Just before 7:00 P.M., after the five-thirty show had ended with the Americana finale that made Vivi cry with joy and pride every time she saw it, and after the cast was back in the dressing rooms, grabbing a snack from the sandwich and fruit trays set out for them, Vivi followed the audience out of the amphitheater and was absorbed into the parade of thousands of fairgoers. She decided to walk a bit, perhaps pick up dinner from one of the many stands. And clear her mind.

It was Saturday night and the crowded pedestrian avenues were filled with New Yorkers who had come by subway and tourists who had come from across the country and across the world. Plus, there was a lot of extra activity, such as stanchions and grandstands being set up, that Vivi figured was in prepa- ration for the King and Queen of England's visit that coming Monday. She'd read all about it in *Today at the Fair*. She thought it would be fun to watch them parade by, but knew she wouldn't have the opportunity with her rehearsal schedule.

Fairgoers were smiling, walking fast, excited to see for themselves everything they'd heard about and read about. For the world was talking about the fair. And if you paid attention, you would be unable to stay away. You'd feel a pull toward the thousand-plus acres of spectacle, as if the fair had its own gravitational draw. It was a moment in history and the clock was ticking. Get it all in or never have the chance.

CHAPTER SIXTEEN

✲

Vivi & Max

Saturday, June 3

As Vivi and Max each walked through the fair that night—Max through the central axis of the fair toward the grand avenue called the Court of Power to hear Elizabeth Dorchester's speech, and Vivi on her way to tour the Democracity exhibit inside the Perisphere just beyond the Court of Power—they couldn't help but be swept up into the energy of all that was transpiring around them.

Neither Vivi nor Max knew that their lives were about to intersect. A collision dictated by the universe that would have long-lasting implications for both. Chance encounters—seeming coincidences of place and time—were fickle. Sometimes such encounters embodied a chemistry and mind of their own, resulting in relationships that were momentous. And sometimes those encounters had as much energy as a speck of inconsequential dust, meant to be overlooked and immediately forgotten.

The universe had plans for Vivi and Max. But the two young women were unaware, as was the case before any two strangers converged. Instead of tingling with the sensation that everything was about to change, they were consumed by their own thoughts of the day.

First, Vivi.

The feelings of wonder and joy Vivi had felt earlier that night while watching the two Aquacade performances began to fade, bulldozed by overbearing feelings of doubt. Doubt that she'd be ready by Friday, due to the extent of what she had to learn. Doubt that even if she did pick up all of the moves, which was unlikely, she'd never cut a line in the pool as gracefully as Ruby, would never live up to Ed's or Billy Rose's exacting standards for Aquabelle Number One. It came down to math: TimeAvailable < AmountToLearn. The equation did not compute in her favor.

Vivi had been doing everything in her power to avoid giving up entirely, but she was beginning to feel that it had all become too much. She realized she might just have to explain the situation to Jack, who, as her agent, would then have to tell Mr. Green and Billy Rose. She understood the potential consequences—Mr. Green had been quite clear—but this situation was untenable.

For now, though, Vivi would try to enjoy the fair.

Then, Max.

As Max walked, dark thoughts began to consume her overactive brain and she convinced herself that she'd be fired from *Today at the Fair*. Because she'd missed that day's five-o'clock deadline, she'd cost the paper a bucketful and infuriated both Mr. Babcock and Mr. Collier.

She knew the appropriate thing to do would be to telephone Professor L. and tell him what had happened so he wouldn't be caught off guard if he were indeed contacted by Mr. Babcock or Mr. Collier. Professor L. would not appreciate being caught off guard. If it were even possible to preserve any shred of their relationship after the stunt she'd pulled, she'd need to get to him before either of her bosses did. She wondered how late she could call him on a Saturday night and how she was going to manage to get his home number. She'd find a way.

For now, though, Max would try to enjoy the fair.

The Court of Power was breathtaking, its expansive pedestrian avenue hugged by lush gardens. Everywhere Vivi and Max looked there were statues, fountains, flags, and benches; endless green space brightened by colorful flowers and specimen trees of all varieties; vendors and crowds and massive stone buildings bedecked with logos of well-known companies. There were groups of giggling teenage girls headed toward the attractions in the Amusement Zone, a uniformed marching band eight abreast most likely on its way to perform at the Hall of Music or in one of the fair's many expansive plazas, young couples about to enjoy dates they'd remember as the most memorable of their lives, and children whose eyes shone like Christmas morning.

A crowd had already gathered and Max gently pushed her way to the front. At the same moment, Vivi, curious to see who was behind that booming voice, wound her way among those assembled, until she was standing next to a cute redhead, practically an entire foot shorter than herself.

"Who's the speaker?" Vivi whispered to the redhead.

"Elizabeth Dorchester. She's from the National Woman's Party," Max said without turning to see who was addressing her. She couldn't take her eyes off Elizabeth Dorchester.

Max knew all about the NWP. She had written an article for the *Heights Daily News* about a speech that one of their representatives had given at NYU that spring.

Max and Vivi listened intently as Elizabeth Dorchester spoke and the crowd cheered and shouted words of support.

"Being a woman is not a hindrance. It is, in fact, the opposite. Being a woman gives us abilities that make us stronger than male employers could even imagine. Being a woman is an advantage to be celebrated, not a disadvantage to feel ashamed of!"

"That's right!" someone called from the audience to a loud burst of applause.

"We need to make sure that women have the same opportunities as men. Opportunities to work hard. To find fulfillment outside of the home if that is what they choose to do. To support themselves. To make an impact upon society!"

Vivi was awed by the cadence of Miss Dorchester's well-chosen words, by her defiant confidence, and especially by how her energetic and powerful voice encircled the crowd in front of her and found the ears that were open to her message.

Max peeled her eyes off the speaker to look around at the other women in the crowd. Some seemed to be in shock, amazed that a woman—an attractive one in a decent dress, no less—could stand outside in full public view of man and God and say what she felt.

A half hour later, when Miss Dorchester had wrapped up her speech to resounding applause, the crowd began to thin.

"That was incredible," Vivi said to the redhead, so stirred up that she needed to talk to someone, anyone.

"You look surprised," Max said.

"I've just never heard a woman give a speech like that. I guess I've been living in Los Angeles for too long," Vivi said, a bit of sarcastic laughter in her voice.

Max wasn't surprised to hear that the woman was from Los Angeles. She looked like a model or an actress or some other sort of ethereally beautiful woman who had the world in her hands and knew what to do with it. Max thought Vivi looked the polar opposite of how she, Max, felt.

"Everything she said was so inspiring, about how women should be treated equally in workplaces, and how they should stand up for their ambitions despite what obstacles might be in their way. But you look like someone who does that already," Vivi said, smiling, thinking Max seemed so confident and self-aware.

"I try, but it doesn't always work. Hey," Max said, taking a closer look at Vivi. "Are you Vivi Holden, from the Aquacade?"

"I am. Have you seen the show?"

"No, but I work at *Today at the Fair*, so I recognize you from some of the stories we've done. I'm Max," she said, holding out her hand to shake Vivi's.

"That's so interesting that you're a journalist."

"Aspiring."

"Still."

"And you're a famous actress, so I think you win the interesting contest."

"Things aren't always as they appear."

"Ain't that the truth."

The two women stood in silence for a moment.

"Do—"

"How—"

"You first," Vivi said, laughing.

"Do you want to grab a drink? The Turf Trylon Café is close and they have a great bar."

"I'd love to."

As the women walked, they told each other a bit about their backgrounds and the jobs they were doing at the fair.

Vivi was enraptured by this petite spitfire of a girl who was as bright as the sky over the fairgrounds during the fireworks show, and she listened intently as Max explained how she was part of a highly selective group of students at NYU who had been placed in summer jobs for different newspapers.

Max always thought women who looked like Vivi Holden would be arrogant, especially women who looked like Vivi Holden *and* were bona fide movie stars. So she was pleasantly surprised by how nice Vivi was. She almost seemed too innocent to be a bona fide movie star.

"Scotch, neat," Max said to the bartender, Patrick, after they'd taken stools in the middle of the long bar. She recognized him from the last time she'd been there and he seemed to recognize her too.

"A glass of champagne, please," Vivi said. She thought of starlet school, where she'd learned how to be a refined representation of the studio. She'd been taught that proper young ladies, and future leading actresses, should always order champagne, should never order beer, as that would appear indecorous, and should stay away from hard liquors, as they had a tendency to dull a woman's inhibitions and lead her to act in ways she'd later regret.

Ha! Vivi thought to herself as she recalled seeing Katharine Hepburn at a charity dinner—just before the famed but declining actress left for Broadway to star in *The Philadelphia Story*—drinking a clear beverage from a glass that would never be used for water. But Vivi knew that what was tolerated for a woman like Katharine Hepburn was intolerable for someone like herself.

"Back to Elizabeth Dorchester," Max said as Patrick prepared their drinks. "You said you were inspired by what she said. But considering where you are in your career, it seems as if you've already had to confront quite a number of obstacles that I imagine have stood in your way."

Vivi thought for a moment. "It's hard to explain, but I don't really confront the obstacles as much as I stride along beside them. Does that make sense?"

Max shook her head.

"I definitely stand up for myself, but in my business that doesn't make much of a difference if the people making the decisions don't agree with me."

"That's exactly what I'm dealing with."

"So rather than continuing to fight and then losing the battle altogether, which would render me jobless, I keep riding the wave that I'm on. It certainly gets me to the next step in my career, but not without rocky shores along the way. But when I really think about it, I'd rather be on the wave, rough as it may be, than not be on it at all."

When Patrick set their drinks in front of them, Max held hers up. "A toast," she said to Vivi.

Vivi lifted her glass and smiled.

"To two modern working girls, toiling away at the fair for the summer, planting the seeds of our ambition that will bloom into the careers of our dreams."

Vivi clinked her glass against Max's. "Cheers."

"And to those same girls not being afraid to raise a little hell," Max said.

They laughed and touched glasses again. They both appreciated being seen by someone else who was striving, who was on a path, who was becoming the woman she wanted to be.

Vivi and Max spent the next hour talking about their concerns and frustrations with their respective situations.

"It seems like your biggest problem, Vivi, is that you sometimes criticize your inner voice instead of listening to it and letting it guide you to what you really want out of life," Max said, her elbow resting on the bar as she slowly swirled her glass, the amber liquid practically hypnotizing Vivi as Max sagely explained precisely how Vivi felt.

Vivi tilted her head and raised her eyebrows. She nodded slowly. "That's quite astute of you, Max. You're pretty observant, but I guess that's typical for a journalist. And though I'm just a paltry actress, I'll attempt my assessment of you. It seems like *your* biggest problem is that you don't want to play by the rules as they exist in your industry or possibly even in life in general. You want to break them all and get to the top before you turn twenty-five. Perhaps your determination, admirable though it may be, is leading you to make decisions that aren't exactly serving you right now."

Max smiled at Vivi, impressed that she was able to know her for such a short time yet sum her up so well. "What do you say we make a pact?"

"I'm listening."

"How about I help you become more of a bull in a china shop and you help me stop breaking all the dishes?"

Vivi smiled, lifted up her glass, and clinked it against Max's.

"I have a crazy idea," Vivi said. "How would you like to go see the fireworks?"

"If that's your idea of crazy, I have a lot to teach you."

They paid their bill and walked arm in arm toward the Government Zone, giggling all the way from the alcohol, from the warm air, from the energy and electricity their bodies were conducting. They bought fifteen-cent double scoops of chocolate ice cream from a vendor and sat on a bench, enjoying their treats and each other. And at precisely nine o'clock, they stood shoulder to shoulder with thousands of fairgoers around the Lagoon of Nations, which they both agreed was an unnecessarily ostentatious name for a man-made lake with a fountain in it. They marveled at the spectacular water-and-fireworks show, performed to the thunderous sound of a live forty-five-piece orchestra. They laughed like carefree children as they felt the spray of the water on their faces and heard the boom of music in their ears.

They both delighted in the exhilaration, the excitement. The bursts and booms reminded them that they were alive and that the setbacks they had both experienced didn't define them. Instead, those setbacks fueled them, making them more of who they already were.

And when the night was over, they walked, again arm in arm, toward the closest gate, the sweet smell of roses and tulips and violets following their every step. And they were both as certain as the sunrise that the night had been special. That the fair was seeping into their bones, becoming part of the blood that flowed through their bodies, nourishing them as they became who they were.

TODAY *at the* FAIR
Sunday, June 4, 1939
By Charlie Hull

NATIONAL WOMAN'S PARTY ROUSES FAIR

She spoke and everyone listened.

A large crowd gathered last night in the Court of Power to hear noted National Woman's Party member Elizabeth Dorchester.

It seemed as if there wasn't an inch of space left on that grand promenade, jammed as it was with women who came to the fair from near and far to listen to Dorchester's spirited talk under the watchful gaze of the Trylon and Perisphere.

Dorchester, one of the founders of the Women's Suffrage Caucus, worked tirelessly in the effort to pass the Nineteenth Amendment. Since then, she has devoted her time and energy toward ensuring the passage of the Equal Rights Amendment, with the goal of providing women the same opportunities as men.

"I feel it is my duty to engage women in their futures, to encourage their dreams, to lead them to challenge the way things are in order to create better spaces to learn, to work, to thrive. I believe all women, young and old, rich and poor, of all colors and of all creeds, deserve to excel in society and become untethered by antiquated beliefs that prevent them from moving forward. We have accomplished so much in our efforts. And yet, there is still so much to do."

After the speech, Dorchester joined Mrs. P. Littlejohn, president of Equal Rights International, and Elvy Kalep, well-known Estonian aviatrix, for a reception at the National Advisory Committees Building, where they welcomed members of their organizations and dignitaries in an evening of gaiety and laughter while discussing issues of particular interest to women.

TODAY *at the* FAIR
Monday, June 5, 1939
By Charlie Hull

WELCOME! YOUR MAJESTIES!

The biggest moment in the history of the World's Fair, past or future, comes at noon today when, to the rumble and roar of a 21-gun salute, Their Britannic Majesties, George VI and Elizabeth, arrive at the Fair Grounds, escorted by sixty motorcycle policemen.

Grover A. Whalen, president of the Fair Corporation, and Mrs. Whalen will be at the entrance to welcome their majesties. They will ascend to Perylon Hall in a private elevator, walk through the main lounge and on to the royal reception chamber, specially decorated for the occasion with antiques and period furniture valued at $1,000,000.

Along the left wall has been placed a platform six inches high, covered with a red carpet and containing two antique chairs upholstered in Gobelin tapestry. On these the King and Queen will be seated during the reception that will be held.

Among the guests will be fair and New York City dignitaries (including Mayor La Guardia and Governor Lehman) and their wives. Sir Ronald Lindsay, British Ambassador to Washington, will attend the royal couple.

The King and Queen will sign the Fair's royal guest book, which already contains the names of the Crown Prince and Princess of Norway and the Crown Prince and Princess of Denmark.

The King and Queen will have their first glimpse of the half-mile stretch of the Mall, gay with flowers and trees, with water cascading through the pools and about the many sculptured groups of the Moods of Time and others. The 65-foot statue of George Washington will gaze down serenely on the procession, while far beyond the Lagoon of Nations fountains will leap high into the air.

TODAY *at the* FAIR
Monday, June 5, 1939
By Max Roth

THE VISIT OF THEIR MAJESTIES TODAY

12:00 noon—Royal party arrives at World's Fair Boulevard Gate, receives 21-gun salute and is met by mounted escort.

12:05 P.M.—Enters Perylon Hall for reception and signing of Distinguished Guest Book.

12:35 P.M.—Leaves Perylon Hall for Court of Peace by way of Court of Communications and Constitution Mall.

12:50 P.M.—Enters Court of Peace and receives military honors. Reviews guard of honor.

1:00 P.M.—Enters Federal Building for luncheon given by United States World's Fair Commission.

2:00 P.M.—Appears on the terrace of the Federal Building. At this time the first daylight show of colored fountains will be given in honor of Their Majesties. The display is entitled "The Ballet of the Crown Jewels." A special program of British music will accompany the fountain display.

2:05 P.M.—Walks down steps of Federal Building and crosses to Irish Pavilion. Daylight fireworks display will be staged. British and American flags will be released to float over Court of Peace.

2:14 P.M.—Leaves Irish Pavilion.

2:19 P.M.—Enters Canadian Building.

2:27 P.M.—Enters Canadian Art Exhibit.

2:30 P.M.—Enters Southern Rhodesia Exhibit.

2:40 P.M.—Arrives at Australian Pavilion. Visits Australia, Colonial Hall, and New Zealand, in turn. Leaves New Zealand and enters the British Pavilion.

3:40 P.M.—Leaves British Pavilion and drives via Petticoat Lane to Administration Gate, where military detachments will stand at attention and a farewell salute of 21 guns will be fired.

CHAPTER SEVENTEEN

Max

Thursday, June 8

Max was rushing through the event listings edits that morning. She was meeting Vivi for lunch at twelve thirty and she wanted to finish as much as possible before then. After their time together Saturday night, they had exchanged phone numbers so they could make a plan to meet again and this, five days later, was the first chance they had gotten. But her focus kept getting interrupted by Charlie's constant sighing at the desk next to hers.

"Charlie!" Max said in frustration. She had tried to ignore him, but each time he sighed it made her skin crawl.

"I'm sorry, Maxine," he said, sighing again and putting his head in his hands.

"Sorry, I didn't mean to yell. What's going on?" Max asked, beginning to feel empathetic toward Charlie. She knew he had a lot on his plate. More so than he'd had during their first week at the paper.

After Max's failed scheme on Saturday, she had brought two neatly typed letters of apology into the office, hoping that they would demonstrate enough remorse for what she had done. Neither Mr. Babcock nor Mr. Collier had arrived yet for the day, so first she went into Mr. Babcock's office and placed one of the letters in the middle of his blotter. When she entered Mr. Collier's office next, she was surprised to find it was completely empty.

Later that morning, she'd learn that Mr. Collier's mother had fallen ill and he'd traveled to Cleveland to be with her. It apparently was quite serious, and Mr. Babcock had told Charlie and Max that Mr. Collier wasn't planning on returning to the paper.

Thus, Mr. Babcock had given Charlie more responsibilities in the form of additional articles to write, but he hadn't done the same for Max, a situation she found neither sensible nor favorable.

Max felt bad for Mr. Collier's mother, but quietly thanked her, figuring it was on account of her declining condition and Mr. Collier's departure that she, Max, hadn't been fired. And Max was glad she had decided not to call Professor L. to tell him of her indiscretion. Mr. Babcock accepted her letter of apology and had chosen to forget, or at least overlook, her insubordination and how much she had cost them. She assumed that there was just too much work to do and they didn't want to lose her.

Since then, she'd kept her head down and done her job. She'd earned back Mr. Babcock's trust by coming in early, having her work done on time, and asking him periodically if there was anything she could help him with. He always said no.

Now, talking with Charlie, she realized just how overwhelmed he was. She heard his assignments every morning in the editorial meeting and knew his workload was tremendous.

Charlie looked around. Marianne was on the telephone, and

the door to Mr. Babcock's office was closed. Still, Charlie lowered his voice considerably before he began talking. "Mr. Babcock is really loading it on. I seriously don't like that guy."

"Maybe I can help you," Max said. When the words came out of her mouth, she hadn't had any motive other than wanting to help a classmate, a friend in need. Now that she had a moment to think, she couldn't help but see this situation as an opportunity.

"Would you?"

"Sure. I've got the hang of my sections. Let me write a few of the articles for you."

"You don't mind?"

"Of course not. I need an article with my byline to enter into Mr. Bing's contest, so you would actually be doing me a favor."

"But I couldn't put your byline on it. You'd have to write the article and then let me put my name on it."

"Are you joking? Why would I let you do that?"

"Well, because Mr. Babcock—Oh, never mind. I'll stay late or something."

"*Mr. Babcock* what? What were you gonna say, Charlie?"

Max paused and waited for him to answer. Instead, he chewed on a pencil, a distressed look on his face.

"Just tell me," Max said, gently touching Charlie's shoulder to get him to look at her.

"He said that the reason he's only assigning articles to me is because he's had bad experiences with every female reporter he's ever worked with. He mentioned one lady who was very bossy and who was always hysterical over this thing or that. He said that men are just better writers—"

"Jesus Christ, Charlie!"

"Shhhh!" Charlie whispered, looking around again to make

sure the office door was still shut. "I didn't say it! Mr. Babcock said it. I'm just telling you."

"I know," Max said, more calmly now. "Go on."

"Anyway, he basically told me that you were better off doing event listings, and that he felt better knowing that I was writing all of the articles."

Max looked up at Charlie and didn't say a word. She knew she shouldn't be shocked. She knew that's what she had to expect if she became a journalist. But still. But still.

Max rolled her eyes and turned back toward her work.

"Don't be mad."

"It's frustrating that just because I have these," she said, cupping her breasts, "I'm automatically at a disadvantage."

"Maxine!" Charlie said, shocked that she would do something so indecent.

"Oh, please, Charlie. Don't *Maxine* me. They're just breasts."

"Well, if it makes you feel any better, not all men are like Mr. Babcock. And when guys our age are the bosses, none of this stuff will happen anymore. Actually, girls like you will probably be the bosses telling guys like me what to do."

"Now you're making sense."

Charlie continued biting on his pencil, and Max contemplated her next move. She thought of Elizabeth Dorchester and wondered what she would suggest Max do in this situation.

"I'll tell you what, Charlie. I'm looking to get some writing in just to keep the muscles working, so I'll write a couple of your articles and you can still put your byline on them. It'll be our little secret."

"Would you really do that for me?"

"We're friends. Of course I would."

The piece Charlie asked Max to write was about a new set of

twins who had joined the baby incubator exhibit in the Amusement Zone. He thought she'd be better at an article about babies than he would. She was thrilled and looked forward to interviewing Dr. Couney, the head of the incubators.

As Max hurried to finish the listings edits, she was excited thinking that with the Dr. Couney article, she'd have something to enter into the contest. There was just the pesky problem that it would be published with Charlie's byline. The contest rules said that the article had to be published under the student's name. But, maybe if Professor L. knew her situation, he'd allow her to enter one with Charlie's byline, seeing as Charlie could vouch for her. Perhaps Professor L. would explain the quandary to Mr. Bing himself and he'd give her extra credit for her tenacity. And if she and Charlie could maintain their scheme without Mr. Babcock detecting it, she could have more articles to decide among as well, since the deadline wasn't until July 15, more than a month away.

She wasn't concerned she was being careless by doing the listings edits too quickly. She had, by this point, mastered her responsibilities, and she usually even slowed down her work lest she be left with nothing to do for the remaining hours of the workday.

A couple of hours later, when she was done with her own work, Max left the office to see Dr. Couney.

"I've just come from the most fascinating interview," Max said as she joined Vivi on the bench they'd arranged to meet at outside the Venezuela Pavilion in the Government Zone. There was a snack stand that Max had heard sold delicious sandwiches and she wanted to give it a try. Plus, Venezuela was across Continental Avenue from the Gardens on Parade, as pretty a place as any on the grounds to have lunch with a new friend.

They walked to the stand, ordered a sandwich and a Coca-Cola each, and brought their paper bags back to the bench. The sky was a clear turquoise and the air was warm. Max figured it was somewhere in the low seventies. She was glad she'd left her sweater in the office. A light breeze was blowing but not enough so that the ladies passing by, walking toward the Government Zone, needed to hold on to their colorful hats.

"Does this mean you're writing an article?" Vivi asked.

"Yes! Remember how I told you that I wasn't being assigned any?"

Vivi nodded.

"Well, it's a long story, but now I am, and this is my first one."

"That's wonderful, Max. Elizabeth Dorchester would be so proud of you. What's the article about?" Vivi asked.

"Have you been to the baby incubators exhibit?" Max asked Vivi. "It's right near the Aquacade." They were seated and had unpacked their lunches—a cheese-and-lettuce sandwich for Max and a ham sandwich with pickles for Vivi—from the bags and onto their laps, their sodas resting on the bench between them.

Vivi shook her head, her mouth filled with the first bite of her sandwich.

"It's a fascinating place. Dr. Martin Couney has been taking care of premature babies for more than forty years, and he's run exhibitions like this one at more than twenty other expositions."

"And he's got live human babies in there?" Vivi asked.

"Yes, and each one is wrapped up in a blanket and tied

with either a blue bow or a pink bow, depending on if it's a boy or a girl. They're the tiniest things. You just wouldn't believe it."

"Are their mothers there?"

"No, just nurses and wet nurses. It's a pretty complicated operation going on. And the incubators these babies are in! I didn't know machines like that even existed. Anyway, you should visit."

"I think it would be too sad. To see those babies, I mean, crying, and without their mothers."

"You're a softy, aren't you, Vivi?"

"You figured me out," she said, smiling and trying to sound light.

Mothers walked by, pushing carriages and holding the hands of children who strained their grips, wanting to take advantage of all the open space to run free. There was a little boy, about five years old, sitting on a bench across from them, his feet dangling off the edge, licking a chocolate ice-cream cone, his mother hovering with a napkin as she tried to prevent the drips from staining his crisp white shirt.

Max wondered if that little boy would remember the fair in 1984, when he was fifty years old, or in 2009, when he was seventy-five. If his mother would remind him of what he'd seen and how he'd enjoyed himself. If she'd show him the snapshots she'd taken that day. If she'd save that crisp white shirt in a keep-sake box along with their ticket stubs and a souvenir toy she'd buy him later that afternoon.

Max took a sip of her Coke and turned toward Vivi. "Did you have an opportunity to see any of the royal festivities on Monday?"

"I tried to see the procession during lunch, but it was too crowded and I couldn't get close enough. It was all anyone was talking about during rehearsal, though, and we sold more tickets than usual that day, so that was good."

"Speaking of, have things gotten any better for you at work this week?" Max asked.

"Definitely. After our night together Saturday, I felt inspired and motivated to change my outlook. Plus, it reminded me that I'm a fighter. And fighters don't walk away from a challenge. They stay and fight."

"Attagirl!"

"Why, thank you," Vivi said, smiling and giving a little bow of the head in Max's direction. "I started hustling during rehearsals and ignoring the criticisms from Ruby, the swimmer who I'm rehearsing with. That seemed to make her soften her approach. She hasn't eased up on her demands of me; she just isn't so harsh when I miss a count or forget a mark. The repetition is sinking in, and I'm learning the pieces. I haven't exactly shed the self-doubt, but I'm getting there. And hopefully when I debut tomorrow night, it'll all come together."

"What time is the show? I'd love to come and see you."

"Please don't," Vivi said in a serious tone. "Let me get through this first night and if I do well, I promise I'll get you a ticket."

"Are you sure?"

"One hundred percent."

"Okay, I'll respect your wishes, but I do want to come and see you."

"Hopefully I'll do well enough to warrant a second show. Now, how about you? Sounds like things have been going well for you considering you got assigned an article."

"It may sound mad, but I almost felt as if Elizabeth Dorchester was placed in that exact spot at that exact time on Saturday night to speak directly to me. It reminded me that I could fail and then I could get right back on my feet and work harder. That it's how I handle the failure that matters, not the failure itself. So I went back to work with a different mind-set and decided to trust the process a bit more. I guess it worked."

They talked a while longer and then Max said she had to leave so she'd have enough time to write the baby incubator piece.

And when she eventually sat down at her desk, Charlie was in a dither.

"Where have you been, Maxine?" he asked in his loud whisper.

"My goodness, Charlie, when exactly did you become my mother?"

"I need that piece written."

"Relax."

"Sorry, it's just been a crazy day. Some Amusement Zone concessionaires came in while you were out and were arguing with Mr. Babcock in his office."

"Really? About what?"

"All I heard before Mr. Babcock shut his door was that they took objection to the article we ran last week about how all of the attractions in the Amusement Zone were doing so well financially."

"Are they not?"

"I don't know, Maxine," Charlie said, frustrated. "All I know is that I have to show Mr. Babcock drafts of all my articles at four."

"Marianne! Coffee!"

Marianne, Max, and Charlie all stopped what they were doing and stared at Mr. Babcock, who had flung open his door to shout his demand at Marianne and then had slammed it shut.

Max gave a sympathetic look to Marianne as she stood quickly and rushed to get him his coffee.

"Have you noticed how mean he is to her?" Charlie whispered to Max.

"I have. And she always seems so nervous around him."

"Think we should say anything?"

"Like what?"

"I don't know. But he shouldn't be able to get away with treating her like that."

"I'll talk to her later and ask her if everything is okay."

"That's a good idea," Charlie said, glancing at Marianne as she knocked quietly on Mr. Babcock's door to deliver his coffee.

"Anyway, back to the article. It's only two. I'll have it to you in forty-five minutes."

"Thanks," Charlie said.

"You really need to get a grip, Charlie. I don't want to have to tell Professor L. that he needs to pull you off this job because it's too stressful."

"You wouldn't dare."

Max winked at Charlie and put a sheet of paper in her typewriter.

She wrote the story, slipped it onto Charlie's desk along with the photo captions she'd typed up for him earlier in the day, and then pretended to be busy organizing her papers.

Each day at four o'clock, Max and Charlie met with Mr. Babcock to go over all of the articles and listings they'd prepared that day. This gave them enough time to fix any changes before Max needed to leave for the typeset office at five.

At four o'clock sharp, Max and Charlie knocked on Mr. Babcock's office door, which was usually open. When he eventually told them to come in, they saw him hang up the phone, a scowl on his face. He was snappy with both of them and even snappier with Marianne when she brought him a package that had just been delivered. Eventually he calmed down and reviewed their work. Max waited nervously to hear what Mr. Babcock would say about her Dr. Couney piece.

He told Charlie it was his best piece yet.

BABY INCUBATOR SETS RECORD WITH
THREE SETS OF TWINS

For the first time in his 40 years' experience as savior of babies prematurely born, Dr. Martin A. Couney is playing host to three pairs of twins at his Baby Incubator at the Fair. Although he has cared for a total of 250 pairs during his long career as director of his famous incubators, this is the first time Dr. Couney has had three pairs at one time.

The record was set early yesterday morning with the arrival of a boy and a girl from Manhattan. They joined two other pairs—all girls—who had been brought to the Couney establishment at the World's Fair earlier in the week, one pair coming from Brooklyn, the other from elsewhere on Long Island.

Because the identities of his little charges are never revealed to the public, Dr. Couney—who makes no charge for the care of premature babies—refused to give details as to the family backgrounds of the newcomers. All six of the twins weigh a total of twelve pounds and will remain in his care until they shall have attained a weight of six pounds each.

Twin babies do not seem to be predisposed to premature birth, according to Dr. Couney, but it has been his observation that once he shelters a pair another pair follows soon after.

There are now a total of 19 babies in the incubators, of which only two are boys. Oddly enough, Dr. Couney cannot recall a time when the babies were evenly divided as to sex, there being usually a marked preponderance one way or the other.

The incubators at the Fair were opened a week after the Fair itself. From that time until today 39 babies have found a haven there. Twenty of the infants have thrived so well that they were able to go home.

The daily cost of maintaining a child in the incubators—the service is free to parents regardless of race, creed or color—is $9, and the time a child remains there may vary from two weeks to two months. There are 16 trained nurses working in eight-hour shifts and the most up-to-date scientific equipment for the preservation of human life.

‰

CHAPTER EIGHTEEN

Vivi

Friday, June 9

"You're on in ten minutes, Vivi!" Paul, the stage manager, shouted into the women's dressing room.

"Thanks, Paul," Vivi said, smiling as she put the final touches on her hair and makeup.

A lot had changed in the past week since the horrible *New York Chronicle* review. Now, waiting to go on for what Ed was calling her "second debut" during that night's eight-thirty performance, Vivi felt ready and excited.

Had she any idea of what was going on in the dressing room down the hall, she may have felt differently.

The hair-and-makeup ministrations had seemed daunting the first time Vivi learned them. So she'd watched Sadie that past week, over and over, so that when Vivi had her turn again to take over the leading role, she'd know the drill.

Vivi carefully rubbed the cream-based makeup all over her face, making sure to get right up to her hairline and under her eyes. Then she applied a special powder on top to let it set. Makeup that would typically be used for a theater production was useless for the Aquacade because it wouldn't stand up to all that water. And there was no time in between numbers for touch-ups. Then Vivi applied waterproof eye makeup that lasted for hours but had to be removed with an oily concoction. Sadie had advised Vivi to lay a towel over her pillow at night so the unavoidable remnants wouldn't stain her pillowcase.

After a coat of waterproof red lipstick, a few smacks of her lips, and then another coat, it was time for the hair.

There were big tubs of warm baby oil mixed with Vaseline near the makeup tables. Vivi dunked her hands into the mixture and rubbed the glop through her hair, giggling about the inanity of it all and trying not to drip the slippery concoction onto the floor or her robe. The process seemed extreme, but that was the only way for a swimmer's hair to stay even moderately in place during a show. They only wore swim caps for a couple of the numbers if the cap was part of the costume. After Vivi pinned the front of her hair back with sturdy hairpins, the transformation was complete.

Now, walking toward the stage entrance, Vivi enjoyed the *break a legs* her castmates were calling out to her as she passed.

She thought about how this performance would end in one of two ways: Either she'd be terrible and Ed would kick her off the premises with nary a *ta-ta*. Or she'd be marvelous, securing her position at the Aquacade for the rest of the summer and ensuring that coveted role with WorldWide upon her return.

Despite option one, whose even existence should have filled Vivi head to toe with nerves, she only felt excited. The power of preparation. She'd made the choice to do the work, she'd silenced the negative voices in her head, and now she knew the numbers perfectly.

Over the past week, in between rehearsals and sometimes during, Vivi thought of Maria and Sofia every day, hoping Maria would come back and praying that she wouldn't. And with each passing day, though it seemed less and less likely that Frank even knew Vivi was there, since he hadn't shown up, she still worried that he would. She still thought she saw his face in the faces of countless other men all over the fair. Still hoped that she wouldn't look out into the audience during her first performance and see him staring back.

But all week, despite the misgivings she felt about Maria and Frank, Vivi was able to relish every "Vivi, darling" letter from Gabe and every "Dear Lovey" letter from Amanda as if they were water and she were lost in a desert. She was lonely. It didn't matter how many people she was surrounded by all day, not one of them truly knew her, knew her heart, what made her operate, what made her her.

Vivi shook off these thoughts as she approached her mark next to Paul offstage, and brought herself back to the present, wanting to focus all of her attention on her upcoming performance.

Hearing the opening bars of the orchestra's first song, Vivi felt butterflies in her stomach. There was a roar of applause from the audience as Morton Downey, the master of ceremonies, took the stage. She listened in as he performed his monologue and waited for her cue.

But then—

There was a terrible commotion all around her; voices were raised and everything seemed to be moving.

Vivi saw Thad rushing toward Paul, toward her.

The cast members immediately around them stopped whispering, stopped bustling around.

Vivi noticed Thad looked worried and bedraggled.

"He said he can't go on," Thad said to Paul.

Paul looked as if he'd been struck physically.

"Who can't go on?" Vivi asked, not frantically but by no means calmly.

"Is he sure?" Paul asked Thad.

"Who? Who can't go on?"

"He's sure," Thad said, and rushed back toward the dressing rooms.

"Johnny? Did something happen to Johnny?"

"And introducing Aquabelle Number One, straight from Hollywood, the lovely Vivi Holden!" Vivi and Paul looked at each other when they heard Morton call her name from the stage.

"Go, go!" Paul said.

"But what about Johnny?" Her heart was pounding.

"Just go!" Paul said, practically pushing Vivi out onto the stage, where she quickly composed herself and sashayed toward Morton.

"Well, hello there, Vivi."

"Hiya, Morton."

"Isn't she just the most gorgeous girl you've ever seen?" Morton said to the audience, gesturing toward Vivi. "And those legs."

By the sound of the roar, the audience agreed.

"Why thank you, Morton. So nice of you to say."

Vivi pasted a smile on her face and hoped she was a good enough actress that the audience wouldn't be able to tell she knew something that none of them did: their beloved Johnny Weissmuller would not be coming out on that stage.

They continued their repartee a couple of minutes longer and Vivi did her best not to look into the wings to see what was going on. Just before Morton was supposed to introduce Johnny, Paul, the stage manager, rushed onto the stage and whispered into Morton's ear. Vivi strained to hear, but she could not. Instead, she scanned the audience for Frank, but the faces were too far away, a blur.

"Ladies and gentlemen, I have an announcement for you all. Some good news and some bad news," Morton said to the crowd once Paul left the stage. "Which do you want first?"

The audience cried out its responses.

"The bad news? Fine, just fine. The bad news is that our Aquadonis, Johnny Weissmuller, who some of you might know as Tarzan, is ill, so he won't be joining us here in the pool tonight."

Boos and hisses from the crowd. And one impressive Tarzan jungle call from the back of the audience that was so loud and resonant, Vivi was sure Johnny could hear it from the dressing room or wherever he was.

"That was pretty good up there," Morton said, pointing to where the call had come from, which made the audience erupt in applause again. "Now for the good news."

Vivi couldn't imagine what that was going to be, but she did what Ed and Morton and the audience expected her to do: stand still with her hand on her hip, smile, look pretty, and don't say a word. Despite her motionless body, her mind was anything but. *Who would perform Johnny's role? Who even knew Johnny's role? Is this going to ruin my chance to stay at the Aquacade since I haven't rehearsed with this person and the show is obviously not going to go well?*

"The good news is that Dean Mitchell is going to swim the Aquadonis role tonight."

Dean Mitchell? The diver? Considering Ruby was Vivi's understudy, it should have occurred to Vivi that Johnny had an understudy as well. But it hadn't. It was difficult to imagine that anyone could compare to Johnny in the pool and especially in the minds of the audience.

There was a slight smattering of applause from the crowd.

"Oh, come on now, everyone. You're in for a huge treat. Dean Mitchell," Morton continued, reading now from the little piece of paper Paul had handed him when he'd come onstage, "is an NCAA diving champion from the University of Michigan. Dean, come on out here; let's let our audience have a good look at you."

The audience applauded as Dean appeared in only swim trunks. Johnny usually came out with a cover-up, but Vivi imagined Paul had made a last-minute decision to have Dean ditch it so the audience could see he was as strong as Johnny.

Dean and Morton spoke for a minute or two, which gave Vivi a chance to think about how she was going to approach this huge change in plans. She and Dean had met early in her run and had exchanged pleasantries every time they passed each other, but they hadn't had a conversation.

She'd been impressed watching him during rehearsals. He jumped so high off the springboard and then seemed to float downward in the air, turning and twisting his straight, strong body in ways she'd never seen before. No one could deny Dean was attractive. He was about six foot two, had very dark hair and ice-blue eyes. His skin was tan from hours out in the sun and his physique looked like it had been sculpted from stone.

So that's all Vivi knew about him: that he was very handsome and he was an exceptional and accomplished diver. What she didn't know about him was how well (if at all) he knew Johnny's part. She was about to find out.

"Ladies and gentlemen, boys and girls, I present to you Vivi Holden and Dean Mitchell!"

Morton held his hands out toward Vivi and Dean in a flourish as the orchestra began playing the song for their duet.

"Don't worry, I know the part," Dean whispered to Vivi through his smiling teeth as he took her hand. She felt her stomach drop a bit and she wasn't sure if it was from nerves or from holding the hand of this handsome man. The audience applauded and Vivi thought it was just as loud, if not louder, than when she'd seen Ruby and Johnny strike this same pose.

She took a deep breath and told herself that all she needed to do was swim her part. Dean would deal with his part of the duet and she'd have to trust that he'd be in the right position when she needed him to be. That he'd swim at least as well as Johnny did. And that hopefully he wouldn't mess her up in any way. This was her chance to show Ed that she had put in the work that week and that she deserved to stay at the Aquacade in the lead role.

Vivi gracefully unwrapped her cover-up, stepped out of the high heels she was wearing, flashed a smile to the crowd, and five, six, seven, eight, dove into the water, Dean diving in alongside her.

⚘

CHAPTER NINETEEN

Max

Friday, June 9

Max hurried to the room at NYU where Professor L. held their cohort meetings every Friday at six thirty. It was always tough for her to get there on time, leaving the fair at five and delivering the daily package to Albert at the typeset office.

Today she arrived a few minutes early, as did James, so they caught up before the meeting began. She'd been excited to show him her baby incubator article, and gave him a souvenir copy from one of the many she'd stashed in her bag that morning. She'd felt glorious all day, excited about having her words in print, and eager to persuade Professor L. to consider it a valid entry for the contest.

Charlie sat across the table from Max, looking paler and smaller than he had at the beginning of the summer.

"Before we go around and discuss what everyone has worked on this week," Professor L. began, entering the room at precisely six thirty, "I have an important announcement to make. Mr. Bing, the generous benefactor of our contest this summer, has just accepted a speaking engagement on the Continent. Thus, we need to change the deadline for the contest entries. Instead of submitting your best published piece by July fifteenth, you must now submit it to me at this meeting two weeks from today, on Friday, June twenty-third."

Her classmates began whispering to one another and she heard one boy groan. Max bit her bottom lip and stared at the knots on the wooden table before her. This was not good.

"I realize that's very soon, but you're all competing equally with one another, so it will still be fair. Now, Charlie, if you would start us off, can you please give an update on what you've been working on this week and what you've learned from your efforts?"

Max tuned Charlie out. She knew what he'd been working on.

She looked quickly at James and he gave her a small, empathetic smile, communicating in that one expression that he knew how the change of deadlines complicated things for her.

The baby incubator article was okay; it would do in a pinch. But it wasn't Max's best work. She knew she could do better and she would. She would just need to convince Charlie to let her write more pieces the following week. That wouldn't be too difficult. He was now practically in tears telling Professor L. how much work he was expected to do.

Max continued to listen as her classmates went around the table, discussing their assignments: Ken Selby was researching Admiral Richard E. Byrd's upcoming Antarctic expedition for *Life*. Stephen Reynolds was working with a senior writer at *The New York Chronicle* on a series of New York State education reform articles. And James was spending most of his time working with an editor from the international desk, reporting on the disturbing situation in Europe and how the United States was intent on remaining neutral.

When the meeting was over, after she'd heard about the exciting jobs her classmates had, the many opportunities they were all being given to write and contribute to articles, and the contacts they were making at the big papers and magazines, Max walked straight up to Professor L.

"Miss Roth," he said, "it sounds like your work is going well at *Today at the Fair.* Tell me, have you had an opportunity to see many of the pavilions?"

"Not that many yet, Professor, but there is something important I'd like to discuss with you."

All of the other students were talking to one another or filing out of the classroom, eager to celebrate their Friday night at one of NYU's local bars, which gave Max privacy in her conversation.

"Proceed."

"As I had mentioned at our first cohort meeting, I'm not assigned articles at *Today at the Fair.*"

"Yes, I'm aware that was the original situation; however, I thought you were going to petition the editor to give you a chance."

"As Charlie explained, the editor, who was somewhat open to it, left to care for his mother in Ohio. Unfortunately, Mr. Babcock, the publisher, won't let me write anything."

"I see. So you're concerned that you won't have an article to submit to the contest?"

"Yes, but if you're able to make a small modification to the rules on my behalf, I will have something to submit. Charlie kindly gave me the opportunity to write one of the articles he was assigned. Unfortunately, however, he wasn't allowed to put my byline on it, so it has his. If he tells you that this is what happened, will you allow me to enter that article, or other articles I hope to write this week, with his byline?"

Professor L. paused and stroked his beard. "I understand your predicament, but I, as you know, am a stickler for rules. They are a necessary ingredient of any successful society, and our cohort here is indeed its own micro-society. I challenge you over the next week to convince Mr. Babcock to allow you to publish a piece with your own byline. And then I'd be happy to accept it for Mr. Bing's contest."

"But that's the thing," Max objected, her voice rising a bit in frustration. "Mr. Babcock is against women as reporters. How am I expected to have an equal shot at the contest if I don't have the opportunity to write articles?"

"Find a way, Miss Roth. I can't imagine that will be difficult for you," Professor L. said as he picked up his briefcase and left.

Max remained still for a moment, processing their interaction. She looked around the room and saw that the last stragglers were leaving. James, however, was sitting in his chair.

"How did that conversation go?"

"Awful and then strange. He said he wouldn't change the rules and let me submit an article with Charlie's byline on it even if Charlie confirms that I wrote it. And then he got a bit cryptic."

"Oh?"

"He told me he was certain I could find a way. I'm not sure if he was challenging me to do something bold in my dealings with Mr. Babcock. Or if he was just trying to teach me the hard lessons of life and that things aren't always fair."

"Knowing Professor L., probably a little of both."

"I don't see how I'm suddenly going to change Mr. Babcock's mind and get him to allow me to write articles." Max pushed her lips together and stared out the window, thinking. "I just have to figure out a way to keep up my little game with Charlie. Maybe I can get him to believe that it's in *his* best interest to convince Mr. Babcock to give me a byline. I'm not sure how I'm going to do it, but Charlie's not smart enough to know I'm playing him."

Max heard someone cough, and turned around.

"I forgot my notebook," Charlie said, walking toward the table and grabbing the pad. He fixed a stare on Max and walked quickly out the door.

"Charlie!" Max yelled, chasing after him, but by the time she opened the door to the building, which she'd heard him slam shut, he was all the way across the quad. She knew she wouldn't be able to catch him.

Max looked up at James, who had run out of the building with her. "I can't believe I said that. How stupid could I be?" Max said, shaking her head and staring in the direction that Charlie had run.

"Don't beat yourself up, Max. You didn't know he'd be coming back into the room. Just apologize when you get to work tomorrow, and he'll get over it."

"I don't know about that. And there goes any chance I had at writing articles. He'll have no reason to help me now."

"Except for the fact that based upon what you told me, it's too much work for him to do on his own."

"What a day," Max said sullenly, pushing her hair behind her ears. The air was humid, a warm New York City evening, and that always gave her hair a mind of its own. "It started off so great with my article, but now Professor L. and this."

"I'm sorry," James said, looking at her and smiling sadly.

Max took a deep breath, scolding herself for being so careless with her words. To make it worse, she didn't even think Charlie was dumb. Rather, she admired how hard he'd been working.

"I feel awful. Charlie's a nice guy. I don't know why it's so hard for me to think before I speak sometimes."

"I think I know what will make you feel better," James said, tilting his head at her. "Any plans tonight?"

"What did you have in mind?" Max said, perking up a bit, unable to resist his charm. It seemed to form a layer over her regret about Charlie. She knew there was nothing she could do at that exact moment to fix things with him, and being with James would definitely make her feel better.

"I have something in mind, but I think I may have to convince you to go along with it."

"Try me."

"Believe it or not, Miss World's Fair, our bet-settling drink at the Turf Trylon Café was the only time I've been to the fair, and I didn't get to see much besides the inside of that bar. I'd really like to go and have a better look, and I figured since you're the expert, you could show me around."

Max paused. She didn't exactly want to go all the way back to Queens. But she did want to be with James. And there was something about the fair, the air there, the energy, that she wanted to experience with him. "Fine, but I have a few conditions."

James raised his eyebrows and smiled at her. Then he gestured with his hand for her to continue. She liked the way he looked at her. As if he found her amusing. And somewhat adorable. She'd never seen herself reflected that way in a boy's eyes.

"Number one: no subway. I've ridden that thing for hours already today. The wicker seats have formed permanent indentations on my legs."

"Fine, no subway. I'll find us the cleanest and most fragrant taxicab in all of New York City."

Max nodded. "Number two: drinks on you. My job pays

peanuts, and I know what you fancy *New York Times* boys are making."

"I hadn't considered otherwise. You show me the highlights of the fair and I'll buy you all the scotches your little body can handle."

Max nodded again. "Number three: I'm exhausted. It's been a long day. So you have to let me nap on your shoulder on the drive to Queens."

"I'll even stroke your hair until you fall asleep."

Max felt all her nerve endings light up. This seemed like more of an official date than the couple of drinks situations they'd had since the summer began, though she felt like James had been sending mixed messages. He sometimes acted as if he really liked her, but she felt that if he really did—like, really, really did— he'd ask to spend much more time with her. It was complicated, she decided, because she was Jewish, and his family, a very old and established New York family, was not. Max hadn't heard the best things when it came to the Worthington family and their feelings about Jews. Not that she thought James was like that, but she couldn't imagine he'd ever be able to bring Maxine Roth home to meet Mums and Dad.

CHAPTER TWENTY

Vivi

Friday, June 9

"Vivi, dear, you were gorgeous out there. It was like watching a swimming angel!"

"Thank you, Ed. I'm so pleased that you thought so."

Ed had been waiting for her outside of the dressing room after that night's eight-thirty show.

Now she was sitting at her dressing table, wiping off her makeup and blotting the grease from her hair. They had canceled the ten-thirty performance. Once they'd put the sign out front that said Johnny Weissmuller wouldn't be performing the final show, tickets stopped selling. Ed decided to call it a day and send everyone home early for the night. Vivi was ready to swim again, especially with Dean, but she didn't mind getting some rest. She'd be doing four shows a day for the next four months.

She felt like there were fireworks going off inside her. She had accomplished what she had set out to do. She had learned the part and she swam it well. She didn't miss a mark or a stroke and the audience rewarded her with applause and shouts.

Dean was a marvelous partner, even better than Johnny. It was hard to explain, but she likened Dean to a generous lover. Johnny went out there, swam his part, and expected Vivi to hold her weight and be there for him when he needed her. Dean was different. He swam in a way that made her feel like she was shining, as if he were supporting her, as if he were reading her body and responding intentionally.

Once the show was over, Vivi learned Johnny was suffering from severe gastrointestinal distress. Ed reassured the cast that Johnny would be fine tomorrow and the show would go on.

She delighted in the comments and congratulations she was receiving from the other cast members.

"Every time I wasn't in the pool, I watched you from the wings," Sadie said, sliding a chair next to Vivi's and locking eyes with her in the mirror. "And you were incredible, better than Ruby or Eleanor had ever been," she said, whispering the last part so she didn't have to deal with any side-eye from a Rubette.

"Oh, thank you, Sadie. You have no idea how much that means to me," Vivi said, doubting the comparisons to Ruby and Eleanor were true but enjoying the compliments nonetheless. When Sadie asked if she wanted to join her and some of the other swimmers and divers at the Rheingold Bar in the Sun Valley Pavilion, Vivi felt bad turning her down, but she was already imagining her bath and her bed and the luxurious sleep she would have, dreaming about how well the show had gone.

"Not bad."

Vivi looked up and caught eyes in the mirror with Ruby, who was standing behind her. "Thank you, Ruby," Vivi said kindly. "You taught me everything I know."

"You didn't let me down, so that's good. You girls coming to the Rheingold for drinks?"

"I am," Sadie said, "but Vivi needs her beauty sleep."

"I'll join you all next time," Vivi said as she finished packing up her bag so she could leave.

After the show, Vivi had looked for Dean to talk to him about how it all went. She wanted to thank him for being such a wonderful partner, but she hadn't seen him. Now, though, as she walked out of the dressing room, he walked out of his at the same time.

"Dean!" she cried as she saw him, walking toward him to give him a hug.

"Vivi, congratulations. You did great," he said, hugging her back.

"Thanks, you weren't so bad yourself," she said, punching him lightly in the arm.

"Going to the Rheingold with everyone?" Dean asked as they walked out of the Aquacade gate.

"No, I thought I'd call it a night. I'm headed back into Manhattan. But have fun and we can talk about everything tomorrow."

"Let's share a cab. I'm not going for drinks either," he said as he linked her arm in his.

They walked through the crowds toward the fairground exit, the air thick with the smell of flowers and the laughter of the fairgoers.

"So how—" Vivi started to ask when all of a sudden she was stunned into silence as a man wrapped his arm around her neck.

"Stop!" she screamed, a thick panic engulfing her entire body, making it hard for her to breathe. She knew Frank would find her sooner or later. She flailed her arms and threw him off of her.

"Relax, lady. What's the big idea?"

Staring into the eyes of the stranger, Vivi tried to catch her breath. She smelled alcohol seeping from his skin, his mouth. But it was not Frank.

"Get outta here!" Vivi heard Dean yell.

"I just wanted to tell you you're gorgeous and I love you and we're gonna get married!" the man declared to Vivi as he backed away from her and Dean, his palms up in surrender, to the amusement of his group of male friends, who absorbed him, slapping his back and laughing in approval.

"Are you okay?" Dean asked, his hands on Vivi's shoulders as he looked into her eyes.

Nodding, Vivi forced a smile, not wanting Dean to know the real reason why she was so alarmed. *It wasn't Frank. You're okay.* Vivi repeated those words to herself as her breath slowed.

"I know you're beautiful and all, but do those sorts of things happen to you often?"

Vivi couldn't help but laugh, grateful to Dean for relieving the tension. "Almost every day," Vivi joked back. She shook off the feeling of the last few minutes and willed herself to act normal. To act as someone would when a harmless drunk man at a fair proposed marriage. "Now, what were we talking about? Oh yes, how did everything unfold tonight with Johnny?"

"We were all getting ready for the show and Johnny was nowhere to be found. One of the guys finally found him, or rather heard him, sorry for my crassness, in the bathroom."

"Oh boy," Vivi said, playing along. *It wasn't Frank. You're okay.* She scanned the crowd, the adrenaline still stinging her veins.

"Exactly. He was not doing well."

"I didn't even know you knew his part."

"I learned it during rehearsals back in the spring. I had been a swimmer in high school before I became a diver, and they said I had the right look or something dumb like that—"

"Oh, don't be so modest!"

"I am modest. It's kind of my thing, Vivi Holden."

"Go on, Dean Mitchell." Vivi felt her cheeks redden and she had a hard time not smiling. The crowds were thinning now that they were close to the exit, and Vivi felt more like herself.

"Anyway, they thought I could fill in for Johnny because we have the same build, so I learned the part, but tonight was the first time I ever swam it during a performance."

"No one would have ever known."

"That's kind of you to say."

"It's true."

"Thanks," he said, laughing as they were about to walk through the gate. "By the way, I enjoyed swimming with you tonight, but, and don't take offense, I hope Johnny gets better because I really prefer diving."

"No offense taken," she said.

They stared at each other a moment. It wasn't awkward, but it seemed heavy with something. Potential? Curiosity? Admiration? Or was Vivi just considering him that way because he had defended her earlier? Because he had been able to make her feel safe in his presence?

"You know," Vivi said, biting her bottom lip unintentionally, "I'm not tired in the least. In fact, I feel completely energized. Want to go for a drink after all?" There was no way she wanted to go back to her hotel room. And she knew the alcohol would calm her nerves, which were still piqued.

"I'd consider that," Dean said, his face lighting up, "but only if we go somewhere a bit more civilized than the Rheingold and you let me buy."

"Deal."

Dean suggested the Turf Trylon Café and Vivi agreed immediately. Once inside, Vivi immediately noticed what an elegant crowd had assembled. As she and Dean made their way toward the long bar, heads turned and eyes followed them as they walked.

⋎

CHAPTER TWENTY-ONE

Vivi & Max

Friday, June 9

As soon as Vivi and Dean took seats at the bar, Vivi felt a tap on her shoulder.

"Max!" Vivi exclaimed, and the two women stood up to hug each other.

"James, this is Vivi, the Aquacade star I was telling you about," Max said, and then to Vivi and Dean: "I took him on a tour of the fair tonight and we heard quite an uproar coming from the amphitheater. I presume that means everything went well?"

Vivi and Dean smiled at each other. And then Vivi and Max introduced Dean and James. Handshakes and kind greetings all around.

Vivi couldn't help but scan the bar for Frank, but she didn't see him. And something about their party of two now being a party of four gave her comfort. She chided herself for being so paranoid. Even if Frank did find her, what could he possibly do to her in public? She made a conscious decision to put him and the earlier incident out of her mind and enjoy the rest of her night. She'd certainly earned it.

"So?" Max asked Vivi.

"It was amazing!" Vivi said, bouncing on her toes.

"She was perfect," Dean said, smiling at Vivi.

"Looks like we're all celebrating, but James is buying, so what'll you have?" Max asked, laughing. She'd chosen, with assistance from the drinks she'd already consumed, as they'd been sitting at the bar for quite some time already, to focus on the joyful part of her day, seeing her article in print, as opposed to the situation that had occurred earlier that night when Charlie had overheard her calling him "not smart."

"That's awfully nice of you," Dean said, looking to James, who nodded. "And as long as I can get the next round, James, I'll have what you're having, Max."

Max smiled as if Dean had said the magic words that opened a gate that led to a tunnel that went straight to her heart. "Patrick," she said to the bartender, "when you have a chance please, another round of scotches, including two for my friends Vivi and Dean, here. Neat."

"Oh no, not for me. Just a glass of champagne, please, Patrick," Vivi said. "I need to ease into things a bit," Vivi said to Max, not wanting her to make a big deal over the fact that Vivi wasn't drinking scotch. The teachings of the WorldWide starlet school, and in this case its admonition against a proper lady drinking spirits, still had quite a hold on her.

"We really are a party, aren't we?" Max said, her face lighting up with delight.

"I almost forgot!" Vivi said. "Did your article get printed today? I didn't have a chance to pick up a copy of *Today at the Fair*."

"It did! So we're celebrating the advancement of my journalism career," Max said proudly, holding up her drink in the air.

"I'll drink to that," Vivi and Dean said at the same time as Patrick set Dean's scotch and Vivi's champagne in front of them.

The four of them toasted and then turned when they heard a group singing "Happy Birthday" at a large table in the middle of the lounge. A photographer was snapping pictures and it seemed everyone in the bar had taken a minute from their own business to stare.

"Is that Lizzy Baker?" Max whispered to Vivi.

"I think so. I didn't know she was in New York."

"Yeah, starring in *Leave It to Me!* on Broadway."

The two women watched as the well-known Hollywood and now Broadway star accepted adulation, requests for autographs, and refills of champagne as if it were all a normal state of affairs for her, which it probably was.

Max then asked what Dean did, and Vivi couldn't help but answer for him.

"He's in the Aquacade too," she said excitedly.

"Vivi is the *star* of the Aquacade," Dean said, looking quite proud. "I'm just a lowly diver hoping the audience will have some applause left every night after watching the swimmers."

"Really, Dean, the modesty. We have to work on that," Vivi said, shaking her head as if he were an errant boy and she his much more experienced tutor. And then to Max and James: "Johnny Weissmuller got sick tonight, so Dean swam the lead with me. He was really something."

"That's marvelous!" Max said. "Vivi wouldn't let me come to her performance tonight, but I can't wait to see you both perform."

"Me too," James said. "We should go, Max, sometime next week perhaps?"

"It's a date," Max said.

Vivi saw something pass over Max's face, but she couldn't quite describe what it was.

"I'll get you seats right up front," Vivi said.

"So tell us about this journalism career, Max," Dean said, scooping nuts from the dish Patrick had set before them.

Max explained the cohort she and James were in and her job at *Today at the Fair.* "Unfortunately, I work for a man who doesn't think girls should get to do the very important and difficult male jobs like writing articles. Apparently, our brains can't handle such strenuous exertion," she said, rolling her eyes. "So I've just been editing the event listings. But I snuck my way into writing an article, and, hopefully, if I didn't mess things up with my coworker Charlie"—she gave James a knowing glance—"I'll be able to continue in that direction."

Vivi and Dean and James all clinked glasses with Max and let her continue explaining how she'd said something mean about her coworker that afternoon or something like that. Max was speaking so fast and slurring just the tiniest bit, Vivi couldn't entirely follow. Plus, she was distracted by what was going on at Lizzy Baker's table.

Will that be me someday? Vivi wondered. Would *she* command a table like that or be confident enough to wear a red slink of a thing that resembled the slips she usually wore *under* her dress, not *as* her dress? If she did well in the Aquacade and Mr. Green kept his promise, would she be closer to being like Lizzy Baker than she could even imagine? Part of it seemed glamorous and wonderful, and it was everything that Vivi had been working toward. But, and maybe for the first time, Vivi saw something that she could only explain as looking, well, sad.

That feeling would be confirmed when Vivi excused herself to the pale pink velvet jewel box of a ladies' lounge and found, when she emerged from the stall to wash her hands, that Lizzy Baker was standing in front of one of the individual vanity tables, staring at the mirror and dabbing her eyes with a tissue. She looked like she'd been crying.

Vivi minded her own business and turned toward her own reflection as she rubbed soap on her hands and accepted a plush white hand towel from the restroom matron. Not knowing what she hoped would happen, Vivi delayed her exit by moving to a vanity table, taking a tube of red lipstick out of her clutch, and then applying it with great precision, slowly.

"Can I borrow that?" Lizzy Baker asked. She swayed a bit, and Vivi thought of the countless champagne bottles crowding the woman's table and surrounding it in gleaming, sweating silver buckets on stands.

"Of course," Vivi said, handing her the lipstick and thinking already about the exhaustive letter recounting the whole interaction she'd write to Amanda the next day. "I'm a big fan," Vivi said, reprimanding herself silently as soon as the words were out of her mouth. But what else do you say to a star like Lizzy Baker?

"Smoke and mirrors, darling. None of it's real. Just a big fat illusion to make young dears like you line up at the box office and buy tickets to our pictures." She was applying the lipstick well outside the boundaries of her lips, making them seem larger than they were.

Vivi wondered if she should mention something about the lips, but instead she smiled politely. She didn't really know what to say.

"You're a pretty girl. I'm sure some man has told you that you oughta be in pictures, am I right?"

Vivi nodded, and decided not to tell Lizzy Baker that it happened almost every day.

"Whatever you do, run the other way. Be a teacher or a nurse or a goddamn prostitute for all I care; just don't put yourself in front of a camera. It looks innocent, but it'll suck out part of your soul every time you face it until little by little your soul is gone and you're a goddamn shell."

"But you're a big star, Miss Baker." *For God's sake, so trite, Vivi.*

"Was. *Was* a big star. Why do you think I'm in New York? If I were a big star, MGM wouldn't have let me go more than ten miles outside of Los Angeles. No, darling, I'm just a washed-up old thing at the age of forty-two. But you," she said, pinching Vivi's cheeks a little too hard, "you have your whole life ahead of you. You goddamn lucky little bitch."

With that, Lizzy Baker tossed Vivi's lipstick onto the vanity and strode out of the bathroom. Vivi, her mouth agape, turned to the washroom matron to see if she'd heard their conversation, but the woman was carefully folding her towels, not revealing that she most likely had heard every word and that their conversation wasn't even the most noteworthy or scandalous of the night.

Vivi retrieved her lipstick, composed herself, and returned to the bar. Lizzy Baker was back at her table and her crowd didn't appear to be slowing down.

"You look like you've seen a ghost," Dean said when Vivi took her seat. Max and James were engaged in their own conversation.

"The ghost of my future, maybe."

"What is that supposed to mean?"

"Nothing, just the champagne getting to me. Forget about it. Tell me, Dean, all about you. What are you going to do once the Aquacade ends in the fall?"

"I might be off to Hollywood, actually."

"I didn't know that. Start from the beginning."

"I don't know if you know, it's pretty embarrassing actually, but I was on the cover of *Life* because of a dive I did at my college championships."

"I may have seen a copy being passed around the dressing room to the oohs and aahs of the admiring girl swimmers."

"How embarrassing!"

"Go on."

"Well, you probably know how this Hollywood stuff works better than I do, but without my knowing it, some fancy agent in LA wanted to see if I was 'movie star material,' as he put it, so he had a journalist friend run a photo spread of me in *Photoplay*. Apparently, it was a big hit, and the agent called and said he'd set up a meeting for me at MGM. It all seemed a little suspect, but then when an agent from New York called to say *he* was interested in representing me, he made it all sound more legitimate. Anyway, so that I don't go on all night, I signed with the New York agent. The rest happened so quickly. I got the call from Billy Rose to be in Aquacade and then Trevor, my agent, got a few meetings with studios. Those went well, and now I'm under contract with MGM to start making films in the fall. I'm still not sure this is the right move for me, but Trevor convinced me to strike while the iron's hot."

"That all sounds very exciting!" Vivi said, her smile genuine and warm. "And we can be friends in LA. I'll show you all the best spots."

"I'd like that."

Vivi thought of Gabe and how he'd feel if he knew she was sitting at a bar with a handsome man, promising to show him around Hollywood. He'd never know about this drink, or whatever it really was, but still, Vivi felt as if she were doing something behind his back. And that she should probably put an end to it. But then another voice in her head became louder: *Relax, Vivi. Have another glass of champagne.* So she decided to stay.

"Tell me more about yourself," Dean said after he'd ordered another round, for Max and James as well. "How did you get yourself into this racket?"

Vivi wondered how much she should reveal. He seemed like a nice guy, trustworthy, but the reality was, they'd just met. "I grew up in Brooklyn, a normal girl. After I graduated, I decided to go to LA for a change of scenery. I worked as a lifeguard, and also took acting classes when I could afford them. I was 'discovered' one day by my agent, Jack Stern, and the rest, as they say, is history. I signed with WorldWide, and I've been training and working small roles ever since."

"How did you end up here?"

Vivi took a long sip of her drink, thinking back on the moment in Mr. Green's office when he told her she wouldn't be in *Every Last Sunset.* "I was about to start a big role, one that would have launched my career, but I got pulled off the picture at the last minute." The memory of those feelings, that rejection, rushed up suddenly and caused her eyes to fill with tears. Dean noticed and put his arm on her shoulder. "Instead, the studio head told me he had a great opportunity for me in New York. And, well, here I am." Vivi took another sip of champagne, pushed the disquieting thoughts of her lost role from her mind, and fixed a proper movie-star smile on her face.

"Will you be swimming in the Aquacade next summer too?"

"Next summer? I thought this was a one-year fair," Vivi said, concern tingeing her voice.

"There's talk that they might extend the fair through 1940."

"I didn't know that. I . . ." Vivi became flustered and thoughts of what that meant made her mind feel sticky, as if it were filled with glue.

"I didn't mean to alarm you, Vivi."

"No, it's fine. I just—I just had been told that if I did well this summer, there would be a part waiting for me when I returned to Hollywood in the fall." She wondered if Mr. Green had been leading her on, if he would tell her in October that he wanted her to stay in New York longer. That she'd done so well and it was so good for her image, they were keeping her there for just one more year. *And then, Vivi dear, and then when you come back, do we have a role for you.*

Vivi turned to look at Lizzy Baker. Her red lipstick had smeared in the corners of her lips, making her look like a sad clown who wasn't in on the joke.

"What are you two talking about?" Max asked, turning to Vivi and Dean.

Dean looked carefully at Vivi, as if to make sure she was okay.

"We were just discussing the fair and how much we love working here," Dean said, diverting attention from Vivi. "What about you, James? Tell us about your job."

James told them about his work at *The New York Times*, about the articles he'd written on Germany and Poland, and about how he had just begun tossing around the idea of becoming a war correspondent after graduation. It all sounded very exciting to Vivi. And real. No smoke and mirrors in journalism, she thought.

The night continued with the four of them talking about what they'd seen at the fair and promising to get together again.

"Where are you staying, Vivi?" Dean asked after they'd said good night to Max and James and were walking toward the closest fair exit gate.

"The Stafford on the Upper East Side."

"It's on my way home. Let's share a cab, and I'll drop you off."

"Are you sure it's on your way?"

"It is. And even if it weren't, it's late and I would never hear the end of it from my mother if I didn't escort you to your door."

"So you're gonna tell your mother about me?" Vivi asked coyly.

Dean laughed and hailed a taxi.

"What are you smiling about?" Dean asked Vivi once they were settled in the back of the cab.

"Tonight."

"You were marvelous."

"I had a pretty marvelous partner."

Dean reached over and squeezed Vivi's hand.

"Any regrets about not going out with the other swimmers to celebrate?" Dean asked.

"Not one bit. I had a wonderful time tonight," Vivi said, smiling at Dean.

"I did too. It was nice getting to know you."

Was it electricity that was passing between them? Vivi wondered. Or just the spark of a friendship? Either way, something about it, everything about it, if she were honest, lit her up inside.

"I know you said you hoped never to swim with me again," Vivi said.

"You know I didn't mean it like that," Dean said, protesting.

"I know," Vivi said, laughing. "But I hope we can become better friends."

"I wouldn't have it any other way."

The drive seemed only to take a minute and then they were in front of the Stafford.

Vivi felt a bit awkward. The whole night with Dean hadn't really been anything, but it also hadn't been nothing.

"Good night, Vivi."

"Good night, Dean."

He leaned over and kissed her on the cheek.

Vivi got out of the car and waved good-bye through the window as the cab sped off down the street.

What was that? Vivi thought as she smiled to herself and then turned away from the curb. She froze when she recognized the tall man standing by the hotel entrance, staring at her.

⎯⎞⎛⎯

CHAPTER TWENTY-TWO

Vivi

Friday, June 9

"Vivi, darling."

"Gabe!"

She ran to him and they embraced. His familiar scent elicited a strong response from her. She had missed him so much.

"It's wonderful to be back in your arms," Vivi said, smiling up at him. "But what are you doing here?"

"I came to see your debut," Gabe said, cupping Vivi's cheek in his hand. "But I arrived later than I thought I would, so unfortunately I missed the whole thing. How did it go?"

"Better than I could have hoped."

"I had no doubt that you would shine out there once they gave you the time to learn the role. How about a glass of champagne to celebrate?"

Vivi was exhausted, but Gabe had come all this way to be with her. He put his arm around her shoulders and together they entered the Stafford.

"There's a beautiful little bar right off the lobby," Vivi said.

"I'm already a step ahead of you."

Vivi looked at Gabe quizzically.

"When I arrived in New York, I knew I was too late to see you perform, so I came straight here. I waited outside for a while thinking you'd return any minute, but then I gave up and came in for a drink before I went back outside."

"I went out after the show," Vivi said, scrunching up her nose. "Had I known you were here waiting for me, I would have rushed right back."

"I know you would have, but I wanted to surprise you."

"You certainly did that," Vivi said, leaning over to give him a kiss. "And it means the world. Thank you."

They ordered champagne and Vivi excitedly told Gabe all about her night, how nervous and excited she'd been just before going on, the situation with Johnny, and details from each of the numbers she swam. She glossed over the parts about Dean. Now that she was with Gabe, she felt guilty for thinking anything at all about her time with Dean.

"I'm sorry I called Jack on your behalf, Vivi. I know that wasn't my place."

"That's okay. You were just looking out for me."

"Always."

"How long are you staying?"

"A week."

"A week!"

"Is that okay?"

"Okay? That's marvelous. How did you get the time off work?"

"I set up meetings with our New York office. I figured, while you're rehearsing, I can be productive and then I'll watch all four of your shows every day and wine and dine you in between."

"I have to warn you, my schedule is terribly crammed up. I don't have much time—"

"I understand and I don't want you to worry about it. I even got my own room so I wouldn't interfere with your sleep."

"You are the most thoughtful man," Vivi said, smiling at him, realizing how lucky she was to have a boyfriend like Gabe, who would spend days on a train to come see her and then allow her to do her job without making her feel guilty that she wasn't spending enough time with him.

"While I'm here, I might as well see the fair too. All the secretaries back at the office in LA have given me lists and lists of the souvenirs they want me to bring back. They couldn't believe it when I told them you were in the Aquacade. They've been reading all about it in their gossip magazines."

"Gossip magazines? I had no idea—"

"Isn't Jack sending you clippings?"

"He hasn't yet. Maybe he has and the package was held up in the mail for some reason. I'm sure the newsstand on the corner will have the same magazines."

"I'll pick up an armful for you tomorrow morning."

"Thank you, Gabe."

Gabe glanced around the bar as if he were looking for someone. The room had an old-world scheme, with dark wood paneling, dim lighting, and melt-into chairs arranged around tiny marble-topped tables each aglow with the welcoming flicker of votives.

"Looking for someone?" Vivi asked.

"Just seeing if there's somewhere more private we could talk."

The room wasn't crowded at all, but most of the patrons were sitting at the bar.

"Come," Gabe said. He stood, picking up both of their champagne glasses, and gestured with his chin toward the corner table in the back of the room.

"Is something wrong?" Vivi asked, concerned, once they had settled.

"I lied to you, Vivi."

"Oh?"

"I didn't come here just to see you perform. I came here to ask you something."

Vivi's hand involuntarily rose to her mouth as she watched Gabe rise from his seat and get down on one knee next to her.

"Vivi Holden, you are all of the brightness in my world. I have never met a woman like you. You are beautiful and strong, gentle and kind. Would you do me the honor of becoming my wife?"

Staring down at Gabe, Vivi felt a rush of thoughts inundate her head. Gabe continued his proposal. She imagined he assumed that her silence, rather than a resounding *Yes!*, meant she needed additional convincing.

"Darling, I know I've asked you before. And I know what you've always said. But being away from you these past few weeks has been torture. I understand that you have your own dreams, and I don't want to take those away. I'm not asking you to give up everything you're working toward; I'm just asking you to continue doing all of those things *while at the same time* being my wife."

Vivi swallowed hard.

"Is it because there's no ring? I didn't want to travel with it, but it's waiting for you back in LA."

"No, Gabe, it's not that at all. . . ."

There were so many reasons she'd always said no. But lately some reasons to say yes had seeped in, making a mess of things and confusing Vivi.

Gabe was absolutely right. Just because she wanted to work didn't mean she couldn't also be married. There were plenty of married actresses. And there was no rule that she had to have babies straightaway.

She also realized that Gabe wouldn't stick around forever. How many times could a man be rejected before his ego got the better of him? Perhaps, Vivi thought, she'd pressed her luck too many times by putting him off.

Plus, she needed to be in Hollywood. And this talk about a 1940 show? Certainly Mr. Green couldn't keep her in New York if she were a married woman. (Billy Rose might not even allow her to stay in his show once there was a ring on her finger, based upon what Sadie had said about the rules.)

Mostly, though, she loved him. And being in his arms tonight, spending time with him, reminded her of that.

Vivi mined her brain for all the reasons that had seemed so rational and convincing all of the other times she'd turned him down. But those reasons had disappeared.

It could have been a minute or it could have been ten. Either way, Gabe was still down on one knee, still staring up at her with an expression filled with love. With hope.

Vivi took a deep breath. "Yes."

"Yes?" Gabe's face was pure shock.

"Yes!" Vivi said, laughing.

"Champagne all around," Gabe said loudly, standing up. "We're getting married!"

The people at the bar clapped loudly as the bartender opened a bottle of champagne and lined up glasses along the bar.

Then Gabe pulled Vivi close and whispered so only she could hear.

"I love you, Vivi. You are my everything. You've made me the happiest man on earth tonight."

Vivi bit her lip as tears filled her eyes. This felt right. Yes, she thought, this finally felt right.

TODAY *at the* FAIR
Saturday, June 10, 1939
By Max Roth

OFFICIAL PROGRAM OF TODAY'S SPECIAL EVENTS

10:30 A.M.—See the Panda

Feeding time for Pandora, the giant panda from China, at the New York Zoological Society Exhibit in the Amusement Zone.

2:30 P.M.—"The Battle of the Centuries"

Mrs. Drudge and Mrs. Modern compete in an epic dishwashing contest. Bets are on Mrs. Modern, who uses an automatic dishwasher in the kitchen of tomorrow, and against Mrs. Drudge, who relies on her hands. At the Westinghouse Building.

6:00 P.M.—Miss Americow

Results are in for the winner of the Miss Americow contest. Also, see Elsie the Cow and 150 of her bovine friends being mechanically milked on the Rotolactor. At the Borden Company Building in the Food Zone.

(Events continue on p. 2.)

CHAPTER TWENTY-THREE

Vivi

Saturday, June 10

"There you are, Vivi. Ed's waiting for you in his office," Thad said to her with a smile as she entered through the cast gate the morning after Gabe's proposal.

"Is he happy?" Vivi asked warily.

"Seems to be, but you never know with Ed," Thad said. "By the way, you were fantastic last night. Don't tell anyone I said this, but you were better than Eleanor or Ruby had ever been."

"Really? You thought so?" Vivi wasn't fishing; she was genuinely surprised.

"I did."

"Thanks, Thad. That's so nice of you to say."

As she entered Ed's office, she saw that Dean and Mr. Mackey, the Aquacade spokesman, were there as well.

"There she is, our gorgeous Vivi. Come, dear, and have a seat." It was clear to Vivi, just from the difference in tone from last Saturday to today, that Ed was much happier with his leading lady. This put Vivi's nerves to rest and she took the chair next to Dean, smiling at him. Mr. Mackey stood behind Ed, his hands clasped in front of him.

Vivi looked at Dean, who smiled back at her but then turned away quickly. Vivi thought he seemed a bit agitated. She'd soon find out why.

"Fabulous performance last night, Vivi," Ed said, flicking ash from his cigarette. "Billy called me this morning and asked me to congratulate you on his behalf. He also apologized for not having been here in person last night, but he's been on the coast in meetings and hopes to get back soon."

Vivi smiled and exhaled the breath she'd been holding. This meant she would keep her job in the Aquacade. Her hard work had paid off.

"Now," Ed continued, resting his cigarette in his ever-present ashtray, "about these." He took a newspaper that was set before him, turned it around so it faced Vivi and Dean, and pushed it toward them.

Vivi couldn't see which paper it was; from the tabloid size, she knew it could have been the *Daily News* or the *City Chronicle* or any one of a dozen daily New York papers. It didn't matter. What mattered was the full-page of photographs of Dean and her.

"Oh my goodness!" Vivi said, her eyes suddenly wide as she pulled the paper closer to get a better look. She looked at Dean, but she couldn't read his expression. It seemed, due to his lack of surprise, as if he'd already seen the pictures.

The photos were of them at the Turf Trylon Café the night before: clinking glasses, laughing, and leaning into each other. And there was one showing Dean's arm on Vivi's shoulder. She had seen a photographer in the lounge, taking photos of Lizzy Baker's party, but she hadn't noticed the lens trained on her.

"This is awful," Vivi exclaimed, thinking only of what would happen when Gabe saw the photos. She pictured him heading to the newsstand that morning to buy the gossip magazines for her. He'd certainly pick up a couple of newspapers for himself, as was his routine. *And when he saw these . . .*

"This is marvelous!" Ed exclaimed, smiling and excitedly banging the palm of his hand on his desk.

"It is," Mr. Mackey agreed.

"I don't—I don't understand," Vivi said, looking again to Dean, who was now looking at his hands in his lap, as if he knew something she didn't.

"The phone has been ringing off the hook," Ed said. "Mackey's been getting calls all morning requesting interviews with the two of you, asking how long you've been dating. The whole shebang."

"And because of that, we're making the two of you a couple."

"A couple!" Again, Vivi looked at Dean. He was shaking his head slowly, his eyes still in his lap. She didn't know why he wasn't participating in this conversation. It was maddening.

"Yes, a couple," Ed continued. "You may not be aware, but ticket sales have dropped considerably since Eleanor left the production. And the damn rain has been affecting sales as well. We've been trying to think of ways to turn things around, and your date last night with Dean might solve our problems."

"It wasn't a date," Dean said quietly, finally playing a role in the conversation.

"Whether it was a date or wasn't a date, everyone who woke up to these photographs today thought it was," Ed said. "So here's what we're going to do. I don't know what's going on between the two of you, and to be honest, I don't really care as long as it doesn't affect your performances, but we're going to set up dates a few nights this week and alert the media as to where you'll be and what time you'll be there. You'll look happy, you'll be affectionate with each other, and crowds will begin lining up to see Aquabelle Number One and champion diver Dean Mitchell swooning at each other across the pool. We're even planning on having you swim Johnny's part during the eight-thirty every Friday night, Dean, so audiences can see the electricity between you and Vivi during your duets."

"This is impossible. I'm engaged!" Vivi said, her voice cracking angrily.

The three men in the room turned to stare at her. Dean tilted his head in a question.

Vivi looked at her lap and began picking at her cuticles. "It's not been officially announced yet, but, yes, I am engaged to Gabe Grant."

The room was quiet for a moment and Vivi felt as if she could see through Ed and Mr. Mackey's skulls, watching their brains swirl and pulsate, figuring out a way to deal with this latest hiccup, to steamroll over it as men like them did, caring little for what was flattened, destroyed, as a result.

"That doesn't matter one bit," Mr. Mackey said. "The public doesn't know about your engagement and the public doesn't care. Apparently, they care very much that you and Dean have begun a relationship. In our business, Miss Holden, photos don't lie. And these photos, of the two of you looking very much in love, don't seem to include your fiancé."

"Does my agent know about this? I don't think he would think this is okay," Vivi said, suddenly standing up so she could tower above these men who seemed to think it was all right to tell her whom she was dating.

"Calm down, Vivi, dear," Ed said, a condescending edge to his voice. "I spoke with Jack this morning. Actually, it was his idea."

Vivi sighed loudly and turned around to face the back of the office. She couldn't look at any of these men, including Dean, who sat there silently. And then it struck her. What if Frank saw these photos? Maria had said she wasn't sure if Frank would recognize her, but appearing in so many newspapers would certainly increase the chances he would see her, recognize her, and show up to cause trouble, or even worse. But how could she explain all of this to Ed and Mr. Mackey? Even if she did, it was likely they'd shush her and tell her not to worry: *Fanciful thinking, doll.*

"And you're okay with this, Dean?" Vivi asked, turning to face him, her hands folded across her chest.

He looked up at her slowly, as if she were a child he needed to pacify. "From what I understand about this business, Vivi, I don't think we have a choice."

Vivi sighed again and shuffled her feet, turning back to face Ed and Mr. Mackey. She knew Dean was right, but she was not happy with the way he just accepted the situation as if they had absolutely no say.

"Dean's right, Vivi. This is how show business works," Ed said, a roguish grin filling his entire face from his eyes to his lips. "Surely you don't think all the couples you see in the tabloid photographs are really dating, do you? Surely you understand that when a studio has a film to promote, they often fabricate a relationship between the two leads. Or when an agent is trying to cover up a male film star's relationship with an inappropriate girl, or even worse, an inappropriate boy, this is how he does it. It's just for a little while anyway, and then you can marry your boyfriend. But right now we need to sell tickets, and you two are going to help us do that."

Vivi listened to the men arranging her life for a few addi-

tional moments before Ed finally dismissed her. She left, trying
to process what had just happened and what it all meant.

Knowing she'd be late for rehearsal but not caring, Vivi
rushed out of the amphitheater and found a pay telephone.

She would speak to Gabe and explain everything to him.
Hopefully he hadn't seen the photos yet, but if he had, she'd tell
him it was all a big misunderstanding.

"He checked out half an hour ago," the front desk attendant
at the Stafford said.

Checked out?

"Did he leave me a message?"

"He did. It's in a sealed envelope in your mail slot."

"Can you please open it and read it to me?"

"I'm sorry, Miss Holden. We aren't allowed to open guest
mail."

"But I'm asking you to."

"Even so. I'm terribly sorry, but I could get fired."

"I promise if that becomes the case, then I will personally
speak to your manager. Now, please, open the damn letter and
read it to me."

Vivi regretted that she had risen her voice, but she felt so
desperate. She heard the attendant sigh and then she heard the
sound of a letter opener slicing through a sealed flap. The man
cleared his throat and spoke quietly.

"Vivi, I saw the photos of you with that man. How dare you?
You know what I went through in my last relationship, and I never
thought you'd do this to me. And on the night we became engaged? I'm
going back to LA today. How could you be so manipulative?"

"Thank you," Vivi said, her voice breaking, and she hung up.

She had no way of getting in touch with Gabe. It would be
days before he was back in Los Angeles and by then, if this fake

relationship moved forward, which it seemed like it was going to, photos of her with Dean would be everywhere.

She would write a long letter to Gabe that night so he would hear the truth from her when he returned to Los Angeles. But she knew by then it would be too late.

Gabe had once been engaged to a woman who'd had an affair with his business associate. It had destroyed him, which had made it difficult for him to trust Vivi at the beginning of their relationship. Regardless of what was really going on with her and Dean, Gabe would fixate on the appearance of it all. On the fact that his fiancée was gallivanting around New York City with another man, and an attractive one at that. Her heart broke at how she knew this would affect him. Hurting Gabe was the last thing she wanted.

She hoped she'd be able to convince him. She pledged to do everything she could. Now that she'd said yes to him, she couldn't wait to marry him. She couldn't imagine that could all be taken away.

Vivi was distracted throughout rehearsal, even kicking Johnny in the head at one point.

And just before the three-thirty show, her first for the day, once her face was made up and her hair oiled, her swimsuit smoothed against her pretty curves, and her opening number cover-up wrapped around her tightly, Vivi hoped Gabe had reconsidered getting on the next train back to LA and that he'd show up backstage and let her explain.

But he hadn't.

She stood next to the stage manager, Paul, at the edge of the stage and waited for Morton Downey to call her name.

"And introducing Aquabelle Number One, straight from Hollywood, the lovely Vivi Holden!"

Vivi knew she had to put her thoughts of Gabe aside for the moment and do her job. And she decided in that moment that if the Aquacade was going to use her to achieve its goals, she'd do the same right back, so she raised herself to her full height and strode out onto that stage as if it belonged to her.

"Well, hello there, Vivi."

"Hiya, Morton."

"Isn't she just the most gorgeous girl you've ever seen?" Morton said to the audience, gesturing toward Vivi. "And those legs."

The crowd erupted in applause.

"Why thank you, Morton. So nice of you to say."

WESTERN
UNION

Received at Worlds Fair, New York
=Hollywood, CA 1939 June 10 9:08A

MISS VIVI HOLDEN C/O BILLY ROSE AQUACADE

HEARD ABOUT YOUR MAGNIFICENT PERFOR-
MANCE LAST NIGHT. WE KNEW YOU COULD DO
IT. BRAVA.=
JACK

⭒

CHAPTER TWENTY-FOUR

Max

Saturday, June 10

"Charlie . . . ," Max began, her tone remorseful, when he came into the office that morning.

He looked at her and then turned his head, settling himself at his desk and shifting his chair away from her.

Max felt terrible that he'd overheard what she'd said the previous evening after the cohort meeting, and she wanted to apologize. Plus, he was way in over his head at work. The last thing he needed was Max making his life more difficult as well.

"Charlie, Max, in my office now, please."

Charlie and Max both stood up when they heard Mr. Babcock open his office door.

"I've made a decision I'd like to share with you both," he said when Max and Charlie were settled in the chairs opposite him.

Max's mind raced through the options of what that decision might be. Was he retiring? Was Mr. Collier coming back? Had he finally realized how he was overloading Charlie with work and had decided to assign articles to Max?

"As you both know, it was quite a shock to our operation when Hugh left. I know you're just students, but you have both stepped up considerably in his absence. I've decided to name one of you editor in chief."

Max and Charlie, despite the tension between them, couldn't help themselves, and looked at each other, shock and curiosity registering on both of their faces.

"I'm going to give you both forty-five minutes to write three hundred words about the importance of the World's Fair to glo-balization and world peace. I will promote whichever of you writes the best article."

Max was shocked that Mr. Babcock hadn't automatically pro-moted Charlie. But she appreciated his effort at fairness and didn't say a word. Instead, she sat quietly and waited for Mr. Babcock to continue.

"Forty-five minutes," he said, looking at his watch. "Go."

Max and Charlie looked at each other again, stood, and walked quickly to their desks. Max looked at her watch and grabbed a pencil and her pad to start outlining what she was going to write. But her hands remained still.

After a minute of that inaction, she chastised herself for wasting valuable time, took a deep breath, and began furiously taking notes.

She heard Charlie load a piece of paper into his typewriter and immediately start typing.

"Damn it," he said, and started loudly opening and closing drawers in his desk.

Max, in frustration, looked over to see what his problem was and saw he had broken the pencil he was using to cross things out as he typed.

Without a word, she took three of her own sharpened pencils and gently placed them on his desk. It was the least she could do for him, and she hoped she'd have the opportunity to apologize to him in a much better way than that.

"Thank you," he muttered, and they both returned to their work.

Max spent several more intense minutes outlining, and then quickly inserted a piece of paper into her typewriter.

She pushed her chair forward and tried to drown out all of the noise around her: Marianne on the telephone, Charlie banging away, the persistence of a clock ticking somewhere in the room, and the sound of Mr. Babcock's eyeballs on her back.

She bent her arms and rested her fingers on the keys. And then she began, her fingers moving as if she were a pianist playing Chopin allegro.

She quickly came up with a lede, and the words began to flow, the narrative clicked. She felt the pressure but it catalyzed her, which she found surprising until she told herself to stop thinking about that and focus on the article.

Max made sure to insert her voice, the part that she'd always found most challenging. She was well versed in the Five Ws, but voice was something you couldn't learn. It had to be coaxed out of a journalist, honed, like a sculpture from marble. The art of a story wasn't just the individual words and sentences, just as the art of a sculpture wasn't just about the chisel and the rasp. You either had it or you didn't. And Max would need to have it if she wanted any chance at impressing Mr. Babcock.

The implications of this exercise and its resulting decision were much more critical for her than for Charlie. He'd already told her that winning Mr. Bing's contest wasn't important to him, and that he didn't think he even had a shot considering the entries he expected from their classmates. She had the most to gain. And the most to lose.

"Five more minutes," Mr. Babcock said loudly.

Max heard Charlie groan.

She read through what she'd finished typing a few minutes prior, released the paper from her typewriter, and exhaled.

She was proud of her piece. She felt that it addressed the assignment and combined her own distinct style with the upbeat and breezy voice of *Today at the Fair*.

"Time," Mr. Babcock said as Charlie typed a few more words. "Come to my office with your articles, please."

Max stood up and pushed her chair back confidently, taking her article and walking toward Mr. Babcock's office. Charlie followed closely behind.

Mr. Babcock sat behind his desk and quietly read the two articles. Then he looked up into Max's and Charlie's expectant faces and read them again, this time making edits with a red pencil.

Eventually he looked up and nodded at them. "Thank you both for your effort. I purposefully didn't give you a lot of time. I wanted to see how you'd act under pressure and what you'd come up with. Now, for my decision."

Max bit her lip and looked intently, hopefully, at Mr. Babcock.

"Maxine," Mr. Babcock said, and stared at her, grasping her article in both of his hands.

Max heard Charlie slump in the chair next to her, and she felt a rush of joy that tried to escape audibly from her mouth. She

clamped her lips tightly so that it wouldn't as she smiled back at
Mr. Babcock.

"Maxine, your article was vivid."

Vivid?

"And I appreciated how you explained your thoughts."

But.

"But, ultimately, I think you, Charlie," he said, turning toward Charlie and replacing Max's article with his, "had the superior piece, and I will be awarding the editor-in-chief assignment
to you."

Charlie sprung out of his chair and thrust his hand toward
Mr. Babcock, who shook it energetically.

"Congratulations, Charlie," Max said kindly. "Thank you,
Mr. Babcock, for the opportunity."

Max walked quietly back to her desk, while Charlie stayed in
Mr. Babcock's office. Mr. Babcock shut the door, presumably to
have a private conversation with Charlie about his new responsibilities. She realized this meant that Charlie would now be
in charge of assigning articles, which he'd probably do happily
to lighten his workload. So despite the fact that she was disappointed that she wouldn't be editor in chief, that she wouldn't be
gaining valuable managerial experience, she'd still get something
out of it. Namely, articles to enter into the contest.

Max sat down and stared at the huge stack of papers in her
in-box, the event and program listings memoranda from the different fair departments.

It would be yet another full day of editing the listings, of
writing the photo captions, of creating the final package, and of
taking a cab into Manhattan to see Albert at the typeset office.
It was her turn to bring him a gift; their game was going strong.

"Sorry about that, Maxine," Charlie said, not an ounce of

sarcasm in his voice, when he came out of Mr. Babcock's office and sat down in his chair. "I know that would have meant a lot to you."

"Thanks, Charlie, but congratulations. I mean it. And I'm so sorry about yesterday. You know I don't think you're not smart. Everyone who Professor L. chose for that cohort is smart. I was just showing off a little for James, I think. I really didn't mean what I said."

"I know you think I'm a big lug, Maxine, but what you said hurt my feelings."

Max nodded at him remorsefully. "I know. And I'm sorry." And then she lightened her tone. "Can I take you to the Chicken Inn for lunch to celebrate your big promotion?"

"That sounds good, but would you like to go out for dinner with me tonight instead?"

Max tried not to laugh. She was so happy he'd accepted her apology, but she still didn't want to go out with him. She reminded herself to be nice. Besides, he was her boss now.

"I think," Max said, "that we should keep our relationship purely professional since we're working together. But if you're still up for a chicken lunch, it's my treat."

"Great plan."

"When would you like to talk about the articles?" Max asked, looking at Charlie expectantly.

"What articles?"

"The articles I'll be writing. Now that you're editor in chief, aren't I going to be . . ." Max realized her mistake as the words left her mouth.

"I'm still gonna be writing all the articles, Maxine. Mr. Babcock just went over that with me."

Then Charlie pushed his chair back from his desk with a loud screech and stood up.

"Where are you going?" Max asked.

"Into my office."

Charlie extended his arms in a big circle around the perimeter of his desk and then gathered up his mess of notebooks, pens, broken pencils, and paper in one big swipe. He carried it all into Mr. Collier's old office, like a giant would carry a tree trunk, and dumped it on the desk.

Max and Marianne had both followed his journey with their eyes.

"I guess it's just us girls now," Marianne said to Max.

"Guess so," Max said, smiling politely but feeling as if she wanted to punch the wall.

TODAY *at the* FAIR
Saturday, June 17, 1939
By Max Roth

OFFICIAL PROGRAM OF TODAY'S SPECIAL EVENTS

9:15 A.M.—Speed Demonstration

The World's Largest Typewriter stands 18 feet high, weighs 14 tons, and types letters that are 3 inches high. Part of the Underwood Elliott Fisher Company exhibit in the Business Systems and Insurance Building.

1:30 P.M.—Elektro

The 7-foot-tall, 260-pound Moto-Man performs 26 tricks, including smoking a cigarette and playing with his Moto-Dog, Sparko. Come early to get a spot, as Elektro draws quite a crowd. At the Westinghouse Building.

4:00 P.M.—57 Varieties

The Sampling Station within the Heinz Dome will offer tastings of Heinz's 57 Varieties, including soups, beans, spaghetti, and chilled tomato juice. Don't forget to pick up your free miniature pickle pin. In the Food Zone.

(Events continue on p. 2.)

CHAPTER TWENTY-FIVE

☀

Vivi

Saturday, June 17

Vivi had now been at the Aquacade for three full weeks.

The swimming had become as familiar to her as brushing her teeth and tying her shoelaces. She'd performed in enough shows by that point to know that each day, when Morton called her out on that stage, she was ready. She knew every kick and every scull she had to do and exactly when to do them, and she knew which costume changes she had to rush through and which ones allowed her an extra moment to grab a sip of water and to reapply her lipstick.

And she'd developed a routine every morning when she arrived at the amphitheater. She sat high up in the grandstand with Dean, drinking coffee before rehearsal started.

"Gabe finally picked up his phone last night," Vivi said to Dean that morning, sipping her coffee and looking down at the stagehands and technicians as they swept and repaired and prepared the sets and systems for the day.

"And?" Dean asked, turning to her, a concerned look on his face.

"He hung up as soon as he heard my voice."

"Oh, Vivi, I'm sorry."

"So I kept calling back. Finally he picked up and I burst into tears, explaining to him, again, that this was a staged relationship, et cetera, et cetera. He was furious and said that even though he believed that it was staged, even though Jack had confirmed that it was staged, he didn't believe that there was nothing going on between you and me. He said he knew me too well, knew my expressions and how I used to look at him, to believe that I had no feelings for you."

"So that's it?"

"I don't know what else to do. I've written every day since he left New York last week. I explained all I could on the phone. I would hope that now that he's back home and can think about it all more rationally, he'll realize how irrational he's being."

"I have a theory. Promise you won't get mad?"

"Promise."

"I can't help but wonder if he loved the chase. He kept proposing. You kept saying no. Men like the pursuit. Once you said yes, you took all the fun out of it for him."

"Seriously, Dean?" Vivi asked, scrunching up her nose. "That's a horrible thing to say."

"You promised you wouldn't get mad."

"I lied."

"I'm sorry. I'm not trying to make it worse."

"I know," Vivi said, giving him a small smile.

Her new friendship with Dean had helped her through the situation with Gabe. Vivi enjoyed talking to him and realized she hadn't had a friend like Dean since Amanda. Someone she could really open up to, someone who was kind, someone who didn't seem to have an agenda when it came to their friendship. She'd written to Amanda, explaining the whole situation, even asking her to try to explain things to Gabe. Vivi hadn't yet received a response.

In the past week, since their relationship had been decreed by those with the power to do so, Vivi and Dean had gone on three photo-op dates: a quick excursion to an ice-cream stand between the eight-thirty and ten-thirty shows on Monday night; another late-night drink at the Turf Trylon Café, making it their official "spot" after Tuesday's ten-thirty show; and a walk, hand in hand (per the request of the photographers), through the fairgrounds on Thursday to get photos with some of the more notable landmarks.

The girls in the dressing room thought Vivi and Dean were the most darling couple. No one had any idea that the relationship was a hoax.

Ed and Mr. Mackey wanted even more from Vivi and Dean. The photos were showing up in newspapers and magazines (everyone, apparently, wanted to get a good look at Aquacade's new couple), but there hadn't been an uptick in ticket sales. Vivi worried about what Ed and Mr. Mackey would have them do next.

Vivi also felt the whole thing was a bit confusing. Despite the *reasons* she and Dean were going out frequently, they were still going out frequently. And she couldn't deny she'd begun to develop feelings for him. These were incredibly surprising, since she was devastated over the situation with Gabe. But her brain had no control over her heart.

The photographers were always yelling things like *Let him taste your ice cream, Vivi!* or *Hold his hand, Vivi!* or even *Give her a kiss, Dean!* She had to act like she liked Dean and he had to do the same. But she wasn't quite certain, for herself or for Dean, where the acting ended and the reality began. The normal cues at the beginning of a relationship, at least the ones Vivi was familiar with, were missing. Dean was a true gentleman. Once the cameras were gone, they sometimes had good-night kisses, but he was always proper. Always knew when the night was over.

One of Vivi's two main fears when Mr. Green had sent her to New York to star in the Aquacade was that it would be detrimental to her relationship with Gabe. The other was that it would be detrimental to her career. With one fear fully realized, Vivi worried about the second.

And that didn't even include the uncertainty she felt about going to New York in the first place. Back to where all of the pain and guilt and regret she felt on a daily basis had begun.

That morning, Vivi was distracted thinking about Gabe, worrying about her career, and trying not to reanalyze the situation about Maria.

It had been two weeks since Maria had come to see her. Vivi wondered if her dismissal of her sister that day had been too harsh. If Maria wouldn't ever come back. Or if she was just waiting for Vivi to get used to the idea. If she was just giving Vivi time to realize they could be a family again.

Vivi had also realized that Maria's, and her own, fears about Frank showing up were unfounded. He either didn't read any newspapers, or didn't recognize her if he did. There was also the chance that Maria was entirely wrong and that Frank had washed his hands of Maria and Sofia and, for that matter, Vivi.

The only positive was when she allowed herself to anticipate the "date" she had with Dean that night.

When rehearsal broke for lunch, Vivi found Thad waiting for her at the exit to the pool. He asked if he could speak with her in private.

"Sure," Vivi said. "Give me ten minutes so I can dry off and change."

"I'd like to talk to you now, actually."

"Okay," Vivi answered, drawing out the word, wondering what could be so important. She wrapped her towel around her and took off her bathing cap, squeezing the water out as they walked toward the audience seating and took the stairs to the third row. There was no one else around.

"What's this all about?"

Vivi noticed that Thad seemed nervous. He slid his clipboard between his legs and began talking. He didn't look at Vivi, but instead stared straight ahead at the pool and stage where some swimmers and dancers were taking their time leaving for lunch. "I know we're not terribly close friends, Vivi, but . . ." He paused and Vivi thought she had an idea where this was going. She'd heard men make similar proclamations since she'd been sixteen. "I need to tell you something."

"Sure, go ahead."

"You can't tell anyone you heard this from me."

"Pinkie swear."

The two of them linked their pinkies and smiled awkwardly.

"I was in a meeting this morning with Ed and Jack Stern."

"Jack Stern, my agent? He's here?" Vivi asked, narrowing her eyes.

Thad finally turned to face her. "He got in late last night, and came to see Ed early this morning. I had been meeting with Ed when Jack came in, and Ed didn't ask me to leave. I heard some things I think you should know."

Vivi nodded, encouraging him to continue.

"Did you know that the fair has been extended to the 1940 season?"

"I'd heard rumblings."

"It's confirmed now. And Ed and Jack were negotiating your salary for next summer."

"But I'm only supposed to swim this summer. And then I'm supposed to get a role in a picture," Vivi said, mostly to herself. Her mind was moving a mile a minute. *Jack is here? And I'm being promised to the Aquacade for another season?*

"That's why I thought you should know."

"Why are you telling me this, Thad?"

"Let's just say I'm not a fan of some of Ed and Billy's behind-the-scenes actions and dealings, and I'm just trying to do my part to help out some of the people they're affecting."

"I appreciate that," Vivi said softly, trying to figure out what all this meant and what she should do with the information. "Thank you for telling me. I wonder why Jack hasn't come to see me."

"Last I'd heard, he and Ed were going to the Government Zone for lunch. He said he didn't want to interrupt your rehearsal this morning and that he would see you after."

"I see. Well then, thank you," Vivi said, standing.

Thad stayed in his seat. "There's more, Vivi."

Vivi sat back down.

"I'm so sorry to have to tell you, but I really do think you deserve to know. Jack said something about the part you were supposed to get this fall at WorldWide, but that they'd decided to give it to another girl and he was now representing her. He said some pretty nasty things about you."

Vivi exhaled loudly, putting her elbows on her thighs and

her face in her hands. She had done everything WorldWide had asked. She'd given up her life, her future marriage for God's sake, to be in the Aquacade. She'd practically swum her legs off and dazzled in the shows. And now she was doing the grand tour of the World's Fair with a fake boyfriend, all for their publicity. And this was the thanks she was receiving? This was the big reward for all of her hard work?

Fear number one: ruined relationship. Check. Fear number two: ruined career. Check, check.

"I'm really sorry, Vivi. I hate to see you so devastated. I hope you're not angry that I told you."

"I'm not angry at you," Vivi said, giving him a small smile despite the burning in her eyes. "I'm glad you told me. You're right: I do deserve to know what people are deciding on my behalf."

They both stood up to go.

"Oh, I almost forgot," Thad said, looking off to the right side of the stage.

Vivi followed his eyes and almost fell down the steep stairs when she saw what—who—he was looking at.

"He came to the cast gate this morning and said he was your brother-in-law. I hope it's not a problem that I let him in."

"Oh my goodness."

Thad must have interpreted her exclamation as one of happy surprise, because he muttered something about leaving them and walked back toward the stage. Vivi was too shocked to ask him to stay.

Catching her footing, Vivi inhaled sharply and paused.

"Alessia," the man said, approaching her. "How nice to see you after so long."

"Frank," she responded in a firm voice. She didn't want him to think she was afraid. Didn't want him to feel as if he had any power over her at all. Based upon what her sister had said, she knew he wasn't harmless, but they were in full view—though out of earshot—of many cast members and stagehands, so Vivi didn't think she needed to be worried that he would harm her physically.

"I'm offended you didn't look me up when you got to town," he said in a mocking tone. "I had to see your picture in a newspaper. I like your hair, by the way." He smiled and reached out his hand to stroke her hair.

Vivi lifted her chin abruptly, turning her head quickly so he couldn't touch her, and focused her eyes on the scar that extended from the left side of his lip all the way toward his ear.

"Why so jumpy? I'm not gonna hurt you."

Vivi stayed quiet. She thought about walking away, but she knew Frank. He'd come after her until he said what he'd come to say.

"Did you know Maria left me?"

Vivi shook her head. "I haven't seen or spoken to her since I've been in New York."

"And you expect me to believe that?" He was practically hissing at her, and she felt his spit hit her cheek.

"I don't really care what you believe, Frank," Vivi said, wiping her cheek. "You know as well as I do that she made it very clear when I left that she never wanted to see me again."

"You wouldn't know where she is and be hiding it from me, would you?" He took a step closer to her.

"No." Vivi took a step back, but almost stumbled as she slammed into the seats.

"You have to tell me, Alessia. I love her and I know I messed up and I just need to talk to her. Please tell me where she is."

"I don't know where she is, and if you can't find her, then it seems as if she doesn't want to see you ever again as well. So look at that: you and I actually have something in common."

"You know I always liked you, Alessia," he said, trying to reach out to her again.

Again, Vivi avoided his touch and crossed her arms in front of her chest.

"I'll tell you what," Frank said, leaning his face close to hers until she could smell the sourness of his breath, "you tell me where Maria is and I won't bother you ever again. I know she would have come to see you. After you left, she wouldn't stop crying. She followed you in all of those stupid Hollywood magazines, so she definitely knows you're here."

Vivi hoped Frank hadn't noticed the surprise that registered in her eyes, hearing that about Maria.

"Can't help you. I don't know where she is either."

"You stupid bitch, tell me!" he said, raising his voice. Vivi noticed he was clenching his fists, his arms straight down by his sides.

"If I were you," Vivi yelled in a whisper, "I'd lower my voice, unless you want a bunch of people running up here to see why there's a man harassing me."

Vivi looked down at the stage and happened to make eye contact with Dean, who was staring up at her. She hadn't intended to look as if she needed help, but he immediately started walking quickly to where she was.

Frank noticed as well.

"This isn't the end of our conversation. I'll be back in a few days. By then she'll either have come to see you or you will have realized that it's in your best interest to tell me where she is. Because if you don't tell me, then I'll get it out of you somehow. I need to see her. You have to believe me that she's safe with me. Please, Alessia."

Dean was a step below where Vivi and Frank were standing. Frank rushed off to the side, across the row of seats and down through the exit, Vivi and Dean staring at him the whole way.

"Are you okay?" Dean asked, touching her shoulder gently. "Who was that guy? And why did he call you Alessia?"

"I don't really know. He thought I was someone else and got pretty angry when he realized I wasn't."

Dean stared at Vivi, who tried to look nonchalant. She could tell by the way he was looking at her that he didn't believe a word she'd said.

⚜

CHAPTER TWENTY-SIX

Max

Saturday, June 17

Max had now been at *Today at the Fair* for three full weeks.

Her responsibilities had become as familiar to her as her morning subway ride and her (almost) nightly dinners with her family. She knew how long the listings edits would take and where the best sandwich stands were for lunch. She knew what kind of surprises put the biggest smiles on Albert the typesetter's face and that their time together always cheered her up despite what had happened in the office that day. She knew how to work well with Charlie and was pleased that their friendship was growing stronger. And she knew that the likelihood of her having an article to enter into the contest by the deadline at the end of the week was lessening each day.

She also decided that pining after James was becoming more and more pointless. They'd only seen each other once that prior week, yesterday at the cohort meeting.

She'd hoped they'd have a chance to go out afterward, but

he'd had to rush off to his mother's birthday dinner. He gave her a kiss on the cheek and told her he was looking forward to the following evening. And so it was that Max was looking forward as well.

After an hour or so, as Max did the event listings at her desk, she heard Charlie calling her into his office.

"Maxine, can you come in here, please?"

Max collected her notebook and pencil from her desk and walked to his office.

She shut Charlie's office door and slumped into one of the chairs across from his messy desk. The office looked as empty as the day Hugh had left, nothing on the walls or in the bookcases. Just a disarray of papers and broken pencils with teeth marks along their wooden bodies, as if they were so many tree trunks that had been destroyed by savage squirrels working out the frustrations from their little squirrel jobs.

"That's not how you sit in Mr. Babcock's office."

She gave him a look and then sat up straighter. "Better?"

"Much," he said, nodding and smiling widely at her.

Max rolled her eyes.

"I need to discuss photo captions with you," Charlie said, a little more loudly than necessary, but Max understood that was his cover in case Mr. Babcock was paying attention to the bang-up subterfuge happening on the other side of his office's back wall.

"What's up, Charlie? You look like you just swallowed spiders."

"Shhhh," Charlie said, wildly gesturing his hands toward the wall behind him, the one that abutted Mr. Babcock's office.

"I know I should be happy that I was promoted," Charlie said much more quietly, his head in his hands, "as you insist on telling me every day, but I don't know how much longer I can take all this extra work."

"This is ridiculous," Max said.

"Keep your voice down," Charlie said, sneering at her. "And what's ridiculous?"

Charlie was clearly stressed about this whole situation, and Max noticed sweat forming on his brow though the heat of the day was still several hours away and the office had air-conditioning.

"What's ridiculous is that Mr. Babcock isn't letting me write articles. He knows I can write and you're in over your head, so why are we putting up with this? You're the editor now, Charlie. Tell him you're assigning me articles."

"I can't do that," Charlie said, shaking his head nervously.

"Why not?"

"Because, as you know, Maxine, he told me that I have to write them all," he said, his voice getting angry. "It's not so simple."

Max looked out the window, her brain working the problem over, trying to find a solution. After a few minutes of sitting quietly, as Max focused on a bird flitting from branch to branch on a tree outside of Charlie's office, and as Charlie bit on a pencil, Max told him she had an idea. "Come with me," she said, standing up and opening Charlie's office door.

"Maxine!" he said urgently. "Where are you going?"

"To Mr. Babcock's office," she whispered. "Whatever you do, just agree with me. You might not like the plan, but it's going to get you out of your situation."

"Wait!" Charlie said, but she was already entering Mr. Babcock's open office door.

"Mr. Babcock, Charlie and I were hoping we could discuss something with you?"

"Of course, have a seat," he said.

She glanced at Charlie and he looked back at her, a terrified expression on his face.

"Mr. Babcock, I'm not sure if Charlie has mentioned it to you yet, but through our summer cohort at NYU, we both have the opportunity to enter a special contest, which has as its prize, tuition for our senior year. As I'm sure you would agree, the prize is quite substantial and something I both hope and need to win in order to continue my studies at NYU."

Max paused for a moment. Mr. Babcock sat patiently, nodding once in a while, encouraging her to go on. Charlie stared at her, questioning looks shooting out of his eyes: *Where are you going with this, Maxine?*

"The contest requires the student to enter an article that has been published by the publication he or she is working at for the summer and the article must contain the student's byline. As you know, I do not have an article with my byline that has been published by *Today at the Fair*, and I was hoping, sir, that you might allow Charlie to assign me a few articles this week so that I might have one to enter into the contest before the deadline on Friday."

Max couldn't imagine a scenario in which Mr. Babcock would say no. He had to see that Charlie was drowning. Had to find this a perfect solution to that and realize that by giving Max a few assignments, he would be helping his star employee, Charlie. And why wouldn't he want to help her out with her education?

Max knew better than to keep pleading. The silence was awkward, but she let it wash over her. She accepted the discomfort, certain that in a moment it would have all been worth it.

"I understand your predicament, Maxine. But I've seen your writing and I don't think it's up to the level that I need for our reported pieces in *Today at the Fair*. I'm sorry, but you'll have to work out another arrangement with Professor Lincoln that will allow you to enter the contest."

Max's took the blow without changing the expression on her face. But her mind was racing.

She didn't want to hurt Charlie. She really, really didn't. But she had imagined this scenario. She gathered her resolve and moved to plan B. Her stubbornness, her inability not to fight for herself, was moving her forward with its own force. And as long as Charlie backed up what she was about to say, it would all go fine.

"With all due respect, Mr. Babcock, that's not what you said a week ago."

He looked at her strangely.

"Jesus Christ, Maxine," Charlie said softly, perhaps only for Max's ears. He shrank in his seat and turned his body away from hers as much as he could in the small office.

"What's not what I said a week ago?" Mr. Babcock asked, a confused look on his face.

"You said that the baby incubator piece was the best Charlie had written, and it made the front page of the paper. However, I wrote that piece, and I have my notes in my handwriting to prove it."

"Is that true, Charlie?" Mr. Babcock asked, his voice rising an octave.

Max turned toward Charlie, raising her eyebrows, trying to remind him with her stare that he should just agree with her. Mr. Babcock would be mad at him for a few minutes, but he could just explain that he was overloaded. And then Mr. Babcock would realize Max could write up to his standards, and he'd allow Charlie to assign pieces to her, easing his load. Win-win.

Max tried to convey all of this. Charlie stared back with a hateful expression.

"What's true, sir," Charlie said, sitting up tall in his chair, "is that Maxine did interview Dr. Couney. Considering I was busy writing all of the articles, I thought it appropriate to delegate the Dr. Couney interview to her. She then provided me her notes and briefed me on the conversation they'd had and what she'd observed, but I can guarantee you that I wrote the article." Charlie folded his arms across his chest and glared at Max, daring her to contradict him.

"That's just not true, Mr. Babcock. I wrote that piece, and I can prove it." Max looked at Charlie and jutted her chin out at him. *Charlie, seriously?*

Mr. Babcock looked from one face to the other and abruptly stood up.

"This is outrageous, and I will not tolerate lying of any sort in this office. Maxine, I don't know what type of little game you're trying to play, but I know Charlie's writing style and I know he has the highest integrity. You, however, have already tried to pull one stunt at this paper, and I'm not going to allow you to pull another. I am inclined to let you go immediately, but we have too much work to do. So despite my preference not to have a girl of your quality tainting our work, you will remain for the time being. Yet you will do only the tasks to which you've been assigned. Do I make myself clear?"

Max sat quietly, his words ringing loudly in her ears. She didn't dare look at Charlie, knowing exactly what she'd find on his face.

"Sir, I—"

"No, Maxine. You've said enough. And consider yourself on

probation. If you commit one more transgression at this paper, you will be fired."

Max nodded contritely, apologized to Mr. Babcock, and stood up, intending to walk back to her desk with her head held high. She was angry at herself for being so impulsive and not thinking through the consequences of revealing all of that to Mr. Babcock before she went into his office. And angry at Charlie that he didn't tell the truth. Though she understood that he was trying to protect himself, and that he still might be mad at her for calling him dumb, surely he could help her out knowing how important the contest was to her.

Just before she walked out of Mr. Babcock's office, though, she stopped and turned back around. And though she tried to keep the words inside, knowing they would do her no service, she couldn't help herself. "I'm sorry you feel the way you do, Mr. Babcock. I'm not lying, and I know one day you'll realize that to be true."

CHAPTER TWENTY-SEVEN

Vivi & Max

Saturday, June 17

That night, Max and James stood with the crowd, applauding as the cast of the Aquacade took their final bow. Vivi had been true to her word and had secured front-row seats for Max and James for the eight-thirty performance.

"That was incredible," Max said, smiling, clapping, and stamping her feet on the ground.

"I'm so glad we came," James said, giving Max a strange look.

"Why are you looking at me like that?"

"I've just never seen you so enthusiastic," he said, laughing.

Max cocked her head to the side and smiled at him. "Maybe I'm evolving," she said, raising her eyebrows.

"Could it be?" James asked in feigned shock. "Anyway, where are we meeting Vivi and Dean? I have to imagine you'll be more comfortable in that outfit at the restaurant than you are in these wooden seats."

"That's for sure," Max said, looking around at the rest of the crowd. She was clearly overdressed. "We're meeting them outside the gate in half an hour."

The photographers had been asking Mr. Mackey for shots of Vivi and Dean at a real dinner date, in a fine restaurant. Ed had complied and had given Vivi and Dean the ten-thirty show off. They were going to the most expensive restaurant at the fair, which was in the Italian Pavilion in the Government Zone. And they had gotten permission to bring their friends along—all on Billy Rose's tab.

When Vivi had heard about this plan earlier in the week, she told Mr. Mackey that she had nothing appropriate to wear. He said he'd take care of it. And he had.

The next night, when she'd arrived back at her hotel exhausted and hungry, as was always the case when she emerged from the taxi around midnight, she had been excited to find a black garment bag with the B. Altman & Co. logo printed in silver across the front. (The front desk clerk would report to his coworkers that Miss Holden, the long-term guest from Hollywood, clapped her hands and bounced on her toes in delight.) Inside, there were six dresses in a rainbow of colors, all her size, and each one prettier than the next. Plus, matching shoes and handbags. And there were instructions from B. Altman & Co. that she should keep her two favorite ensembles and they'd pick up the rest in the lobby the next day.

Vivi forgot how tired and hungry she was and tried on every single outfit, checking her reflection in the mirror and adjusting her hair into different styles depending on the neckline. It was difficult to choose just two. But such are the hardships a star must endure.

Now, in the scarlet off-the-shoulder silk, Vivi emerged through the cast gate where she'd told Max and James to meet her and Dean. A moment later Dean joined them in a dark suit that fit him beautifully (she wondered if he'd had a similar garment bag delivery, but perhaps from Billy Rose's personal tailor). Max and James were also dressed in fancy attire and the four friends admired one another, lobbing compliments and buzzing in anticipation about their exciting night ahead.

It was decided, due to Vivi's and Dean's fatigue from the three shows they'd performed that day and due to Vivi's and Max's high heels, that they'd hire guide chairs to push them the considerable distance from the amphitheater to the Italian Pavilion.

Unfortunately, the chairs only held a maximum of two people, so the foursome split up into couples. The photographers, choosing not to pay seventy-five cents to be pushed to the Government Zone, walked quickly beside them, trying to keep up, snapping photos of Vivi and Dean along the way.

Vivi tried to maintain a smile despite how upset she still was over Gabe and also by what had happened earlier in the day: the news from Thad and the appearance of Frank. Now, riding on the chair in the most elegant dress she'd ever worn, she felt as if she were being watched. But she tried to brush off the feeling, telling herself she was being ridiculous.

So Vivi smiled for the photos and tried to think instead about how excited she'd been to experience what was written up and talked about constantly: the fancy restaurant in the Italian Pavilion.

Max also was trying to quiet the chatter in her own mind. It had been a horrid afternoon since her failed attempt to get Mr. Babcock to assign her articles. Charlie wasn't speaking to her, accusing her of trying to get him in trouble. She tried to be optimistic and convince herself that Mr. Babcock would come around, that he'd want to lighten Charlie's load. But it didn't seem like that would happen. Max had resigned herself to not having an article to enter into the contest and was contemplating what jobs she could apply for, since she wouldn't be able to enroll at NYU in the fall. At home, her father was avoiding having conversations with her, which confirmed to Max that there had been no positive developments in his job search.

All she could hope for was that Mr. Babcock wouldn't call Professor L. to complain about her. She still needed her professor's letter of recommendation, and it would do her no favors if he knew what she'd done.

So Max smiled for James, hoping not to put a damper on what would be their first real dinner together in a restaurant.

"Isn't it magnificent?" Vivi said to Max as they disembarked from the chairs, the men paying the pushers the fee and possibly a bit more in a tip.

They looked up at the pavilion, which seemed to be one of the highest buildings at the fair, certainly in the Government Zone. There was a cascading waterfall out front that was lit up beautifully. It was difficult not to stare, not to just ask for a table to be brought outside to that very spot so they could have their dinner with a view.

"I think the dining room is on the second floor," James said as the handsome group climbed the steps into the pavilion, trailed by the photographers and the eyeballs of fairgoers wondering who the beautiful and important young people were.

The maître d' led them to a table in the center of the room and told the photographers they could take a few photographs while the couples had appetizers and then again during the dessert, but in the meantime, they were to wait outside the restaurant, down the hall to be exact, and to please not bother the other diners or include them in the photographs. This was an exclusive establishment, and many of the patrons expected discretion. *Molte grazie. Scusi, per favore.*

"This might be the nicest restaurant I've ever eaten at," Vivi said quietly to Max as they placed their cloth napkins on their laps.

"Me too," Max said, looking around at the mirrors on the walls, the intricate light fixtures, and the sculptures that stood on podiums scattered throughout the room. "I researched the restaurant today and found an article from *Today at the Fair* that said it's run by the Italian Line, and that this room is an exact replica of the main dining salon on the *S.S. Conte di Savoia.*"

"Oh, how I'd love to travel on a cruise ship one day, ideally the Italian Line. I'm dying to go to Rome," Vivi said, the candlelight glimmering in her eyes.

"Compliments of Mr. Billy Rose," the waiter said as he held a bottle of champagne out before him.

"How nice!" Vivi said as she watched the waiter open the bottle with a flourish and pour four glasses.

"I say we each go around and give a toast," Max said.

"As long as you go first," James said.

"No need to twist my arm," Max said, her face brightening at the opportunity to have the spotlight shine on her. "I'd like to make a toast to—"

"New rule," James said, interrupting. "The toast can be no longer than ten words."

James and Dean nodded at each other, smiling, and they all turned back to Max, who stuck her tongue out at James.

"Not a fan of rules lately, but, fine." She thought for a moment. "To new friends who make me so happy, I couldscream," Max said, counting out the words on her fingers.

"That was eleven!" James said, pointing at her, but smiling.

"I combined the last two," Max said, lifting her chin, daring him to defy her.

"Well done, Max," Dean said. "I'll drink to that."

They all lifted their glasses and clinked them together.

"Now you, Dean," Max said.

"To the world of today and the world of tomorrow."

"Here, here!" James said.

Again they all clinked glasses.

"Extra credit for incorporating the theme of the fair. Quite poetic," Vivi said, winking at Dean.

"Your turn, James," Max said, and they all turned to look at James.

He paused, silently counted words out on his fingers, and proceeded. "May a pack of blessings light upon thy back."

"Shakespeare. Nicely played," Dean said.

"That was only nine words," Max said.

"I know. I always like to come in just under my word count."

"Ha-ha," Max said.

"Journalist joke. Sorry," James said to Vivi and Dean.

They clinked glasses, and then all eyes turned to Vivi.

Vivi wasn't good at this. She was glad to go last, as she hadn't known what to say. And then it came to her. "Let's stop this game right now. I need a drink."

Dean, Max, and James all cheered and said, "I'll drink to that," in unison.

The evening, so far, was splendid. What could be more ideal about the situation? Four beautiful young people glowing like starlight at the finest restaurant at the largest, most expensive world exposition ever held. Their futures were bright, their bodies were lithe, their dinner was being paid for. It was the type of night they thought they'd look back on when they were older, much older, as one of the best of their lives.

They had the world in their hands, or so they thought. And what was the harm in letting them think that, at least for a few more years, until the realities of official adulthood and the atrocities of war would settle upon their shoulders like heavy weights demanding complete attention and steadfast vigilance?

For just as unaware as they were about what was happening, truly happening, across the ocean, they were unaware about what was about to shatter their idyll.

There would be scotch (even for Vivi), there would be secrets, and then everything would change.

๛

CHAPTER TWENTY-EIGHT

Vivi & Max

Saturday, June 17

For now, let's allow the two couples to enjoy their charmed time together.

James and Dean took over the ordering, consulting with the waiter and eventually allowing him to decide for them, seeing as they were all unfamiliar with the delicacies. Max ordered more drinks for the group, and then she placed her hands on the table dramatically and looked from Dean to Vivi with a sly smile on her face and a twinkle in her eye. "So, how long have the two of you been dating?"

Vivi and Dean gave each other a look.

"What? What was that look?" Max asked, her voice suspicious.

"My, you're a perceptive one," Dean said.

Max tilted her head and narrowed her eyes at Dean.

"Vivi?" Dean said, a question in his voice.

"Go right ahead," Vivi said, gesturing with her hand.

"We're not really dating. The Aquacade people are having us fake a relationship for publicity."

"What?" Max exclaimed a little too loudly as the diners around them turned, and then she lowered her voice. "Do they really do that?"

"I had no idea that actually happened," James said.

"Oh yes, the flacks do all sorts of things, creating relationships and situations when they'll improve box office sales, and covering up relationships and situations when they won't. Big entertainment companies, especially the movie studios, couldn't operate without their fixers."

"So this is all for show?" Max asked, waving her hand at the two of them.

"You're the only two who know," Dean said, giving Vivi a smile she couldn't interpret.

"How about the two of you?" Vivi asked. "How long have you been together?"

Max and James started speaking at once, and then looked at each other and laughed.

"We're just old school chums," James said, smiling at Max.

"Chums? What is this, 1870?" Max said, teasing James, retreating into their comfortable banter to avoid giving too much away.

"Then let's drink to true love. May we all find it," Vivi said, lifting her glass.

"To true love!" the others toasted.

"So, dear Vivi, what was so bad about your day that you needed a drink so desperately?" Max asked.

Vivi had drunk her two glasses of champagne very quickly and was already feeling the effects.

"I got some bad news today," she said, watching as the waiter set down drinks. Four scotches, neat.

"I hope these are okay," Max said, gesturing to the drinks. "I thought they would make for a lively evening."

Vivi shrugged and took a sip. Her face contorted involuntarily, and the others laughed. "As I was saying, two pieces of bad news. First, WorldWide gave my part, the part they'd promised me, to another actress. And second, they made a commitment to the Aquacade that I would swim in the 1940 production."

"I thought the fair was only for one year," James said, taking a sip of his drink.

"It was supposed to be," Vivi said, "but the Fair Corporation decided to extend it. Apparently, the attendance numbers haven't been as high as they'd hoped, so even though they're still closing at the end of October, they'll reopen in the spring to recoup more of the investment."

"That's interesting," Max said. "We've had a couple of articles in *Today at the Fair* about how attendance numbers are right on track. Anyway, how come you don't want to swim in the Aquacade next year? I thought you loved it."

Vivi was quiet for a moment. There was so much to say. "I don't love it as much as I should."

"You sure work hard for someone who doesn't love it," Dean said.

"I was motivated because if I did well, I was told WorldWide would bring me back to Hollywood in the fall and I would be given a plum role. But I'm so confused, because I don't even know if I want to act anymore."

"Whoa, what?" Max asked, a shocked expression on her face.

"Sure, Hollywood has its allure. But it's like a boyfriend who's not good for you. He takes you to wonderful places and makes you feel adored, but it's all empty. And you find out in the end that he didn't have your best interests in mind, only his own.

Elizabeth Dorchester's speech opened my eyes to how things really are. How all these men who tell me they're guiding my career are really just using me to advance their own careers. I have zero control over my life at WorldWide. I realize that's how it works, and I appreciate the opportunities it's afforded me, but I'm just not sure if this is what I want anymore."

Dean, who was sitting to Vivi's right, put his hand on her arm, sensing how difficult this all was for her. Vivi turned to him and gave him a small smile, feeling tears prick her eyes. It wasn't the emotion of all this honesty that brought the tears; it was the kind man sitting next to her, telling her with his eyes and with his touch that he saw her, that he was hearing her, and that it was going to be okay.

They all fell silent as four waiters brought appetizers, setting the plates before them in one synchronized movement.

"I understand what you mean about the false allure of Hollywood," Dean said, once the waiters had left. "I'm just tasting it for the first time, and you described it perfectly."

Vivi smiled at Dean.

"Can we have another round, please?" Max said, stopping a waiter who was headed to a different table. "This got deep fast."

"Sorry!" Vivi said, laughing, which felt good.

"No, no, don't be sorry. So what are you going to do?"

"I'm not really sure. My agent is here in New York. I only saw him briefly today, so we didn't have time to get into it all, but we're supposed to meet for breakfast tomorrow morning. I guess I'll see where that conversation goes and take it from there."

"Not to change the subject, but oh my heavens, this is the best food I've ever eaten," Dean said, practically moaning over his pasta.

"If you like this, then I know of a restaurant in Greenwich Village to recommend to you," James said to Dean.

"I took you for a hot-dog-and-hamburger kind of guy for some reason, Dean," Max said, giving him a sly smile.

"No, not at all. I love to cook and I love to eat, the more exotic the food, the better."

"So what are you doing diving?" Max said, her eyes wide. "You should train to be a chef!"

"Trust me, I think about that almost every night when I go to sleep. But I was good at diving and it's taken me on a path that I feel like I have to continue on."

Vivi looked at Dean and felt sad. Here was someone, like her, who had been swept up in the whirlwind of the entertainment machine and felt compelled to stay because it would lead to success. And financial independence. But would it lead to happiness? Did that even matter?

"Anyway, let's change the mood. Sorry I was such a downer. Max, tell us what's going on with your job," Vivi said.

"I have a story too. It's not nearly as tragic as yours, Vivi," Max said, smiling. "But I'm doomed nonetheless. I tried to pull off another scheme in my office so I could be assigned an article, which I need to enter the contest I've told you all about. But my plan failed and I'm officially persona non grata. Wait, is that Italian? Did I just speak Italian at an Italian restaurant?"

"Latin," James said. "But close! Very, very close."

Max smiled. "Anyway, I almost got myself fired, again, and I'm well on my way to being a complete failure with no future in journalism because I won't be able to pay for school next year. And if my boss calls my professor to tattle on me, there's no way he's going to write me a letter of recommendation."

"My goodness," Dean said, and they all paused for a minute, taking bites of the delicious food.

"James, are things this dramatic over at the *Times*?" Vivi asked.

James laughed. "Not even close."

"Well, hold on," Max said. "It's not entirely a fair question, since James is male and he's not being treated as unfairly as I am."

"True," Vivi said, "But, Max, I—" Vivi stopped, deciding to think about how to best frame what she wanted to say.

"What?" Max asked. "What were you going to say?"

All eyes turned to Vivi as she took a sip of her scotch, part delay tactic, part courage grab. She thought back to the night she and Max had met at the Elizabeth Dorchester speech. Afterward, at the Turf Trylon Café, they had made a pact that Max would help Vivi become more assertive and Vivi would help Max tamp down her boldness when it did her more harm than good. Perhaps this was an opportunity to help her do just that.

"I was going to say that maybe you should let things play out. You know, instead of trying to make it fit into your idea of what it's supposed to be."

Max sat back in her chair and laughed.

"What's so funny?" Vivi asked, raising her eyebrows.

"Nothing," Max said, trying to restrain herself from saying what she was thinking.

"No, say it," Vivi said.

There was a small part of Max that knew she shouldn't lash out at Vivi, that Vivi wasn't necessarily attacking her, even though, at the moment, that's exactly how it felt. But the alcohol loosened her tongue and hindered her ability to act composed.

She ended up going full-on Max. And once she started, she couldn't stop.

"First of all, it's ironic that you refer to Elizabeth Dorchester as opening your eyes to what you deserve in your career, but you criticize me for acting boldly and trying to have a say in mine. And second, it's amusing to get career advice from you at all. Someone who doesn't want to be an actress or a showgirl or whatever it is that you are, but you keep going in day after day, in a tiny bathing suit, so all the men can gawk at you."

"Whoa, whoa, Max. Is that really necessary?" Dean asked, looking vexed.

"It's okay, Dean, I can handle it," Vivi said, patting his hand. "Where is this coming from, Max? Can we just have a calm conversation about it?"

"Sure," Max said, a combative tone in her voice as she crossed her arms across her chest.

"Let's just forget it," Vivi said. It hadn't been her intention to get Max riled up and she hadn't expected Max to become so defensive so quickly.

Vivi noticed that James and Dean both looked slightly uncomfortable.

"No," Max said. "Let's not forget it. You have something else to say to me? Say it."

"You know what, we can talk about it tomorrow. We were all having such a nice time. I don't want to ruin it. Let's change the subject," Vivi said.

"What did you work on this week at the *Times*, James?" Dean asked.

Vivi felt relieved that he was trying to help her out.

"Well—" James began.

"I can't do this," Max interrupted. "I can't just act like you didn't start in on me. Just say what you want to say, Vivi."

Vivi knew Max was feeling defensive and attacked, but she decided that maybe it would do her good to hear another perspective besides the one she kept convincing herself was true. Looking to Dean and James, who both shrugged, Vivi continued. She tried to make her voice as calm and nonconfrontational as possible. "The first night we met, you asked me to help you become, and I think these were your words, less of 'a bull in a china shop.'"

"Right. And I was going to help you become more of one."

"Well, here I am, growing horns, and if you want me to be perfectly honest with you, which I would think you'd prefer than all of us just agreeing with you because we're scared to tell you the truth, then I think you're making a mistake."

"Do you agree with her, James?" Max asked.

James looked into Max's eyes and gave her a small smile. "I do."

"Nice," Max said, rolling her eyes.

Vivi continued. "You can't mold everything in life to how you want it to be. You can't manipulate it all to your own advantage. That's not how life works. Sometimes you have to play by the rules, let things fall into place, and then deal with them where they are."

"And how's that working out for you?"

"I'm doing the best I can right now."

"Really?"

"Really."

"That's not how it appears."

"And how exactly does it appear to you, Max?"

"It appears as if you're too afraid to stand up for yourself.

That you're so caught up in this glamorous Hollywood lifestyle that you're willing to sacrifice what's meaningful to you just so you can become rich and famous. Like blowing off your sister."

"You don't know anything about what's going on with my sister," Vivi said, her voice deepening with anger. She'd briefly told Max about Maria, but hadn't gone into it to the extent that Max could assess the situation with any ounce of insight.

"I know that you're working your rear end off to do well in a show that you now say doesn't even mean anything to you and all the while you're ignoring your sister, who should be the most important thing."

"Come on, Max. Lay off," Dean said.

"I'm just trying to help you, Max," Vivi said.

"Well, while you're out there having all of these opportunities with your Aquacade and your big film career, I'm just trying to do everything I can to figure out a way to go to school next semester. So until you know what that feels like, I suggest you let me be."

Max stood up, threw her napkin onto her chair, downed the rest of her scotch, and stormed out of the restaurant.

Vivi and Dean turned toward James, expecting him to follow Max out. But he remained in his chair, looking as if he didn't know what he should do next.

Soon after that, they left the restaurant. Vivi and Dean took a few final photos for the waiting photographers. And the three of them said their good-byes.

Dean rode in the taxi with Vivi back to her hotel, putting his arm around her shoulders and stroking her hair. They spoke quietly, trying to figure out how things had turned sour so quickly. Mostly, though, Vivi was quiet, trying to process her thoughts alone. She felt a little bad that the evening had ended so abruptly and so vastly different than how it had begun, filled as it had been with promise and bonhomie, but she didn't regret a thing she'd said. She hoped that when Max took the time to process it all, she'd realize that Vivi was just looking out for her best interests.

And Vivi realized, though what Max had said hurt and though she didn't exactly have all the facts correct about Maria, perhaps Max had done the same.

The New York Chronicle
Sunday, June 18, 1939
By Pierce Hayes

IT'S OFFICIAL: FAIR EXTENDS TO 1940

It's been no secret that attendance at the World's Fair has not met the lofty expectations put forth by Grover Whalen and his Fair Corporation. In fact, the numbers are downright dreadful.

During the first several weeks of the fair, low attendance numbers were mostly blamed on the damp and cold weather. Other factors contributed, such as school being in session and high prices. But, as the summer has progressed, attendance and profits have not followed. They hover around 50 percent of initial projections.

Corporate exhibitors, Amusement Zone concessionaires, and international governments have all filed grievances with the Fair Corporation complaining that they don't foresee recouping their investments based upon the current circumstances.

The Fair Corporation has responded by confirming that the fair will extend to the 1940 season, and, in the coming weeks, they'll begin offering less expensive admission packages.

The official closing date for this year is October 31, 1939. Adjustments and renovations will be conducted over the winter months, with the fair reopening set for early summer 1940.

TODAY *at the* FAIR
Sunday, June 18, 1939
By Charlie Hull

THE MORE FAIR, THE BETTER

What's better than a one-year World's Fair? A two-year World's Fair, of course!

Future and current fairgoers will be thrilled to learn that Grover Whalen and the Fair Corporation have made it official: the 1939 World's Fair of New York City will be extended through 1940.

Exhibitors and concessionaires have expressed their delight at the decision, thrilled to be able to share their offerings with more visitors in the 1940 season.

CHAPTER TWENTY-NINE

⫰

Vivi

Sunday, June 18

Vivi woke up early, despite having gone to bed late the night before, after dinner at the Italian Pavilion. When she'd finally said good night to Dean and rested her head on the pillow, her mind raced with thoughts of the night she'd had and what would happen the next day.

The sky was dark and cloudy, and as Vivi glanced out her window, which was covered with glistening beads of rain, she looked down upon the tops of the trees that lined the street outside. People were walking on the sidewalk below (quickly, always so quickly) with umbrellas. The weather had been improving over the last few days, with warm nights, which made the conditions in the dressing rooms a bit stuffy, but at least Vivi and her castmates weren't cold and shivering, as wet as they were all the time.

Vivi showered, put on a pair of dark trousers, a starched white blouse with gold buttons, and her highest heels. She was dressing to command a presence.

At precisely eight, Vivi emerged from the elevator into the lobby of her hotel and walked into the dining room, where she immediately spotted Jack sitting at a table for four.

"Are we expecting two more?" Vivi asked, looking down at her agent and keeping her voice steady.

"No. I just like to spread out," Jack said, smiling, and then he stood. "Now a proper good morning to you, Vivi. You're looking gorgeous, as always. Surprising, considering what you were up to last night."

Vivi wondered how he knew what she'd been up to. Then she looked down and saw the newspapers spread open upon the table. She moved closer and saw the photos of her and Dean in the guide chair, outside the Italian Pavilion, and in the restaurant itself. And there was a sweet one of the four of them, hamming it up over champagne.

"It was quite a night," Vivi said, taking the chair that Jack had pulled out for her. "You should go to the Italian Pavilion for dinner if you have a chance before you return to LA."

"Unfortunately, I'm heading back this afternoon." Jack sat down and motioned to the waiter to bring coffee.

"What'll you have, Vivi? I'm having eggs myself."

"Just the coffee."

"You were marvelous last night. I know you couldn't see me in the audience, but I'm sure I was cheering the loudest. I was impressed. You've worked hard and it shows."

"That's kind of you to say. So I guess you'll be putting in a good word to Mr. Green. I can't wait to get back to LA, to that role he promised me for the fall."

"Actually, um, I wanted to talk to you about that."

Vivi sat quietly as she watched Jack squirm in his chair. She thought about what Thad had told her the day before. She'd had no reason to doubt Thad, but she wanted to at least give Jack the benefit of the doubt.

"About the role?"

"Did you hear that they're extending the fair through next year?" Jack asked, ignoring her question.

And that's when Vivi knew Thad had been telling the truth. "I did."

"Have you thought about staying?"

"No, Jack. I'm planning on going back to LA for the role."

"Uh, about that . . . ," Jack said, beginning to stammer.

Vivi was disgusted by this man, who'd assured her on numerous occasions that she should trust him, that he'd always look out for her best interests.

"Is there a problem?"

"Um, no. No problem at all."

Jack changed the subject and made small talk about the fair and about Vivi's experience in the Aquacade, all the while acting as if things were dandy. As if he weren't audaciously lying to her about every single thing that came out of his mouth.

And when their meeting was over, Vivi placed her hands flat on the table, stood up, smiled down at Jack, and walked out of the dining room without so much as a good-bye.

When she returned to her room, Vivi stared at herself in the bathroom mirror. She wondered when everything had become so complicated. And then she picked up the telephone to call Gabe, to tell him all about her meeting with Jack. She began to place the call and then she hung up, realizing that she couldn't call Gabe. She had forgotten for a moment what had happened between them. Had forgotten that he was no longer her Gabe. That he wouldn't want to hear every last detail of her conversation with Jack.

No, Gabe had made it clear that he didn't want to speak with her. She hadn't given up on their relationship yet, far from it, but calling him early on a Sunday morning—it was just past 6:00 A.M. in LA—was not the way back into his heart.

Screw it, Vivi said to herself, and placed the call anyway. Gabe may have given up on her, but she wasn't ready to do the same with him.

"Hello?" Gabe answered, his voice groggy. She'd definitely woken him up.

"It's me," Vivi said softly.

"Jesus, it's six A.M."

"I know. I'm sorry. I just wanted to talk to you."

"Who is it, lovey?"

Vivi recognized the voice as soon as she heard it. And if she hadn't, the "lovey" would have given it away instead.

"Is that Amanda?" Vivi asked, too shocked to allow the disgust she was beginning to feel seep into her voice.

"What the hell did you expect? You cheated on me, Vivi, and humiliated me. Everyone I know saw those pictures," Gabe said, his tone rising.

"I didn't cheat on you. I explained the whole situation. Amanda?" Vivi was now furious.

"Relax," Gabe said.

"Let me talk to her," Amanda said, her voice carrying across the pillows, which Vivi was now picturing in her mind.

Gabe muttered something that Vivi couldn't make out, and then Amanda was speaking. "Vivi, hi, lovey. It's been ages. Let me explain."

"You know what, Amanda? You can have him. You two are perfect for each other. I hope you have beautiful little conniving babies together."

Vivi hung up the phone. She felt betrayed. Sick to her stomach. Exactly, Vivi realized, how Gabe must have felt when he saw the photos of her and Dean.

Walking back toward the window and looking out at the rain, at the colorful canopy of umbrellas below, Vivi tried to process the fact that her fiancé, which she still insisted on calling him, was bedding her best friend. If she had thought there was a possibility that she and Gabe could get back together, she knew now that was no longer the case.

Amid the overarching feelings of pain, Vivi realized that Gabe had just made things easier for her. She hadn't cheated on him. But he had cheated on her. And with a woman who had always disliked him—at least that was what Amanda had told Vivi. Perhaps discovering them in flagrante delicto was the best thing that could have happened. Perhaps, Vivi thought, knowing what they were capable of would make it easier for her to realize she didn't need to waste another minute caring for people who didn't care for her. And perhaps it would allow her to start fresh when she was ready.

Still, it hurt.

Wiping her eyes, Vivi took a deep breath. She cursed quietly when she looked at the clock. She was going to be late for rehearsal. The day had already been more eventful than she could have imagined. And it was only nine fifteen in the morning.

On her way to the fairgrounds, Vivi was able to think clearly for the first time in weeks. The car sped toward Queens and Vivi rolled down her window a bit, the fresh breeze a welcome relief from the taxi's stagnant air. The rain dripped in, the way it does on a summer morning in a New York City cab, and she was getting wet, but she didn't care. It all seemed to elucidate her thoughts. *Funny how rain can do that*, Vivi thought. A thorough wash of the dark film that had been blocking any light from shining through.

Knowing she was going to be very late, Vivi walked quickly across the grounds once she exited the cab. The rain had stopped and the flowers were heavy with the drops of water resting on their petals. The sun looked as if it were about to poke through the clouds.

The amphitheater was just ahead, but seeing Maria, Vivi stopped short. She didn't think she could deal with this now. Besides, having a conversation with Maria would make her even later than she already was. She'd tell Maria to come back before the three-thirty show.

And then she saw Sofia.

Vivi approached slowly. When she drew closer, she locked eyes with the beautiful little girl with dark curls and golden-brown eyes. She knelt down and smiled at her.

"Sofia, this is Alessia. Can you say hi?" Maria asked, bending over at the waist.

Sofia hid behind Maria's legs.

Vivi and Maria both stood, smiling cautiously. Maria's smile apologizing that Sofia wasn't friendlier. Vivi's smile saying she understood and that it was perfectly fine.

"She's beautiful, Maria."

Maria smiled, glancing down at Sofia as well. "She resembles you."

The two sisters stared into each other's eyes, and Vivi felt her walls coming down.

Vivi wanted only to spend the next hour observing every inch of Sofia. But there was a more urgent matter.

"You need to be careful here, Maria. Frank came yesterday. He's looking for you."

Maria appeared worried and instinctively looked around. "Is there somewhere private we could go?"

"Come with me."

Vivi walked quickly toward the cast gate as Maria picked up Sofia and followed behind.

When they entered the amphitheater, Vivi saw that the cast had already assembled for rehearsal.

"I'll be right there!" Vivi shouted in the general direction of Johnny and some of the other swimmers. They waved at her, and she led Maria and Sofia into the dressing room. They'd have privacy there, and she had to change into her swimsuit anyway.

Placing Sofia in front of a rack of dancers' costumes, Vivi smiled as the little girl twirled among the long skirts and scarves. Maria sat in one of the chairs in front of the makeup mirrors, and Vivi began to undress.

"I would have stayed. I wanted to stay," Vivi said, her breaths shortening. "I didn't care what people said. I wanted to raise her. Now that I think about it, it wasn't your decision to make. Just because Mom and Dad died, it didn't automatically allow you to make those decisions for me." Vivi began to cry uncontrollably.

"It would have been a mistake. You needed to go."

It all came back in a rush. So much pain. So many regrets. She stood still, trying to make sense of it all. And then she couldn't help herself. "And you wanted a baby."

"That's not fair."

"But it's true, isn't it?" Vivi took measured breaths and calmed her voice. Still, her eyes were sharp.

"Frank was dangerous. You were in danger," she said slowly, clearly, as if it still wasn't sinking into Vivi's head.

"He still is, Maria, but you left him. And we could have left him back then too. Now two years have gone by, and I missed everything," Vivi gestured toward Sofia and spoke more softly. "I missed everything."

The two sisters were quiet for a moment.

"You had opportunities, Alessia. And look at you. You made something of yourself."

"But that's not what's important." The words came out of Vivi's mouth without much thought, but she knew the moment she said them that they were the truth. Her success, her film potential, the clothes, the money . . . none of it meant anything. Everything that meant anything was standing right in front of her. "She's my daughter, and you shouldn't have forced me to go."

"I wish it had all been different, and I'm sorry things turned out the way they did, but you have to believe me that at the time I thought I was protecting you."

Vivi glanced down at Sofia, who was smiling as she held a pink shoe out toward Maria. She felt her guard come down.

"What's she like?" Vivi asked, looking at Sofia. The tears had begun anew, and now Vivi wasn't even trying to hold them back, now that she was looking at her daughter. Her daughter. Maria had told Vivi that Sofia would be better off without her real mother in her life. Had convinced Vivi that Sofia would be safe in the house with Frank. That she'd spoken to Frank and he was going to change. Remembering that interaction hurt just as much now as it had when it had happened. But Vivi knew Maria. Knew that the cruel way she'd sent Vivi to California wasn't the real Maria. *This* was the real Maria. And now that Frank was gone, perhaps Vivi and Maria could be sisters again.

"She's wonderful," Maria said, her smile lighting up her face. "She's smart and gentle and opinionated and she scrunches up her nose whenever she's thinking hard about something."

The sisters laughed, and Sofia looked up.

"What funny, Mama?" Sofia asked in the sweetest voice.

"Sofia," Vivi said, "would you like to see yourself in this big mirror with all the lights?"

Sofia nodded and let Vivi lift her up in the air. Vivi paused before she set Sofia back down and allowed herself to feel the lovely weight of Sofia in her arms. Allowed herself to smell her baby hair and touch her baby skin. And, for a moment, allowed herself to wonder what it would be like to be in Sofia's life on a regular basis.

For a moment Vivi imagined that staying at the Aquacade for another year might not be so bad. She'd have a job that would allow her to be with Maria and Sofia.

That blissful feeling was interrupted by the appearance of Ruby.

"I was sent in to get you. You're late for rehearsal. And, by the way, you shouldn't have such personal conversations, Vivi—or is it Alessia?—unless you're certain no one can hear you," she said, a sinister smile on her face. Ruby bent down and smiled at Sofia, ruffling the curls atop the child's head.

Vivi's heart sank. She couldn't be sure how much Ruby had heard. Ruby, who could use this against Vivi and get the starring role back, a role she'd always felt she deserved.

"I don't know what you think you heard, Ruby, but you must have been mistaken," Vivi said, moving closer to Ruby, crossing her arms across her chest and staring down at her.

"I heard enough to know that if Ed or Billy Rose knew the truth about you, they'd fire you on the spot. Everyone knows having an unmarried mother in a production is a scandal. To be honest," Ruby said, narrowing her eyes as if she were trying to get a better look at Vivi, as if she were seeing her for the first time, "I'm kind of surprised. I didn't know you had it in you."

CHAPTER THIRTY

✴

Max

Sunday, June 18

The morning after the dinner at the Italian Pavilion, Max's day off, she was still in bed at 11:00 A.M. when she heard a knock on her bedroom door. She'd been up for a couple of hours, unable to stop thinking about how things had ended with Vivi, and with James, the night before. She didn't particularly want to face the day.

"Maxine, honey, can I come in?"

Max didn't even know why her mother bothered knocking, considering she always just waltzed right in instead of waiting for an answer.

"What is this?" Mrs. Roth asked. She was holding up a newspaper and had a sour look on her face.

Max had forgotten that photos from the night before might be in the paper. And she hadn't considered, as she was goading on the photographers to take shots of her, that her parents would ever see them. And that they'd blow her whole lie wide-open.

"Oh my goodness," Max said, feigning surprise as she looked at the photos. "Would you look at that! These were at my dinner last night. I thought the photographer worked for the restaurant. I had no idea they'd be in the paper. I'm glad the lighting was good at least." She smiled up at her mother, waiting for Mrs. Roth's expression to change.

"Why does it say in the caption that you work for *Today at the Fair*? Why would they write such a thing?"

"Maxine!"

Max and her mother both turned as they heard her father stomping down the hall toward her bedroom.

"Maxine, what is this?" he asked, holding a newspaper out to her, his voice rising. "I was just down on the second floor at the Cohens' apartment having coffee, and Dora Cohen showed me this newspaper with your picture in it. What's this about working at the fair? You told us you were working at *The New York Times*."

Max sat up in her bed and looked from her mother to her father, wondering what the best course of action would be. She stared an extra beat at her father, thinking that he was one to talk about lying, but she knew her situation was vastly different than his. And if she'd learned anything from last night, it was that she had to be a bit more gentle with how she handled things.

But the reasons she had originally told her parents she was working at the *Times* still held. She didn't want to add to their concerns then, and she certainly didn't want to now, especially now that she knew the truth about her father's job.

She also knew that it would be hard to come up with a story to refute what was printed in the paper. And she was too tired to even try.

"I've been working at *Today at the Fair* all summer. I didn't get the job at the *Times*. I'm sorry I lied. I didn't want to disappoint you both and give you more to worry about. I'm really sorry." Max tried to read her parents' expressions. They both looked stunned.

"Oh, Maxie, why would you think you were disappointing us?" her father asked, sitting on the edge of her bed.

"Because I know what high expectations you have of me, that you've always had of me. And I have them of myself. And I know you're worried about my future, and let's be honest, a job at the *Times* sounds much more promising than one at a paper at the fair."

"We're proud of whatever you do, darling," her mother said, picking up items of clothing off the floor and folding them.

"Ma, thank you, but I'll take care of it all," she said, smiling at her mother, who placed the stack on Max's bureau.

Max felt her heart soften. Last night she thought Vivi had been so cruel, but all morning, as she ran over the conversations again and again in her head, she realized it was she who was just too stubborn.

"Maxie," her father said, "let me tell you something. Don't think twice about what your mother and I think. It's not your responsibility to keep us from worrying. No matter what your sisters and you do, we will worry. We can't help it."

Max laughed quietly and was happy to see her mother laugh as well.

"You could be the president of the United States and we'd worry," her mother said.

"It's true," her father said. "Not that we'll live long enough to see a woman president—a Jewish one at that—but still, we'd worry."

"Just do what's best for you, and we'll support whatever it is.

You want a job at a fair? Get a job at a fair," her mother said in a singsong tone. "You have a good head on your shoulders. You'll do the right thing."

"I'm not always so sure about that," Max said.

"What are you talking about?" her father asked.

"When I was little, was I as outspoken as I am now?"

"You were the bossiest girl in the building. None of the other girls would even play with you," her mother said, laughing fondly at the memory.

"They were a bunch of little sissies," her father said.

"David," said Mrs. Roth, shaking her head.

"What? It's true."

"Maybe it's not so good to be bossy. Have you ever thought of that?" Max asked.

Her father shook his head. "You've got it all wrong. Being a bold and determined girl is neither good nor bad. It depends on how you use it, Maxie. It depends on how you use it."

They were interrupted by the telephone ringing in the hall. Mrs. Roth rushed out of Max's room to pick it up.

"For you, hon," her mother said, returning to her room. "It's a young man."

Max's stomach dropped, thinking it must be James. Who else would it be? She was so angry the night before that he hadn't followed her when she'd stormed out of the restaurant. She realized it was a childish move, but, at the time, she just couldn't help it. She had to get out of there.

She'd waited a few minutes at the exit of the Italian Pavilion, hoping James would come looking for her. But he hadn't.

Thinking about it all that morning, she didn't blame him. Despite what she hoped was happening between them, they weren't a couple. He didn't really owe her anything. And by not following her, she realized he must have agreed with what Vivi was saying. Or maybe he just thought Max was better off clearing her head alone.

Either way, Max was excited he was calling. She would apologize for being so insolent. And she hoped he would tell her that he understood and she should forget it had ever happened.

"Hello," Max said into the receiver, wrapping the cord around her finger.

"Hi, Max. This is Arthur Zeitlin. Um, I was wondering if you'd like to come to the fair with me tonight?"

During the subway ride to the fair, Max wondered why she'd even accepted Arthur's invitation.

She hadn't at first. When he asked her, Max thought the last thing she wanted to do on her day off was to go to the fair. She felt so tired, and her mind was still reeling about what had happened the night before. So she'd thanked him very much and told him that maybe they could meet at the Rheingold after work one day that week.

She didn't mean it, though. She liked James, and she didn't want to give Arthur the wrong idea.

"Who was on the phone?" her mother had asked when she hung up.

"Arthur Zeitlin."

"I saw his mother at the butcher just the other day!"

"He works at the fair. He asked me out for tonight."

"That's wonderful! What time is he coming to pick you up?"

"I said no."

"Now why would you do a thing like that, Maxine? He's very handsome and his mother told me how successful he is."

Max rolled her eyes. "I'm not interested in him that way, Ma."

"How do you know if you've never gone out with him? Call him back and say yes, Maxine. I don't want you moping around the house all day."

Max stared at the piece of paper she was holding with his phone number on it. He'd given it to her in case she changed her mind, and she'd written it on the pad of paper her mother kept by the phone.

Max thought it would be a good way to clear her mind. And since things might not actually go anywhere with James, she would be an idiot not to keep her options open. And Max's mother was right: he was handsome.

So Max had called him back, accepted his offer, and they'd decided to meet in the Amusement Zone in front of the Aquacade at eight. It didn't make sense for Arthur to pick Max up at her apartment, because he lived with a few of his fair coworkers in an apartment near the grounds in Queens.

Now Max was on the subway. She tried to read a small paperback she'd tossed into her bag but was finding it hard to focus on the words. She kept thinking about what Vivi had said to her. To distract herself, she looked at the advertisements on the placards near the ceiling for Shinola shoe polish, Nathan's Famous hot dogs, and even the World's Fair itself.

There was a new set of placards she'd seen in recent months for a contest she'd read about in the newspaper called Miss Subways. Some pretty girl got her picture posted next to a pithy description of her ambitions. Max stared at the photograph for this month's winner, a gorgeous girl named Mary with short dark hair, lovely facial features, and a smile that seemed to illuminate her entire face: *Meet Miss Subways, Sparkling Mary Gardiner. Thank County Mayo parents for this Washington Heights beauty. An Aquinas graduate, she loves her secretarial job in airline office. Now 19; stands 5'7 1/2"; skates, swims, and paints in oil.* Max made a mental note to tell Vivi to enter. She'd be perfect. Then she remembered, feeling sad, she probably wouldn't ever talk to Vivi again.

During dinner, Arthur mostly talked about himself, and Max found the whole thing boring. They did reminisce about when they'd worked together on their high school paper, but Max felt as if he were speaking to her, *at* her actually, as if she were still a lowly teen coed who looked up to the powerful editor. She tried to explain that she'd grown up a lot in the last six years and she wasn't the same girl she'd been, but he kept referring to her as Little Maxie and reminding her of how he thought she was so pushy back then.

"Why do you call it *pushy*? I was just asserting myself, doing what all the boys on the paper were doing."

"I guess, but it was hilarious coming from you because you were so tiny and had that high-pitched voice."

When Max called him out on what he'd said, he just shrugged and laughed. She considered leaving right then, but she didn't want to deal with her mother's questions about why the date had ended so soon. Didn't want to hear her mother say how it would have been so nice to have the Zeitlins as *machetunim* and how embarrassed she'd be the next time she found herself ordering brisket next to Mrs. Zeitlin at the butcher.

So while Arthur was going on and on about what he would be doing after the fair closed in October, she made a mental checklist of what she was looking for in a man. James beat out Arthur in every category.

After a couple of drinks at the Rheingold, they decided to go on the Parachute Jump. For the first time during the entire date, Max was excited; in her three weeks at the fair, she hadn't yet had a chance.

There was a long line because everyone wanted to be on the ride during the fireworks show to see it from that vantage point. Arthur and Max were warm in body and spirit from their time at the bar, and they were enjoying talking to the equally cheerful people in front of and behind them in line. Every time Max had a couple of drinks, she realized what it must feel like to be someone who lived without cynicism. And to her surprise, each and every time, she thought she preferred feeling cheerful. She knew the high expectations she and her parents had for her caused undue stress. So those moments when she allowed herself not to overanalyze things, not to feel like she should be accomplishing something—those moments were bliss.

As they neared the front of the line, Max thought she'd have preferred to be standing next to James, especially in this setting. The sights, smells, and sounds of the fair had a way of seeping into Max's skin, infusing her with a glow she didn't feel anywhere else. She admonished herself to stop thinking about James and concentrate on Arthur, who actually wanted to be with her.

As the line moved, Max suddenly felt nervous. She'd never gone on anything like this in her life. Arthur seemed more nervous, though, but she decided not to point that out to him. She didn't want to make him feel worse.

"Welcome to the Life Savers Parachute Jump!" the red-vested ride operator said when Max and Arthur reached the front of the line.

Max smiled at Arthur and sat down on the black canvas bench.

"First time?" he asked them.

They both nodded.

"You have nothing to worry about," he said as he strapped them in. "There's only been one case of the ride getting stuck and the people only had to wait five hours until the ride was fixed. But they were nice about it and got to ride for free the next day."

Max and Arthur nodded wanly, as if that had been a pep talk meant to encourage them.

"You both feel snug in there?"

More nodding.

"Fantastic. Once I set you off, you'll rise up for a few minutes. That's a nice, pleasant ride. Once you feel it reach the top, pull this rip cord and you'll float to the ground. Ready?"

Before they had the chance to ask any questions, the man pushed a button and sent them up. They both gasped and then turned to each other and laughed uncomfortably. Max watched the other ten or so parachutes on the ride around her rising and falling, rising and falling, and was reassured by the untroubled operation of the ride.

"Are you okay, Arthur? You look a bit green," Max said, a concerned expression on her face.

He nodded quickly and pursed his lips.

Max thought it better to leave him to his own thoughts, so she tried to concentrate on the view, which was magnificent. She was captivated by the pristine layout of the fairgrounds, by the stately pathways and courtyards, and by the enormity and grandeur of it all.

Max felt a jolt when they reached the top. She looked at Arthur and he just nodded quickly again to her.

"Ready?" Max asked.

He nodded again. So she tugged on the rip cord as the operator had instructed and held her breath. Nothing happened. Arthur looked at her with a pained expression on his face.

"It's not working! We're stuck!" he cried.

Max grabbed the rip cord again and tugged harder. She closed her eyes tightly, waiting for the drop to thrust them to the ground. Again nothing happened.

"Hey! Hey!" Arthur started yelling.

"Who are you yelling at? They can't hear us down there."

"There's a workman on the tower. I'm trying to get his attention."

Max turned her head toward the direction Arthur was shouting, and saw a man with a tool belt climbing the lattice-like tower at the center of the ride. But it didn't appear he could hear Arthur.

At this point Arthur was crying and Max realized she really would have been better off with James. She didn't think he would have had this type of reaction. No, he'd probably be climbing up the ropes to the top of the ride to see what the issue was.

Max reached up to try once more, but right then she felt a lurch and then they were dropping. The parachute captured the air in its billows. She and Arthur both screamed, but while he looked terrified, Max had a huge smile on her face. She loved the exhilaration, the fear, the excitement. She felt the adrenaline in her veins, reminding her that she was alive.

When they reached the bottom, the parachute stopped with a jolt and they bounced uncomfortably in their seats, straining the tenuous straps.

"Where's the manager? I need to report this parachute. The rip cord doesn't work!" Arthur said to the operator, who began unstrapping them.

He began laughing. "Relax, buddy, that's just a little joke of mine I like to tell. We control the whole thing from down here. Gave you a little thrill, did it?"

"It wasn't funny," Arthur said curtly as he walked, unsteadily, from the ride.

Once they were a safe distance away, Max asked Arthur if he was okay. When he said he was, she apologized that she had to rush off and go home.

They said good-bye to each other, and Max headed toward the exit. Turning to see if Arthur was watching her and confirming that he had taken off in another direction, she turned around and started walking quickly back to the Amusement Zone.

Sure, Max thought as she walked with intention, she was bold. Sure she was a little difficult. But wasn't it also those traits that had gotten her to where she was? That had allowed her to work so hard at NYU and had gotten her accepted into Professor L.'s cohort in the first place? Maybe her personality got her into trouble, but she knew that if she used her strong will in the right way, as her father had said, it could work to her favor. No, she wouldn't stop being her. No matter how hard she tried, she would never be a truly well-behaved, play-by-the-rules type of girl. She also knew, though, that what Vivi had said could also be true. She could be herself without being so reckless. She would start cleaning up the messes she'd made.

A few moments later Max arrived back at the Parachute Jump and proceeded to ride it two more times, swelling with a new-found feeling of power, and giggling with joy when the fireworks began.

֍

CHAPTER THIRTY-ONE

Vivi

Monday, June 19

The morning after Maria and Sofia had come, Mr. Mackey told Vivi and Dean they had a photo shoot during lunch that day at the Parachute Jump and that the photographers would meet them there at noon. Vivi knew better than to object. She was on borrowed time at the Aquacade anyway. As far as she knew, Ruby hadn't yet told Ed what she'd seen in the dressing room the day before. Or if she had, Ed hadn't yet done anything about it.

Now, as she and Dean approached the entrance to the Parachute Jump, they looked around for the photographers, but didn't see any.

"Do you think Mr. Mackey had the time wrong?" Dean asked Vivi.

"I don't know, but let's get in line, and I'm sure they'll be here when we get to the front."

It was a beautiful, sunny day, practically perfect except for a slight wind that made the clouds look as if they were racing to get somewhere important.

As usual, there was a long line for the ride. Vivi watched as a man selling balloons tied a blue one onto the wrist of a little boy, and then she noticed a uniformed janitor with a broom bump into the balloon seller, seemingly on purpose. The balloon man gave the janitor a dirty look, which the janitor returned with a strange laugh.

And then Vivi got a closer look at the janitor's face as he approached her, and she saw a long scar. Realizing it was Frank, she felt a tightness in her chest and instinctively moved closer to Dean.

"So we meet again," Frank said, sneering, once he was standing in front of Vivi. "I got a job at the fair so I could watch you. I know Maria will come see you at some point, and I'll be here waiting." Frank narrowed his eyes. Vivi could smell alcohol on his breath.

"Get away from me, Frank. I have no information for you. Don't you understand that she doesn't want to see you?" Vivi's voice was stern, but she felt fear take over her body. She was all too aware of how dangerous Frank could be.

"What's going on? Who is this guy, Vivi?" Dean asked, his voice filled with concern.

"He's my sister's ex-husband."

"Butt out, mac. This is a family situation," Frank said to Dean, sticking his finger in Dean's face.

"Easy," Dean said, putting his hands out in front of him. "Vivi?" He turned to Vivi to make sure she was okay. She nodded at him.

"And for your information," Frank said angrily, turning back to Vivi, "we're still married."

"Not in her eyes."

"You goddamn bitch," Frank snarled, coming closer to Vivi.

Vivi noticed the crowd around her getting agitated. A woman in line whispered to Vivi that she was going to get a policeman.

"How do you know she doesn't want to see me if you haven't seen her?" Frank asked, growing louder, more aggressive.

Vivi felt emboldened by the protection of the crowd and the impending arrival of police. "If she wanted to see you, do you think she would have ever left you?"

"Just tell me where they are. You don't want me to hurt them, do you?" he asked, his voice taunting. Frank reached into his pocket clumsily and pulled out a switchblade, gesturing with it in front of Vivi's face.

"Don't you dare!" Vivi shouted, taking a few steps back. The thought of Frank hurting her sister or Sofia, the thought of him getting anywhere close to them, made her frantic. She knew what he was capable of.

"Hey, hey, buddy, watch it," Dean said, his voice indignant as he bravely placed his body between Frank and Vivi. Dean was much taller than Frank and got right up to his face. "I suggest you put that thing away, leave this area right now, and don't bother her again."

"Oh yeah, and what are you going to do about it, pretty boy?" Frank said, stepping around Dean as he released the blade and pointed it at Dean and then at Vivi. "Tell me where she is!" Frank yelled at Vivi.

"I don't know!" she yelled back.

"You little whore. Did you tell your boyfriend here about your baby?" Frank was waving the knife now and acting more agitated than Vivi had ever seen him. Then he turned and saw a policeman rapidly approaching them. "I know you know where she is!" he shouted at her, spit flying out of his mouth.

Vivi saw the policeman getting closer and then Frank threw his broom and ran off into the crowd.

"Are you okay, ma'am?" the policeman asked, searching to see where Frank had gone.

The policeman quickly wrote down what Vivi and Dean said in a little pad and told them he would immediately issue a top-priority alert that there was a potentially dangerous man with a knife in the Amusement Zone. When two more officers arrived, he dispatched them in the direction Frank had run so they could try to apprehend him. He also said he'd file a report with the personnel department that hires the grounds janitors so they could further deal with the situation as well, in the unlikely event the officers weren't able to locate Frank.

"Shouldn't you cordon off some areas or close the rides or something?" Dean asked the policeman.

"Once we have a better assessment of the situation we might decide to do that, but my colleagues are probably arresting him right now, so I wouldn't worry about a thing," the policeman assured them, rushing off in the direction the other officers had gone.

"What do you want to do?" Dean asked Vivi, placing his hands gently on her shoulders.

"I want to ride the Parachute Jump." Vivi was shaken up, but her thoughts were clear. She felt she was safest right where she was, as more policemen and the photographers had gathered in the area.

Vivi decided as soon as she got off the ride, she'd call Maria and tell her not to come back to the fair. She was relieved Maria had written down her telephone number on a piece of paper before she and Sofia had left the day before. It also occurred to her that she should discuss her own safety concerns with Ed. Frank knew exactly where she'd be every single day and night.

Dean tried to calm Vivi as they waited in the line by telling her funny stories about some of the antics that went on in the men's dressing room at the Aquacade.

When they reached the front of the line, they were directed around the tower to one of the twelve parachute loading areas.

"Welcome to the Life Savers Parachute Jump!" the red-vested ride operator said.

Vivi and Dean sat down on the seat in a little basket below a wide parachute, and the man strapped them in.

"It's not too windy for the ride to run?" Vivi asked, feeling a little on edge. The wind had picked up while they were in line.

"Nah, not too bad yet. They'd shut the ride down if it was. Plus, the wind makes it more fun up there. First timers?"

They both nodded.

"You have nothing to worry about. Here's what's gonna happen. I'll pull this lever here and you'll go floating up. I control your chute from down here, so after I think you've had a good enough view, I'll release you and you'll float down gently. Ready?"

Vivi and Dean nodded again. Vivi's adrenaline was pumping. It was triggered by the encounter with Frank, and now that she was about to rise 250 feet off the ground, it was even more pronounced.

She turned to Dean, and he grabbed her hand.

"You okay?" he asked.

She gave him a small smile, and then they floated up.

Looking out over the fairgrounds, Vivi tried to distract herself by picking out buildings and landmarks she had walked by. She saw the Aquacade and couldn't believe how impressive it looked from above. She tried to focus on the loud carnival-type music being pumped out of speakers positioned on the central tower behind them.

Vivi felt a jolt and realized they had reached the top.

And then she saw something move out of the corner of her eye. Normally a brain would register that as a bird flying by. Or a billow of the parachute next to theirs. The brain might not even make a big deal out of it, dismissing the stimulus as nothing of much import at all.

But the hairs on Vivi's arms were raised. So she turned to get a better look. And when her eyes focused on what had actually caused her to look in the first place, she felt her stomach drop.

"Dean!" she heard herself scream, and Dean turned toward where Vivi was looking.

Frank had climbed all the way up the lattice central tower and was now quickly scaling the metal bars toward their parachute. Vivi realized that when he'd left them in the line, he'd ascended the tower to wait for them.

It only took a split second for Vivi to notice the knife in his hand again.

She also realized that they were too far up for anyone down below to notice what was going on, and the music was too loud for anyone to hear them scream. Even if it hadn't been, the wind had picked up, making their chute billow violently.

"He's coming at us!" Vivi yelled to Dean.

Dean stood up, unstrapped their safety belt, and told Vivi to switch seats with him so he was the one closer to Frank.

Vivi slid over and felt their basket tilt to Dean's side as he leaned over to shout at Frank.

Vivi watched as Frank maneuvered his body along the bars so he could get closer to their parachute. She looked to the parachute next to theirs and saw that the billowing nylon was attached to the top of the ride with thick cables. Even if Frank's knife couldn't cut through the cables, he could damage their parachute enough to make their basket drop to the ground with no resistance.

"Hold on!" Dean yelled to Vivi as he started swinging their basket, trying to get it close to the tower.

But with each attempt, the wind pulled them away before he could grasp the metal bar.

Vivi had no idea what he would do if he did catch hold. Meanwhile, she was screaming at Frank to leave them alone.

And then Dean grabbed hold of a metal bar on the tower. Vivi heard him groan as he tried to maintain his grip while the wind pulled the basket in the opposite direction.

Their basket tilted violently and Vivi felt as if she were going to fall out. "Dean!" she yelled.

It registered with Vivi that Dean was trying to maneuver his body so he could climb out of the basket without tilting it too far over to put Vivi in more danger. And that he was somehow going to confront Frank on the tower itself.

"Dean, stop!" she yelled, trying to make her voice carry over the wind and music.

Frank was now right above their basket, barely ten feet from where Dean was still straining violently to maintain his hold on the tower.

Vivi had no idea how much time had gone by since they'd reached the top of the ride. Shouldn't the ride operator be releasing them by now?

She panicked, thinking that if the ride operator did release them, the jolt would fling Dean from the basket.

And she panicked thinking that if the ride operator didn't release them, Frank would puncture their parachute or cut their cables or, even worse, somehow climb into the basket and threaten Vivi with his knife.

Vivi screamed as she saw Frank slash Dean's arm. Dean cried out in pain but didn't loosen his grip.

Then the music suddenly stopped and what happened next seemed to occur in slow motion.

Vivi looked down, and though the people on the ground were tiny, she could see some of them waving frantically in her direction. They must have been able to see what was going on.

And then she felt the basket release, which jolted Dean. He lost hold of the tower but fell back into the basket.

And Frank, who had gotten so close that he was holding on to Dean's arm, lost hold of Dean.

As Vivi and Dean floated down, incongruously slowly and gracefully, they watched Frank's body plunge to the ground and land in a heap.

Vivi barely had a moment to comprehend what was going on. She saw Dean's bloody arm. A flash of a man plummeting to the ground. And then their basket and parachute came to a stop back on the ground where they had begun.

Vivi couldn't move. She saw people rushing up to her. She heard voices shouting but couldn't understand what they were saying. Dean lifted her up and she looked into his eyes. His mouth was moving and he was staring at her urgently. Vivi knew what was happening but she couldn't actually feel or see or say a thing.

And then in what could have been a split second or an hour, everything became clear. Vivi was shocked. She'd been threatened. Dean had been hurt. They'd been in danger. A man had died. But she was safe and alive. Dean's wound would heal. And the man who had died had wanted to kill her. Had been a danger to the people she loved most in the world: Maria and Sofia.

A policeman brought Vivi and Dean to the fair police station to give statements. When Vivi told Dean she was okay, he left her for a bit to tell Ed and Mr. Mackey what had happened. They'd been completely sympathetic and had given Dean and Vivi the rest of that day and the next off and more if it turned out they needed it, urging Dean to go to a hospital to see if he needed stitches. It would turn out that he did. Sixteen, in fact. And he wouldn't be able to get his arm wet for weeks, a difficult diagnosis for someone whose job required him to dive into a pool for four performances each day.

While Vivi waited at the police station for Dean to return, she felt a great sense of relief. Of intense emotion. Of acute introspection. The type of introspection that makes people wonder how everyone around them can go on with their lives as if the world hadn't tilted a bit. How are those people still holding on? How can they look so undisturbed?

Dean brought Vivi back to her hotel. She immediately called Maria, who rushed over with Sofia. The sisters hugged and cried, clinging to each other, as Dean kept Sofia busy in a corner of the room.

And as the night wore on, as Vivi and Maria discussed what Frank's death meant for both of their lives moving forward, Vivi had an idea. At first it seemed inappropriate on such a day, and perhaps a little morbid; a man had died, after all. But eventually Vivi decided that Frank had made decisions that put him in the situation that caused his death. And Frank had treated them disrespectfully, abusively. And that, as adults, they were all responsible for choosing the directions of their lives. Sure, different circumstances dictated people's realities and opportunities, but knowing what they knew about Frank, he had chosen his destiny without regard for the consequences of his actions or the people they most affected.

So Vivi picked up the telephone in her room and called down for a bottle of champagne. They were free of Frank and the threat he represented. They were finally able to think about the future. And that, oh indeed, *that* was worth celebrating.

DELUSIONAL MAN DIES AT FAIR

According to World's Fair police, fair janitor Frank Walters, 29, of Brooklyn, died yesterday after plunging 250 feet to his death from the tower of the Life Savers Parachute Jump in the Amusement Zone.

Prior to ascending the tower, and much to the dismay and concern of bystanders, who alerted the police, Walters was observed threatening Miss Vivi Holden, Aquabelle Number One in the Aquacade, and her companion, diver Dean Mitchell.

Walters fled when approached by police, who were unable to locate the man until he was observed behaving erratically and dangerously while wielding a knife at the top of the Parachute Jump tower. Allegedly, he was attempting to damage Holden and Mitchell's parachute. Instead, Walters apparently lost his grip on the tower and fell. He was pronounced dead at the scene.

Holden was unharmed while Mitchell received treatment for a deep wound sustained at the hand of Walters.

Police and Parachute Jump officials have blocked off the base of the tower in order to avoid future access by unauthorized persons.

CHAPTER THIRTY-TWO

Vivi

Wednesday, June 21

Vivi had spent most of Monday night, after Frank's death, with Maria and Sofia, making plans. But there were still things she needed to figure out. One thing was clear that night: despite how shaken up she'd still felt about the events the day before, she'd wanted to return to work.

Which is how it came to be that she was back in the water on Tuesday night, when, during the finale of the ten-thirty performance, she came up with the idea. She nearly forgot her moves, stunned as she was by what her brain had concocted. After the number, she analyzed the plan step-by-step to see if it had legs.

She thought about it while she changed into her street clothes, as she signed a few autographs outside the cast gate, during the taxi ride back to her hotel, and in the shower as she tried her best to wash the thick Vaseline out of her hair.

Now that the plan had seen the light of day, Vivi decided she'd go for it.

When rehearsal broke for lunch on Wednesday, she quickly dressed and rushed across the fairgrounds to the Administration Building.

It had been four days since Vivi had last seen Max at their dinner at the Italian Pavilion. She still felt sad that things had ended as they had, but she'd decided that if she and Max had a chance to talk, they could clear things up.

Max had left a message for Vivi at her hotel on Tuesday once she'd heard about Frank's death. But with all that was going on, Vivi hadn't felt ready to phone her back.

Now Vivi knocked on the *Today at the Fair* office door and turned the knob. She'd never visited Max at work—they'd always met somewhere on the grounds—so she was surprised that the office was so small. Despite all the work she knew Max carried on her own shoulders, she figured producing a daily publication like *Today at the Fair* would require a much bigger operation.

"Can I help you?" the woman at the front desk asked. Vivi thought she looked vaguely familiar, but she didn't think they'd met before.

Vivi looked into the main room of the office and saw Max, who had turned around when the door opened.

"I'm here to see Max," Vivi said kindly.

Max stood up and walked toward Vivi. They smiled sadly at each other.

"Can I talk to you somewhere private?" Vivi asked.

Max nodded, told the receptionist she'd be right back, and led Vivi outside the Administration Building to a shaded bench on the path out front.

"Vivi, I'm—"

"Max, I'm—"

They both stopped and laughed quietly.

"Please, I'd like to say something," Vivi said, and Max gently nodded at her to go on. "I'm sorry I was so harsh with you on Saturday night. Regardless of the pact we'd made to help each other, you're an adult and I have no right to tell you how to behave." Vivi clasped her hands together and nervously picked at her nails.

"Thank you, Vivi. I appreciate your saying that. And I'm sorry that I was harsh right back to you. I can get a little defensive when I feel like I'm being attacked. It was ridiculous of me to run out of there. You were just trying to help me, and it's very clear that I could use the help. I know everything you said was true and I'm really trying to figure out how to rein myself in a little better."

"I'm glad."

"And everything that happened Monday," Max said, disbelieving what Vivi had gone through.

"It was awful, but it's over and we're all the better for it," Vivi said softly, keeping it to herself for the time being that the man who had died had been her brother-in-law.

"Still—"

"Anyway, friends?" Vivi didn't want to talk about what had happened Monday. Actually, she never wanted to talk about it—or Frank—again.

"Friends."

The two women hugged and then laughed when they both exhaled loudly at the same time.

"By the way, is everything okay with you and James?" Vivi asked.

"There never really was a 'me and James,' so things haven't changed in that regard. He called me yesterday to check in on me and we talked for a while about what had happened at dinner Saturday night. He felt bad that I was upset. Anyway, he's busy during the week at work, but we'll see each other Friday at our meeting with our professor, so we'll talk more about it then."

"I hope things work out for the two of you. I think you're adorable together."

"I wish he agreed."

"I see something in the way he looks at you. I wouldn't be so sure there's nothing there."

"I guess we'll both just have to wait and see."

"I came by today for another reason as well. I have a plan that I'd like to discuss with you."

"Plans are my very favorite things, but I've sworn off them for a while. They tend to get me in trouble."

"That's why I think this one is so good. If all goes well, it will get you out of trouble."

"Do tell."

Vivi explained her plan, which would involve Max writing an article to be published in *Today at the Fair* with her byline. An article that would put Vivi out of a job. Or so she hoped.

Max was stunned when Vivi told her what the article would be about, as Vivi expected she would be, so Vivi took a deep breath and explained. "I found out I was pregnant at the be-ginning of my senior year of high school. The father was a boy from Texas who was in New York for the summer and staying with cousins."

"Did you ever tell him you were pregnant?"

"God, no. By the time I found out, he was back in Dallas. After I'd, you know, with him, he was awful. He didn't speak to me the rest of the time he was in New York. So when I found out, I couldn't imagine telling him."

"Sorry I interrupted; please go on."

"Since my parents had both died, I was living with my sister, Maria, and Maria's husband, Frank. Maria sent me upstate to a home for the duration of my pregnancy and told everyone I was going to an acting academy. When I had the baby—her name is Sofia—Maria convinced me that Sofia and I were both better off if Maria became her mother. Words were exchanged, and I listened to my sister, who said that she couldn't support me and that I had to make my own money. Becoming an actress, 'using your looks,' as she said, was my best and only option. I believed that she somehow knew what was right for me, that I should trust her instincts over my own."

Vivi paused for a second, surprised that all of that had come out of her. She'd never told Amanda, never told Gabe. She'd tried to bury her past, but now that she'd been confronted with it all, she realized that hiding it had been a folly. It was part of her. Like her skin. Like her breath.

When Max remained silent, shocked as she seemed to be by the story, Vivi continued. "My sister and Sofia came to visit me on Sunday—"

Max gasped and then apologized, gesturing to Vivi to continue.

"And seeing them, being with them, made me realize there was nowhere else I wanted to be. We can talk about it all more later, but I don't have much more time before my lunch hour is over, so what do you think about my idea?"

"First, oh my goodness. That is quite a story, and I want to discuss it further with you. But since you're in a hurry, I'll answer your question. I love the idea, but I'm not allowed to write articles. Maybe I could try to get Charlie to write it for you."

After the episode in Mr. Babcock's office a few days prior, when Max admitted she had written the baby incubator article, she and Charlie had talked it out calmly. Even though they both stood behind their arguments, they decided that since they had to work so closely together, they needed to figure out a way to coexist. So they agreed to a truce. Albeit a delicate one.

"But," Vivi continued, "part of this plan is that *you* would then have an article with your byline to submit to the contest. I thought I was giving you a big exclusive."

"Maybe whoever submits the press release to Mr. Babcock and Charlie could insist on my writing it," Max said, and then shook her head, reconsidering. "No, that won't work. Mr. Babcock has made it very clear that he won't allow me to write any articles."

"Press release?"

"Well, yeah. All the different departments know that you have to submit a request for an article in a press release on the department's, in this case the Aquacade's, letterhead."

"Oh," Vivi said, scrunching up her nose. "I hadn't thought of that. I thought I could just tell you what the article was about and you could write it. This isn't going to be as easy as I had planned. I'm sorry, Max." She threw her hands in the air. "I thought I was going to be able to help you."

"That's okay. I appreciate the effort."

"Couldn't I just give you the information, you write it, and then you sneak it into the paper somehow?"

Max thought for a minute. "If you had come to me last week with this, then yes, I might have done it. And I could have, but after I made Mr. Babcock mad on Saturday, he took away my production responsibilities, so I'm not the one who goes to the typeset office anymore. Plus, at your suggestion, I'm trying to restrain myself from breaking rules."

"Fair enough," Vivi said, but she wasn't going to let this go.

"So your classmate Charlie goes to the typeset office? Would he help us?"

"He doesn't, and he probably wouldn't help me anyway. Marianne, the receptionist, is the one who goes, but she could get fired for sneaking an article in, and there's no way she wouldn't get caught. I wouldn't even ask her to consider it."

Just then Vivi noticed that the receptionist was walking out of the Administration Building and approaching Max and her at the bench they were sitting on.

"Off to lunch, Marianne?" Max asked.

"I am. Can I get you anything?" Marianne asked.

"That's nice, but I'm fine. I brought something from home. Marianne, this is my friend Vivi. Vivi this is Marianne."

Vivi smiled and stuck out her hand to shake Marianne's.

"I thought that was you. Vivi Holden from the Aquacade, right?" Marianne asked.

"The famous star in the flesh," Max said proudly.

"My sister Ruby swims in the Aquacade," Marianne said.

"You never told me you had a sister in the Aquacade," Max said.

"Your sister is Ruby Lancaster?" Vivi said, her voice sounding a bit more stunned than she had intended.

"I know she can come off a little strong. Trust me, I've been living with her my entire life."

"No, I didn't mean it like that. I'm just surprised for some reason," Vivi said, looking at Marianne a little harder and understanding now why she had looked familiar when Vivi had first encountered her in the office. They had the same hair, the same face shape, but Ruby had a sparkle that Marianne didn't have. Marianne's eyes looked sad.

"It's okay," Marianne said. "I know you two have had your differences. She goes on and on about it. In fact, she never shuts up, that one. But, Max, I didn't know you and Vivi were friends."

The three women spoke for a little longer and then Vivi rushed back to the Aquacade so she wouldn't be late to afternoon rehearsal. Max promised she'd come to the five-thirty performance and they could talk more after.

"I just met your sister," Vivi said to Ruby as the two of them entered through the cast gate at the same time.

"Which one? I have two sisters who work at the fair."

"Marianne," Vivi said.

"Oh, she's the sweet one. Good thing you didn't meet Evie. She wants to bust your kneecaps so I can have your part," Ruby said, laughing.

"Well then, I guess it *was* a good thing I didn't meet Evie."

"Where did you meet Marianne?"

"My friend Max works at *Today at the Fair*, and I was at their office."

"I've heard about Max. Marianne thinks she's really nice. But Marianne hates working there, because the editor is handsy; poor girl can't get him off her sometimes. I always wish it were me or Evie working there instead of her. One day we're gonna walk in there and give the guy a piece of our minds."

"That's awful for her!" Vivi said, wondering if Max had been dealing with it too.

"We've been trying to convince her to stand up for herself, and the worse it gets the more she seems to listen to us, but she's scared. It'll all be over soon there for her, though."

"Why?"

"Marianne has to leave to take care of our father. His condition has gotten worse, and she's the best with him. She hasn't told her boss yet, but next week is gonna be her last."

"Huh," Vivi said, a thought coming to her.

"Huh, what?" Ruby asked.

"Regarding what you think you saw with me and that little girl on Sunday, have you said anything to Ed yet? Or to anyone?"

"Not yet. I was trying to figure out what to do with the information. You're starting to grow on me, Vivi."

Vivi paused and stared at Ruby.

"Why are you looking at me like that?"

"Remember on the first day you started rehearsing with me after Camilla had left?"

"Yes."

"When I said that if you teach me the part well, I'd make it up to you somehow?"

"Yes," Ruby said impatiently.

"I think I may know how to do that. But I'm not sure I can trust you."

"Now why would you say a thing like that?" Ruby asked, laughing.

"My idea has a lot of benefits for you. And maybe, if you agree to go along with it and if you agree to get your sister to go along with it, you might just get to be Aquabelle Number One after all."

⋎

CHAPTER THIRTY-THREE

Max

Wednesday, June 21

After Vivi had presented her plan to Max and headed back to the Aquacade for her afternoon rehearsal and shows, Max ate her lunch at her desk and worked on the next day's listings. She turned when she heard a commotion outside the main door an hour or so later.

"I ran into them outside as I was coming in," Marianne said to Max as she entered the *Today at the Fair* office. "They want to talk to us." Marianne gestured to the two women standing behind her: Vivi and Ruby Lancaster, whom Max recognized from seeing the Aquacade.

Ruby pushed past Marianne and peered first into Charlie's office and then into Mr. Babcock's, both of which were empty, as the two were still out for lunch together. "Which one is the bastard's?"

"Ruby!" Marianne shouted.

"What? Don't get so huffy. I just want to know where he sits so I can loosen the wheels on his office chair or something."

"Don't you dare!" Marianne said. "Now, let's go outside so if they come back, I don't get in trouble for entertaining family at work."

"Does it really matter? You're leaving anyway," Ruby said.

"Ruth Helen Lancaster!" Marianne growled, and huffed out of the office.

Ruth? Vivi mouthed at Ruby as they followed Marianne, Max trailing behind.

"I wouldn't talk, *Alessia*," Ruby whispered back.

Vivi introduced Max to Ruby as they walked.

"What does she mean, you're leaving?" Max asked Marianne when they caught up with her down the path that fronted the building. "And why would she want to loosen desk chair wheels?"

Before she could answer, Ruby started talking. "Marianne, we need your help with something. You're not gonna like this, but I will do anything you ask if you say yes."

"We thought of a way to get the article printed," Vivi said to Max.

"Oh no, you can't ask Marianne to do this. I won't allow it."

"Ask me what?" Marianne asked, looking confused. It was clear she was annoyed just being around her sister.

"It's okay, Max. Trust me," Vivi said.

"We need you to sneak an article into tomorrow's edition of *Today at the Fair*," Ruby said, putting her hands on her hips.

"And how exactly would you like me to do that?" Marianne asked.

"She could get fired for that," Max said, shaking her head.

"She's quitting anyway," Vivi said.

"Why are you quitting?" Max asked Marianne, confused.

"You told Vivi that?" Marianne said to Ruby, ignoring Max's question.

Ruby shrugged. "Why do you care? This will just accelerate your timeline."

Marianne sighed loudly.

"Here's the deal," Ruby said to Marianne. "Vivi has an article she wants in *Today at the Fair*. She wants Max to write it with her byline so she has something to enter into some contest thing that she has to do for her college."

"And what's in it for you, Ruby? I know something has to be in it for you," Marianne said, crossing her hands in front of her chest.

Max liked this side of Marianne.

"The article would get Vivi fired. If Vivi is no longer in the Aquacade, I get her part."

"Aha. I knew you had to benefit in some way," Marianne said. "But wait," she added, turning to Vivi, "why do you want to get fired?"

"Long story," Vivi answered.

"Marianne, why are you quitting?" Max asked again.

"My father's condition has taken an expected turn for the worse, and he needs someone to care for him during the day," Marianne said, her voice soft.

"I'm so sorry to hear that," Max said. "But you still can't do this. Mr. Babcock will be furious, and he won't write you a letter of recommendation for your next job."

"I don't think he'd write me one anyway, Max."

"Of course he would. You're a perfect employee. You do everything he asks."

"Not everything," Ruby snorted.

"What does she mean?" Max asked.

Marianne bit her lip. Max realized there was something she didn't want to say.

"Her editor behaves inappropriately with her," Vivi said, trying to lighten things up and wanting to prevent Ruby from being unnecessarily explicit. "Let's leave it at that."

"Charlie?" Max said loudly.

"Shhh!" Marianne said, looking around and then lowering her voice and her head. "No, not Charlie. Mr. Babcock."

"Marianne, you told me everything was fine when I asked," Max said, putting her hand on Marianne's shoulder.

"I couldn't just come out and tell you what was really going on."

Max felt awful. She should have known it was worse than Marianne had let on.

"Okay, okay, you two can cry on each other's shoulders all you want later, but Vivi and I only got a short pass to leave rehearsal, so we need to figure this out. Marianne, this could be your big chance to stand up to the asshole and do something bold for once in your life."

"It could work, Marianne," Max said, thinking. "Take the editorial package when Mr. Babcock gives it to you, but then substitute the article I'll write about Vivi for one of the other articles that's supposed to get printed."

"Oh, and it's about Dean too," Vivi said.

"What about Dean?" Max asked.

"Something he asked me to put in the article. I'll explain later. We don't have much time."

"But what about Albert?" Marianne asked Max.

"He won't mind. You've had to substitute articles before at the last minute, haven't you?"

"Yes," Marianne said. "But I don't know. . . . There are too many things that could go wrong."

"Albert's so fond of both of us. I'm sure he'd go along with it all if you explained the situation to him."

Ruby rolled her eyes at her sister. "Vivi, why do we even need an article? I'll just tell Ed what I overheard, remind him of the rules of the production, and poof, you're fired."

"He'll never believe you. He knows you want my part. If it's in an article, then he'll believe it, and he won't think it's coming from you."

"True." Ruby paused and then looked at her watch. "We have to go. Are you two in?"

"I'm in, but I don't want to pressure Marianne," Max said as they all turned to look at her.

"I've never done anything like this," Marianne said, biting her bottom lip and looking anguished.

"Marianne," Ruby said in a soft voice. "Think about all the horrible things you've told me about that man. Don't you want to be the one in power for once? Go out in a blaze of glory?"

Marianne thought for a minute and shut her eyes tightly. She opened them, her expression completely changed, and took a deep breath. "Fine. I'll do it."

"That's my baby sister," Ruby said, hugging Marianne.

"Wait," Max said, a thought suddenly coming to the surface. "There's a problem. Getting my name on an article is great, but as soon as Mr. Babcock sees it in the paper and realizes we went behind his back, he'll fire me. That'll ruin my standing with my professor, which defeats the whole purpose."

They all stood silently for a moment.

Think, Max, think. There's got to be a way around this.

"I may have a solution," Marianne said in a small voice, and they all huddled around her to find out what it was.

֎

CHAPTER THIRTY-FOUR

Marianne

Wednesday, June 21
Four Hours Later

"There are two last-minute articles that need to go into to-morrow's issue," Marianne said calmly after she handed Albert the sealed package. "We'll have to make room in the layout."

On the way over to the typeset office, Marianne had rehearsed what she'd say and how she'd say it. Now that she was there, she felt so nervous that Albert wouldn't go along with the plan, despite Max's insistence that he would. She worried he'd see what she was doing, be furious with her, and then, and then . . . She could barely bring herself to think of the consequences.

"Okay, let me see what you've got."

Marianne pulled two sheets of paper out of her pocketbook, handing them over to Albert.

He skimmed the first one, about Vivi and Dean, not even noticing that Max had the byline. "Interesting," he said, putting the article down on the desk in front of him.

Marianne took a deep breath when he started reading the second one.

After he'd finished, he looked up at Marianne and narrowed his eyes at her. "Are you aware, Marianne, that company policy requires me to call Mr. Babcock any time there are changes to the front page that are unaccompanied by a signed letter from him?"

Marianne shook her head. "I was not."

Albert scratched just above his eyebrow and seemed to be thinking about something.

"Albert, I realize you could get in trouble for this, and I'm so sorry to put you in this position"—Marianne said, speaking quickly, trying to make up for the horrible silence in the room and the look that Albert was giving her—"but I wouldn't be asking you if it weren't really important and—"

"Is this true?" he asked, holding up the article.

"It is, and I have proof." She took a minute and explained herself.

"Have a seat, Marianne. We have work to do."

Marianne raised her eyebrows at Albert, and her face broke out into a smile.

There were currently two long stories on the front page, one of which would have to be deleted to make room for the two new, shorter articles.

Marianne and Albert debated the merits of keeping each. But ultimately, they decided that the one about the performance by little Eli Metzger, age six of the Bronx, who was a prodigy composer, would have to go. He was young. He had plenty of time in his life to be famous. It had been either Eli's story or the one about the Ninety Club, which was a group of ninety-year-olds who were all celebrating their birthdays together at the fair the next day. They had less time, Marianne and Albert gathered. Their story would run.

And when they were done, Marianne picked up her pocket-book and walked toward Albert's office door. "I really appreciate your help with this."

"I always thought there was something off about that guy. Something tells me he's getting his due."

As Marianne rode home on the subway, toward the house she shared with her father and many of her siblings, she thought of how good it felt to stand up for herself. Finally.

SCANDALS DISGRACE AQUACADE

Each day, thousands line up to witness one of the most talked-about attractions at the World's Fair. But now, that attraction, Billy Rose's Aquacade, will be talked about for all the wrong reasons.

The Aquacade has been disgraced by a pair of scandals involving two of its stars. This information was provided by a member of the Aquacade who wishes to remain anonymous, for fear of professional and personal repercussions.

Vivi Holden, Aquabelle Number One, a Hollywood star lent to the Aquacade by WorldWide Films, was found to be an unwed mother who abandoned her child at birth two years ago. Holden's sister now cares for the toddler. Holden had been hiding this fact from the Aquacade producers, knowing that if it came to light, her positions with both the Aquacade and WorldWide would be in jeopardy.

In addition, Dean Mitchell, the noted diver, is also concealing an important truth about his personal life. Mitchell is in an intimate relationship with another man. Mr. Mitchell is set to start his career with MGM once the Aquacade ends its run in the fall. It is expected that MGM will release Mr. Mitchell from his contract based upon that revelation.

The romantic relationship between Miss Holden and Mr. Mitchell, oft photographed and much heralded in the New York press as of late, was revealed to be a sham, put forth only for publicity purposes.

Billy Rose and Ed Tandy, the show's general manager, were both unavailable for comment. The Aquacade is expected to resume its normal schedule with Ruby Lancaster most likely assuming the role of Aquabelle Number One.

TODAY *at the* FAIR
Thursday, June 22, 1939
By Max Roth

TODAY AT THE FAIR PUBLISHER GUILTY
OF ACCEPTING BRIBES

Stanton Babcock, the publisher of *Today at the Fair*, has been taking bribes from the Fair Corporation, says a source who wishes to remain anonymous for fear of retribution.

Mr. Babcock was allegedly printing misleading stories about the financial stability of the fair in return for significant monetary rewards.

At various times, representatives from different fair departments, especially concessionaires in the Amusement Zone, have filed complaints with *Today at the Fair* saying the figures used in articles have been incorrect, and as such the difficulties they are experiencing financially haven't been accurately covered. The concessionaires report that representatives from the Fair Corporation haven't been taking appropriate measures to help these concessionaires, as they are contractually required to do, citing positive attendance numbers reported by *Today at the Fair*.

According to Amusement Zone concessionaires, if attendance numbers fell below a certain threshold, they would be allowed to exit their contracts without penalty. Their own receipts showed a significant dip in attendance, but this wasn't reflected in the numbers published by this newspaper and attributed to the Fair Corporation.

Records proving the bribery claims have been turned over to the authorities for further investigation.

This is a developing story.

⎯ ⎯

CHAPTER THIRTY-FIVE

Vivi

Thursday, June 22

Having awoken early the day after enacting the plan to sneak in the articles, thinking about what the day would bring, Vivi thought back upon her career over the past couple of years. Specifically, to the day she signed her contract with WorldWide.

A film studio contract was a blessing for an actress like Vivi because it guaranteed work and training, typically for a term of seven years. But, as Vivi learned quickly from her own experiences and those of her fellow actresses, a contract could also be a curse because the studio had full control of every aspect of the actress's life: typecasting her regardless of her wishes; forbidding her from marrying if it would endanger her sex-symbol status; forcing diet pills, cigarettes, and verbal abuse on an actress to control her weight; even changing her name and her appearance to hide her ethnicity.

Vivi also knew a contract with a studio like WorldWide was impossible for an actress to break, say, if she wanted to move to another studio or if she wanted to stop acting altogether. And most actresses would never dream of doing so, having been fortunate to land a contract in the first place and getting to live the rarefied life of a Hollywood actress, regardless of its less glamorous realities. But if a scandal about that actress, circulated by the gossip magazines, would keep American audiences away from that star's pictures, or if she were detrimental to the studio's reputation, then a studio head, like Mr. Green, would release an actress from her contract faster than she could draw in her fake beauty mark.

Vivi was counting on that fact.

Surely Mr. Green would never imagine Vivi had anything to do with exposing her own transgression. Why, that would be suicide for an actress. No actress in her right mind would ever make such a choice knowing she'd never hold another script in her manicured hands. No. Not a soul would ever suspect that Vivi Holden had outed herself.

But Vivi had. And so had Dean.

That morning, Vivi didn't set her alarm. She figured she'd be awakened by a phone call. And she had been.

It was the front desk calling up to say she had a visitor. She hoped it was the one she was expecting.

"Good morning, sleepyhead," Dean said when Vivi, still in her robe, opened the door to her hotel room.

"Do you have it?"

"Right here."

Dean held up that day's *Today at the Fair* and wiggled it in his hand. Vivi's stomach dropped as she took the paper and headed into the bathroom to brush her teeth, reading Max's Aquacade article as she did, while Dean called downstairs to have breakfast for the two of them delivered.

"I have to be honest, now that it's out there, I'm a little bit in shock," Vivi said, getting back under the covers, her white robe tangling around her legs.

"Just a little bit? I feel like my insides are being processed through a meat grinder, over and over and over again."

"Yeah, now that you mention it, mine too."

Vivi and Dean stared at each other, both disbelieving what was actually happening.

"Max really pulled it off," Vivi said.

"Are you surprised?"

"Not one bit. That girl is all-powerful."

"Still, this is big."

"Huge." Vivi paused, letting it all sink in. "I can't believe no one's called yet."

"Who do you think will call first?" Dean asked, as if they were betting on a boxing match, not witnessing the end of their entertainment careers.

"Jack."

"Me too."

"Any regrets?" Vivi asked.

Dean put his hand over his chin, and Vivi could tell he was thinking hard about her question. "I was a mess yesterday knowing what was being orchestrated. And last night when I wasn't tossing and turning, I dreamed about a printing press exploding. People like me aren't exactly accepted in polite society these days. But, no, all in all I don't regret it. If it results in allowing me to live the life I've decided I want, if I can maybe become a chef, and if I can live in the same city as Trevor, then I won't regret it at all. The only thing I regret is kissing you during our press outings to try to throw you off the trail," he said, laughing. "Can you ever forgive me?"

"Of course. Already forgiven. But . . ."

"But what?"

"It was a pretty good kiss."

"Why, thank you. Now, how about you? Any regrets?"

"Not really. There were parts of my life in LA that I really loved. But I am one hundred percent positive that I'd rather have a life here with Maria and Sofia than back in LA. And when I spoke with Maria last night to tell her what was happening, it confirmed that I was absolutely doing the right thing. I'm not letting those two out of my sight ever again. I don't know what that life will look like yet, I don't know what kind of job I'm going to get, but I know it will be quieter. There will be a lot less noise without all those loud voices around me: Jack's voice, Gabe's voice, Carl's voice, Ed's voice. Even Frank's voice. All those men talking, talking, talking. I look forward to the quiet so I can hear my own voice."

She started to tell Dean more about the conversation she'd had with Maria but was interrupted when the telephone rang.

"This is Vivi Holden," she said confidently as she picked up the receiver. She held the phone out a bit so Dean could hear. He'd gotten into the bed next to her to hold her hand and give her strength.

"For crying out loud, Vivi, what the hell is going on?"

"Good morning, Jack. It's quite early for you, no?" Vivi smiled at Dean.

"I got woken up at the crack of dawn. What the hell is the deal with that article?"

"What article?"

"Do you really not know?"

"Jack, I don't have time for this. I'm rushing to get to the pool for rehearsal. If there's something you want to talk to me about, just tell me."

Dean gave Vivi a thumbs-up and clapped quietly.

"There's an article in the World's Fair paper that says you have a baby. Tell me that's not true, Vivi."

"How did they know? Damn, Ruby. Is WorldWide going to find out?" Vivi asked, trying to sound shocked.

"They already have. I've been on the phone all morning trying to work this out. Ed saw the paper when he got to the amphitheater early this morning. He called Billy. Billy called Carl, and Carl called me. So you can see," Jack said, practically yelling, "that this is a huge problem. Just tell me the truth, Vivi. Do you have a daughter? If not, Carl will put his fixers on this. But if you do, and you lie to me, the consequences for us both will be our worst nightmares."

"I do have a daughter. What does this mean?" Vivi said, affecting her voice to convey dismay.

"Damn it, Vivi," Jack said in a tone that sounded as if it were a mix of disappointment and anger. No, not anger. Rage. "It means that you'll be dismissed from the Aquacade and WorldWide. It means that unless I can work some pretty difficult magic, you're going to have a reputation trailing you around, and your career as an actress might be over."

And here's where Vivi decided to go in for the kill.

"I thought that's what you were trying to do anyway, Jack," Vivi said, changing course, emboldened.

"What the hell are you talking about?"

"I heard that you told Ed at the Aquacade that the part I was promised was given to another actress, and that you'd committed me to the Aquacade for next summer. And that while you said all that, you delighted in it. Is that true, Jack? Did you really have that information and make that decision without bothering to tell me?"

"I was going to tell you, Vivi."

"Oh really. When? It seemed like during our breakfast Sunday morning would have been a good time. But you chose to lie to me instead."

"You have to understand, these things happen behind the scenes. Decisions are made that are out of my control. I just have to negotiate them on your behalf for your own benefit."

"But wouldn't you agree, Jack, that those negotiations don't really benefit me?"

"Let me come back out there, Vivi. We can discuss this in person. I don't know what kind of game you're playing, missy."

"It's no game, Jack. It's life. And now I have the upper hand on you instead of the other way around."

"How so?"

"Because I have another piece of information that I'm sure you don't want made public," Vivi said, savoring the moment. The day before, Thad had approached her again, remembering another tidbit that he thought Vivi should know.

"And what is that?"

"I know for a fact that Billy Rose is paying you five hundred dollars a week for me, but that you're only giving me a hundred and twenty-five of that. We both know that your commission isn't seventy-five percent. Not even close."

"Who told you that?"

"So it's true."

"I didn't say that."

"Oh, Jack, you're just like the rest of them. Now, let me tell you what's going to happen."

Vivi heard silence on the other end, so she continued.

"You're going to get me out of my WorldWide contract in a nice, congenial way that saves my reputation and keeps any information about my daughter out of the news. And you're going to write me a check for all of the money you stole from me. You do those two things, and I won't tell any of your other clients that you're probably stealing from them as well. Have I made myself clear?"

"Yes," Jack said, and hung up his extension.

Vivi hung up and then flung herself back on the pillow.

"Oh my goodness," she said, feeling elated.

"That was incredible!" Dean said, laughing and bouncing on the bed.

"I can't believe I just did that," Vivi said, feeling better than she had in a long time.

They both turned to a knock at the door, and Dean jumped up to open it.

"Coffee?"

Vivi turned to see the man delivering room service. He was quite attractive and wasn't in a uniform.

Vivi watched as Dean kissed the room service waiter.

She was confused when the waiter walked in and another man, this one in uniform, followed, pushing a table on wheels.

"Vivi," Dean said, leading the first waiter toward the bed, "this is Trevor Abbot."

Vivi started laughing and then hugged Trevor, understanding now what had gone on at the door.

"The front desk attendant tried to call up," Trevor said, "but your line was busy. I told them I had a very important meeting with Miss Holden and that she'd be very angry if I were even a minute late. So they let me up," Trevor said, clearly pleased with himself.

"Well done," Vivi said.

"My goodness, you two," Trevor said as Dean began pouring the coffee. "We have a lot to discuss."

"We do. First things first, please call me Alessia."

Later that morning Vivi telephoned Max at her office, and they decided to meet at the Aquacade entrance at noon to have lunch. Vivi wanted to thank Max in person for the article and tell her what had happened with Jack and Maria. And Max wanted to explain how everything had gone down with the articles the night before.

Vivi hadn't noticed Max's second article at first, consumed as she was with the one about Dean and her, but when she took another look at *Today at the Fair*, she read the piece about Mr. Babcock and the bribery. Vivi was happy that Marianne had been willing to reveal the information she knew about Mr. Babcock, which would result in his firing rather than Max's. And she hoped Marianne was able to regain a small piece of herself that she'd lost to that man.

It had all gone exactly to plan.

Vivi dressed in her favorite red blouse. She always wore red when she wanted to feel her best. She wore red on her birthday and for important auditions. She'd worn red on her first date with Gabe and to the dinner with Dean at the Italian Pavilion. Today, then, felt like a perfect day to wear red. A rebirth of sorts.

Now, as she and Dean approached the entrance to the Aquacade, she wasn't sure what to expect. They'd gotten there a little early so they could collect their things from the dressing room before their lunch with Max. Trevor had joined them for moral support.

Ruby was the first person they both saw when they walked through the cast gate.

"I can't believe Max and Marianne pulled it off," Ruby whispered to Vivi. They'd all agreed that no one could know about Ruby's involvement in the plan. They moved toward the back of the dressing room building so they could speak privately.

"How is Marianne?" Dean asked.

"I've never seen her so happy. We were all worried about her last night, but she seemed fine. She placed a letter of resignation on her desk before she left the *Today at the Fair* office last night, and Evie stayed home from work today to be with her in case Babcock decides to telephone or pay a visit."

"I hope it doesn't come to that," Vivi said. "What's been the talk around here?"

"Absolute pandemonium. I think I saw someone's head explode. *Vivi and Dean, Aquacade darlings with deep, dark secrets.* No one knows what to do with themselves."

They all laughed.

"Actually, what happened is when we all arrived this morning, Ed gathered the whole cast together and explained that he has people looking into the allegations, but that the show must go on and he'd like to congratulate *moi*, Miss Ruby Lancaster, on assuming the role of Aquabelle Number One."

"That's great, Ruby. I'm happy for you. I know it's what you always wanted," Vivi said.

"And Ruby Lancaster always gets what she wants," Ruby said, a sly smile on her face. "So, what's next for you two?"

"For now," Vivi said, "we're going to get our things and then we'll fade into the sunset. But first, a final lunch for old times' sake at the Midway Inn."

"I wish I could join you, but duty calls," Ruby said, turning away and flinging her wrist in a dramatic way behind her.

"I must get that girl's number. She's got quite a future in show business," Trevor said, sounding impressed.

After Vivi and Dean gathered their belongings, relieved to have avoided Ed, whom they knew they'd have to deal with eventually, they walked out of the Aquacade cast gate for the very last time, holding hands, neither of them taking even a small glance back.

CHAPTER THIRTY-SIX

✲

Max

Saturday, June 24

"How are you doing?" James asked Max quietly, a sympathetic tone in his voice, as Max settled into the seat next to him at the cohort meeting.

It was Saturday morning, two days after Max's articles had come out in *Today at the Fair* and the day after they'd all submitted their contest entries. "Things are still a little crazy, to be honest."

"I still can't believe everything that happened with Vivi and her brother-in-law on Monday."

"It's truly unbelievable. Thankfully, Vivi and Dean are okay, and that's all that really matters."

Max looked around to find Charlie. And when they made eye contact, he smiled at her.

On Thursday morning, the day the articles had come out, Max had arrived at the *Today at the Fair* office at her normal time. Charlie had greeted her at the door with a copy of the paper in one hand, Marianne's resignation letter in the other, and a stunned expression on his face.

"Let me explain," Max had said, and proceeded to detail the series of events that had led them to that moment.

"I—I—I don't even know what to say," Charlie had said, shaking his head and looking like a six-year-old who'd just found out Santa wasn't real.

"Are you mad? You look a little mad."

"Mad? Absolutely not. Just the opposite. I'm so proud of you and Marianne for being so bold. I only wish I'd been able to help you girls stick it to the bastard."

Then, an executive, Mr. Southerly, from the Fair Corporation, entered the office and told Max and Charlie that Mr. Babcock wouldn't be coming back. Mr. Southerly also said he'd called Mr. Collier to see if he could return from Ohio, and would Max and Charlie be okay running the paper for the time being? Max said of course they would, which seemed to satisfy Mr. Southerly, who promptly turned and left, mumbling under his breath that this was not in his job description.

Charlie panicked about the additional workload, asked Max to figure out what the hell they should do, and stormed out of the office saying he needed to go for a walk. By the time he returned an hour later, looking calmer and carrying a Coke for Max as a sort of peace offering, she had devised a schedule, created a document that fairly distributed their workload, and called Marianne to ask her if she could spare a few hours over the next few days just until things settled down.

Today Mr. Collier would be back in the office to resume responsibility, and Max and Charlie would have a moment to breathe. But Max had loved the pace of putting the paper out over the last couple of days and hoped Mr. Collier would trust her with more than just the event listings when he returned.

"Are you nervous about the contest results?" James asked, interrupting Max's thoughts.

Max was about to tell him that she was, exceedingly so, when Professor L. walked into the room.

"Good morning, everyone. I apologize for the early hour, but I wanted to ensure that those of you who have to work today could get to your offices by a reasonable time. I am grateful that Mr. Bing was able to judge the contest entries so quickly. He apologizes for not being here today, and he asked me to tell you all that he was impressed by the caliber of your articles and regrets only being able to award the grand prize to one student. I know you're all eager to find out the winner, so let's commence the proceedings."

Max watched Professor L. pull an envelope out of his briefcase. She felt her heart beating and looked down at her wrist to see if her pulse was visible, thinking it certainly had to be for how loudly it was pounding in her ears.

Professor L. opened the envelope and unfolded the paper inside. Max realized he didn't know the winner yet either, and she had a difficult time interpreting his expression as he read the winner's name to himself silently before announcing it to them.

"I'm pleased to announce," Professor L. said, clearing his throat, "that Ken Selby is the winner for his *Life* magazine piece about Admiral Richard E. Byrd's upcoming Antarctic expedition."

Max felt herself exhale and then joined the rest of the class in a round of applause for Ken, who looked surprised and delighted, receiving kind words and praise from classmates as they got up to pat him on the back and shake his hand.

"May I speak with you, Miss Roth?" Max looked up and saw Professor L. glaring at her.

She walked to the corner of the room where he waited for her.

"Regarding the article you submitted about the Aquacade scandal—"

"I know. It wasn't my best work."

"Not even close."

Max nodded. She abhorred letting her professor down. But she hadn't had many articles to choose from to submit to the contest. The few articles she'd written on Thursday for Friday's paper weren't all that interesting, and she hadn't wanted Professor L. to see the bribery article.

"I saw your article about Mr. Babcock. Before I make my thoughts known, is there anything you'd like to say for yourself?"

"How did you see it?"

"It was sent to me by the person at the Fair Corporation whom I worked with to arrange your and Charlie's placements."

"I'd like to explain to you why I did it."

"Miss Roth, you are neither an investigative reporter nor are you employed by an outlet such as *The New York Times*. A fair newspaper is not the place for takedown articles that lack corroborating sources."

"I saw the evidence myself."

"That isn't the point. Did you question the motive of the anonymous source?"

Max paused, realizing that Marianne did, in fact, have a motive to expose Mr. Babcock, but he really was doing the things the article accused him of. Marianne showed Max the file of documents that revealed everything. "I realize that Mr. Babcock is your colleague and his reputation is now damaged, but I couldn't stand by while he was doing something so unethical and potentially even illegal, so I—"

"Miss Roth, let me stop you there. I may be challenging you about some of your less professional journalistic methods, which I will certainly revisit at a later date, but I'm not upset with you."

"You're not?"

"I never liked that guy. He's always been deplorable. The only reason I even agreed to place you and Charlie there is because I thought working at the fair would be a momentous opportunity."

Max smiled at her professor.

"The only thing I'm upset about is the quality of your writing. I know you can do better."

"Does this impact your willingness to write me a letter of recommendation?"

"Not one bit. Plus, you will have plenty of opportunities to show me better work when the fall term begins. I look forward to that very much. Now if you'll excuse me."

Max hadn't been prepared to tell Professor L. that, because she didn't win, she most likely wouldn't be returning for the fall term. She watched him go and then walked toward James. He was the only student who remained in the room.

"What was that about?" James asked.

"Oh, I'm sure you can imagine."

"I'm so sorry, Max."

"For what?"

"That you didn't win."

Max smiled and looked into James's eyes. "You are so kind to be concerned about my feelings, and you have no idea how much I appreciate that. But what's done is done. I tried my best with what I had, and now I'll figure out a way to deal with the repercussions. No use crying about it now."

"You really are something," he said.

She smiled at him and felt happy despite all that had transpired over the past few days. She actually couldn't remember feeling this light, this free.

Max took a deep breath, picked up her handbag, and walked toward the door, ready to go to work and see what Mr. Collier had in store for Charlie and her.

Then she stopped and turned around. "James?"

"Yes."

She eased her bag off her shoulder and took a step toward him. He looked at her with a question in his eyes.

Then she took her right hand and placed it upon his cheek. She couldn't believe what she was doing, but, in typical fashion, once Max started something, she couldn't stop herself.

She brought her lips to his and kissed him, putting her hands on his shoulders and drawing him closer to her. He felt like her dreams.

When they pulled apart, he looked down at her and smiled. "I've been wanting to kiss you for a very long time."

"You have?" she said, laughing, relieved that he hadn't pushed her away, relieved that he'd kissed her back.

"I have."

"So why didn't you?"

"You intimidate me a little," James said with a small laugh, raising his eyebrows and tilting his head at her.

"What could possibly be intimidating about me?"

James laughed again and put his hand on her cheek. "Absolutely everything," he said, and then they kissed again.

∿

CHAPTER THIRTY-SEVEN

Vivi & Max

Saturday, August 5

Six Weeks Later

Vivi and Max had decided to meet directly under the arch at three thirty.

A heavy and resplendent sun had broken through the clouds hours earlier, and now Washington Square Park was filled with families and lovers, children wading in the fountain, and old men playing chess under the shady elms.

Vivi spotted Max immediately, dancing alone to a band that was playing a patriotic march. Not a song typically dance-worthy, but Max had found a way, as Max always did. And always would. Her smile seemed convinced, her entire presence was light.

"Happy birthday!" Vivi said.

"You're here!" Max said, hugging her friend. "When you told me Elizabeth Dorchester was speaking, I couldn't think of any better way to spend the day."

"I'm sorry we didn't get to spend the whole day together," Vivi said.

"Unfortunately Mr. Collier is not a fan of the day off, regardless of whether one wants to celebrate the anniversary of one's birth. At least he let me go early!"

"And everything is set for tonight?" Vivi asked.

"We have a reservation at seven."

"Can't wait. But now, birthday girl, Elizabeth Dorchester awaits."

The two women linked arms and marched off to the beat of the band, toward the crowd that had gathered in the southeast corner of the park.

They got spots up front, and at precisely four o'clock they cheered along with the other women who were excited to see Elizabeth Dorchester, excited to hear a woman speak about things that were important to them. She called for women to join political movements, to claim their spots in the workforce, to join together and make their voices heard as a united force.

Vivi and Max agreed later that they thought a lot of what Elizabeth Dorchester had said seemed a bit unrealistic for the times. It was difficult for women to get jobs, after all, and the idea of a mass of women having prominent roles in government seemed like a far-off dream. But they couldn't help but be inspired by this woman, who spoke so confidently and with so much fervor.

Vivi had come to the park that day with a spark of an idea, but after listening to Elizabeth Dorchester's speech, she was certain that she wanted to fan that flame. Make it a full-blown, raging fire.

With Max by her side, Vivi approached the women who had set up a table to promote the work of the National Woman's

Party. She felt something stirring in her as she spoke with them, a sense of belonging. Purpose. And when they asked her if she would like to volunteer with the organization, she signed up to help at a rally they were having the very next weekend.

Vivi didn't imagine at that point that it would turn into a profession for her, that she would ever work full-time for an organization that promoted the work of women, an organization that supported a woman's dream to have lofty ambitions, to want more from her life than society currently wanted her to have. No, at that point, she just wanted to be in an environment that celebrated women listening to voices of women. An environment that celebrated women listening to their own voices. Because that's what Vivi had finally begun to do. And that voice sounded like a song.

"Ready to go or do you want to supplicate at the feet of Elizabeth Dorchester herself?"

"You're quite amusing, Max, but I'm ready for the next event on your very busy birthday schedule."

As they rode the subway, Max pointed out the Miss Subways posters to Vivi, encouraging her to enter the contest.

"Maybe I'll send in your picture," Max said, her eyes lighting up.

"Don't you dare," Vivi said, turning to Max with a serious expression on her face. "Best of luck to all those girls out there who want this sort of thing, but I'm going to take a break from the spotlight for a while. Now that you've brought this to my attention, though, I think I know a pretty young thing who should have her picture up in the subway."

"Who?"

"Oh, don't be so coy."

"I wouldn't stop you from sending my picture in if you absolutely, definitely felt the urge to do so," Max said, laughing.

With that, Vivi took her camera out of her pocketbook, and the two embarked on a photo shoot right there in the subway, with Vivi enjoying being behind the camera and Max hamming it up and adoring the stares of the other passengers.

When the subway stopped at the fair exit, Vivi felt nervous. She hadn't been back to the fair in six weeks, since the day she and Dean had gone to collect their belongings.

"You okay?" Max asked. She had known Vivi was ambivalent, and almost changed the venue for her birthday dinner because of it, but Vivi had insisted on going to the fair.

"I am," Vivi said, nodding. "I really am. To be honest, I'm a little surprised at how excited I am to be back here."

"Do you miss being in the Aquacade?"

"It was a fun experience in a lot of ways," Vivi said. "I do love to perform, and who wouldn't enjoy applause from a crowd? But I don't miss feeling like I'm under the control of people I don't trust. It's been a relief to be away from all of that. And my nails have never looked better!"

"At least you had an experience you can talk about when you're old and gray."

"When I'm old and gray, no one will ever believe I used to look like this and that I was capable of doing what I did in that pool four times a day."

Standing at the fair gate, Max held her hand out to Vivi. "Ready?"

"Ready."

"We have a bit of time and there's something I want to do before we meet everyone for dinner," Max said.

"Great, but hold on one second," Vivi said as she released Max's hand and ran to a nearby souvenir stand. She returned with two matching charm bracelets, and Max squealed with delight as she and Vivi immediately clasped the trinkets onto their wrists. "Now that we're bonded to this fair—"

"And to each other."

"And to each other," Vivi said, smiling, "forever, where is it you want to go?"

"Have you seen the time capsule at the Westinghouse Building?"

"I haven't, but I want to," Vivi said, an excited tone in her voice.

When they eventually stood in front of the time capsule replica, Vivi asked Max to read the sign out loud.

Max cleared her throat. "Welcome to the Westinghouse Time Capsule. The original Time Capsule, an 800-pound, 7-foot torpedo-shaped non-corrodible copper alloy tube, was buried on September 23, 1938. It rests at the bottom of the glass-covered Immortal Well, which is illuminated for your viewing ability. It includes a condensed record of our present-day civilization for the inhabitants of the Earth in the year 6939. Included, and assembled by noted archaeologists, are microfilm containing 10,000,000 words and 1,000 pictures revealing a condensed record of our present-day civilization along with 100 items that represent a comprehensive cross-section of life as we live it today. After the fair, the shaft will be filled solidly with pitch, concrete, and earth. There it is hoped the Time Capsule shall remain for 5,000 years."

"How will anyone know it's there in five thousand years?" Vivi asked.

"There's a Book of Record," Max said. "Three thousand copies are scattered around the world in libraries and museums."

"How can anyone even fathom what the world will be like in five thousand years? I can't even imagine where I'll be in ten years," Vivi said. "I know where you won't be, Max. You won't be making meatloaf and playing blocks with your three children while you wait for Daddy James to come home from his day at the paper, that's for sure."

Max laughed. "You know me very well. I'm hoping instead that I'll be the first female editor in chief of *The New York Times* in ten years."

"That's my girl," Vivi said. "It is kind of interesting to think about where we *will* be in ten years," she continued, wistfully, staring down into the well. "I don't even know how to begin thinking about that. So much has happened in the last few months that ten years sounds like a lifetime."

"I have an idea!" Max said, her eyes lighting up, as they tended to do. "Let's go into Westinghouse's writing room."

"What's that?"

"Fairgoers can go into their writing room, use their stationery, and write a letter to anyone in the world. Let's write a letter to ourselves ten years from now about what we hope we will have accomplished by the time we read the letters and what we want our future selves to know. Then, in ten years, on my thirty-first birthday, we'll get together and open our letters together."

"I love that idea," Vivi said, holding her hand out to Max as they walked toward the writing room.

After they'd written their letters, sealed the envelopes, stuffed them into pocketbooks, and shaken hands, swearing they'd meet up in ten years' time, Vivi asked Max if they could take one more short detour before they met up with the others.

"Follow me," Vivi said, walking east. A few minutes later, Vivi and Max stood before the Photo-Garden outside the Eastman Kodak Building, where there was a painted backdrop and miniature replicas of the Trylon and Perisphere.

Vivi handed the attendant her camera and asked if she would take a photo of them.

Vivi and Max sat on the edge of the platform, their arms around each other. Two friends who had shared an extraordinary experience, an extraordinary summer. Two friends who would each keep this photo in a frame for the rest of their lives, moving it from home to home, and staring at it fondly, nostalgically, as a memory of that summer of rebirth.

"That was a perfect idea, Vivi," Max said, giving her friend a kiss on the cheek. "Now, let's go to the restaurant. I'm sure the others will be waiting for us."

And they were. Max's parents, David and Sarah, and her sisters, Anna and Leah; Vivi's sister, Maria, and little Sofia; Albert from the typeset office with his wife, Gloria; and James, Dean, and Trevor. Marianne and Charlie sent their regrets. They were visiting Marianne's grandmother in New Jersey and enjoying their budding romance.

James had booked a large table at Le Restaurant in the French Pavilion, which had a terrace overlooking the Lagoon of Nations. It was extravagant, and Max had protested when he had made the suggestion, but he insisted. Their relationship was flourishing, and Max was scheduled to have dinner with James's parents the following weekend.

After the maître d' had led their lively group to a table, Anna and Leah insisted on plopping Sofia right in between them. Albert regaled David and Sarah Roth about his experiences as a typesetter. Maria and Gloria bonded over their shared love of needlepoint. Dean introduced Trevor to everyone and entertained them all with stories of the restaurant he was now working at, which was owned by one of Trevor's friends. The head chef said if Dean showed aptitude, he would consider taking him on as an apprentice.

The meal was delicious. Afterward, Vivi and Max, who were seated side by side, turned to each other and smiled.

"Are you having a good time?" Vivi asked.

"This might be the best birthday I've ever had."

"Have you made any decisions about next year?" Vivi knew the topic of Max's father's job was sensitive, and though they'd spent the whole day together, Vivi had hesitated to bring up the issue. But now, after drinks and laughs, Vivi thought it was okay if the conversation turned a bit more serious.

"Things are the same with my dad," Max said quietly. "He finally told my mother that he'd lost his job. She was supportive, and I know he feels better that he doesn't have to lie about it anymore. I've officially put in for a leave of absence from NYU for next year. Mr. Collier said I could stay on at *Today at the Fair* until the fair closes in October, if I don't find a different job before then."

"Did you talk to your professor yet about what's going on?"

"I did. He was very supportive, and the next day he called me at home to say that he'd just heard that the *Heights Daily News*, our student paper, has a paid administrative position open. I applied for the job, and I should find out if I get it next week. It would be nice to work for a newspaper rather than waitressing or something like that, so I can stay close to what's going on at NYU. I was really disappointed about not going back to school, but I've come to terms with it. I realize a few swerves in the road are fine. Not everything has to be a straight path. Straight paths, if you really think about it, are pretty boring."

"That sounds perfect. And things are going well at *Today at the Fair*?"

"They really are. It's busy, but I love writing so many articles each day, and, you'll be happy to know," Max said in a serious tone, but laughing as she spoke, "I've been working really hard to behave so I don't get myself fired."

"Oh my goodness, Max, you're growing up right before my very eyes," Vivi said, laughing. "Just don't stop being bold."

"I won't. I used to feel ashamed of my confidence and my ambition, that they were what got me into trouble. But now I realize that it's my confidence and ambition that make me who I am and that have gotten me where I am. I know I can't always let those wild animals out of their cages, because they like to break things, but I can let them roam and give them the air they need."

"And you absolutely should," Vivi said, laughing, and then she changed her tone. "I noticed you looked sad earlier when you were talking with James. Is everything okay?"

Max took a deep breath and looked around to make sure no one was listening to their conversation. "He told me last night that he's enlisting."

"What?" Vivi said. She was shocked, but she tried to keep her voice down and her expression calm so no one would notice.

"He spent his entire summer covering the conflicts overseas. Initially, as he mentioned to you one of the times we all went out, he was thinking about becoming a war correspondent, but he doesn't feel like that would be contributing enough. He said he feels that it's his duty to serve. I don't want to get into too much detail right now, but he's leaving soon."

"Oh, Max, I'm so sorry to hear that."

"Don't get me wrong, I'm proud of him. His father was in the Great War, and James has always been interested in the military. But with everything going on in Europe, it worries me."

Vivi put her hand on Max's and gave her an understanding smile. "You have me. We'll get through it together."

"Tell me about you. How has everything been going?"

"I'm all settled in with my sister and Sofia, trying to get used to being called Alessia again. I know it's gruesome, but we're so grateful that we no longer have to worry about Frank. And I absolutely love being around Sofia every day."

"Have you decided what you're going to do about her in terms of telling her you're her mother?"

"It's so complicated. But we have to do what's in Sofia's best interest. Right now that means Sofia and I are getting to know each other. Maria and I are going to talk to someone who's trained in these situations and get advice about how we should handle it. I failed my daughter once, leaving her in a home with a dangerous man. I'm not going to fail her again."

"Knowing you, you'll handle it perfectly," Max said, taking a sip of the coffee the waiter had brought.

"Maria has been able to go back to her job now that I'm around to watch Sofia, and I've got enough money saved up so I can take some time to decide what I want to do next. I don't want to jump into anything too quickly."

"That sounds wise."

"I'm also really excited about volunteering with the NWP."

"Elizabeth Dorchester made quite an impact on you."

"She did."

"Look at us," Max said. "Do you remember what I said to you the first night we had drinks at the Turf Trylon Café after Elizabeth Dorchester's speech?"

Vivi smiled. "I do, but say it again."

"I said we were two modern working girls, toiling away at the fair for the summer, planting the seeds of our ambition that would bloom into the careers of our dreams."

"Those two girls could never have imagined what was going to happen to them," Vivi said, lifting her eyebrows.

"I still don't think they can."

Max and Vivi looked at each other, their stares heavy with understanding, with respect, with appreciation for what had happened to them both that summer.

Three months prior they were two girls on opposite coasts who hadn't gotten what they wanted. Who had lost out on the jobs they *thought* were their dreams. Instead, they'd been sent to the fair, a place that Professor L. had said, in his wisdom, could be life-changing. And it had been.

The fair's flags soared. Its flowers bloomed. It took hold of the imaginations and got under the skin of all who witnessed its energy and promise, its sights and sounds and smells. Its scientific advancements astounded. Its global unity promised hope. Its vision inspired those who visited to do something bigger, to be someone better. Girls became women. Boys became men. All lit up by sunshine and optimism and a belief that the future and the better days it promised were just around the corner. The fair had a way of touching everyone who passed through its gates.

As for Vivi and Max, the fair transformed a chance meeting into friendship, into love. Cementing itself in their hearts forever.

Historical Note

I first learned about the 1939 New York World's Fair while reading Esther Williams's autobiography, *The Million Dollar Mermaid*. Williams writes vividly about her experience swimming in Billy Rose's Aquacade at the Golden Gate International Exposition in San Francisco in 1940. *Wait. Aquacade? What's an Aquacade?*

A couple of hours of deep-dive Internet research later, I learned that Billy Rose's Aquacade, which got its start at the 1937 Great Lakes Exposition in Cleveland, Ohio, was the highest-grossing attraction of the 1939 New York World's Fair and a showcase for Eleanor Holm and Johnny Weissmuller, both celebrities of the era. Not only was I fascinated by the accounts of the Aquacade—its elaborate production, the behind-the-scenes intrigue—but I also became enchanted with the history and details of the 1939 fair itself.

I immediately conjured the idea of writing a character who swam in the Aquacade, and the novel developed from there.

To research the fair, I read books, pored through websites

and newspaper archives, and watched endless hours of newsreels and amateur videos of the fair. I placed order after order on eBay for souvenirs, maps, actual copies of *Today at the Fair*, and the official fair guidebook.

My favorite part of the research was visiting the fairgrounds in Flushing Meadows–Corona Park, Queens, and the nearby *World's Fair Visible Storage* exhibit at the Queens Museum to get a feel for the scope. How extraordinary it was to actually walk the paths that my characters did, to appreciate firsthand how massive the fairgrounds were, and to see remains of the fair, though there are few.

The historic details of the 1939 New York World's Fair are impressive—the story of its conception, the planning and construction, President Roosevelt's personal outreach to foreign governments, the specifics of each and every pavilion and exhibit, the esteemed visitors, the strategy behind the lighting and sound . . . I could go on and on. It's also critical to understand what was happening in the United States and abroad during the late 1930s to fully appreciate how the technological, scientific, and social advances celebrated at the fair were received by fairgoers and the media. Due to length and story constraints, I was unable to include all of the particulars of and fun facts about the fair, but I encourage you to investigate further, as discovering those particulars is worth the effort.

While reading *We Came Here to Shine*, you probably wondered what actually took place on those grounds in 1939 and what came from my imagination. A few specifics in order of appearance in the novel:

The Fair: All of the details I included about the 1939 World's Fair—the facts and figures, the attractions, the physical layout—are true. It was the largest, most expensive fair ever held costing $155,000,000 and covering 1,216 acres in the borough of Queens in New York City.

The Trylon: The *Official Guide Book New York World's Fair 1939* and many other publications list the height of the Trylon at 700 feet. Other sources, including *The 1939–1940 New York World's Fair* by Bill Cotter (Arcadia Publishing, 2009) and 1939NYWorldsFair.com, note that due to budgetary constraints, construction goals weren't met and the tower reached only 610 feet.

WorldWide Films: The studio, its films, and its employees are fictional, though they were inspired by the workings of the famed, and at times controversial, Hollywood studio system.

New York University (NYU): Due to overcrowding at its campus in Greenwich Village, NYU expanded to a new campus in University Heights in the Bronx in 1894, moving much of its operations there, including the undergraduate College of Arts and Sciences. Thus, when Max was a student at NYU, her classes were located at the Bronx campus.

Alessia/Vivi: It was not uncommon for a movie studio at that time to "whitewash" an actress. For instance, Rita Hayworth was originally Margarita Carmen Cansino. In the late thirties, when 20th Century Fox thought she would be more marketable if she were cast in less "exotic" roles, they changed her name, lightened her hair, and raised her hairline through electrolysis.

Billy Rose's Aquacade: The Aquacade was an entertainment and technological sensation at the time. Billy Rose was known as an impresario and had a long history in entertainment. His first marriage was to comedian Fanny Brice (Barbra Streisand depicted Brice in the 1964 Broadway musical and the 1968 film *Funny Girl*). The actual historical figures mentioned in the story are Billy Rose, Eleanor Holm, Morton Downey, Johnny Weissmuller, the Vincent Travers Orchestra, and the Fred Waring Glee Club; the rest, including Ed Tandy, Thad Muldoon, Camilla, Mr. Mackey, Ruby Lancaster, and Dean Mitchell, are fictional. Videos taken at the Aquacade can be found online if you'd like to see actual performances.

Eleanor Holm: An Olympic gold medalist in swimming in 1932, Holm was selected by Billy Rose to star in his first Aquacade at the 1937 Great Lakes Exposition in Cleveland. She successfully completed the 1939 season in the Aquacade; her unfortunate fall, which created a vacancy in the role that Vivi fills, is fictional. She and Billy Rose did get married in November 1939.

Today at the Fair: This was an actual daily newspaper at the fair. Very little is documented about the operations of *Today at the Fair*, so my descriptions about the office and staff are entirely fictional. I did, however, have access to multiple issues of the newspaper and spent hours reading articles and listings to learn what went on at the fair on a daily basis. The sections "Official Program of Today's Special Events" and "Around the Clock Today at the Fair" actually existed as they're described in the book. The event listings featured between chapters highlight real fair events or exhibits. And the article about Dr. Couney and his baby incubators that appears before chapter eighteen is from the August 22, 1939, issue of *Today at the Fair*.

The New York Chronicle: There was not a newspaper called *The New York Chronicle* in 1939. Thus, all of the *Chronicle* articles featured in the novel aren't from a real paper, but their content (except for the articles about Vivi) is based on actual news stories about the fair. For instance, the May 29, 1939, article before chapter six about the lousy weather at the fair and attendance size is based on real reporting from *The New York Times* and other publications.

The Famous Chicken Inn: This was an actual, and very popular, restaurant in the Amusement Zone. The Milk Fed Southern Fried Chicken platter "with all the Trimmins" was its specialty and cost sixty-five cents (about twelve dollars in 2019 dollars), just ten cents less than the seventy-five-cent cost of admission to the fair. It cost ten cents more to get the chicken charcoal-broiled.

Royal Visit: On June 10, 1939 (five days later than depicted in the novel), King George VI and Queen Elizabeth toured the fair. That day, in a front-page story in *The New York Times*, Foster Hailey wrote, "A reception fit for a king and queen was being prepared by New York City for the five-and-a-half-hour visit today of Their Britannic Majesties, George VI and Elizabeth, as they traveled toward the city from Washington on their special train last night." The details of their visit—the arrangements, security, press coverage—are fascinating and can be explored online. The *Today at the Fair* article and event schedule before chapter seventeen are adapted directly from the June 10, 1939, issue of *Today at the Fair*.

Mickey Rooney and Judy Garland: As mentioned in chapter fifteen, Rooney, eighteen, and Garland, sixteen, huge Hollywood stars of the time, did visit the fair for a promoted event with New York City mayor Fiorello La Guardia, though it was on August 24, later than depicted in the novel. During their interview with La Guardia, they admitted that they had come to the fair in disguise two days prior to tour the Amusement Zone and go on the Parachute Jump. The two teens were in New York to promote Garland's new film, *The Wizard of Oz*.

Elizabeth Dorchester: The National Woman's Party is an actual organization formed in 1916 with the mission of securing voting rights for women. It later focused on the Equal Rights Amendment. Elizabeth Dorchester is fictitious, but her positions in the novel reflect what female activists were fighting for during that time period.

Miss Subways Contest: During her subway ride in chapter thirty, Max observes Mary Gardiner's Miss Subways poster. Miss Subways was an advertising campaign that ran in the NYC subway system from 1941 to 1976. Since it's the subject of my previous novel, *The Subway Girls*, and because I find the topic so interesting, I took the liberty of including the contest two years before it actually debuted. Mary Gardiner, whom I interviewed while researching *The Subway Girls*, was an actual Miss Subways, though not until May 1953.

Today at the Fair **Bribe Controversy**: I haven't seen any evidence that Fair Corporation president Grover Whalen conspired with *Today at the Fair* to publish misleading articles. What is true is that Whalen remained publically optimistic about the fair's first-year viability even when attendance numbers came in below projections and concessionaires complained that they weren't recouping their investments.

During the research phase for *We Came Here to Shine,* and even while writing and editing the manuscript, I often found myself surrounded by a pile of opened books and multiple browser tabs of websites, highlighter out, taking furious notes and becoming more and more enthralled and captivated by the fascinating details of the fair. I recommend all of these books and materials I consulted during my research.

- 1939NYWorldsFair.com by Paul M. Van Dort
- *The 1939–1940 New York World's Fair* by Bill Cotter (Arcadia Publishing, 2009)
- Billy Rose's Aquacade 1939 program
- *The Fixers* by E. J. Fleming (McFarland & Company, Inc., 2005)
- *The Good Girls Revolt* by Lynn Povich (PublicAffairs, 2012)
- *The Million Dollar Mermaid* by Esther Williams (Simon & Schuster, 1999)
- *The New York Times*
- *The New York World's Fair 1939/1940* by Stanley Appelbaum (Dover Publications, Inc., 1977)
- *New York World's Fair in Pictures* (Quality Art Novelty Company, Inc., 1939)

- *Official Guide Book New York World's Fair 1939* (Exposition Publications, Inc., 1939)
- *Today at the Fair* (multiple issues) (Exposition Publications, Inc., 1939)
- *Uncommon Type* by Tom Hanks (Alfred A. Knopf, 2017)
- *Wine, Women and Words* by Billy Rose (Pocket Books, Inc., 1948)
- *Women in American Journalism* by Jan Whitt (University of Illinois Press, 2008)
- *The World of Tomorrow* by Larry Zim, Mel Lerner & Herbert Rolfes (The Main Street Press, 1988)
- WorldsFairPhotos.com by Bill Cotter

To learn more, please visit my website, www.susieschnall.com, where I've compiled a special section about the fair.

Acknowledgments

Writing a novel is a solitary pursuit: endless hours alone in a quiet room imagining, crafting, plotting, writing, revising, and editing. But to turn a finished manuscript into an actual book requires a band of merry and accomplished book lovers who work tirelessly, and without whose help this novel would not have been published.

Thank you to the team at St. Martin's Griffin: Lauren Jablonski for all of your hard work and effort shaping this book into what it became. I will always appreciate your dedication to the story and your thoughtful input. Alex Sehulster for carrying this novel over the finish line. I'm grateful for your steady stewardship and early enthusiasm for the project. Mara Delgado-Sanchez for your tireless coordination. Also to the rest of the talented team who worked on this novel with great care: Anne Marie Tallberg, Brant Janeway, DJ DeSmyter, Clare Maurer, Michelle McMillian, Olga Grlic, Chrisinda Lynch, Kaitlin Severini, and Janine Barlow.

Thank you, Alicia Clancy, for acquiring *The Subway Girls* and what would become *We Came Here to Shine* for St. Martin's. You saw something in my writing and in me, and that changed the trajectory of my life.

Thank you to my agent, Carly Watters. I got supremely lucky the day you chose to represent me, and I will forever be grateful for all you've done for me and my career. I appreciate your guidance, dedication, and friendship.

Thank you, Crystal Patriarche. Our fourth book together, lady! You have been the one constant since SparkPress published my first. I love being on this journey with you, and I am consistently blown away by your efforts on my behalf.

Thank you, BookSparks, the most dynamic, creative, dedicated *book babes* on the planet, for all you've done for me.

Thank you to Addison Duffy at United Talent Agency for your love for and resolute dedication to my work.

Thank you to all who assisted me in my research of the World's Fair, especially Vickie Karp, director of public affairs for the NYC Department of Parks and Recreation; Ken Frenkel, who graciously toured me around the site of the 1939 fair and answered all of my questions; and to those who I worked with on securing photo rights: Bill Cotter of WorldsFairPhotos.com, Paul M. Van Dort of 1939NYWorldsFair.com, Andrea Felder of the New York Public Library, and Kay Peterson of the National Museum of American History.

Thank you to the talented Silvia Gherra for creating the gorgeous map of the fair at the beginning of the book. You are an absolute joy to work with!

Thank you to my bold and brilliant author friends. I found my tribe when I found all of you. I am grateful for your friendship, encouragement, and for being fantastic venting partners. I have never met a group of women who are more genuinely supportive.

I have been fortunate to connect with many authors, but special thanks to Cristina Alger, Jenna Blum, Amy Blumenfeld, Jamie Brenner, Jennifer Brown, Jillian Cantor, Georgia Clark, Fiona Davis, Camille Di Maio, Abby Fabiaschi, Liz Fenton, Elyssa Friedland, Jackie Friedland, Jane Green, Nicola Harrison, Jane Healey, Elise Hooper, Sally Koslow, Emily Liebert, Lynda Cohen Loigman, Annabel Monaghan, Amy Poeppel, Taylor Jenkins Reid, Alyson Richman, Kaira Rouda, Meredith Schorr, Allison Winn Scotch, Lisa Steinke, Beatriz Williams, and Lauren Willig.

Thank you to the book champions who have supported me in immeasurable ways: Cindy Burnett of Thoughts from a Page, Andrea Peskind Katz of Great Thoughts Great Readers, Suzanne Leopold of Suzy Approved, Zibby Owens of *Moms Don't Have Time to Read Books*, Jenny O'Regan, Jamie Rosenblit of Beauty and the Book, and the Jewish Book Council.

Thank you to the readers who choose my books, write reviews, attend my speaking events, and send me thoughtful notes. Your support means everything.

Thank you to the librarians, bookstores, booksellers (especially Patrick at Arcade Booksellers in Rye, New York), book clubs, reviewers, and bookstagrammers who have done so much for me. I appreciate your efforts tremendously.

Thank you to my early readers Mike and Rene Benedetto, Amy Burke, Fiona Davis, Lynda Cohen Loigman, and David Shorrock, and to my friends and family who generously hosted events for *The Subway Girls*: Sara Blakely, Terry Gevisser, Jesse Itzler, Penny Kosinski, Elizabeth Moyer, Joanne Norris, Nancy Norris, Kerry Rosenthal, Dorothy Sifford, and Lisa Smukler.

Thank you to my loving family and friends. I am astonishingly lucky to have such supportive and wonderful people in my life.

Thank you to my husband, Rick, and our three boys. How

much fun was it to plot Frank's demise around the dinner table? It's never boring loving you all. Thank you for being my people.

And a special thank-you to the women who step outside of their comfort zones, who stumble or outright fail and get back up, who believe in themselves and their strength and then use that strength to do great things, who show up, who embrace their authenticity, who work hard at what lights them up, who own their badass selves, who stride boldly into the arena. You inspire me and make me better. Thank you.

WE CAME HERE TO SHINE

by Susie Orman Schnall

About the Author

- A Conversation with Susie Orman Schnall

Behind the Novel

- Fun Facts About the New York World's Fair of 1939

Keep On Reading

- Recommended Reading
- Reading Group Questions

Also available as an audiobook
from Macmillan Audio

For more reading group suggestions
visit www.readinggroupgold.com.

 ST. MARTIN'S GRIFFIN

A Conversation with Susie Orman Schnall

Could you tell us a little bit about your background, and when you decided that you wanted to lead a literary life?

I've loved books as long as I can remember . . . Shel Silverstein, Beverly Cleary, Judy Blume. I've read them all. And though my favorite authors have changed, that love of reading is still strong today. After college, I worked for magazines, internet companies, advertising agencies, and nonprofit organizations doing marketing and corporate communications. It wasn't until after my youngest son started kindergarten that I even considered writing fiction. Four books later, I'm so happy I pivoted and became an author.

Is there a book that most influenced your life? Or inspired you to become a writer?

At the time I was writing my first novel, I was highly moved by and influenced by *The Middle Place* by Kelly Corrigan. Throughout the years, though, so many books have influenced me—the way I think, the way I see the world, the way I see my place in the world. And so many books have provided me an opportunity to laugh, cry, and connect with humanity at large. Some of my all-time favorite books include: anything by Jane Austen or Jeffrey Archer, *Becoming* by Michelle Obama, *Eat Pray Love* by Elizabeth Gilbert, *The Help* by Kathryn Stockett, *Homegoing* by Yaa Gyasi, *Daisy Jones & The Six* by Taylor Jenkins Reid, and *Small Great Things* by Jodi Picoult.

How did you become a writer? Would you care to share any writing tips?

I had been writing freelance articles for magazines and websites and I felt like my next challenge would be to write a novel. So I signed up for a course to provide structure and discipline. As the day of the first class approached, I almost talked myself out of attending—the idea of writing an entire book seemed intense and daunting. As encouragement, I told myself that if I hated the first class, I didn't have to do the homework. I went to that first class, I did the homework, then I went to the next class, and by the end of the course I had written several chapters of what would turn out to be my first novel, *On Grace*. Today, upon the publication of this, my fourth novel, I look back and feel astonished by and proud of what I've accomplished.

A Few Writing Tips

1. Read around and read up: Read books in the genre you hope to publish in. It's important to know the expectations and conventions of the genre—not that you have to follow them exactly, but so you know what readers and editors are looking for. And read books that are more advanced than the level you currently write at. That's where all the juicy learning takes place.

2. Don't hem and haw. If you want to write, write. It's just like anything else in life. Learn as much as you can about the industry and the craft, put in the hours doing the actual work, understand that rejection is part of the business, set goals, keep going until you've achieved them, and then set new goals.

3. Do your research. People come up to me at my events all the time and ask me questions: How

do you find an agent? What should I do with my children's book manuscript? There are a bazillion blog posts, and courses, and magazine articles galore on everything you want and need to know about book publishing. Use those resources to help you get where you want to be.

What was the inspiration for this novel?

It all began when I read Esther Williams's autobiography, *The Million Dollar Mermaid*, and learned about her experience swimming in Billy Rose's Aquacade at the Golden Gate International Exposition in San Francisco in 1940. I had never heard of Billy Rose or his famous show, so I did some research and fell in love with the history of the Aquacade and the New York World's Fair of 1939 in particular. I thought it would be fun to write a character who had a similar experience to Esther Williams, and the story developed from there.

Can you tell us about what research, if any, you did before writing this novel? Do you have firsthand experience with its subject? Base any of the characters on people from your own life? What is the most interesting or surprising thing you learned as you set out to tell your story?

I did a great deal of research on the 1939 World's Fair before I began writing the novel and during as well. I wanted to ensure that the details were accurate and that readers didn't have to question whether something that is presented as factual in the story really happened. Similarly, I wanted everything that came from my imagination—the characters, the story lines—to be rooted in the actual history of the fair, the people who attended, and the contemporaneous events that were

happening in the United States and abroad.

I began by reading a number of books, websites, and newspaper articles about the history of the fair: about how it was conceived, the players, pavilions, attractions, daily events, food, overall look and feel, etc. I especially enjoyed firsthand accounts—written and filmed—so I could absorb what it would have been like for children and adults in 1939 who were lucky enough to experience this slice of history.

One of my favorite ways of understanding the fair was through eBay! I purchased memorabilia, including Heinz pickle pins (the most popular souvenir from the fair), postcards (blank and filled out), guidebooks, maps, and even an original Aquacade program. The most exciting finds were actual copies of *Today at the Fair*. It was remarkable and transporting to turn those yellowed pages and to have a real-life keepsake of what my character Max worked on every day.

The cherry on top was a visit to Flushing Meadows—Corona Park in Queens. There are few remains from the 1939 fair (and only a bit more from the 1964 fair), but being able to see the footprint of the fair and to walk the paths that my characters walked was extraordinary. It brought it all to life!

Are you currently working on another book? And if so, can you tell us what it's about?

At press time, I'm still in the conceptualization and plotting phase for my next novel, which will stay true to my past work by exploring themes of women realizing their professional dreams against evergreen workplace challenges all set against an interesting slice of American history. In this case, the world of culinary school.

Fun Facts About the New York World's Fair of 1939

I was able to include many details about the fair in *We Came Here to Shine*, but there were so many aspects of the fair I found fascinating that didn't make their way into the final version of the book. For instance:

An Oasis: The Fair Corporation spent $1,500,000 on landscaping and considered the endeavor a serious and important undertaking; thus, the grounds were lush with trees and flowers. Plantings around the fair's 1,216 acres included 10,000 live trees, 400,000 pansies, 500,000 hedge plants, 250 acres of grass, and a million tulips given as a gift by Holland.

Rainbow of Colors: The colors of the buildings were part of a master plan conceived of by the fair's Board of Design. Thus, from the Trylon and Perisphere (the only true-white buildings on the grounds), the structures on each of the main thoroughfares extended in a particular color, deepening toward the darkest version of that color the further it was from the center. For example, the buildings along Constitution Mall progressed from rose to a deep burgundy. Additional colors were utilized in murals, sculptures, and other effects.

The Daily Count: The National Cash Register Company erected the world's largest cash register (forty feet tall) atop a building in the Amusement Zone. It displayed the real-time attendance of the fair in giant numbers that measured two-and-a-half feet tall.

Introducing . . . Television: At its exhibit in the Communications and Business Systems Zone, RCA, the Radio Corporation of America, revealed television for the first time. With the assistance of

RCA employees named Miss Television, fairgoers were able to participate in a demonstration that allowed them to see themselves on the screen. In addition, the first commercial television broadcast in New York was of the fair's inaugural ceremonies on April 30, 1939.

Meet the Middletons: The Westinghouse Electric Company created an hour-long film as a clever way of advertising their exhibit at the fair. It starred the fictional Middletons of Indiana, who were meant to represent the typical American family visiting the fair, and is still available for viewing on the internet. Today's observers have argued that the film is a piece of corporate propaganda and an argument for capitalism over communism, but it serves as an important audiovisual relic of the fair in its glory.

Masterpieces of Art: This art exhibit was worth $30,000,000 and was heralded as "one of the most important exhibitions of old masters ever displayed under one roof." There were approximately five hundred paintings and sculptures spanning the years from the Middle Ages to 1800 and featuring artists such as da Vinci, Titian, El Greco, Rembrandt, Goya, and Michelangelo. Artwork was lent from museums around the world.

Do Not Open 'til 6939: Westinghouse buried the first time capsule on September 23, 1938, for display at the 1939 fair. More than one hundred items meant to represent life at the time were inside, including Bausch & Lomb eyeglasses, a slide rule, a plastic Mickey Mouse child's cup, Elizabeth Arden makeup, Camel cigarettes, asbestos cloth, a dollar bill, wheat seeds, a leather-bound rag-paper copy of the Holy Bible, and messages from noted men, such as Albert Einstein and Thomas Mann. The capsule also included a fifteen-minute newsreel containing speeches by President Franklin D. Roosevelt, Howard Hughes, and Jesse Owens; clips of sporting events, such as a Harvard-Yale football game and the Big League All-Star baseball game of July 1938; a fashion show in Miami; and a demonstration of the United States's military prowess from an event at Fort Benning, Georgia. Westinghouse also created a time capsule for the 1964 New York World's Fair that was buried on October 16, 1965. A monument at the site of the time capsules still stands at its original site at Flushing Meadows—Corona Park in Queens, New York.

Fun Facts About the Aquacade

Trudy: Another star of Billy Rose's Aquacade was Olympic gold medalist (Paris 1924) Gertrude Ederle. She is known as the first woman to swim across the English Channel. On August 6, 1926, she departed Cap Gris-Nez, France, just after 7:00 A.M. and arrived at Kingsdown, England, fourteen hours and thirty-one minutes later, beating the records of the five men who had accomplished the feat prior to her.

Brrr: May temperatures in New York City in 1939 were colder than normal, which resulted in unpleasant pool conditions for the swimmers. Thus, Billy Rose installed an expensive heating system in the pool to keep the water at seventy-five degrees. As fall weather crept in, Rose put in an additional $10,000 to increase the pool temperature to eighty-two degrees. Rose also spent around thirty dollars a day on steaming hot coffee to keep his swimmers warm.

Heading West: After the Aquacade's great success in New York in 1939, Billy Rose also staged the

show at the 1940 Golden Gate International
Exposition in San Francisco. He chose seventeen-
year-old Esther Williams, a champion swimmer
who would become a Hollywood film star, to be
the female lead, and she was joined by male lead
Johnny Weissmuller. (Olympic gold medalist and
film star Buster Crabbe took over Weissmuller's
role in New York to swim alongside Eleanor
Holm—at that point, Mrs. Billy Rose—during
the New York fair's 1940 season.) Williams's
Aquacade audition was held at the Los Angeles
Athletic Club pool during her lunch hour from
her job at the I. Magnin department store, where
she earned seventy-six dollars a month. During
that audition, Williams wanted to show Rose how
strong she was, so she dove into the pool and
handily completed one hundred meters. Rose told
Williams that instead of swimming fast he wanted
her to "swim pretty" and offered her the job on
the spot. She boarded a train to San Francisco the
very next night. In her fascinating and informative
autobiography, *The Million Dollar Mermaid*,
Williams recounts episodes when she was seduced
by Rose and Weissmuller. She tells of confidently
rebuffing them both.

Thwarted Dreams: Before swimming in the
Aquacade, Eleanor Holm was a champion swimmer
who had won a gold medal in the 1932 Los Angeles
Olympics and was a member of the 1936 U.S.
Olympic team. However, in what would become a
scandal of the time, while on the SS *Manhattan* en
route to Berlin for the Olympics, Holm was kicked
off the team after being accused of being drunk and
breaking the 9:00 P.M. curfew.

Aquabelle Number One's Salary: Esther Williams
was swindled by her unethical agent while

swimming in the 1940 Aquacade. She entrusted her agent with her finances and was unaware of what her salary was. Billy Rose issued Williams's weekly $500 paychecks to this agent, but he took more than his fair share and paid her only $125 a week. Master of Ceremonies Morton Downey (another man that Williams, in her autobiography, accused of harassing her) revealed that information to her. Holm apparently made $2,000 a week in the same role, but, according to Williams, this didn't bother her as Holm was more accomplished. Williams would go on to confront her agent, and this episode became the inspiration for a story line between my character Vivi and her agent, Jack.

Recommended Reading

The Million Dollar Mermaid by Esther Williams

This is the book that piqued my interest about Billy Rose's Aquacade. It also gives a great behind-the-scenes account of being a movie star in the middle of the last century.

The Good Girls Revolt: How the Women of Newsweek **Sued Their Bosses and Changed the Workplace** by Lynn Povich

This book tells the story of the discrimination suit filed against *Newsweek* in 1970. Though it's set thirty years later than *We Came Here to Shine*, if you're interested in the topic of women in journalism, it's a must-read. Also, I loved the TV spin-off, *Good Girls Revolt*, and was disappointed that it was canceled after the first season.

The Devil in the White City: Murder, Magic, and Madness at the Fair That Changed America by Erik Larson

If you love world's fairs then check out this book that tells the stories of two men—one a famed architect, the other a serial killer—and their ties to the 1893 World's Columbian Exposition in Chicago.

The World of Tomorrow: The 1939 New York World's Fair by Larry Zim, Mel Lerner & Herbert Rolfes

I read a lot of books about the New York World's Fair of 1939; this is the most comprehensive and has hundreds of photographs.

1939NYWorldsFair.com

A breezy, enlightening, and well-organized website created by World's Fair historian Paul M. Van Dort that contains everything you've ever wanted to know about the New York World's Fair of 1939.

Uncommon Type: Some Stories by Tom Hanks

This book is a collection of short stories. One in particular, "The Past Is Important to Us," is about one man's visit to the New York World's Fair of 1939. The story has an interesting twist and wonderful descriptions of the fairgrounds and exhibits.

📖 *Reading Group Questions*

Note: Many of these questions contain spoilers.
Please don't read them until you've finished the book.

1. The World's Fair plays the role of another
   character in the novel. Have you ever
   attended a World's Fair yourself or know
   someone who has? If you haven't attended
   one, based upon the description in the novel,
   do you think it's something you would have
   wanted to go to? Why or why not? And how,
   if at all, did the fair's depiction in the novel
   teach you about, or change your impression
   of, this important event?

2. The New York World's Fair of 1939 took
   place as the Great Depression was winding
   down and as World War II was beginning.
   What do you know about the political and
   cultural landscapes of the time that inform
   the story lines of the characters and the
   timing of the World's Fair in general?

3. If you could time travel back to 1939, which
   exhibits or buildings would you visit? What
   souvenirs would you buy?

4. One of the opening quotes is by Eleanor
   Roosevelt: "You must do the thing you think
   you cannot do." What does that quote mean
   to you?

5. Are you more of a Max or a Vivi, or neither?
   Why? How did your impressions of each
   character evolve while reading the book?

6. What job would you have pursued at the fair
   during the summer of 1939? Would you have
   wanted to work for *Today at the Fair*, swim

in the Aquacade, work at one of the exhibit buildings, or something else entirely?

7. Were you surprised to learn that Sofia was Vivi's daughter? What else surprised you while reading the novel?

8. Do you blame Vivi for leaving her newborn daughter in the care of her sister, Maria, even though Vivi knew Frank was a dangerous man? Or do you think Vivi did what she had to do because Maria pressured her to leave?

9. How do you think Max handled the situation she faced in not receiving comparable work assignments to her coworker Charlie? How would you have handled her plight?

10. While reading the novel, did you hope Vivi would end up with her Los Angeles boyfriend, Gabe, or the Aquacade diver Dean? Or did you think she wasn't well suited for either?

11. Did you think Max and James were a good match? How did you feel about their relationship when the novel ended?

12. If you were asked to create a time capsule of the present day, what items would you recommend be included to represent our society?

13. What can we learn from Max's and Vivi's experiences about the challenges women faced professionally and personally in the late 1930s?

14. Have you read any of Susie Orman Schnall's other novels? How would you compare this one to those?

15. If you were making a movie of this novel, whom would you cast?

16. Did you take away any message from the story?

17. Reread the last paragraph of the acknowledgments. Why do you think this sentiment is so important to the author? Is it something that you find inspiring or interesting, or that you identify with in any way? Why or why not?

Enhance Your Book Club

- If your book club is near New York City, go as a group to the grounds of the fair at Flushing Meadows–Corona Park to see the site of the World's Fair. Better yet, take one of the many tours offered of the grounds. And be sure to visit the Queens Museum to see their extensive World's Fair collection.

- Wear late-1930s fashions to the book club meeting and play music from the era.

- Screen World's Fair videos. Suggestions include *The Middletons at the Fair*, scenes from the Aquacade, and the seventeen amateur films by Philip Medicus that show a tremendous amount of the fair and its attendees (the Aquacade portion begins at time stamp 13:46 on Reel One). All can be found through a simple internet search.

- Visit 1939NYWorldsFair.com, search "Famous Chicken Inn Menu," and look at the first image that shows up. Ask everyone in the book club to bring an item from the menu so you can all enjoy a meal that commemorates a crowd favorite from the fair.

About the Author

Tiffany Oelfke

SUSIE ORMAN SCHNALL grew up in Los Angeles and graduated from the University of Pennsylvania. She lives in New York, with her husband and their three sons. *We Came Here to Shine* is her fourth novel.